Travel Page

Every publication from Rippple Books has this special page to document where the book travels, who has it and when.

The Label Maker

MacKenzie Stilton

First published in 2012 by
Rippple Books

Editor: Jeff Kavanagh
Cover design: Claudia Bode
Layout: Susanne Hock

Rippple Books
Postfach 304263
20325 Hamburg
Germany
www.rippplebooks.com

A CIP catalogue record for this book is available from the British Library.

ISBN: 978-3-9814585-5-8

Lexicon

ceeville
A website which combines social networking and gaming. Users create personal, themed cities and invite others to become ceevillians and help build the city. Unlike other social networking sites, ceeville encourages removing people; exes and unwanted friends can be killed off and buried in a city's cemetery. Despite presenting itself as completely unedited and unsupervised, ceeville uses strong word scanners to match ads with certain themed pages. Companies and brands are very active on ceeville in order to target consumers.

Denoris
Mid-sized pharmaceutical company located in Montreal. Big sellers include Liftomex (a male consolidator), Sailiun (an anti-depressant) and Dozoxin (a sedative). In the age of makeovers and reinvention, vanity drugs and mood pills are a major growth industry. Competitors include Natrofield and Massobix. Natrofield is at the forefront of research and development and has the political clout required to get drugs approved faster than smaller companies like Denoris.

Idntphi
Face recognition software available for computers and smart phones. Allows users to identify or verify people from a photograph taken with the user's device. The software searches for a matching photograph.

Mayola
Three-star hotel chain popular with companies trying to reduce their travel expenses. Was big in the 1970s and all the decor remains from that time, in the colours avocado and brown. A recent strategical shift was to market the brand as 'retro luxury'.

Plasher
Online discussion website designed to offer access to expert information, opinion and advice. A user creates a 'pond' and other users can 'make a plash' in that pond by commenting or participating in the discussion. Each plash has a maximum 88 characters. A lot of users on Plasher are actually social media managers from companies

trying to push their brand and protect their brand image. While it was started with noble ambitions, nearly every discussion on Plasher turns into a playground shouting match, making it troll heaven.

Raising Pokerzona
Online poker site popular with tweens, teens and college kids. Very low bets and no age limits. It has survived repeated attempts to be shut down, but as it operates out of the tiny Pacific island nation of Kiribati, the cards continue to be dealt.

The-t-wall
Website where anybody can write anything about anyone, and do it anonymously. Has become very popular with teenagers, students and low-level office monkeys.

Veedus
Website where users can post videos and comment. Has a special 'live' feature where video can be posted as it happens. It's like a wide-reaching, unedited version of reality TV, without the scripting and fancy production. People really do broadcast their lives 24-7 on Veedus.

Half dinner with Baggage Handler

"Simplicity is the answer. That's what you used to say. A lot. Well then, yeah, I don't think you'd like her, Pops. She's not in any way simple. Don't worry. I won't bring her back tonight. She likes home field advantage, but not double-headers. I know. Complicated. She's got all these little hang-ups. I'm sure she's been confused for quirky or cute, but she's a mess. You don't notice at first, but you pick up on it. You can't not pick up on it. I think she wants you to pick up on it. It's like she was chewed up by nineties pop culture and spat out as some twenty-first century alpha-female, wearing the neuroses of every rom-com and sit-com lead of the last twenty years as badges of honour. Or maybe hoisting them up as defense shields. You won't get close to me, oh no."

He dries his hair and puts in some organic product. He gives the fringe a spiky tuft, clumping short strands together, and ruffles it to look stylishly unstyled, just-out-of-bed.

"Sorry, Pops. I had tough day at the office. Just another day, and now I gotta go out again. I'd rather stay here. Look, she's not that bad. I actually like her. She's nice. But to get to that nice, you have to wade through so much...pretending. I don't know what's actually her and what she's putting on. And what she's taken on. Then there's all the crap she carries with her. Guess that means she's not that different than me. But I don't have a handbag. I'm carrying mental crap, but she's all physical. A gatherer. You should see her handbags. You could live in one. Huge, weighty, jammed with stuff, too big even to be a carry-on. And she carries them so the label shows, even spinning the bag around so the world can see. Gucci. Louis Vuitton. I guess I should see the funny side of it. Because she's showing off fakes. Single stitching. I checked. Like the ones the Africans sell on the streets of Rome, spread out on a bed sheet or a blanket. That was something to see. When the police came, the sellers would tie the four corners of the bed sheet together, heave the massive sack over their shoulders and run for it. With the right soundtrack, it would be comical. A pantomime robbery. A giant sack with dollar signs on it."

He pads through room naked, opens the wardrobe and surveys.

"You'd like Rome, Pops. Ancient. Maybe I'll take you there one day. You like to fly? Me neither. We could hit the road instead. Grit our teeth through the flight to Europe and then rent a sidecar. Grand tour. But not to Spain. No fucking Spain. I'd take you east, behind the curtain. Croatia, Montenegro, Macedonia, Albania. Where there aren't any gap-yearers burning holes in their mum's mega handbags. Yeah, head east. Always toward a new sun. Make the days go faster."

He pulls on a pair of white briefs.

"What? Tighty whities not sexy? Don't look at me like that. It's just dinner. This is what people do. They go out, talk, eat. I like it. And I like her, a bit, but that's not the point. She's Enora's friend. I can't just blow her off. She'd have it all over the office before the water cooler burps its last bubble."

He slips on a tight undershirt, pausing to admire his physique in the mirror. He flexes a little.

"I'm going. I know she's complicated, but so am I. And so are you. The whole world is complicated. Look. Even the weather is complicated. Rain, sun, rain, sun."

He goes to window and peers out into the evening. There are dark clouds blending with the shadowy outline of the trees on Mont Royal.

"What do you think? Should I take the bike? We're meeting at some place in the Vieux Port. Her idea. It's probably some converted factory serving quasi-cuisine. Jamaican-Nepalese-Sushi fusion, or something like that. Small portions, arty trapezoid plates, terracotta wine goblets, wooden cutlery. All at my expense. She never carries any cash. A massive handbag and not a toonie in there. She's a plastic girl."

He slips into a pink shirt. "Gimme a break, Pops. She likes pink. Pink is the new white. That's what she said. Everyone wears them at work. Xav's got a dozen shirts in every shade. Yeah. He looks ridiculous. But if everyone's wearing them, then I look like an idiot in a white shirt. Too late. I'm wearing it. Fine. Walk away. Can't keep her waiting."

***

"I've been waiting twelve minutes already."

"Sorry. I got held up."

"Robbed?"

"Delayed. Missed the bus."

She offers a cheek to kiss and he obliges, bending down self-consciously but still getting a slight buzz of enjoyment as his lips brush against the ripe fuzz of a bruised peach.

"You're such a bad liar."

The stool opposite her is low and cushioned. He's forced to sit on it like it's a toilet, hunched forward, elbows digging into the table cloth, hands holding an imaginary newspaper.

"I ordered already."

"I can see that."

"But not for you."

"I can see that too."

"I don't know what you want."

"I think I'll just have a salad."

"You eat like a girl, Joe. Have a steak. Something real. Like all the other guys in here. They're carnivores."

She swishes her hair – those fake-looking extensions – in the direction of the four manned-up tables, pausing long enough to eye a few of the men. Joe follows. He sees she's right. The suited automatons are convinced they need their protein. They hack into it, backs bents, faces close to their plates, modern cavemen gathered in tight circles around tables instead of fires, sitting on stools instead of their haunches. Hunters still, tearing flesh from bone, barely chewing, grunting agreements. He finds it fascinating to watch, and graphic, and he feels pity and jealousy at the same time. At one table, four men – three of them in pink shirts – are waging a sombre war over the salt shaker; using it and placing it next to their own plate, forcing another to reach across the table for it. Their table is cluttered with printouts, phones, folded-open reports, empty glasses and picked clean bread baskets, and through it all swims the salt shaker.

"I'm not big on meat."

"I don't get that."

"It is what it is, Siobahn."

"Fine. Have your salad. You want apple juice with that? Maybe a glass of milk?"

She laughs, covering her mouth with long fingers. She has the hands of someone twice her age: gnarly knuckles, ligaments taut and straining, rainbow coloured veins ready to burst. Yet still she puts these unattractive hands so often into view, gesturing, twirling, emphasising, pointing.

Her phone buzzes on the table, rattling the glasses briefly. She tilts her head and slips the phone under a massive cresting wave of hair.

"Hi, Stace...Can't. I'm having dinner with Joe...Yeah, he did...I know. It's sooo pathetic...Okay, call ya later."

She puts the phone back down on the table, the screen facing her. "That was Stace."

"Who's she?"

"No one you know."

"But she knows me."

Siobahn eyes the phone. "Why were you late?"

"Like I said, I missed the bus."

"You were late for the bus too."

"No. Not my fault. Something happened at the bus stop."

"Did it?"

"A guy had a heart attack. Really."

"Right. Where's the waiter? I hate it when people monopolise waiters. They're not personal servants. All of us need service in here."

"They should hire more staff."

"Waste of money. The people shouldn't be so selfish. Ah, at last."

A waiter places Siobahn's creamy looking soup in front of her, taking her knife and fork in the process.

"Wait. Where's the bread?"

The waiter slouches away.

"Hey, I didn't get to..."

"Don't worry. He'll be back. But no tip from me, or you."

She roughly takes up her ceramic spoon, struggling a little with it, her long nails slipping and scratching against it. In the end, she has to hold it like a farmer, in her fist, and starts shovelling soup into her mouth.

"Don't wait for me."

"It'll get cold."

The waiter drops a basket of bread on the table, with one lonely roll cut into three big slices. He raises his eyebrows at Joe, a look somewhere between exhaustion and hatred.

"I'll have the Mongolian Caesar salad, thank you. And a glass of whatever light beer you've got on tap."

"Slow down, Joe. It's a school night."

Slurp. Cracking of bread. A shower of crumbs on the table as bread goes from basket to bowl. She tears it and dunks it in the soup, not delicately, but like she's trying to drown the bread, water-boarding it. As she bites into it, a white drip escapes the corner of her mouth. She catches it with the nail of her left thumb and then licks it.

He'd like to sit back, get some distance, but there's nowhere to go. "I got an early train tomorrow."

Through a mouthful: "Whe?"

"Toronto."

"Why are you taking the train?"

"I don't have a car."

"No wonder you're always late. Anyway, it's a business trip, right? Rent one."

"I'd rather take the train."

"What on earth for?"

"I like trains. They're comfortable. I can work a bit, stare out the window, chat with people. And I don't have to deal with any traffic or stressed out drivers."

"Rent a car, Joe. With sat-nav. It'll be sooo much easier."

Slurp. More bread torture. She's almost finished, and is sliding the last bit of bread around the bowl, lapping in a spiral, herding the remaining soup into a white pool at the bottom. He wonders if she will lick the bowl.

"Good?"

She pushes the bowl away, almost in disgust. "Ordinary."

His beer arrives. It's cold, but the glass is warm and smells faintly of pine detergent.

"To soft landings."

"What?"

"It's something Max used to say."

"Who's he?"

"My dad. He always said it as a toast."

"You've lost me. Can't he just say cheers like a normal person?"

"He was a runner. Did a stack of marathons."

"I still don't get it."

"A soft landing keeps your legs fresh. Your joints don't hurt, you don't cramp up, don't get any blisters. It means you can last the race."

"I had a boyfriend who was a runner. Terrell. Got up every morning at six."

"It takes commitment."

"He was sooo boring. All he could talk about was how fast he could run, and about all the injuries he'd had to overcome. Duh-hull."

Joe raises his glass. "Well, anyway, to soft landings."

"That's not really worth drinking to."

"Max thought so. And he hated to fly as well. Maybe that's what he meant."

She laughs. "You certainly come from a line of brave men. Now, why were you late?"

"The guy at the bus stop? The heart attack?"

"Right. He die?"

"No, I think he'll be all right. But I don't know what happened after they put him in the ambulance."

"And how did this impact you? You know him?"

"I called the ambulance. It took ages to get there."

She throws her hands in the air in geriatric frustration. "Why is it sooo hard for people to be on time?"

"There was too much traffic. Sainte Catherine was jammed."

"You should've called me."

"Instead of the ambulance?"

She taps the table with her right index finger, the strings of ligaments flexing and pulsing. "I rushed here to be on time, you know."

"Sorry. I didn't mean to be late. I was really looking forward to this, but I couldn't just leave the guy."

"You just left me here."

"I didn't even want to be involved. I just got caught in the middle of it. When I got to the bus stop, he was already arguing with some other guy."

"About what?"

"You won't believe it."

"I'm not sure I believe any of it."

The waiter places Joe's salad in front of him.

"Thank you."

"You're welcome. Anything else?"

Siobahn eyes the salad. "That looks good. Another fork."

"You can use mine."

"Ew. That's like sharing toothpaste."

"You mean a toothbrush."

"That's worse. I had a boyfriend who used to squeeze the toothpaste right into his mouth. Dequawn. Sucked it out when it was nearly empty. Disguh-husting."

The waiter gives her a fork from a nearby table and she attacks Joe's salad.

"About this so-called argument at the bus stop to hell. It was over...?"

"Cigarette butts."

"Hah. What a story. Joe, why don't you just admit you were late? You can tell me you took an extra ten minutes doing your hair."

"Forget it."

"No, no. Go on. I like a good story."

Joe pokes at his salad. Siobahn parries his fork aside.

"I think the guy was a little crazy."

"Well, he's in hospital now so who cares."

"The other guy. He was yelling at the guy to pick up his cigarette butts. The ground was covered with them."

"You got something against smokers?"

"No. People can smoke if they want. That's their choice. I'm fine with it. I'd probably smoke too if I didn't swim anymore."

"And? What happened?"

"They shouted at each other. The guy who had the heart attack stubbed out a cigarette right at the feet off the other guy, really got in his face. So, the crazy guy scooped up a handful of butts and threw them at him."

"Definitely crazy."

"Yeah, but he had a point. There was a trash can right next to the guy who was smoking."

"Don't take the moral high ground. This has nothing to do with littering. Sometimes you've got to stand up just to let people know you're not their bitch. But you probably wouldn't know the first thing about that."

He chews slowly, wondering why Siobahn even goes out with him. Maybe she fears Enora's wrath as well. "The whole thing seemed pointless. Since when are cigarette butts worth fighting over, worth defending?"

"You still have to stand up."

"There's gotta be more important things in life than that. It was totally weird to see these two guys arguing over something so trivial, and the smoker talked on his phone the whole time."

She stabs at Joe's salad again, with some trepidation, like she knows she shouldn't, and feels guilty doing so, but also feels she deserves it. "Interesting guy. Knows what he wants. Shame his heart went on him."

"Huh. What bad luck."

"So, the crazy guy made a completely unnecessary scene and then the cool guy's heart gave up."

"Well, he pushed him a little."

"The crazy guy?"

"The other guy. He shoved the crazy guy to the ground and then turned his back on him. Still talking on his phone too. He was giving a running commentary of what was going on."

"I like this guy. I'm starting to believe this all actually might've happened."

"The whole thing could've be avoided if the guy had just put his butts in the trash."

Siobahn gets a fork-load of salad. She holds it up in the air between them, fork in her granny hand, like a trophy. The lettuce drips. "They're not just his butts."

"That's true. People litter every day."

"Yes, so think of it as creating a job for someone. There you go. Littering's good for the economy."

"We should all dump our trash on the streets. Nuclear waste too."

"Now you're being melodramatic. It's just a cigarette."

"Yeah, maybe you're right. But it's the action that gets me. The fact he doesn't care."

"But the crazy guy, he cares."

"Yeah."

"So, to summarise. You were late because an idiot got annoyed with some innocent guy who dropped one pathetic cigarette butt? And then tried to educate him about not littering when there's, like, a thousand other more important things for a person to learn, and he got pissed and started defending his actions, like a rational person would?"

"And got so worked up about it, he had a heart attack."

"And all the while I was sitting here waiting for you. That's me, who works sixty hours a week."

"Sorry."

"You should be."

Siobahn keeps talking, but Joe is at the bus stop. The man is lying on the ground. Joe reaches down to grab the man's phone, but he holds onto it, clutches it to his chest. Joe takes out his own phone and calls an ambulance. While on hold, he looks down at the man. He's clenching and unclenching his jaw, all the small muscles on his cheeks rippling. The man grunts, once, as a man would when lifting something too heavy, grunting with failure. Joe watches the internal fight, some obscure battle taking place at rapid pace, a life playing out with only the good stuff remembered. Or only the bad stuff. Resentment, anger, bitterness, injustice, an unending list of all things unfair. Not even a glimmer of satisfaction, a sense that it's okay to go now and to be happy with all he's done. No. Just a look of leaving behind so many things unfinished, undone, unachieved. But then that fades and regret creases his face, cracking lines on his forehead that appear like crossed out sentences, corrections of mistakes made years ago, or yesterday. Yes, everything in your life has come down to this, lying on the ground next to the trash can you should have used. Joe finally gets through and shouts for the ambulance. The man looks up at Joe. He reaches up to grab the sleeve of Joe's pink shirt. His eyes glaze and widen, trying to look ahead with hope but seeing nothing. No tunnel, no light, no silver and gold escalator, no judgement gate. Emptiness. Darkness. So the fear becomes frustration, a knitting of the eyebrows so severe it makes a deep squiggle between his nose and forehead that resembles a question mark. Why indeed? He looks at Joe again, his skin paling, his face softening, letting go, giving up. What's that? Gratitude? Nothing left to worry about, nothing to fear, no one to please. The day-to-day battle of getting and satisfying is over, and all that hassle and pluck, all those hard fought small victories, it was all for nothing. Relief.

Buzz. Buzz.

Joe snaps out of it. Siobahn drops her fork and snatches at her phone.

"Hi, Leahnee...At Ralph's...Francine recommended it...No, not so good. But you might like it. Lots of wieners on the menu."

"Siobahn, do you mind?"

She cups her wizened hand over the phone, giving him an irritated look. "I'm done already."

"Yeah, but I'd like to talk to you. This is our date."

"Sorry, Leahnee. It's just Joe...Yeah, it's like I told you. Sooo many issues...Um, what time is it?"

Joe reaches for the phone, but Siobahn pulls back.

"What the hell are you doing?"

"I'm sorry. I didn't mean...Look, we're having dinner."

She stands up, the stool sliding a little and the cushion falling to the floor. "You know what, I think I will meet you for a drink. Joe just flipped on me. He went from girly to psycho in half a salad. See you in five."

She palms the phone and shoulders her massive handbag, which bulges with weighty contents.

"Siobahn, wait a minute."

She turns and leaves, like she's exiting a stage, heels clacking, extensions flowing, walking in that strange way girls do in very high heels; leading with her knees and looking like she's about to topple over with each step.

Joe looks down at the remains of his salad. She polished off most of it, methodically pushing the slithers of radish to one corner of the triangular plate, so they lay there in a neat pinkish pile. In his pocket, his phone buzzes.

"srry, j. its not working. lets go our own wayz."

Selling solutions to Cool Hand Lou

A large man enters the pharmacy.

Joe looks at Louis. "Your turn."

"I could play this all day, but let's say winner takes all with this guy. Loser buys lunch."

"That's how we used to do it in high school. Shooting free throws."

"Those cafeteria lunches weren't worth anything."

"And you always missed the one shot that mattered."

"Don't remind me. What's the score?"

"Two all."

"You go first this time."

Joe shakes his head. "You've got home field advantage. You go."

"All right. Hmm. That stance. That look on his face. My money's on haemmorrhoids."

"You really think so?"

"Yeah, he's a backdoor man, I'm sure of it. Gives him haems too, because he likes it rough."

"That's disgusting."

"I'll be glad to be wrong, but maybe I'll put on some latex gloves if his prescription makes its way up here."

"He's got one. Look at him, waving it like it's a winning lottery ticket."

Louis screws up his face. "But he's so nervous. Maybe it's something sexual. He looks a little limp."

"Liftomex?"

"Could be?"

"You can buy all those dick pumpers online. That's not the kind of thing you go into a pharmacy for."

"Or they send in their wives or girlfriends."

"The beneficiaries."

"Geez, Joe, can you imagine those old hags getting worked over from every angle?"

"Well, you're parents made you at some point, probably with a fair amount of chemicals in their system."

"Are you calling my mother an old hag? Anyway, I went from petri dish to test tube. No intercourse involved."

"So, you're going with Liftomex?"

Louis nods. "Yeah. You?"

Joe looks down at the man. He's sporting Joe's hairstyle except it looks like he got it directly from the pillow and not from application. There's something dishevelled about him, as if he just roused himself but took his time doing so. His pants are creased in the right places, but his shirt is half hanging out. He's fidgety and impatient. His hands constantly move over the top of each other, like he's trying to keep them warm, or simply trying to keep them active. He slides up the sleeve of his jacket a few times, looks past the people waiting at the counter in front of him.

"You think he's nervous because he's embarrassed?"

"For sure. A third peg minus the wood."

"I think he's just insecure. And not because he can't get it up. Looks like getting up in the morning is hard enough."

"Anti-d's?"

"Some kind of fire extinguisher. Put out the flames in his head. Probably Sailiun. All the doctors are prescribing that these days. It's like a miracle cure."

The man gets to the counter and the prescription is passed up to Louis.

"And the drugs go to...Sailiun. Jesus, Joe, did you stop him in the street?"

"I'm right?"

"Jumbo pack. But not for Denoris."

"Natrofield?"

"Yep. Amazing how people stick to a brand. When it's all the same stuff."

"Don't forget generics, Louis. Same pills, half the price. But you didn't hear that from me."

"No one buys generics."

"That's because they think they're getting an inferior product."

Louis opens a draw and pulls out a box of Sailiun. "Sorry. Have to follow the docket."

"Natrofield bribes doctors to prescribe their brand. Organise all sorts of junkets."

"I know. I've been on a couple."

"Traitor. Where's your loyalty?"

"In my other lab coat. But how did you know it was Sailiun?"

"Lucky guess."

"It wasn't."

"Let's just say he's showing some of the signs. I was involved in the clinical trial as an intern. We actually developed it first, but Natrofield pulled strings to get approved faster and beat us onto the market. They also poached the developer behind it. Drove up to his house with a dump truck full of money."

Louis laughs. "I'm still glad you came down. To visit."

"Gotta go after the people I know to get some sales."

"Ah, ulterior motives. A man low down on the sales count."

Joe pulls out a large binder from his leather satchel. "I also came down to deliver this."

"The new catalogue. Denoris helping people forget their troubles."

"It's mostly just new packaging. Rebranded solutions."

"All comforting blues and greens. Yellows for hope and sunny days."

"Something like that."

Louis takes the catalogue. "You could've mailed this, but I'm glad you didn't. Always good to catch up."

"Yeah."

"Nice bag by the way."

"The satchel?"

"I never noticed it before. Where'd you get it?"

"Found it at a fleamarket in Berlin about a hundred years ago. I like to tell myself some old spy used to own it. Carried around top secret documents in it. A gun with a silencer. A laser-firing pen."

"Still Captain Fantasy. Day-dreaming Joe."

"I don't have time for that anymore."

Down at the cashier, the man shouts; "What's taking so long?"

Louis sneers. "He better pop one before he leaves."

"Easy. You don't wanna know the statistics of people who are on this stuff."

"Enlighten me."

"Half of Canada. Most of the States. A frightening number of kids."

Louis whistles. "Jesus."

"They used to look to him. But now it seems the answers are at the bottom of a white box."

Louis slips out of his white coat and leads the way down the short stairs. He drops the box of Sailiun on the counter as he passes.

"Cover for me, Sandra. I'm going to lunch."

Outside on busy Spadina Avenue, they wait for the green light.

Joe has to shout over the traffic. "I'm not gonna hold you to that bet, Louis. Lunch is on me."

"Before Natrofield buys me a hybrid?"

"If they haven't already."

"In that case, you can buy me dinner as well."

"Deal. Let's burn through my extremely limited expense account."

They cross the street towards the bagel shop.

***

The Toronto Mayola boasts a swimming and spa complex, but this turns out to be a portable, toilet-sized sauna that only works at restricted times and a six metre wading pool that's a little on the green side. All downstairs in the basement. Disappointing. So he abandons his corporate burqa and walks over to the university to churn out his three Ks in the fifty metre pool on Harbord Street.

A couple of groups are training. Teenagers, college kids, crammed in ten to a lane and swimming close enough for fingers to touch toes, mechanically sweeping through the same style, without passion or joy. Robots, with great technique. Duck-walking coaches are patrolling the edges. One coach is standing on the starting block of lane three. He has a stopwatch around his neck, a whistle and a grey hint of chlorine in his pallor. Looped over his right wrist is a plastic bag full of inhalers.

The groups are making it a fast pool. While stretching, Joe watches the handful of adults in lane four giving everything to keep up with the machines in three. The three public lanes are set by speed – slow, medium, fast – but nobody's keeping to them. It's chaos.

He sits down next to the block of lane six, the supposed fast lane. He dangles his feet in the water and makes small circles with his legs. He puts on his swim cap, presses in his ear plugs and breathes in and out. He spits in his goggles, rubs them with his thumbs and rinses them in the gutter. Goggles on, he stretches the skin around his eyes to get a good seal. The ear plugs silence the splashing and echoes, dull the screech of whistles and the shouted demands of the coaches. He counts to three, moving his arms in a few strokes, trying to imagine them gliding through the water.

He can hear his heart.

The end of the pool looks far away, but he will get there, flip, and then come back, flip again, until he reaches sixty. No stopwatch, no lap splits, no heart-rate monitors. There's nothing to do but swim to the end and flip. To breathe in and out. Solitude, silence, one arm in front of the other, climbing the ladder, kicking without effort. An easy forty-five minutes of swimming.

He wishes the pool was empty, that he had a lane to himself, but that's not how life works. There are always people around. Life is a shared experience. Nothing's private. Everything is open to comment, blogged and gossiped about as it happens.

"Complicated."

Yes, he thinks, complicated. Over-complicated. And that goes into everything we do, even into the pool. Look at them, sinking under the weight of all the crap they carry with them, thrashing their arms and kicking like mad to stay afloat. It looks so hard. Sooo hard, as Siobahn would say.

He feels bad about what happened last night, sabotaging his own date. He should've just let her talk on the phone, should've let it go.

He takes another deep breath and lowers himself into the water. It's cold. He wants to get out. He pushes his face into the water and blows bubbles at his goggles, to be sure of the seal. One bubble manages to squeeze through, but that's okay; it will keep that side from fogging up.

He waits for the next swimmer to hit the wall. He'll pass him before they get halfway, but it's polite to wait and say hello. The guy pushes a wave of water against the wall, slaps his hands against it and stops. He turns his back to Joe and hangs on the lane rope, breathing loudly.

"All right if I join you?"

The guy turns his head slightly and looks over his shoulder. His goggles are orange and too small for his face, making him look beady-eyed and sinister. "What?"

"Can I swim in the lane with you?"

"Sure. It's a free country."

"Always polite to ask."

"Buddy, it's a pool."

The guy turns his back again and hangs on the lane rope.

Joe stares ahead, his face half submerged. From this view, he can't see the end. He imagines the pool as a deserted lake, somewhere in

New England, down a dirt path wide enough only for motorbikes.

"Be the Russian."

He pushes off from the wall, dolphin kicks underwater, hands clasped, then launches smoothly into freestyle.

***

The Toronto Mayola continues to disappoint. It claims to have free wireless internet, but the connection is so weak in his room, he's forced to take his notebook downstairs and sit in the lobby restaurant. It's a miserable enclosure, dotted with corporate transients at varying stages of sobriety, all spying the waitress with one-night eyes. He's one of them, in a business shirt open at the collar, with nowhere to go in this strange city, at least until Louis shows up.

A group of transients has collected at the bar, like suited fence posts strung together in a tight ring. It sounds like they're attempting to laugh through their misery. They look like the kind of men who got married for career reasons and whose small children now live in other cities. Men who hang their suit coats from the little hooks above the back windows of their cars. Men who frequent laundromats on Friday nights, and have cleaning ladies, and have half a dozen local Chinese take-outs on speed dial. Men who have profiles on dating websites. Men who wake up at three in the morning and stare at the ceiling, wondering how their lives came to this, wondering where they're going, and wondering why they're even bothering to try to get there.

He'd like to chat with them, to hear what they've got to say, to have them hear what he's got to say. Therapy of sorts. But it's easier just to turn his chair to face the window. The waitress appears at his shoulder, a pained, bored look on her face.

"Do you have any tea?"

"Sure."

"Green tea, with honey. Thanks."

"I'll see what I can do."

In the reflection, he can see the dark lines under his eyes left by his goggles. A good swim, he thinks, even with all those idiots trying to ruin it.

He boots up his notebook. The tea arrives, accompanied by a single serving of what looks like breakfast honey; the difficult-to-open kind given to airline caterers. He lifts the tea bag out and squeezes it.

It's not very hot. After several tries, he gets the top off the honey and spoons some into the cup. He stirs and sips. It tastes papery and thin, as tea bag tea always does. Worse, it's barely warm. He wonders if the waitress used tap water. He drinks it in a gulp.

He clears his email, copying and pasting in the standard replies from his special drafts folder. It's a real time-saver, especially for work stuff. He'll deal with the invitations on the train back. Any conference has to be cleared with Supe first.

"Anything else?"

"Yeah, same again. But could you please boil the water this time?"

"I did."

"Well, unfortunately, on the journey from the bar to here, it got cold."

"Fine."

She trudges away. In the reflection of the window, he watches her make a show of filling the kettle and turning it on. Some comment to the suited automatons cracks them up and they huddle closer to the bar, shoulder to shoulder, corralling the waitress.

He focuses on his screen, reads the news of the day. He jumps over to ceeville and scrolls through all the billboards, comments and happenings. There's an announcement from Siobahn, accompanied by a small gravestone: "Siobahn decided she had one too many architects in her city and buried you in her cemetery."

"Huh. That was quick."

Siobahn is still on his list of ceevillians. He clicks on her photo. Her page comes up, but he can't see anything except her photo: big sunglasses, pink lips, one vile granny hand clutched around an extravagant fruit cocktail raised in a toast.

"To soft landings."

He sees she's changed her title to Princess. The last time he checked it was Queen. How many dates did they have? Five? Five and a half. And they slept together once. He grimaces, remembering that night: the awkwardness, the acting, the expectations, the intense feeling that there was a film crew in the room, and the let down as he discovered she was yet another girl schooled in sex being about the man doing everything to please her. Those looks of consternation and disappointment threw him off, turned him off, but actually made him last longer. And, ironically, she was impressed, even if she didn't show it. Throughout the whole act, he just wanted to pat her shoulder and tell her everything is all right. He wanted to hug her more than fuck her. Seeing her naked was not like seeing her as she really was. She even accessorised her nudity, with a few strings of beads, assorted bracelets and necklaces, and a pierced navel, and she turned the lights off and pulled the sheets up before he could even get a decent look. Her turn, his turn, unnatural positioning; like something drawn with stick figures in a guide book. Then after, wondering if he should stay the night. He opted to sleep on the edge of the bed as a sort of compromise. In the morning, he woke up to see that Siobahn actually looked a lot better in the pure light, her eyes closed, her face serene. But she made for the bathroom, leaving the door ajar so she could talk to him. A half hour later, she reappeared, her face set, looking like a stranger and, interestingly, behaving like a different person.

Now she was a princess waiting to become a queen again. He feels sad that it ended that way it did. He really should've just let it go, the whole phone thing. His fault.

The waitress drops the tea on the table. Again, he lifts the tea bag out and squeezes it, but nearly burns his fingers.

"Hot enough?"

"Yes. Thanks."

This is what life has come to, he thinks, wiping his hand on a napkin. A battle of wills, everyone trying to impose their way of thinking onto everyone else. Each single person working overtime to claim victory. Still, at least it's hot. I got what I wanted.

He stirs in some honey and slides the saucer over the top of the cup. In his pocket, his phone buzzes.

"yo bro. where you at????? comin to pland soon????? b gr8 2 c ya."

He writes: "turonno. have invite to conf in seattle. clear with boss 1st. get back to studying."

The phone buzzes again.

"okok. c u in hb."

He puts his phone away. "Crap. The wedding."

He goes back to the screen of his notebook. He has an invitation to join Nate Morrison's get well page. He clicks on it, recognising the man from the bus stop last night, and wonders how he got the invitation. Nate's tribute city has over a thousand ceevillians. No wall has been built around the city so Joe can read all the comments posted.

"All the best, Nate. You'll be back better than ever."

"The Boob Bar isnt the same without you."

"Nate, your the last person sumthing like this should of happened to."

"Why? Why? Why? Why? Why?"

"Get well, Nate, from all the girls at BB."

"Nate's the GREATEST guy. So undeserved. So shokcing."

And so on in that vein. He goes to Plasher and puts Nate Morrison into the search box. There's a conversation happening about Nate. It's moving fast, with experienced plashers able to punch out the short comments in a few seconds.

"Great guy. We went to school together."

"I met him at a party once. Funny, charming, total stud."

"I dont understand. I dont understand."

"Is he really the owner of the Boob Bar?"

"Co-owner."

"May be a femminist got her revenge?"

He laughs at this, but the plashes come thick and fast in Nate's defense. According to the comments, the guy's an absolute saint. Joe decides to make a plash in the pond, as buttman.

He writes: "Great guys shouldn't drop cigarettes on the ground. That's karma for you."

He sits back, sips his tea and waits.

"What's that got to do with anything, arsewipe?"

"Nate told me at NY he was given up the coffin nails."

"You don't know shit about Nate buttman."

"Buttman's got his finger so far up his own arse he can tickle his tonsils."

"Get a life. Nate never dropped his trash. He helpt everyone."

"Go to the top of the nearest building, buttman, and jump."

Louis knocks on the window and gestures for him to come outside. Joe closes the page and shuts down his computer.

Hot drink with Solo Snapper and the Multitasking Failure

"That was good, Xav. Thanks for making me go."

Xav stretches, hamming it up for the girls walking out, cracking his neck and trying to look serene. "I feel so loose. You wanna get a coffee?"

Joe checks his watch. "Why not?"

"Where you got to rush off to? Another date with Enora's pal?"

"That's dusted."

"What'd you call her?"

"Baggage Handler."

"Yeah. Hah."

"My fault. I messed it up."

"You're probably better off. Anyone from Enora's clique is bound to be a big old can of crazy. Girls with issues have friends with issues."

"You are who you hang out with."

They stare at each other, briefly, as this statement hangs awkwardly between them.

"Yeah, well, let's meet at Steamers, eh?"

Joe walks to his bike and unlocks it. "Text Francois. Last one there pays."

Xav hits the switch on his key, making the indicators of the Calamity flash once. "You're on. Warm up your wallet."

Joe clips the heavy lock around his waist. He shoulders his satchel, turns on his lights, puts on his helmet and leather gloves, and tucks the right jeans hem into his sock. On the bike, he slaloms on the sidewalk before taking a driveway to get onto the street. The road is wide enough, but there's no bike lane marked. He rides cautiously, hands on brakes, checking over his left shoulder for the traffic and eyeing every parked car in case a door flies open, which happens a lot more often than it should. No matter how many luminous jackets and straps he wears – not even if he attached a 200-watt stage spotlight to his handle bars – the people just don't look for him.

It's a lovely spring evening, chilly and clear. Everyone seems glad to be putting winter behind them.

The first traffic light turns orange and he pedals hard, getting across just as the cars start to stream over the intersection like glowing liquid metal. He turns and sees Xav stuck at the light.

It's still early enough for the traffic to be heavy, for all the high-potentials and ultra-motivated to be scurrying home after an eleven hour day. There's nothing unusual about all the hurrying and urgency, the near-misses and impatience. Everyone's got somewhere better to be, some place more important than here. Drivers take risks to get ahead, ducking around double-parked cars when the space is barely wide enough. More dangerous than the cars are the people who just start walking across the street, appearing from in front of stopped buses like apparitions or ghosting through the narrow gaps between parked cars. Ignoring every rule they were taught as children, they cross the street, maybe bothering to check left or right once half way. Joe is forced to brake and weave. The people aren't remotely apologetic; some scowl like it's his fault, that he's getting in their way.

Xav zooms past, leaning forward in his seat, frowning, and so concentrated on his texting he doesn't even notice Joe.

Other bikers slow Joe down, but he cheats a couple of times to make a race of it, sneaking across when the lights are red – to a chorus of shouts and horns – and once getting off his bike to walk across with the pedestrians. He manages to pass Xav again but when he gets to Steamers, the Calamity's out front, parked hastily so its right bumper is sticking out like a broad blue arse. Cars have to wait until the road is clear before zipping around it.

He locks his helmet to his bike.

"You're completely mad to get around on that thing."

"Global warming, Francois."

"Please. That's a theory. And I've seen your apartment. It's not exactly a shining example of plastic and glass separation."

"I'm reducing my carbon footprint by riding. If only everyone else was so eco-friendly."

"Then there might be a song about our city."

"Hum a few bars."

He sings: "There are thirty-five bicycles in Montreal. No, doesn't sound quite right."

"You've got yourself a hit, with the right software."

"And the right branding and marketing."

"Don't start. And don't use the b-word in front of Xav."

"Still, we could shoot a funny clip and stick it on Veedus. Become an overnight internet sensation."

"Pass."

"Yeah, making a funny video is a lot harder than it looks."

They head inside. Steamers is decorated like an old railway station café. Maps and signs on the walls, a menu board that looks like a timetable, train knickknacks picked up at fleamarkets, a dusty model train set behind glass that attracts kids but disappoints because it doesn't work, photographs of trains winding around and through the Alps, and a print copy of Monet's smoky and foggy rendition of the Gare St Lazare. On one wall, there's an enormous Roman numeraled clock stuck at 9:53. The lighting is dim. Most of the patrons are slouched over notebooks and tablets. A few have headsets on and are talking animatedly, like they're alone in the room. One girl is holding an e-reader in front of her face and seems caught in indecision; as if she doesn't know what to read or doesn't know why she's even reading.

They see Xav huddled over his phone in a booth by the window, which has thin frilly curtains in front of it and a pull-down shutter.

Joe moves towards the booth. "Looks like I lost."

"Lost what?"

"We raced here, but we both lost at yoga."

"How do you lose at yoga? Couldn't touch your toes?"

"Actually, Francois, I can touch my toes, now."

They fall into the booth. Xav looks up briefly.

"Bon soir. That's a latte, Mr. Solitus. Jumbo size."

"Feel free to order the lobster as well."

Xav continues texting, manipulating the screen with deft touches of his fingers, sliding and pressing with fast-learned dexterity. "Not hungry."

"I'm not paying for anything until you put that thing away."

"Just clearing my email."

Francois leans over the table. "He's on ceeville. 'Managed to put one leg behind ear at yoga but no girls impressed. Licked own eyebrows and that got their attention.'"

"It doesn't say that."

Joe laughs. "Come on, Xav. Tech off the table. You're in the real world now, with real friends."

Xav presses the phone a few times and then puts it in his pocket. "My people wanted an update from their king."

"Right. Joe says you lost at yoga. That means you actually raised your blood pressure."

"No sign of the redhead from last Friday."

The waiter, in a conductor's uniform replete with old-fashioned cap, slightly askew, and his fly half open, stands at their booth.

Xav points at Joe. "My latte's on him."

"An unlucky latte."

"Green tea, please, with honey."

Francois offers a cheesy grin. "I'll have an express-o."

The waiter looks up blandly. "That is so funny. You're the first person ever to say that in here."

The waiter chugs to the next booth.

Francois picks up a spoon and uses it as a microphone. "Ladies and gentlemen, there will be no service on this train. Now, back to yoga. What about this redhead? She get the dirty job done?"

Xav screws up his face. "What?"

Joe smiles. "He's quoting Springsteen. I called the redhead Swami Scully. Xav says she gave him a soulful look last week."

Xav nods. "The eye and then some."

"She was probably in a trance."

"It was definitely a look, Francois. I'm gonna talk to her next week."

"When she's there."

"She'll be there. On Friday, like last week. You in, Joe?"

"Can't. I'm going to Boston."

Francois drums the table with his fingers. "What for?"

"Some indie developer is giving a presentation about his product."

"What is it?"

"Some vanity pill. A quick fixer, or something like that."

"You staying the night?"

"No."

Xav puts his phone back on the table. "Good. Then you'll be back for yoga. Swami Scully is sure to have a friend."

"I won't make it. I'm heading up to Harbrook after the presentation."

"Why? Someone die?"

"My ma's getting married. Remarried."

Xav taps the screen of his phone. "A Vermont wedding. Great place to meet some country lass and have a roll in the hay."

"It's New Hampshire."

"I knew that. I was joking with you."

The waiter puts their drinks on the table.

Joe goes to work on his tea. "Don't worry, Xav. Everyone mixes them up."

"There's plenty of people that think Canada is a state of America."

Francois sips his espresso, delicately. "And plenty of Americans who think Europe is a country. How you gonna get there, Joe?"

Outside, a horn blares. A truck is stuck behind the Calamity's arse.

"Eddie."

"Will she make it?"

"Hope so. She should be full of go after her winter hibernation. And she's better on the open road than in the city."

Xav looks out the window, watching the truck edge around his car. "Forget the bike. Rent a car. I'd let you take mine but I need it."

"To race the bus to work?"

Xav taps at his phone. "Rain on Friday in Boston. You better drive. No. Fly to Boston and rent a car at the airport. Charge it all to Denny. Visit a pill house in Westbrook."

"Harbrook."

"Right. Make up some reason to be there and charge all your expenses."

"Can't. I promised Eddie."

Francois drains his espresso. "You looking forward to it?"

"The trip, yeah. The wedding, not really."

"How come?"

"She's marrying Len."

"Who's Len?"

Francois runs his hands through his hair. "You're an idiot, Xav. Don't you ever listen?"

"What? I can't ask? I don't know who Len is."

Joe holds up a calming hand. "It's all right, Xav. Len's the idiot. They've been friends for ages. Worked together. They were a couple, but tried to convince the whole town they were just friends. No one bought it. I just never expected them to get married."

"He'll be your step-dad."

"That's an incredible deduction. Did the internet tell you that?"

Francois laughs. "Is Gordie flying in?"

"Yeah. I think Len paid for his ticket."

Xav slurps his latte. "That's nice of him. He bankrolling your bro's education too?"

"Maybe. Max had life insurance, but I think Len's contributing."

"Not such an evil step-dad after all."

"He didn't offer to buy me a ticket."

"Then be nicer to him at the wedding. Maybe he'll introduce you to some of his nieces."

"Doesn't have any. He's an only child."

"Still, there should be some tail to chase out in the back woods."

Francois drums the table again. "Xavier, when was the last time you actually had a date?"

"Hey, work takes up a lot of time. I went out with one of Enora's gal pals a couple of weeks ago. Disaster. She wasn't worth the bill."

"What happened?"

"She brought all these hoops for me to jump through. Stopped short of setting them on fire."

"Who's Enora?"

"She has the cubicle between me and Joe. We can't have a conversation without her butting in."

Joe nods. "The Corporate Hipster."

"Why hipster?"

"She tries to dress retro, lot of greys and flannel, like she's the fifth Beatle. But she's also a bit on the hip, which kind of detracts from the skinny sixties look she's going for."

Xav looks out the window, eyeing his car again. "She's always trying to set us up with her friends."

"She has a limitless supply, like she's part of ten different singles support groups."

"And they've all been schooled on *Sex and the City*. You don't have a chance. It's over before they even tell you their name."

Francois grins. "Maybe you're not what they want."

"What they want doesn't exist. I'm willing to compromise and they should too."

Joe sips his tea. "I'm done with that."

"What about Stephanie?"

"Siobahn."

Xav's phone beeps and he starts playing with it. "Right, Siobahn. Come on. I'm listening."

"I wasn't too happy when she talked on the phone during dinner."

"Rude bitch."

Francois laughs. "You should take her out, Xav. You're made for each other."

"I can do this in front of you guys, but I would never do this on a date."

"What about that billboard you posted a couple of months ago? 'Looks like the king is in.' And that was during a date."

"That was a mistake."

"Because she was your ceevillian."

"Yeah. She went to the bathroom before dessert and came back all flustered and pissed."

Joe turns to Francois. "Enora said she poured a drink over his head."

"That's a lie. I won't be making that mistake again."

Francois shakes his head. "Could you go one day without using that thing?"

"He couldn't go an hour."

"Sure, I could. I lived half my life without it. If they all disappeared tomorrow, I wouldn't even miss it. But as long as we have the technology, we might as well use it."

"I'm sure you'll be first in line to have that thing implanted in your palm."

"You're just as bad, Joe."

"When I'm at work, yeah, but that's because I have to."

"You're like a little kid. Fine. I'll put it in my pocket."

"You know, Siobahn ended our very brief relationship with a text."

"Yeah?"

Xav shrugs. "There's nothing new about that. My sis told me she has a message saved in her drafts exactly for that purpose. She once sent it to me by mistake."

"What did it say?"

Xav takes out his phone, locates the message and points the screen at them.

"'we aint that gr8 2gether. srry.'"

"That's her brext."

Joe sits back. "Have I met her?"

Xav nods.

"Refresh my memory."

"Female. Everything a little less than me. Not as clever. Not as tall. Not as successful."

"Not as vain."

"Not as ugly."

"You guys gonna take this duo on the road?"

"Did she have really short hair?"

"Yep. Bleached."

"Ah, yeah. She's at UVic, right? Something with computers."

"Computer science and psychology."

Francois rubs his eyes. "Sounds like a nerd."

"No, no. She was really interesting. I chatted with her for most of the night. The others at the party were pretty boring. A lot of work people. But there was something strange about her."

Xav nods. "She's totally weird. A full on tomboy. Plays hockey. Never had an email address."

"That's it. I asked for it but she said she didn't have one. Why is that, Xav?"

"She never needed it. She does it all with her phone and IM-ing on ceeville. She reckons the whole email thing is too nineties."

"What was her name again?"

"Iris."

"Yeah, Iris. That was at your birthday party last year."

Xav frowns. "The big three-o."

"She's definitely not as old as you."

"You'll be there soon, Joe, and let me tell you, it won't be pleasant."

Francois leans back and puts an arm along the booth, behind Joe. "Relax, Xav. Thirty is the new twenty. At the rate people are living, turning thirty pretty much means maybe a quarter of your life is over."

"I guess we're to blame for that."

"No, Joe. Natrofield is. They make all those life extenders and HGH supplements."

"One of their goons will probably be at my meeting in Boston."

Francois turns to Joe. "Why's that bad?"

Xav drains the foam from his latte. "Because, Francois, they're a bunch of dirty thieving pricks."

"Aw, you're just being nice. How do you really feel about them?"

"They're nothing but a brand, and that's everything in this business. Reputation, branding, corporate identity, market leader. Consumers trust the brand because they think it's the best, and they won't change, even when our products are better."

"Are they better?"

Joe smiles. "It's all the same stuff."

"That's not the point, Joe."

Screech of brakes. Crash.

"Oh, fuck."

Xav leaps out of the booth and dashes for the door. Joe and Francois pull back the frilly curtain to look through the window. Outside, a man gets out of his car to inspect the damage, looking only at his own car. He puffs on his cigarette, flicks it at the Calamity and gets back into his car. He reverses and is about to drive off when Xav puts his hands on the hood.

Francois grimaces. "This might get messy."

"It won't. He's all show."

The driver tries to edge his car forward. Muffled shouting comes through the window.

"Shall we provide the voiceover?"

Francois sits up. "I'm definitely Xav. You stupid dumb bastard. Look what you've done to my precious phallic symbol."

"You're the one who parked with your big arse on the road. It's your fault."

"You're gonna pay for this."

"That heap's not worth twenty bucks. I'll give you ten just to get out of my way."

"It's brand new. I traded in my pink Prius for it last week."

Joe laughs.

Outside, the car is edging forward, pushing Xav down the street. Traffic is backing up, horns sounding. People lean out of their windows to shout. Others have stopped on the street to watch.

"Don't you break my beautiful chicken legs."

"Move. I'm late for little Johnny's class performance of *Hair*."

The car accelerates and Xav is forced to jump out of the way. He gives the man the finger, then walks back to inspect the Calamity's bumper. It's hanging limp and loose, like an arm off the side of a bed. Xav tries to put the bumper back in place.

"Of all the low, despicable, detestable things. He's going straight to hell. Now, if I could just, grunt, grunt, bend it into place, grunt. Oh, this is so heavy."

Xav gets the bumper back on.

"There. Good thing this piece of shit is so easy to fix. And doesn't it look good. My phallic symbol is whole again."

Xav dusts his hands and gives a nod of finality. The indicators of the Calamity flash once. He gets in and drives off.

"And I don't even need to say goodbye to my friends."

"You should be an actor, Francois."

"I'm half way there, pretending to be a photographer."

"How's your week been?"

"Bad. A mag in New Zealand sent me an email offering me five dollars, New Zealand dollars, for my pics of Niagara."

"Does that cover your espresso?"

"Just. But what about my rent? All that money I made doing those school shots in Quebec City is nearly gone. These days, every idiot's a photographer. Flickr, Getty, Free Images. You can get anything you want for nothing, or next to nothing, and nobody gives a crap about quality anymore."

"There's always yearbooks."

"Yeah, but where's the art in that?"

"At least it's lasting. In fifty years, people will still be looking at those photos."

"But they won't care who took them. Anyway, a couple more years and even the schools won't need me. The guidance counsellor will take the photos on her twenty megapixel phone. And the yearbook will be just a file to download. Nothing lasting. Nothing you can hold in your hands."

Joe swills the dregs of his tea. All the honey is at the bottom and the last sip is pleasurably sweet. "That all sucks. How's your love life?"

"Bad too. I know what you think about my life, but believe me, there's no glamour."

"Just be glad you're not a punch-clock Joe, like this Joe."

"That's something. Anyway, enough about me. You all right, with the wedding and all?"

"Yeah. I just wish it wasn't Len."

"That bad? Maybe he's changed. You know, mellowed. Doesn't fear the hand of God as much anymore."

"I think he's worse."

"When was the last time you were home?"

"Christmas, two, no, three years ago. Just after Gordie started college. He was majorly homesick and made me promise I'd go home for Christmas."

"How'd that go?"

"He gave us the wonderful gift of a gambling debt."

"You never said anything about that."

"Been trying to forget."

"Vegas?"

"Online. Raising Pokerzona. Me and Len split the damage."

"How much?"

Joe shakes his head. "Don't make me say it."

"You have that kind of money?"

"I wasn't gonna let Len pay it all."

"You borrowed it?"

"You could say that."

"What happened?"

"Ma forced Gordie to get some help."

"You never said anything about this."

"Who wants to know the inner crap of the average family? Can you imagine all the stories and secrets out there in suburbia?"

"That's the juice reality TV lives on."

"True."

"He still got that ridiculous goatee?"

"Last time I saw him, yep. And his love affair with the backwards baseball cap continues."

"He was into visors when he was here."

"That was embarrassing."

"What about the straw chewing?"

"That's still on. I think he likes the plastic high."

"He'll grow out of it, once he gets out of college and samples the mundane pleasures of the real world."

"Huh. Didn't you just declare that thirty is the new twenty?"

"How old is Gordie?"

"Nearly twenty-two. But he still acts like a teenager. Maybe it's like you said. Because we live to be older, that makes our youth longer. Everyone getting married later."

"Thirty-nine going on thirteen. I know plenty of people like that."

"Sometimes our office is like high school. Cliquey and ruled by popularity. People getting teased for what they wear and what they say. All these judgements passed based on what someone likes. And the only form of humour is thc toilet kind. You know what I mean?"

"Yeah. Well, no. I never worked in an office, but I can imagine it."

"Max used to say, pay attention at school because everything you'll ever need to know about life you'll learn during recess."

Francois coughs. "I guess it won't be easy going home."

"It'll be all right. All my old friends have moved away, but Gordie'll be there. And ma'll be too occupied to trawl through the past with me."

"Maybe this is a chance to talk with her."

"Pass. Can you feed Popov?"

"Sure. If you get back in time for our Sunday swim."

"Are you gonna hold him for ransom?"

"Ha-ha-ha. When you come home, he'll be sitting in my lap and I'll be stroking him, like some criminal mastermind."

Solo gig with Miss Untouchable

The world changes across the line. The dusty flat fields morph into tree-covered hills. There are grey-blue lakes, still chunky with clumps of ice even now in late spring. The straight, vacant highways curve and clog: mum-piloted SUVs, college kids driving with notebooks on their laps, huge pick-up trucks with one person in the cab. Guns which are normally locked away or used only for hunting trips are now under car seats and in glove compartments. Billboard-lined interstates lead to bland cities laid out in unimaginative, mathematically perfect grids, the roads with interchangeable names, and a downtown that's deserted and dangerous after work finishes. Across the line, an open, tolerant, almost European view narrows and jams, like the streets, and becomes one-way traffic.

Down I-89 and then onto I-93, like passing through a makeshift, inaccurate and terribly disappointing theme park of other places: Montpelier, Hanover, Lebanon, Manchester, Derry, New Hampshire, New England, but there's not much that's new about it.

The back roads would be nicer, down towards Hancock and Peterborough, where he and Max went with Eddie to go cross-country running when it was warm enough. He wouldn't have to concentrate as hard, be so aware of all the traffic, or have to make split second judgements of which drivers not to trust. He would wind through the forests, pass over single-lane wooden bridges with the planks rattling against Eddie's tires. But he's on the clock. It's better to be on the interstate, to sit in the slipstream of this truck and save petrol, and keep from freezing.

Eddie is like a hot water bottle between his legs.

It's good to be out of the city, out of the office.

He follows the truck all the way to the outskirts of Boston, until it takes the I-95 south. He thank-you-waves and accelerates to get behind the campervan with Idaho plates up ahead. The uninspiring skyline comes into view, another vaguely familiar city of glass and steel. A sign says "Boston next 28 exits."

He's early, but heads straight for Cambridge, following the arrows to Harvard and negotiating the chessboard of streets until he finds Beacon. Eddie makes it easier to change directions and double back, to make a quick illegal turn without holding up traffic. He tracks the numbers down Beacon and stops in front of a big, rectangular house that looks like it extends quite a way back from the road.

He brings Eddie to a halt and she lets out a final, wheezing gasp.

"You made it girl. I know. You love the open road. Rest up. We still got to get to Harbrook."

He unloops his satchel from around his shoulder and stows his jacket, pants and gloves in the right saddle bag, careful not to break the wine decanter, still in its box with the red "30% off" sticker on it. He swaps boots for shoes and checks himself in the mirror. He'd like to wash his face and hands, but there's not enough time. There's some water in his small travel flask and he uses this to wet his hands and face. He towels himself down with the satin inside of his suit jacket, loops the helmet straps over his right wrist, re-shoulders his satchel and walks towards the house.

On the wall next to the steps, someone has taped a piece of paper with "Sticky Solutions" written on it in pen and an arrow pointing towards the basement steps. He follows.

"Sounds like a porn studio."

There's a greasy switch next to the door, perhaps made greasy by the hands of a thousand pizza delivery boys. He presses it and hears the muffled sound of a lion roaring inside. The door is opened by a young guy with glasses and scraggly hair, worn long and combed forward so it curls upwards from his glasses. He's wearing a t-shirt that reads "True achievers reach high at a young age" and has the simple graphic of a kid hanging backwards from a flagpole by his underwear.

"Name. Company. Projected profit margin."

"Joe Solitus."

"From?"

"Denoris. I got no idea what our profit margin is."

"You're early. That means you're desperate."

"Traffic was light."

"Your better half called from the airport to say she's late. Gloria someone."

"Enora. Yielding."

"That's it."

"Are you Fabian Zambrowski?"

"Call me Fabian again and this meeting ends. I'm Fab."

"Okay."

Fab looks at the helmet. "Sweet fuck. Did you ride here?"

He nods.

"What, all the way from Toronto?"

"Montreal."

"Same dif. When you start?"

"At dawn. There was less traffic."

Fab looks past Joe. "Is that your Enfield?"

"Yep."

Fab pushes Joe aside and jumps up the stairs to get a closer look. Joe is impelled to follow.

"A Bullet. Three-fifty. What year?"

"Eighty-four."

"When the Indians started building them. And sold them back to the Brits. Brilliant. They knew what they had."

"My dad bought it right off the line. Rode it back to Europe and put it on a ship."

"That's a fascinating story."

"Yeah, uh, you ride?"

"I built a site for classic bikes when I was fifteen. Sold it for a mil."

"To who?"

"Bike mag. I was stealing all their traffic. I hit them with a virus a couple of years ago. You know, just for fun. Can I take it for a spin?"

"You know how to ride?"

"What am I, an imbecile?"

"Doesn't our meeting start in a few minutes?"

Fab gets on the bike. He's too small for it, having to sit almost on the tank to reach the handle bars. "It starts when I say it starts."

Joe fumbles in his pockets for his keys, even opening his satchel to look for them. He's saved by a taxi stopping on the street. Enora climbs out, straightens her hip-hugging skirt and waits for the driver to get her carry-on out of the trunk. She wheels this towards the house and walks up to Joe.

"You wouldn't believe the scene at Logan. Some joker left a bag on a carousel. Shut down the whole terminal."

"Nothing blew up?"

"Nothing ever does. This country is drowning in its own fear, and it means those of us who are sane have to sit around waiting all the time."

"Sorry about that."

"Did you really ride here? I thought you were joking."

"No terrorist plots on I-89."

She looks at the house with distaste. "Is this it? Looks like the house for the fraternity no one wants to be in. What's the last letter of the Greek alphabet? That would be the name of this fraternity. Loser, loser, loser. Have you greeted the nerds yet?"

"This one's called Fab."

Astride the bike, one elbow on the handle bars, hand cradling his chin, and surely his testicles burning against the hot tank, Fab tries to look unperturbed and arrogant. "MIT doesn't spell nerd. It stands for millionaire iconic teenager."

Enora steps forward and extends her hand. "Sorry. Someone I know at Natrofield said you were all nerds. It was just an inside joke between me and Joe."

Fab takes her hand. "Maybe you'll see her. She's coming at one."

Enora smiles warmly. "I'm glad you decided to meet with us first."

"Yeah, sure. Whatever you offer will make a useful bargaining tool for when I talk to the big dogs. So? No ride?"

"I think we should get started. I don't want to keep the big dogs waiting. Maybe later."

Fab gets off the bike. "You I like. You not so much."

Enora forces her look of shock into one of enthusiasm. "Let's change that."

Fab leads the way down the stairs. "Sweet fuck, is she always like this?"

Enora waits for Joe to lift her carry-on down the stairs. As he picks it up, she whispers: "I think I'm in love."

"Turn on the charm. Maybe we'll get the account that way."

Enora sneers. "I have to do everything."

It's dark inside, the only lighting coming from low-wattage desk lamps and large monitors. There are no windows and the ceiling is low. It stinks of cigarettes and old take-out food. Sci-fi posters on the walls, naked girls, a cardboard cut-out of Jean-Luc Picard, phaser drawn. It's unwelcoming, disorganised, damp, untidy and personal, like a teenage boy's bedroom.

Fab leads them through the maze of desks, with each occupant slouched in front of a monitor or two, headphones in place. None of them look much older than twenty, and no one is interacting, or working. They are engaged in role player games and online poker, watching movies and TV. One kid is playing a graphic form of battle chess, and cheers and pumps his fist as a bishop is beheaded.

At the doorway to the cramped meeting room at the back of the basement, Fab turns and surveys his domain. He seems proud. His shirt is untucked, his scuffed sneakers poke out of low-riding jeans – underwear showing – that are frayed at the hem from dragging along the ground. Joe looks down and sees small bits of twig caught in the hem, and what looks like a large shard of green glass.

"Welcome to Sticky Solutions. Drink?"

"Water's fine for me."

Fab steps aside to let Enora past. "It's on the table."

"Thanks."

Enora parks her carry-on at the doorway and then turns sideways to shimmy through. Her generous arse brushes Fab's thigh. He gets a good look.

"What about you, Jack? Drink?"

"It's Joe. And I'll take a green tea, if you've got it."

"Tea? Who the fuck drinks tea?"

"I do."

"I wouldn't do this for anyone else, but for someone who rides a Bullet…Hey, Largo. Rustle up this hippie a green tea, will ya."

"Fab, I'm live here."

"Now, or you're fired."

Largo throws off his headphones and stomps towards what Joe guesses is a kitchenette off to the right side of the basement.

Fab gestures towards the chairs. "Sit down."

The table is oval. The chairs have wheels on them but the loose carpet makes it impossible to wheel them closer to the table. Joe sits, further from the table than he would like. He leans back, crosses his legs, and tries to look relaxed, like the last thing he needs is this account.

Fab slouches in his chair. "Let's get straight to it. I'm not gonna bore you with PowerPoint slides and all that crap. I'll put it to you like this. Imagine a world with no more fat people. Sweet-Aid will change the face of dieting, here and all over the world. You want it. Believe me."

"It sounds fantastic."

Joe looks over his shoulder at the darkened room behind him. "Where's your lab?"

"On campus. This here is our ideas lair."

"Do you have any products already on the market?"

"You should know that, Elena."

"It's Enora."

"Whatever."

Joe clears his throat. "A-Plus."

"He's done his homework. The cram patch. Natrofield rebranded it as A-Plus. Huge seller, especially around exam time."

"It could have been more successful if we had marketed it."

Fab looks at Joe. "She's not doing your chances any good."

"I think what she means is that it's not as big a seller as it could be."

"Big enough to have her fly in from Q-land and for you to brave the ice of the interstate at dawn."

"We're interested. A-Plus is a good product. Good marketing too."

Largo comes in and drops Joe's tea on the table. There's nothing to put the tea bag in, so Joe lifts it to the edge of the cup and wraps the string around the handle, to keep the bag out of the water. He sips. It's scolding hot.

Enora helps herself to some water. "Tell us more about Sweet-Aid."

Fab scratches at his three-day beard. He's twitchy, blinking a lot, constantly adjusting his thin, purple-framed glasses, his left shoulder going up and down. But he doesn't strike Joe as nervous; his movements look chemically enhanced, or sleep-deprived.

"You ever see *Supersize Me*? Guy eats McDonalds for a month. He gets fat and barfs it all over the place. That's where I got the idea. Ages ago. It's been mutating in my brain ever since. During the month, he consumes, like, a ton of sugar. It's in everything. We're the fattest country in the world because we eat so much sugar. You want some for your tea?"

"No, thanks."

"Good answer. There's sugar in everything except biker boy's tea. It's making everyone fatter, kids especially."

Joe looks at the gamers behind him. "So it's not from a lack of exercise."

"Ha-ha. Biker boy thinks he's a comedian. Anyway. We're addicted to sugar. It's our drug. And like any addiction, the addict has to be taken off it slowly. No cold turkey. Replace it with something else and lower the dosage over time."

Enora leans forward, trying to take charge. "Like a nicotine patch."

Fab claps slowly. "That's brilliant. Would you like to come work for us? You could answer our phones and turn on our computers. Where'd you graduate, Toronto Remedial? Yes, sweet fuck, of course it's like a nicotine patch. Sweet-Aid has the same principle, releasing sugar onto the addict's skin."

Joe clears his throat again. "Does it look like a nicotine patch? There's a stigma to wearing those, and you can't have kids using them."

"Now you're a sharp one. Where'd you graduate?"

"University of New South Wales."

"You don't sound like a Brit."

"It's in Sydney. Australia."

"I was just yanking your chain. You're an Aussie, fresh outta jail."

"Actually, I'm American. My dad's Australian."

"Two passports?"

"Yes."

"Useful. Bet it's easier travelling on the Aussie passport, what with us at war and drowning in a sea of fear."

"It is. For now."

"Lucky you."

"Lucky me."

Enora again attempts to take control. "Tell us how the patch works."

"It's not a patch. It's a band-aid. Aussie biker boy's right about the stigma. No one wants to be seen as an addict, or a recovering addict. Sweet-Aid looks just like a band-aid. No one will even notice it. And if they do, they won't ask any questions. We even came up with a kids' version, you know, colourful, with potential merchandising angles."

"All you have to do is stop people from eating sugar."

"Sorry, Joe. Not our problem."

Enora claps her hands together. "Sounds really interesting. This is definitely something for Denoris."

"You mean profitable, and it works."

"In the tests you did. We'd have to do our own trials."

"Sure, Elena. We can't do what you can. And we can't get approval. I want this to be over-the-counter."

"That's why you contacted us."

"And Natrofield. They get first bite because of A-Plus, but I'm open to other offers."

***

"What do you think?"

Enora shrugs. "Amateurs. Not for us."

"Because he couldn't remember your name?"

"It's too risky. And all the sugar peddling companies would come down hard on us if we released it. The cigarette lobby is nothing compared Coke, Pepsi and McDonalds."

"And the rest."

"According to that dick, every food company in America."

"There's a market for it. Especially for kids, even if it would be just more chemicals in their systems."

Enora points at the basement door. "They're not for us. Let Natrofield take all the risk. He's gonna choose them anyway."

"Agreed. Sounds like he already has."

"He just brought us here as a bargaining chip."

"The Bohemian Brainiac."

"What?"

"Nothing."

Enora looks at her watch. "What a waste of time. And you killed it with all your wisecracks."

"Your intelligent research and questioning didn't exactly help. Anyway, he'd already made a decision."

"You still could've worked harder."

"You gonna tell Miles on me again?"

"He knows you're not up to it."

A taxi stops in front. A woman in a smart, perfectly creased dark blue pantsuit gets out. She's carrying a small, thin attaché case and is talking on her phone.

"Maybe I can get an earlier flight."

"Unless they shut down the terminal."

Enora charges at the open taxi door and flops herself down. "See you on Monday, Joe. By the way, Siobahn doesn't say hello."

Joe watches the taxi drive away and then looks up at the sky. The clouds are dirty grey and thickening.

The woman in the pantsuit comes up to him. "Who's Siobahn?"

"Huh? Oh, no one."

"Sounds like someone."

"Siobahn's what happens when other people think they know you, know what's best for you."

She puts her attaché case on Eddie's seat. "Been there. Sorry for the line, but do we know each other?"

"If you've got a one o'clock in this dweeb dungeon, then we've probably bumped shoulders at a trade fair somewhere."

"Massobix?"

"Denoris."

"Sorry."

"Don't be."

"Not for the mistake. For the fact you work for Denoris."

"Between you and me, I'm pretty sorry about that too."

"I'm Anita."

"Joe."

"Should we exchange business cards?"

"Probably not a good idea."

"No. I wasn't aware Fab was trying to land a small fish."

"He's not. He just wants…leverage."

Anita smiles, no teeth. "Should I believe that?"

"That's the truth. And those guys in there, they'll talk about making the world a better place and helping others, but they just wanna make money."

"Who doesn't?"

"That's my honest take. And we didn't make him an offer."

"Appreciate it. Thanks."

"You're welcome. Look, uh, you live here, right?"

She nods.

"What do you think? Those clouds, does that mean rain in this part of the world?"

"Are you planning to escape across the border on this hunk of junk?"

"Careful. She can hear you."

"If I say it'll rain, will you stay in Boston tonight?"

"What's the forecast for tomorrow?"

"New England spring."

"Then I'd stay."

She looks at the clouds, then at Joe. "Rain. Heavy. Like a bucket being tipped over. And that means you can buy me dinner tonight."

"What if it doesn't rain? I'll know you lied."

"You should be flattered I'd do that to keep you here. But it's your call."

He laughs.

She opens her attaché case. On a small piece of stiff paper, like a blank business card, she writes down a number. "My bat phone. Call me when you have an emergency."

"Will you appear like a shadow in the sky?"

"The clouds will be too heavy to see."

He laughs again.

"There's a couple of B&Bs over on Cambridge. Anson's is a nice one."

"Anita, stop fraternising with the enemy and let's get this deal signed."

"Hi, Fab. See you later, Joe."

She walks down the short stairs and doesn't look back.

Fab holds the door open. "It's the bike, isn't it? We're well into the twenty-first century and still you chicks can't resist a sleek set of wheels."

"As long as you drive that ridiculous Smart, you'll be dateless."

"Hey, it's easy to park."

The door closes.

Joe puts on his helmet and climbs on the bike. It takes a few starts to get Eddie going. "She said that, not me."

He rides down Beacon and makes a right onto Cambridge.

***

It rains all afternoon, fat drops of water that splatter against the window like they're shot from a paint gun. He kills the afternoon catching up on emails and doing paperwork. Still connected to the company intranet, he lies down on the floor to nap. The plush carpet is more comfortable than the very soft bed. The sound of the rain is soothing. He sleeps.

~~~

They walk through the Common. Overcast, chance of rain. Men in suits sit on park benches eating lunch, the sports section of the *Globe* open in front of them, frowns on their faces as they take in the Red Sox's troubles.

He can think of nothing to say. Talk about her, that's what Max said. Sentences form. They all sound stupid.
~~~

She walks with her arms folded, making it impossible for him to, maybe, just reach it to try, to make contact with her hand, see where that might lead.

Your dad's really cool.

Thanks.

I mean, he's, like, not like other dads, all old and wrinkly. He looks good. How old is he?

Um.

Is he gonna drive us back? That was, like, so much fun driving down. Thanks for letting me sit up front.

No problem.

He knows everything. My dad doesn't know jack. If you ask my dad the time, he'll have to, like, look it up on his computer. But your dad. Wow. I can ask him anything. And his accent is so cool. Why don't you have it?

Uh.

Australia. That's, like, so far away. The other side of the universe.

Planet.

No way. It's further than that. You ever go there? I'd love to go. See all the people fighting crocodiles in Sydney and the Aborigines throwing those sticky things.

Boomerangs.

Right. Zoomerdangs. You should get your dad to, like, take you there. You could bring me back a bear for a pet.

Koalas aren't bears.

Then why are they called koala bears, stupid? You don't know anyway. You haven't even, like, been there. That's so lame. Your own country and you never ever went there. How do you look at yourself in the mirror? I'd hate to be you. Are you, like, adopted?

Um.

Your dad's so cool. I wish our teachers were like him. He rocks. You should get him to become a teacher at our school. Ask him. I would, like, so reward you if you did.

I guess I could…

Do it. He could teach all of my classes. That would be wild. School is such a drag. I hate it, don't you? It's, like, such a complete waste of time. I don't even know why I bother to go. All the homework is so pointless and…

She goes on like this for a while, long enough for them to circle

Frog Pond and start doubling back to the pick-up point at Park Street Station. There's no break in her speech – she can even talk breathing in – and any questions posed are quickly answered. She jumps from school to Max to cheerleading to Max to TV to Max, walking the whole time with her arms tightly folded. Watching her for the past few months across the hall and over the Bunsen burner in the seventh grade science lab, he'd never thought she'd be, like, like this. She seemed quieter, more self-contained, deeper, easier. Now, she was in love with Max.

...Such a cool dad. MaxMaxMaxMaxMaxMaxMaxMaxMaxMax.

~~~

He wakes. The first thing he sees is the frilly pink and orange lampshade hanging from the ceiling. Anson's. Boston. Friday afternoon. Rain. Supposed to be heading for Harbrook. Gordie bound to be disappointed.

He rolls onto his side and gets to his feet. His back is stiff from the ride.

"A swim would sort that out."

In the bathroom, he pees, flushes, splashes water on his face and grabs a fluffy pink towel with Anson's stitched on it. He takes the plastic bag from the trash can and puts the towel inside it, along with his goggles, ear plugs, swim hat and Speedos.

Down at the reception, he rings the bell and waits.

"Can I help you?"

"Hi. Would you happen to have an umbrella I could borrow?"

Grandma Anson points at the door. "Try the rack. People are always forgetting them there. Take one."

"Thanks."

It's a real brolly, a golf umbrella, which two stout pros and their caddies could easily get under, bags and all. It makes negotiating the sidewalk difficult, as everyone else is walking with their faces hidden beneath umbrellas. He has to keep lifting it and tilting it, so he doesn't take out eyes and puncture awnings. Everyone has something to say about it.

"The beach is the next street on the right."

"What's that, a jousting stick?"

"Can my whole family come under there?"
~~~

"Fore!"

In the end, he packs it away and walks in what is now a light drizzle, swinging the umbrella like a cane. Down Quincy, he tries to copy the practiced slackness of the students, to blend in. He looks the part in worn jeans and a sweatshirt, but feels old, doesn't have that carefree gait. He knows he's walking as if there are a million things trying to pull him down.

"Try to travel like a local."

It's not happening. He has more chance pretending to be an assistant professor, or even a janitor.

He cuts down Dewolfe towards Weeks Bridge, walking with his head down to navigate the puddles. Once, the flooded sidewalk forces him onto the street and a car horn blares.

"Get off the road!"

On the bridge, he sees a rowing eight stroking towards the boat houses. To the west, the sun is cutting yellow swathes through the clouds. Better weather tomorrow.

"New England spring."

He tucks the umbrella under his arm and pulls out his phone.

"This is Anita."

"Not Batgirl?"

"Who is this?"

"It's Joe. We met this afternoon."

"Is it an emergency?"

"Does hunger count?"

"The food kind? Yes. Where are you?"

"Weeks Bridge. I'm heading to Blodgett for a swim."

Reminded, he starts walking.

"What on earth for?"

"To knock off a couple of miles."

"Weird. Where are you staying?"

"Anson's."

"But there's a pool right there. War Memorial."

"It's twenty-five yards."

"So?"

"Too small. You spend more time flipping than swimming."

"I have no idea what you're talking about. Anyhoo. Baptist Church at eight. We'll do fish."

"Where's that?"

"Near the corner of Harvard and Mass. You'll find it."

"All right. I'll have a copy of the *Globe* in my pocket."

"I think I'll recognise you."

He crosses North Harvard and finds the entry. Fortunately, there's no meet on. At the gate, the guy asks for his card. Joe hands him a ten dollar bill. The guy pockets it, looking bored.

"Circle swim."

"Thanks."

He changes, pees again, stretches a little and checks the clock. He'll have to go straight to dinner afterwards.

Down at the pool, he gets a shiver of joy when he sees he has lane two all for himself. He rubs spit in his goggles, rinses them and presses them into his eye sockets. He slows his breathing, counting to three, visualising his arms churning through the water with each count.

The water's warm, like urine. He puts his head face first into it and blows bubbles at his goggles. It's a good seal, but he's pressed them in too hard, he knows, and will have some nice purplish rings to show for it later. But it's too late now. He stares at the other end, far in the distance, like another country almost.

"Get to the end and flip. Simple."

The swimmer in lane three hits the wall with a whale of a flip turn, sending a torrent of water over the edge of the pool, and into Joe's face. He watches him struggling towards the other end, hips swivelling, body gyrating, arms bent.

It would be so much easier if someone straightened him out, he thinks.

He breathes in, breathes out and counts to three.

"Be the Russian."

***

"So. How are we gonna do this?"

"Do what?"

"You know, steal each others' secrets and have a good time."

"I'm from Denoris. We got nothing you want."

"Sure you do."

"Is that what we're here to do? Scam each other?"

"I don't know yet. This was very much unplanned."

"How'd it go with Fab?"

"Can't say. You know anyway."
"The FDA will never okay it."
"But we could sell a dumbed down version that doesn't qualify as a drug. Stick it at checkouts next to the gum and candy. Oops. Better stop there. Shall we order?"
She beckons the waitress.
"I'm ready."
The waitress comes to their table. "Yes?"
With the menu still closed, Anita orders first: "I'll have the Maltese octopus salad. And another beer."
"Very good. For you?"
"What's the fish of the day?"
"Salmon."
"Atlantic or Pacific?"
"Not sure. Either way it's salmon."
"I'll take that, thanks, and hold them lemon."
The waitress nods and heads for the kitchen, moving so slowly and languidly between the tables, she seems to glide.
"Don't like lemons?"
"I'm allergic."
"Very funny."
"Seriously."
"Never heard of that. Unusual."
"I'm an unusual guy."
"Three nipples?"
"Not that bad."
Anita sips her beer. "What happens if you have lemon? Do you turn into a yellow Hulk?"
"No idea. Maybe."
"How did you find out you're allergic?"
"I had some tests done when I was a kid. My ma's a nurse. She was a bit paranoid about me and my brother, tested us for everything. Turned out my allergy was lemons. My brother's allergic to responsibility."
"Does that come up on a test? What's he do?"
"He's at college, in Portland. Economics."
"That'll get him nowhere. Unless he specialises, or is he allergic to that too?"
Joe laughs.
"You never had lemons? Not even lemonade?"

"Am I missing out?"

She leans forward, as if to impart a secret. "Real lemonade, and I mean the fresh stuff with lemons squeezed on the spot, well, it's heaven. Back home, we put honey in it, not sugar."

"Sounds good, but not for me."

"Then you're missing out."

"Where's back home?"

"Kansas. You?"

"New Hampshire."

"Really? That's just up the interstate. I thought you were from up north, Yukon maybe, where they eat walrus blubber for breakfast, or even way east, Newfoundland or some place weird. You've got the strangest accent."

"Thanks."

"Or is it part of your whole unusual guy routine?"

"My dad's Australian. I guess I picked up a drawl from him and it blended in with the New England twang."

As she sips her beer, she looks around the restaurant, over the rim of her glass, her eyes darting from table to table, face to face. "You ever go?"

"Where?"

"Australia."

"I studied there."

"Interesting."

"Look, are you expecting someone?"

"What? No. Sorry. To be honest, I'm a little worried someone from work might see me here, see us."

"Why'd you bring me here then?"

"I like it."

"Don't worry. Denoris likes to cultivate anonymity amongst its employees. No one will recognise me. You didn't."

"True."

"But that means this is one of your haunts for pampering. Is there a rub and tug out the back?"

"It depends. The bigger the account, the more upmarket we go. I think we're safe. You don't look very professional in that sweatshirt. Still, you never know who might walk in."

"Say I'm an old school pal from Kansas."

"My high school sweetheart?"

"If you want. What's my story? Was I the starting quarterback?"

"It's easier to lie convincingly if you stick close to the truth. Let's say you were on the swim team. You were a senior and I was a junior. How old are you anyway?"

"Twenty-eight."

"You look older. I can count the rings under your eyes."

He rubs at them, feeling the grooves. "I told you. It's from the goggles. What about you?"

"So, you were a senior and I was a freshman."

"I thought you were a junior."

She picks up her glass of beer and swirls it a little, wistfully. "You were flunking biology and I was top of my class. The swim coach asked me to help you out, so you could graduate and get a scholarship."

"Did we burst into song when I aced that final test?"

"Slow down. My parents didn't like you. But we would text each other and I used to sneak out at night. You had an old treehouse you built as a kid..."

"That's true."

"We lost our virginity up there. What? That part's not true?"

"Go on, and please don't get pregnant."

She takes a sip of beer and is about to continue when the waitress places their plates on the table.

"I asked the chef where your fish came from and he said the delivery truck."

"Well, thanks anyway."

"Enjoy."

A few bones are sticking out. He plucks these with his fingers, lining them up on the side of his plate. He drains his beer and drops the big wedge of lemon in the empty glass.

Anita takes an unappetizing, slimy-looking mouthful and talks through it. "We were the most popular couple at school. Untouchable. You were always writing me these sweet little texts. Four line poems with stupid rhymes, but they were so cute. Roses are red, something, something."

"And you never replied."

"I couldn't. My parents spied on me. Looked at my cell when I was in the shower."

"Did your dad come at me with a shotgun?"

"I was grounded and they took away my cell."

"The treehouse was a one-off night of magic."

"You came to my window the night before the big swim game and..."

"Meet. It's called a meet."

"Sure. The big meet. God, it sounds like a business event. But that night, you came and asked me to run away with you, to, to California. And you were so in love with me that you lost the big race just so you wouldn't get the scholarship and we could run away together."

"How romantic, and sad. Do people really do that in Kansas? It all sounds so misguided."

"It happens. Sometimes to make it in life, you have to run away."

"So, I lost the race. Then what?"

"You said you'd get a job in California and I'd become an actress."

"How closely are you sticking to the truth?"

"Well, I went to New York, not LA."

"Successful?"

"Turned out there's more money in drugs."

He chews. The salmon is dry and requires a lot of chewing. He wonders if it swam in waters much further from the Atlantic or Pacific, or maybe in someone's backyard pool. Wherever it swam, it was definitely a while ago.

"But you've put those acting skills to good use."

"Selling is acting. But I'm not in sales."

"What then?"

"Procurement."

"That's why you met Fab. Did you pretend to be excited about Sweet-Aid?"

"It needs re-branding. More focused on energy. How it makes you more powerful and energetic. Gives a boost instead of curing an addiction."

"Clever."

"Yes."

He checks her plate. She's almost finished, eating fast but seeming not to rush. She has no problem talking and chewing at the same time. Indeed, she seems proud of her multi-tasking.

"Want some salmon?"

"I'm allergic."

"Ha-ha."

She leans across the table, stabs at a square of pink flesh and chews thoughtfully. "Needs lemon."

A phone buzzes.

"Is that you or me?"

"Mine. Ignore it."

"Don't you want to know who it is?"

"Not during dinner. It's probably my brother. He can wait. So? What happened to us? Did you become a big star in LA?"

"Well, even though you lost the last race, you had already won all the others and got the scholarship anyway."

"What about the test? The final celebratory song and dance number with the whole school?"

"They cheated."

"Who?"

"The school. The college gave them some money and they faked your result. You went off to college and we never saw each other again."

"I'm not sure I like myself."

"Also the truth?"

"Not the Kansas version."

"But then today, we accidentally ran into each other in Cambridge."

"And is this just a dinner between old friends or is the flame of teenage love reigniting?"

"Is that how you think it would go?"

"Not sure. I think she might be out for information from the old friend."

"No, it's just a friendly dinner. But the first love is always the strongest." She pushes her plate aside. "Have you ever been in love, Joe? Is there a high school sweetheart sleeping alone in your bed in Montreal?"

"Just Popov."

"The local Russian mafia?"

"Popov's my cat. And he's probably happy to have the whole place to himself."

"Answer my question."

"No sweetheart. No girlfriend."

"I mean about love."

He wipes his mouth on his napkin. "That's a heavy topic for a friendly dinner, isn't it?"

"I'll start then. I've never been in love, and I'm not entirely sure it even exists."

"Not even between Kansas High's untouchable couple?"

"I think people confuse love with convenience. All the pieces seem to fit and they think this is love. You know, like having things in common and finishing each others' sentences. You like The Smiths. Oh, me too. Let's get married. That kind of stuff. Nothing earth shattering."

"Communist love."

"What?"

"That's what my dad called that."

She nods. "I like it. Love from the convenience of commonality."

"Not very romantic."

"Oh, cry me a river. Romance is an invention to sell chocolates and flowers on Valentine's Day."

"Yeah, it is. Still, you're not very romantic."

"I'm pragmatic. What about you?"

"Isn't love used to sell something as well?"

"Pretty much everything from detergent to the American dream."

"My buddy in Montreal, Francois, he says men only get one shot at love."

"That's deep. Go on."

"I can't remember where he got it from. Maybe a movie or a book. But he says once a man has his heart broken, he never loves with the same intensity again. He doesn't want to get hurt, so he doesn't give as much of himself."

She shrugs. "That makes a kind of pathetic masculine sense. But you say it with conviction, like this happened to you."

The waitress appears. "All finished?"

"Yes, thanks."

"Dessert? Coffee?"

"I'm good."

"Me too."

The waitress wraps a claw around each plate and glides back towards the kitchen.

"I know a place around the corner where we can have a coffee that doesn't taste like aquarium water."

"All right. Finish your beer and I'll get the check."

She picks up her glass, but doesn't drink from it. "Not until you tell me what happened. What tramp broke you're precious little heart and left you unable to love with the same intensity again?"

"Don't make fun of Francois."

"I'm making fun of you."

"Careful. Men are sensitive these days."
"Aw. Share your feelings, Mister Unusual Sensitive Guy."
"I'm not really sure if it was love, but it hurt. It still hurts."
"Is it hurting now?"
"When I'm reminded of it, yeah."
"When was it?"
"About ten years ago. So it fits in with Francois's under twenty-three rule."
"What?"
"He thinks guys get their hearts broken before they're twenty-three."
"What about girls?"
"They're doing the breaking."
"Is he playing for the other team?"
"Francois? No. He's single, but... Anyway, does it matter?"
"He sounds pretty soft. What does he do?"
"He's a photographer. You'd like him."
"I hate it when people say that."
"You'll have to trust me then."
"It's a little too early for trust."
"All right. Then let's get back to Kansas."
"I'm sorry, Joe. I didn't mean to offend you."
"You don't look sorry."
"Oooh, you are sensitive."
Joe tries to laugh.
Anita stops the waitress as she drifts past. "He wants the check."
"Isn't this a business expense?"
"Not yet. It's too much fun watching you squirm. So. About this big love who broke your heart. Did you go to school together?"
"Nuh. Book's closed."
"Come on. Please."
"Is this the kind of thing you tell on a first date, go through all the old boyfriends and girlfriends, as a way of warning each other?"
"Is this a first date?"
"What is it then?"
"Call it a peace negotiation between enemies."
"I thought we weren't going to talk business."
"You're right. Let's talk love instead. Pretend I'm your gay pal Frankie."

"Francois."

The waitress drops the check on the table. Anita snatches at it.

"Tell you what, Joe. I'll pay, you talk."

She drops some notes on the table and puts the receipt in her handbag.

He stands up. "I think we're getting too personal."

She comes around the table and kisses him. He tastes the vinegar of the salad dressing; it makes him think of an octopus shooting ink in defence.

"Now it's personal. Come on. Let's get that coffee. And don't forget your damp little homeless man's bag and your beach umbrella."

She shoulders her smallish handbag, which has a long strap, and heads for the door. He follows, retrieving the umbrella and the plastic bag along the way. Outside, he tucks the bag under his arm and leans on the umbrella.

"How far is it?"

"You wanna take a taxi?"

"No."

"Couple of blocks."

"Lead the way."

She locks an elbow around his as they walk down the street. For a Friday, it's surprisingly quiet.

"Tell me everything. I paid, so now you have to. You said it was ten years ago. That would make you, what, seventeen?"

"Eighteen."

"Where did you meet?"

"Look, Anita, can we talk about something else?"

"Frankie's theory made curious. I need proof. Was it at school?"

"After. In Europe."

"A summer in Europe. You're not so unusual after all."

"Yeah, but the further east I went, the better it got. I went pretty much by land all the way to Indonesia and then flew from Denpasar to Sydney."

"How long did that take?"

"About six months."

"But back to Europe. Paris, right?"

"This is real life, not a movie. It was in Portugal."

"How did you meet?"

"By accident."

"No one meets by accident. People meet because they're supposed to. Think of all the events that had to happen for you two to end up at the same place at the same time. Any slight change would've meant you never would've met. Take Francois. He's your best friend, right?"

"Yeah."

"How did you meet?"

"In the pool."

"Don't lie to me."

"I'm serious. We were swimming in the same lane and I kept passing him. He didn't like that. He tried to talk to me, but I wear ear plugs and completely tune out when I'm swimming. When I did a flip turn, he grabbed my leg. I nearly hit him."

"What did he want?"

"He asked me how I could swim so fast without trying. I told him it was technique, that you have go through the water and not fight it. A lot of people don't get that."

"Sounds bizarre to me."

"Anyway, I gave him some tips and we ended up seeing each other a few more times in the pool. He came up to me and told me he was swimming faster, because of my tips. He offered to buy me dinner as a thank you. Then I thought he was gay."

She laughs. "And you've been friends ever since."

"We were friends from the start. It just took a while for us to make it happen. It was like we'd known each other for ages, were friends in another life."

"Or lovers."

"Maybe. We swim every Sunday evening, an hour before closing, when the pool's empty."

"What an exciting life you lead. Now, think of all the things that had to happen for you and him to meet in the pool."

He considers this. "I was there by choice. Francois was there on doctor's orders, to fix his back."

"So, at some point he hurt his back and there followed a long sequence of events on his side and yours until you met in the pool. You can't tell me all that is random. You guys were meant to meet. Like you and the girl. Like you and me."

"Huh. You're starting to make sense. If it hadn't happened in the pool, maybe it would've happened somewhere else."

"Now you're getting it. But back to the girl. Was it in Lisbon?"

"Lagos."

"Where's that?"

"In the south. The Algarve. I was on the train from Faro and this woman sat down in front of me."

"What'd she look like?"

"This isn't her."

"Let's cross the street. It's just around the corner. Go on."

"She couldn't speak any English, but she had this file. It was like a guestbook, with photos and comments from people in a bunch of languages. She had a small guesthouse and she was trying to get me to stay there."

"Sounds like a scam."

"That's what I thought. But I'd just spent the last few weeks slumming it in a variety of dirt-bag hostels and I really wanted a nice bed in my own room."

"Understandable. So you went with her."

"I did."

"And she had a daughter you fell madly in love with."

"No. She was staying in the other room."

"Who? The daughter?"

"Trina. The girl."

"Anita?"

"Oh, crap."

A man waves from the other side of the street. He ducks between the traffic. "Anita, hi. I thought that was you."

"Dwayne. How's it going?"

"Good. What're you up to?"

"Just out for dinner with an old school friend. This is Joe, from Kansas."

Stupid, crappy, lame drunk wedding with dishonest, bald, ugly Pentecostal Philanderer

"You're mega late. A whole day."

Joe gets off the bike and removes his helmet. "Sorry, Gordie."

"Didn't even answer my texts. I thought you weren't gonna show."

"Traffic was intense. Half of Boston heading for the White Mountains."

Gordie comes down the stairs to initiate their one-hand-clasp-forearm-against-shoulder-rap-mogul hug. He's chewing on an orange straw.

"Great to see you, Gordie."

"What happened last night? I waited up."

"Rain happened."

"Not here."

"It did in Boston. Old Testament rain. Biblical."

"Look at it. Weather's perfect."

"Today, yeah. Was Len up all night praying for sun?"

"Leave it alone, bro."

"Definitely up praying for something. Hair perhaps. A miracle overnight growth."

"Wow. You really sound like you wanna be here."

"I'm here to see you."

"Fucking straight."

"How long we got?"

"An hour. Ma's been asking after you."

"What'd you say?"

Gordie laughs. "You wrapped Eddie around a tree."

"That's not funny."

"I'll text her you're here."

He follows Gordie up the short steps and onto the porch. The outdoor furniture is gone, including the hammock that was slung between the beams on the right side. They stop at the door. Gordie's head is bowed over his phone, almost in worship.

"Good to see you shaved off the chin fluff."

"Too much maintenance needed. I'm not into manscaping."

Joe peers through the open door, into the void.

"Is everything gone?"

"Course."

"Power? Hot water?"

"Already off. We're lucky there's water at all. I wouldn't drink it though. Probably been sitting in the pipes the last five years."

"A half decade of living in sin."

"How old are you? Ma's allowed to fuck if she wants."

"God. With Len?"

"Why not? You're the ones selling the magic pills that make it happen."

"So that's my fault too."

Joe turns and looks out from the porch, at the familiar line of trees, the narrow road leading to town, all the memories tied up in this view, this tiny, insignificant part of the world. He feels a pang, regret, something lost, a shiver that tells him things will never be whole again, and the dull reality that even if it was, it would never be quite as good.

"I can't believe she sold it."

"It's falling apart. We'll probably wake up tomorrow morning under a pile of rubble."

"No chance."

"That hero worship's still strong."

"Huh?"

"You can shower at Len's."

"From holy water on tap? I'd rather stink."

"Oh, will you lighten the fuck up. Let it go."

"Sure. Fine. Nothing to worry about."

"Have a cold shower. It'll do you good."

"I'll just wash up."

"You got Eddie all over you. Why don't you sell that piece of shit and buy a real bike. Or better, a car."

"Don't start, Gordie."

"Eddie's the one that don't start."

"She's running like a dream. You just gotta keep her within her limits."

"Whatever."

They move into the house, Joe leading. It's bare, seems huge. Their footsteps echo. Gordie has set up camp in the living room: double air mattress, sleeping bag, his big notebook, clothes spilling out of Joe's old backpack, a few baseball caps hanging from picture hooks, that fuzzy old man smell Gordie has. Joe can hear a generator humming in the kitchen, maybe from inside the pantry.

"Internet, but no hot water."

"Fucking straight."

Joe drops his saddle bags and peels off his riding garb. "At least you've got your priorities right."

"For real. Hey, you look good. You swimming again?"

"No."

Gordie falls on the mattress and stares at his notebook. "What was up in Boston?"

"Product presentation."

"Of?"

"More crap the world doesn't need. Solutions to problems people don't even have."

Gordie taps the keys. "Did you bring some goodies to make the evening a more enjoyable experience?"

"I don't like being your dealer."

"It's either you or someone else. And it's always best to have a dealer you trust. Someone close."

Joe reaches into his satchel and tosses Gordie a line of pills. "Here. But just take one. Xav reckons if you mix it with Pepsi you'll be flying."

"Mos def. Thanks, bro."

"And take it after Len and ma have left. I don't want an inquisition."

Gordie punches a pill off the line and swallows it. "I'll take the second after they go. You want one?"

"Pass. I'm still hungover from last night."

"Nerd party?"

"A pushy procurer. Miss Untouchable."

"What?"

"Nothing. Sat in my room watching porn and draining the mini bar. As the biblical rain fell."

"I'm so jealous of your life."

"I'm gonna get dressed. Lose the cap for the ceremony."

"Fuck you."

But Gordie flicks off his Red Sox cap, revealing a closely cropped head with an even more pronounced M-shape than the last time Joe saw it. Gordie takes out the well-chewed straw as well and drops it on the floor.

There are two towels in the bathroom. Gordie has used them both, with one slung over the towel rack and the other over the shower rail. There's a hand press container of hospital soap, almost full. Joe uses this to wash his hands and then splashes cold water on his face. He considers braving the shower, to wash off the interstate, but the water's so cold it stings, and it has a brownish tinge to it. He takes off his undershirt and gives himself a quick whore's shower, cupping water in his hands and rubbing it against his chest and neck and under his arms. He towels off, rolls on some deo and tries to arrange his hair so it looks fashionably unstyled. He pulls it back to see if it's receding.

Trina's boyfriend is probably completely bald by now, he thinks, if they're still together.

He stares at himself in the mirror, seeing reassuring shadows.

"I didn't know she was gonna sell. And baby bro burned my nest egg so I can't buy it back."

He puts his undershirt back on. In the living room, Gordie is huddled over his notebook. When he sees Joe, he snaps the notebook shut and jumps up.

"Ready?"

"What were you doing?"

"Just crapping on Plasher."

"About?"

"Don't know. The usual whatever."

"What do you think, Gordie? Tie?"

"I didn't bring one."

"You're wearing what you've got on?"

"So?"

"At least that means I can go without a tie and still be better dressed than you."

"I don't have a suit."

"Len didn't offer to buy you one?"

"Why should he? This is all just a formality. A piece of paper."

Joe pulls on the same clothes as yesterday. Grey suit, light blue shirt with the collar open, black shoes. He sniffs at the lapel of the coat and thinks he's getting a faint whiff of the dank basement of Sticky Solutions.

"Where am I sleeping? And don't say that mattress."

Gordie gestures at the dusty hammock piled in the corner. "I didn't hang it up."

"You mean she took it down only for us to put it up again?"

"Len did."

"Moron."

"He thought you wouldn't show."

"He's a believer."

"You haven't exactly tried to be friends with him."

"I don't want to be his friend."

Gordie shrugs. He stands and adjusts his jeans. More precisely, he pulls them down, so his Sponge Bob boxers show and it looks like he has no arse at all. He chooses a cap and spins it around his finger.

"Leave it, Gordie."

"Yeah. Probably right."

Joe picks up the hammock. "Come on. I don't wanna do this later."

They manage to rig it up between the kitchen and dining room, tying one end from the thick beam that separates the rooms and the other from a cross beam near the ceiling.

"Sleeping downhill."

"Better than the floor, Gordie."

"It might pull the whole house down."

Joe loosens the higher end to make it more horizontal. He tests it, sitting. "It'll do."

Gordie checks his phone. "Now we're late. Let's take Eddie and make a real entrance."

"We're walking."

Outside, Gordie gets on the bike. "Keys."

But Joe is already out on the road and walking towards town. Gordie hustles to catch up.

"How's Montreal?"

"Bilingual, as ever."

"You comin in May like you promised?"

"I never promised."

"You did."

"My boss said the conf in Seattle isn't worth the airfare."

"You never told me that."

"Haven't you got enough on your plate at school?"

"It's a breeze. You just have to show up for class and they pass you.

Come to P-land, bro. I'll show you a good time. Fuck, you really look like you need it. So stressed out."

"I'm not. I'm just, just not looking forward to this."

"Why'd you come then?"

"I had to."

"Get over it."

"I don't like Len."

"He's family now. Just don't push his Pentecostal buttons."

"Has ma converted?"

"Not that I know of. What was dad?"

"He wasn't anything. He put religions in the same bracket as biker gangs and the SS."

"What's social security got to do with God?"

"Forget it."

A car comes from the other direction. Joe jumps to the side.

"See. Completely stressed."

"Come on. We're late."

Gordie stops and looks around. "Hold up. It happened somewhere here, didn't it? Where's the rock? Hey, Joe. Wait up."

"Too slow, bro. Race ya to the Woodpecker."

Joe starts running, his business shoes slapping the tarmac and hurting his ankles, like he's running in clogs. He turns to see Gordie easily closing the gap, taking short, quick strides, his upper body perfectly straight and steady. Gordie passes with a wave. When Joe gets to the Woodpecker, Gordie's already hunched over his phone, probably letting all his ceevillians know he can still outrun his brother.

"What do I get?"

"The joy of victory. Are you running track in Portland?"

"Fuck no."

They start walking down Main Street.

"You should take that speed onto the track. You'd nail the four hundred without even training."

"Booooring."

"What a waste."

"Just following in your footsteps, bro."

"Hey, I missed out, but you could've got a scholarship, if you'd tried."

"Great. And then I'd spend the best years of my life getting up at six to run around and around in circles."

Joe stops at the volunteer fire station. Some of the crew are practicing winding hoses. He waves to Louis's dad. "Where is this wedding anyway?"

"Len's house. He's set up an altar in his backyard."

"Tell me that's a joke."

"It ain't."

"Huh. Well, lead the way."

"You don't remember? We used to go there all the time."

"You did. I chose to forget the few times I went, and the way there."

"You need to get a tattoo, bro. 'Get over it' written a thousand times on your arms. You seriously need help. It was ten years ago."

"Gordie."

"See a therapist or take something."

"I'm over it, Stan."

"Don't call me that. Every time I see you it's like you're carrying more of that crap around."

"Hey, it's not easy being back here. You weren't there. I saw it. I watched it."

"Yeah, you like throwing that at people."

"Fuck you, Stan. I'm going back."

Gordie grabs Joe's arm. "No, you're not. I'm not dealing with ma on my own. You're staying, for me."

They're on Len's street. Joe remembers it now: the big take-out dinners, sleeping in the den while the three of them played cards, playing with them when he was older and able to keep up, Max and Len clicking like a comedy duo and looking the part. Fun.

"Sorry, Gordie. Just accept this isn't easy."

"Move on, bro. Ma has."

"I can't believe she sold the place."

"They're moving."

"What? Where?"

"Florida. Len got a job in Naples."

Gordie walks up the drive. SUVs and pick-ups are bumper-to-bumper, most with "Live free or die" license plates. Voices excited by cheap champagne float over the roof. Gordie stops at a monstrous purple-grey Beamer, its windows filled.

"See? They're already packed."

"Does this hippo belong to Len?"

"Yep. They're driving down tomorrow."

"Jesus."

"Don't let Len hear you say that."

Joe shouts: "Jesus."

"It is what it is, bro. Deal with it. If you called ma more often, she would've told you."

"Like she told me when she moved in with Len. And when they were getting married. It all comes from you. She doesn't tell me anything. Jesus fucking Christ almighty. She can call me, you know."

"It's gonna be great visiting. The sun, bro. Len bought a place on the beach. You should see the pics."

"And he paid for it with the money from the house dad built."

"Len's got enough cash."

"He been giving it to you?"

Gordie walks between the cars and towards the side gate. "He helps me out. He's a good guy. Come on."

***

Outside the terminal, Len is waiting.

Joe. Hello, Joe. Look at you. All grown up.

His hair is whiter, thinner, his face more elongated, his forehead stretched. Joe likens him to your friendly, neighbourhood paedophile.

Where's ma?

She had to cover someone's shift. You know her. Never says no.

It's been four years. She couldn't come to the airport.

Sorry. I'm parked over here.

He follows Len across the busy street: taxis, buses, cars, shuttles, people wheeling trolleys piled high with luggage, like they're moving house.

Gordie here?

School.

Well, thanks, I guess, for picking me up.

Least I could do.

Len opens the trunk of the Volcano.

Where's your car?

In the shop.

He hesitates, then drops his backpack and satchel in the back. Len closes the trunk.

Welcome home.

Yeah, home.

He stands at the open passenger door.

Are you getting in? Come on. We have to beat the rush hour traffic.

Len, unconfident and passive behind the wheel, works his way slowly into the streams of cars and trucks, letting everyone in and getting pushed out himself. They get on the turnpike, then go through the tunnel. It takes a while to get on I-93 going north. The merging is slow and complicated, no one giving an inch, except Len, who waves in everybody.

Every man for himself.

What's that, Joe?

Nothing. Take the gap. Shit.

Another car fills the space. Len waits, offering a pathetic attempt at a serene smile.

What's your rush? Show some patience.

No one else is.

Look at these people, Joe. They need our compassion.

He stares out the window. Eventually, they make it out of Boston and head north. The traffic thins as the cars drift to the various exits, workers ending their commute from hectic downtown to secure suburb: no immigrants, good schools, soccer fields, AA and NA support groups, a secret behind every locked front door.

Good flight?

Huh?

How was the flight?

What do you think?

To be honest, I never did a journey like that.

A stack of money to sit in a flying toilet.

Looks like you enjoyed Australia. You got yourself a nice tan there, Joe. You might regret that when you get to be my age.

It's weird to be in the Volcano, with Len behind the wheel, driving this interstate. Len sticks to the right lane, a good five miles under the limit. The miles click off achingly slow. Even the trucks pass.

Joe doesn't want to converse with Len, so he closes his eyes.

When he opens them again, they're off the interstate, on the back roads towards Harbrook. Home. Whatever that means. The towns are familiar, the houses fanning out from the highway, the pick-ups and SUVs parked in driveways and on curbs; nobody walking anywhere. There's snow on the ground, cleared from the road and shovelled from sidewalks in front of the houses of those who can be bothered.

Outside of the towns, the snow clings in scraggly clumps to the trees. Through a break in those trees, he sees a man on cross country skis, just standing, a leash tied around his waist and his dog pulling him forward. Into another town, another condensed strip mall of fast food joints, gas stations, hardware stores and 24-hour supermarkets. A lot of cars, a lot of movement, but no life on the streets. Out the other side. More trees, more snow, a frozen lake.

Len turns slightly towards him. You missed it.

A bit.

But he's missing more the heat, the sand and the salt water. Simple Sydney. The screech of the fruit bats at night as they soared through the darkness only to fry themselves on power lines. Waking up to see a massive spider on the ceiling above and wondering if it is just about to drop down and land on you, or already has and is working its way back to its web. The echoing crash of the surf hitting the rocks at Clovelly. The winds tasting of salt and sewage. The hospital blue-white bottom of the pool at the Bondi Icebergs. The unbelievably refreshing impact of a hot cup of green tea in forty degree heat. The blanket-heavy air of the still, humid nights. The standoffish friendliness of the locals. Hell, he even misses the cockroaches darting between the wheelie bins on Coogee Bay Road.

It's good you're back. What's your plan?

Montreal.

Montreal? That's the first I've heard of it. Visiting?

Relocating.

You never said anything about that.

Surprise.

You got a job there?

Internship. Start on Monday

Who with? And doing what?

Denoris. Sales.

Denoris? Those morons. Make sure you get into their customer service department. Their service is hopeless. You should've said something, Joe. I've got contacts at Natrofield. I could've got you an interview there.

Pass.

Much better company than Denoris. You could have a real career there.

Too late now.

Tell you what, do the internship at Denoris and then I'll help you switch. That way you won't have to start at an entry level position.

Stop trying to make it right.

I don't follow you.

I'm going to Montreal.

Good luck to you. Never been there. Is it nice?

A fuck load better than here.

Wanting distraction, he plays with the radio, getting it off Christian contemporary and searching for something more grating, something that would have a parents advisory sticker on the CD cover. He settles on Gordie's kind of angry, gun-toting, champagne quaffing hip-hop. Len shifting in his seat is a small morsel of victory to be savoured. But it's still all wrong, so many things way off. Four years away and it's Len who picks him up. He wonders if his ma had conjured it that way, to bring them closer, to heal.

Wrong.

Bored, he opens the glove box, wanting something he can put in his hands, something he can lift up in the air and say, hey, this is how it really should be. He fishes around, pushing the small first aid kit and the packets of tissues aside and then clutching a handle that clicks. He lifts it out.

Colonel Mustard.

What did you call me?

Max used this label maker working on site, used to label everything that needed doing, putting these reminders all over the place. Colonel Mustard was his favourite, the leader of his label maker army. The round disc with the numbers and letters stuck half out the side. A little window, just below where the label comes out the top, shows which letter is about to be punched. Above the window, there's a small blade, hidden, for cutting the label when it's finished. The Colonel feels lighter, smaller in his hands.

The tongue of a label is sticking out: L's a motherfucker. Gordie, he guesses. Or did he do it, before he left? He cuts it off and drops it on the floor. He starts to bang off a label, feeling Len's eyes. One letter, another. The wheel is stiff from lack of use and turns better clockwise than counter. He spins, clicks, finishes and pulls the label up so it catches the blade. The old back paper comes off easily. He sticks the label to the dashboard and slides Colonel Mustard into his inside jacket pocket, holstering it, like a gun.

Never trust a borrower? I think you need to brush up on your Shakespeare.

Max used to say that.

Len laughs. But he borrowed everything.

No, he didn't.

Anyway, there's nothing wrong with borrowing. The Lord giveth and the Lord taketh away. Sometimes, everyone needs a little help.

They enter Harbrook.

Where are you going? The house is the other way.

Relax, Joe. You're staying with us.

No chance in hell. Stop the car. I'll walk.

Okay, okay. I'll drive you. You can catch up with Gordie for a while. He can't wait to see you.

Len executes a slow, meandering u-turn, waiting for traffic that's a good hundred metres away. A few people recognise Len and wave to him. Joe wonders if they are having the same sensation as him – this car, this driver – or are they used to it by now?

They pass the Woodpecker. He sees Rex and Lanno smoking in the doorway. They don't wave; just stare, the way the locals do at strangers. The tan, he assumes, or perhaps they don't want to know him anymore.

On the narrow road out of town, they pass the rock. He looks towards the house, perched on that familiar rise, the back of the house pointing to town and the front porch facing the forest. The homestead, modelled after Max's old house in Western Australia. The long veranda, the thick wooden beams, the hammock swaying slightly in the breeze, the red roof with the massive gutters that were such a chore to clean. The sense that this house was far removed from its location, from Harbrook. Another world.

Where are George and Ringo?

What?

The oaks.

Cut em down.

What?

They were rotten to the core, Joe. They had to go. The roots were getting to the foundations.

Who said that was your decision to make?

Tessa decided. Your ma.

The house looks naked without the towering oaks that flanked it and jammed the gutters in fall. It looks exposed, vulnerable, alone.

You've been gone a long time, Joe. Things are going to be different.

Nothing ever changes in Harbrook.

You know that's not true.

Len stops the car in front of the house, but doesn't get out.

I better get back to the hospital. I'll tell Tessa your here.

He retrieves his bags, then watches the square back of the Volcano as it turns and crawls towards town. He goes up the short stairs and breathes in. The front door is locked. He leaves his bags on the porch and goes around to the back. The vegetable patch is gone, paved over and with an 8-foot basketball hoop. The hoop has been bent almost right off and the net is hanging on by a single strand; it doesn't sway in the breeze, and looks frozen. The fields roll down to town, criss-crossed by tracks with deep grooves carved by dirt bikes, now set for the rest of winter. He prays to Len's God that Gordie hasn't been subjecting Eddie to those tracks. He's scared to go into the garage and see the grand old Indian dame has morphed into a pile of mud-caked junk. Near the back door, he grabs the sides of the laundry window and finds the little switch that pushes the window off its rails. Max's secret entry, as useful as ever.

Inside, it's surprisingly clean. Gordie mentioned something about a Mexican or a Guatemalan who comes once a week, or twice. The old X-Files poster is still on the door to his room. The truth is out there. It's still out there, somewhere. He opens the door and pokes his head into the room. The curtains are drawn. Gordie has commandeered it as his play den, having set it up with all manner of technology, old and new: screens, several computers, a tangle of joysticks, cables, long power adapters, boxes of discs, computer game packages in an untidy heap, a pair of massive speakers but no stereo. There are old pizza boxes, empty beer cans, half drunk bottles of spirits, an elaborate bong. The room smells, of dust, of the burps and farts of junk food eaten late at night, of the sweated frustration of not reaching a certain level before having to rush off to school. It smells of tissues rotting with old semen.

He pulls the door closed. Scully and Mulder scowl at him.

The truth is in there.

He moves down the hall and into the kitchen-living room. The counter still has the remains of Gordie's hasty breakfast: the top of the Coco Pops packet still open, the lid of the peanut butter jar not screwed on properly, a knife stuck to the counter with a brown smear on it, a deflated half-loaf of Wonderbread, crumbs everywhere. Over by the sofas, there's a large flat-screen TV attached to the wall.

Max would love that.

All those evenings, all that time spent on the sofa. *Northern Exposure*, *Larry Sanders*, *Quantum Leap*, *Seinfeld*, repeats of *Spinal Tap*, late night marathons of *Blackadder*, and the other weird, off-kilter stuff Max always knew about, always knew first about. He wouldn't let anyone watch crap, turning the TV off when ma tried to watch *Melrose Place*, *Friends* or *Sex and the City*. They would argue, not heatedly, but because it was part of the routine, because it gave Max the forum to deliver his fantastic rants about culture and entertainment and the forcing of ideas onto people. Branding, gender roles, product placements, ad time, white power, stereotypes, capitalism, the American dream, it all got a mention. And it was funny enough for ma to stick around and listen to before going off to a friend's house to watch her shows there.

He hears the echo of Max's voice. I know she does it. But I don't want you seeing that crap. She's ruined already, but you, you're still in development. *Star Trek*'s social humanism is better for you than brand whores living on credit in New York.

The front door opens. Gordie trudges in, baggy jeans and over-sized sweatshirt, a ratted backpack covered in badges and graffiti slung over his right shoulder. He's got big headphones on, a backwards baseball cap over a bandanna, aviator shades low down on his nose, a few pathetic strands combed together in an attempt to make a goatee.

What're you doing here? You supposed to be at Len's.

Joe pulls out Colonel Mustard and points it at his brother. Hey, Stan.

~~~

"Joe? Joe?"

"Huh?"

"Joe."

He opens his eyes and tries to sit up, but his back rebels, locking. The hammock swings a little and the wooden beams creak. He sees his mother standing in the hallway.

"I thought you left already."

"Len had a bit too much to drink."
~~~

"Someone turn water into wine?"

"Stop that. Your smirking at the ceremony was embarrassing. Everyone saw you."

He rubs his eyes. "Great. You've come to tell me again I'm going to hell."

"That's enough."

He pulls the sleeping bag up to his chin. "Sorry. Really."

"Len's outside. I just wanted to say goodbye, you know, properly."

"Have fun in the sun."

"I'm not leaving like this, Joe."

"How do you wanna leave then? You want my blessing?"

"I knew you'd behave like this if I got married again."

"So that's what stopped you. Well, you're way wrong. I got no problems with that. I got problems with Len."

"Ssh. You'll wake Gordie."

"Not just him."

She shoots a concerned look at him and then heads for the living room, her sensible heels clicking on the floor. Joe somehow manages to untangle himself from the hammock, to get his body moving, and to stop her as she firms her shoulders with nursing intent to reach down and wake Gordie. He pulls her back and they both take in the scene. Gordie is lying half off the mattress, his baseball capped head resting in the crook of his left arm. His mouth is agape. He's snoring, and there's a sliver of drool on his forearm. The index finger of his right hand is on the notebook's track pad, thumb on the left mouse button.

"I'd like to read that billboard."

"Who's that?"

A bulky looking girl is taking up most of the mattress and all of the sleeping bag, her hair fanning out and covering her face. She blows a bang or two into the air with each wheezing exhale. Joe points at the black slacks and white apron left crumpled on the floor, then at the various torn open condom wrappers.

He grabs his mother's arm and pulls her from the room. "Let's go outside."

He picks up his suit coat and pulls it on, just managing to move his back enough to get into it. He sniffs the lapel. It stinks. He vaguely recalls all those God-fearing Pentecosts gathered in tight circles much more intent on worshipping nicotine and alcohol.

It's cold on the porch. The sun is out, creeping above the tree line and glistening on the dewy grass. The light hurts his eyes. It feels like there's a prisoner in his brain running a tin cup backwards and forwards against the steel prison bars.

The hippo is parked out front, pointing its fully packed arse at the porch, ready for a fast getaway. Steamy smoke comes out of the exhaust. The engine hums. Through the passenger window, he sees the outline of Len's big head, sees him look at his watch and then start playing with the sat-nav.

She crosses her arms. "I can't believe it."

"He's not exactly a kid."

"He's barely old enough to drink."

"He's been doing that ever since you left him alone here."

"You left him alone here."

"Yeah, you're right. My fault again."

"Can you please stop it. We're talking about Gordie."

"You don't know the half of it. Anyway, it's too late now. Damage is done."

"You were supposed to watch out for him. You always said you would."

"Me?"

"Yes, you."

"Stop blaming me for everything."

"You should've got that scholarship in Burlington. Then you would've been nearby. You would've set the right example. But it was easier to run away, wasn't it?"

He digs a thumb and finger into his eyes and pulls out a few crusty bits. "I'm not gonna fight with you, ma. I'm happy for you. Your life's on track. Congrats. Have a safe drive. Make sure Len doesn't use the phone while driving. Take plenty of rest breaks. I'm sorry if I ruined your wedding."

"You still have so much growing up to do, Joe. This is the example you set for Gordie."

"He's doing all right. He's at college, and he'll graduate and make something of himself. You make it sound like he's blowing guys in a bus station toilet for a score."

"Oh, God. Is that what happens in Montreal?"

"Not just there. You've been living in the sticks too long. Look, ma, what do you want from me? If you wanna blame me for everything, go for it. If it makes everything easier. That's fine. But we're different. I can't let go so easily."

Her face hardens, drawing lines from nostrils to mouth corners, her fluorescent-tanned skin shadowing around the cheeks as the skin is pulled taught. She looks old, worn, as if Len's grey hair, giant prostate, stooped walk and old man's spots have rubbed off onto her, bridging the gap, slapping on another decade and a half in the space of just a few years, bringing them closer.

"You don't know how it was."

"I know what I saw. He borrowed what didn't belong to him."

"That was ten years ago."

"You're lucky I didn't beat the crap out of him."

"That's not your way. And you assume too much. Didn't Max ever tell you never to assume?"

"He did. He stuck that label all over the place."

"Len was there when I needed him. You weren't."

"I'm not sure that a son should support a mother in that way, you know, in a good Christian family."

She slaps him. "Sorry."

"It's okay. I'm awake now."

"I'm trying to make this right."

"Marrying Len was not a good start."

The hippo's engine revs a couple of times. The horn lets out a nasal, high-pitched toot.

"Joe, if you'd just give him a chance. When we get settled, I want you to come down and visit."

"Yeah, I'll come down. Me and Len can play golf, maybe, maybe go for a run together."

"He's not a replacement. Look, you don't have to stay with us."

"You don't have to worry about that."

She lets out a huff. "You are just like your father."

"Good."

"That's not a compliment."

"Better than saying I'm just like Len."

The horn toots twice more.

"The Lord waits for no one."

"Stop that."

"Fine. No more jokes. Send me a postcard."

"Our new house, there's a pool at the end of the street. Olympic size."

"I don't swim."

"Still?"

"Look, ma, I'm always happy to see you. I just struggle with Len, with everything that happened. It was really hard to come here."

She shakes her head. "Then it shouldn't be hard to leave then."

"There's nothing left. It's all sold up and packed away."

"Well, Joe, you better get over it, because I'm going to spend the rest of my life with Len. If you were stronger, you'd at least try."

She moves towards the top of the steps.

"Don't you wanna say goodbye to Gordie?"

"I did last night. He was in a great mood. At least he's happy for me."

Joe laughs. "The better half of the chemical brothers."

"What?"

"Nothing."

"He's coming to visit. In summer. You could too."

"A nuclear family, again. I don't know. Work's crazy at the moment. I'm getting shipped all over the place."

She leans towards him and kisses him on the cheek, grabbing his shoulders awkwardly with her hands and not quite getting him into the hug she seems to want.

"Bye, Joe."

"Bye, ma."

She takes the steps one at a time. "I'm sorry we didn't get the chance to talk last night."

"We did this morning."

"If you do come, tell me as far ahead as possible. We're gonna get a lot of visitors this year."

"I won't throw your schedule into disarray. I promise."

"Yes. Well. Take care."

"Drive safely."

He raises a hand. She boards the hippo and it lurches forward with a squirt of mud. He moves back inside before the hippo turns onto the road.

He packs, folding things tightly so they'll fit in the saddle bags. He takes out the forgotten wine decanter, still in its box, and tosses it aside. In the bathroom, he splashes cold water on his face and tries to piece together the previous evening. It's hazy. He brushes his teeth, the water almost cracking his molars.

"Um, hi."

"Hey. I'm Joe. The brother. Sorry, but there's no hot water."

"Lindsay. Did we meet last night?"

"Probably."

Her long hair is bent almost square on one side and she has a perfect straight line down her left cheek from the groove of the air mattress. Her size lends her a few extra years, but he still wonders if she's legal. He hopes so.

"Any coffee?"

"No. But there's internet."

"What kind of house is this?"

"An empty one. Sold, the ghosts as well. The boxes of memories were set on fire."

"Oh. I guess I better, like, go."

"Where's your ride?"

"My what?"

"Your car."

"Oh, right. My car. At the wedding house, I guess."

"You wanna lift?"

"I can walk."

"It's about twenty minutes."

She nods. "Bye."

"Later."

He rinses his mouth and spits. In the living room, Gordie snores on. Joe packs the rest of his stuff. He takes the saddle bags outside and attaches them to Eddie. He can see Lindsay walking down the road. With a single sweep, he wipes the dew off the seat. Back inside, he puts on his riding clothes, leaving his helmet and gloves neatly by the door. He sits down with his back against the living room wall.

"Bottom scraper, that's you, Stan."

With everything gone, the memories don't sparkle and stab. It's just another empty house. He wonders what she did with it all. Sold it at some Pentecostal fleamarket and bought Len a steak dinner with the proceeds. Maybe Len just borrowed it all. He surely commandeered the tools.

"Every tool has a purpose, Gordie, but you can do a lot with just a hammer, a saw and some nails. And a label maker."

Gordie stirs, snorts, picks his nose with that dexterous right thumb of his, and falls back into a neat snoring rhythm.

"Max built this house. And that means nothing now."

He gets up and stretches his stiff back. He looks down at Gordie, considers kicking him awake, or just kicking him, once, really hard; kick all the crap out of him. He raises a boot, then lets it hit the floor.

He goes through the house, checking every room. It's empty, even the garage. The hammock is all that remains, and Eddie, and the house itself. And all those little labels Max left, stuck to the walls and floors.

In his parents' bedroom, he bends down to the floorboard near where the head of the bed was, the side Max slept on. There's a label: "Sparschwein". The German word for piggy bank. Next to it is the nail that's actually a pop-up pin. He gets his door key into the hole and the pin jumps up. He shimmies the floorboard loose.

"My thirteenth birthday. You remember? You showed me this. I was so impressed. When I got out of hospital, I took everything out. Buried the gun in the veggie patch. It's probably still there. Took all the money and hitch-hiked down to Boston. And I never got to thank you for it."

He feels inside, stretching his arm and grabbing handfuls of dust and cobwebs. It's almost like he's scooping around the inside of his hungover brain. Then he feels it. The plastic handle. The grooves and dents of the wheel. The sharp corners of the label still hanging out. He gets it in his hands and pulls it out. A spider is hanging from the long label and he drops it in shock. The spider scampers back below, into the darkness.

He brushes the dust off, revealing the mustard yellow, faded on top and slightly darker on the clickable handle.

"'The sun will rise, the birds will sing, but only people will let you down.' True. But it's more that we ask too much of people. Expect too much."

Colonel Mustard slides easily into his jacket pocket. He puts the floorboard back in place, the pin popping in and locking with such ease it fills him with remorse and affection. He sniffs as he touches the label with his fingertips.

In the living room, he gives Gordie a light shove. At some point, Gordie moved his head onto the keyboard, and as he raises it, one side of his face is covered with small little squares and the faintest outlines of letters. He groans as he rolls onto his back. The Red Sox cap comes off. He grabs it, spins it around and pulls the visor over his face, bending the sides. He opens his eyes.

"Morn."

"How many?"

"Wha?"

"How many did you take?"

"Don't know. Lost count, heh-heh."

"That's the last time I make the night enjoyable for you. You slip her one as well?"

Gordie rubs his face, rippling all those perfect squares. "Who?"

"It's good you don't remember. Then you can lie with conviction when they arrest you."

"Calm yourself, bro. She's eighteen."

"She tell you that? She doesn't even drive."

"Will you calm the fuck down. God. She gone, yeah? I hope we didn't keep you up."

"That fucking generator did."

Gordie sits up to listen. "You turned it off?"

"I had to."

Gordie jumps to his feet, staggers on the first couple of steps and goes into the kitchen. The generator starts humming again. All the technology in the living room comes to life, beeping and gurgling, lights flashing, a collective machine stretching and getting ready to face the day.

Gordie comes back and flops down on the mattress. "That was some good shit. Your buddy was right about mixing it with Pepsi."

"Is that how you gave it to Linda?"

"I'm not that lame."

"You're the man, Stan. You tell your ceevillians the moment you blew your load?"

"That's crass. What's the matter with you? And what are you all dressed up for?"

"I'm off."

Gordie starts tapping at the keyboard, squinting at the screen. "What? Fuck no."

"Ma says goodbye."

"She was here?"

"Yeah."

"Why didn't you wake me up?"

"It wasn't the most flattering scene."

"She saw Linda?"

"Jesus, Stan, when are you gonna get it together. You're gonna graduate next summer. Then what?"

"If I get a job, I'll turn into someone like you. Stressed and nervy and bad company and screaming in my sleep."

"You gonna stay in Portland?"

Gordie turns the screen towards Joe. "Florida's where it's at. Check the pics."

"Is that their house?"

"Right on the beach. Fucking straight."

"I could get you an internship at Denny."

"No way. I don't wanna be you. I like the free samples, but I don't agree with the evil your company spreads."

"I don't think you would've said that last night."

"Probably not. Still. There's a pill for everything, right? And the people who really need it, can't afford it."

"Who told you that?"

"Len. He hates Denny, but not the other one. Natural something."

"Natrofield."

"That's it."

"What did he say?"

"And I quote, 'Denoris's quick fixes are killing real medicine.' He's real old school."

"Old old old school. His stethoscope is a hearing aid."

"But he's got a point."

"He's way off. Pills are killing doctors, not medicine. The internet knows a lot more than Len does."

Gordie hammers away at the keyboard. He manages to type with his left hand and send a text with his right. "You gotta stick around, bro. I wanna take Eddie for a spin."

"You got your leg over one beast. That's enough."

"Eddie's half mine, remember."

"You forfeited your half when you tried to kill her. I hope you didn't treat Lindsay the same way."

"Who's Lindsay?"

"Your servile conquest."

"Linda."

"Lindsay. I was fucking with you, to see if you knew her name."

"Linda, Lindsay. What's the diff?"

"Huh. When's your flight?"

"Tonight. We can go to the airport together. I'll ride."

"Wrong direction. And there's no way we'll get all of this on Eddie."

"Leave your stuff here. You can pick it up on the way back."

"No."

"Then how am I supposed to get to Logan?"

"Ask Lindsay for a lift. Maybe her parents will take you."

"You just gonna leave me?"

"Get one of your buddies to drive you down. It's not far. They probably don't have anything better to do."

"Lachie wanted to hang today. He'll take me."

Gordie picks up his phone and punches off a quick text.

"I'll leave you to it."

"What the fuck's wrong with you?"

"You don't get it, Gordie. You never did. And I'm not gonna waste my time explaining it to you."

"Be happy for her, bro, and stop thinking about yourself and how everything affects you."

Joe picks up his gloves and helmet.

Gordie stands up. He fumbles in the pockets of his jacket and pulls out a photograph. "Joe, wait. Here. Ma asked me to give you this. Remember that?"

He looks at the photograph: a helmeted and spandexed Len, a fit and lean Max, a skinnier, self-conscious version of himself in the middle, the three of them locked in arms in front of the finish line. Ridiculously, Len has the index finger of his left hand pointing upwards.

"Timberman."

"Ma says she took it."

"Mora did."

"Len's ex?"

"She was in town visiting."

"Remember your result?"

"I was third out of the water. Max had the best run of anyone over 30. Len completely tanked the bike. We could've won otherwise."

"How old were you?"

"Sixteen."

"That's why I can't remember it."

"You were bored out of your brains. Ma didn't have any spare batteries. You cried and made a scene."

"You lie."

Joe looks at the photo again. Max is in great shape. He was tall for a runner, with flamingo-skinny legs made even more pronounced by those short shorts he favoured. But he was able to take long, economical strides, skipping along while the smaller runners pounded the pavement and pumped their arms. Even standing, with his legs loose and relaxed, Joe can see the muscles and taught tendons, shaped and strengthened by all the miles logged. A head full of blonde hair, wavy and healthy, even here in, what, his mid-forties? He and Joe look almost like brothers, with the grey haired, balding, geeky, out-of-shape, neon spandex wearing Len as their embarrassing father. Despite the disappointment of the day, Max is smiling broadly, clutching Joe's shoulder with his left arm, his right arm flexed and bulging a sizeable bicep.

He puts the photo in his jacket pocket with Colonel Mustard. "Thanks, Gordie."

"You wanna get some breakfast? The Pecker does brunch on Sundays now."

"All right. Let's go."

Gordie bangs at the keyboard. "This'll just take a minute. I'm riding."

"No way."

Clicking to enlightenment with Colonel Mustard

They exit the pool.

"You wanna grab a bite?"

"Yeah. Quick one."

"What species?"

"Something light."

"You're not helping, Joe."

"You gonna make me choose? Fine. The Sombrero."

"I knew you'd say that. Let's ride there."

"You came by bike?"

"Yep."

"I didn't even know you had one."

"It was in the basement."

From the Aquadôme, Joe leads the way down Boulevard de la Vérendrye. The going is slow as Francois's tires aren't fully pumped up and his seat is too low, making his knees almost hit his chest. The whole bike is too small and has no lights or reflectors. It's not completely dark yet, but it still helps to be illuminated, at least, Joe thinks, for legal reasons. Francois does have a miner's light strapped around what looks like a kid's helmet, but this doesn't make much difference for cars coming from behind. And the tiny helmet is perched on the back of Francois's head, making the miner's light point straight up.

Francois tries to ride next to him, but it's too dangerous. There's a lot of traffic for a Sunday evening, every single driver in an incredible hurry. Joe finds it fascinating and baffling. He wonders how many babies are being born on those back seats, how many people are bleeding to death, because surely only an emergency could explain such impatience and risk-taking. A couple of cars pass so close that he could elbow the passenger window. One car even passes a car that's passing them, nearly collecting an open car door on the other side.

They cut through Verdun and the suburban streets are quieter. Francois pedals hard to get alongside Joe, who coasts.

"How was the wedding?"

"Pass. Next question."

"That bad? Jesus."

"He didn't make an appearance. A few people thought he might, but I guess he had somewhere better to be. Maybe he had to help some athletes get godly victories."

"Oh, yeah. Len's a bit of a religious quack, right?"

"He stopped half way through his speech to pray."

Francois laughs. "I guess the wedding was full of them."

"And alcohol and nicotine are key components of their worship."

"You have fun?"

"Actually, it was pretty entertaining. Gordie definitely enjoyed himself."

An SUV flashes its lights and Francois moves behind Joe. The driver waves furiously for them to get off the road and gives them the finger through the open sun roof. Joe sees the heads of two small children in the back seat. The blasted horn triggers a chain of dog barks from the nearby yards.

"Respect, Joe."

"Why?"

"This shit is dangerous."

"It's a good reminder that you're alive, that's what it is. It's much worse than this during the week."

"I don't remember it being like this when I was a kid. We didn't even wear helmets. And Montreal was no smaller then."

"Is that the same bike?"

"Yeah. I wanna racing number like yours."

"It's faster, but you get a lot of flats. I put thicker tires on, but that doesn't stop people from dropping bottles on the ground."

"Bastards."

"It's not their fault. The winter stones are just as bad."

They get onto Boulevard Lasalle, go under the freeway, and take St Patrick to Charlevoix. There are white bikes painted on the streets, along with the jagged outline of a bike path, but still the drivers overtake recklessly, blowing their horns as they pass within half an arm's reach.

Joe and Francois are forced to ride single file down Charlevoix, which is buzzing with traffic. They turn right onto Notre Dame and stop in front of the building with the massive sombrero attached to the facade. There are no bike racks. Joe locks his bike to a parking meter, getting the lock around the quick-release front wheel as well.

Francois locks his bike to Joe's. He takes off his kid's helmet and his hair is damp with sweat.

"You look a little hot."

"Gives me a whole new perspective of swimming."

"Why?"

"It's easier. And safer."

"You need to pump up your tires."

"I let the air out. For suspension."

"I'll buy a special haemmorrhoid seat for your birthday."

"How thoughtful."

It's not crowded inside, but the voices echo, making it sound busier than it is. They get a table near the window. Joe hangs the strap of his satchel over the chair, stretches and sits.

"Long ride?"

"I slept in a hammock last night."

"Yo-ho-ho. A parrot on your shoulder?"

"A guilty conscience. I was a bad boy, stuck in a bizarre three-way with the father, son and the holy ghost."

"That would make it a four-way. And very bizarre."

The waitress comes over, her face shadowed by the enormous hat that's part of the uniform. Joe takes a turkey quesadilla, Francois a tofu burrito, both washed down with Coronas. Francois orders a shot of tequila as well.

"To fortify myself for the ride home."

"I don't think that'll help."

"You're right. I'll have another before we go. You said last night. What about Friday?"

"It rained. I stayed in Boston."

"Ah, Beantown. Love it."

"It was fun."

"Did you paint it magenta with your clients?"

"Not quite."

"What then? Come on. You started this. Tell."

"I fraternised."

"At Harvard?"

"With the enemy. Natrofield. She was at the same meeting. Well, after mine."

"More."

"She bought me dinner."

Francois scratches his neck. "Girls don't just do that. What did she want in exchange?"

"I think she was lonely. Or bored. Or both."

The beers and Francois's shot arrive. The waitress also dumps a basket of nachos on the table and salsa in what looks like an old jam jar, a spoon sticking out the top.

"Cheers, Francois. Good swim."

"Not so fast. You're holding back on me."

Joe takes a long drink. It fills the cold pockets of his lungs. The pool had been unusually cold, like they'd turned the heater off at lunch time.

"You know how dates normally go."

"You know I don't date, because of that."

"Yeah, but still, when two people go out like that, they always end up talking about the usual stuff. Where are you from? What do you do? What do you like? What do you want?"

"The interview."

"Right. We didn't do any of that."

"What then?"

"Somehow we got onto love. I told her about your under twenty-three theory."

"Never fails. Everyone I know had it."

"She didn't believe it, doesn't even believe in love, so she pushed me to prove it."

"Oh, no. You didn't?"

Joe raises his bottle. "Si, senor."

"You idiot."

"I know. Still. It did the trick."

"What? A sympathy fuck?"

"You're a classy guy, Francois."

"I do what I can. But you're the one doing one night stands in Beantown."

"I think she just wanted, you know, to connect."

Francois lowers his voice: "How Intercourse Became Connectivity: The Joe Solitus Story."

"We both knew it was going to happen the minute she asked me to dinner. I think she needed it go deeper than just a one-nighter between strangers. Between competitors."

"And did she also tell how her heart was broken?"

"Like I said, she doesn't believe in love. Come to think of it, we didn't talk about her at all."

"Now that is strange."

"Yeah."

"You gonna see her again?"

"At a conference, probably."

"That might be awkward."

"Yeah. We can't really show in public that we know each other. We ran into one of her colleagues on the street and she pretended I was an old high school sweetheart from Kansas."

"I like this girl. What's her apartment like?"

"Didn't see it."

"You take her in the restaurant bathroom?"

"She came to my hotel."

"To or in?"

"You're all class."

"But she lives in Boston?"

"Yeah."

Francois takes a handful of nachos and leans back in his chair. He keeps the nachos in his cupped right hand and eats with his left. "Boyfriend."

"Maybe a girlfriend. Who knows?"

"I don't think ménage à trois is going to make it into the Joe Solitus Story."

"Maybe it already has. The holy trinity."

Francois picks up the shot of tequila and slams it down. He shakes his head and grimaces. "Woof. That's mighty fine sauce."

"How can you drink that stuff?"

"Unlike you, I don't have to get up tomorrow to ride a desk all day. Right. Back to Beantown. You told her about, what was her name again?"

"Trina."

"That's it. You told her about Trina and she came back to your hotel. Man, if only life was so easy. I could tell girls about Emmanuelle and I'd be in."

"She had other motives."

"She wanted money after?"

"No. I woke up in the middle of the night and saw her rummaging through my satchel."

"Maybe she thought you had a picture of Trina."

"She was after company stuff. She's a spy."

"For who?"

"Natrofield."

"They're a company, Joe, not the CIA."

"Sure, but they're still in the intelligence business. How do you think they got so big?"

"Pray tell."

"Stealing the ideas of other companies. Buying smaller competitors. Locking out rivals. Poaching talent."

"She find anything?"

"There was nothing to find. I don't think she realised what a small fish I am on the Denny food chain. She toyed with my notebook for a minute, but gave up when she saw the fingerprint sensor."

"And got back into bed."

"I don't think so. I heard her go into the bathroom. Then I fell asleep. When I woke up, she was gone."

"She leave a note?"

"A text."

He pulls out his phone, finds the message and points the screen at Francois.

"a meet meant 2 b. you're fun. ani."

The waitress slides their plates in front of them. "Bon appétit."

"What does she mean by that?"

"We should enjoy our dinner. Your French is appalling, Francois."

"The text."

"She thinks people don't just meet by accident. They meet because they're supposed to."

Francois bites into his burrito. "She relidgish?"

"Don't think so. I'm not sure good Catholic girls do solo gigs."

"Sounds religious. Oh, it always tastes so good after a swim. Must be the chlorine. Anything that drives away that taste is good."

Joe splits his quesadilla into sections he can pick up with his hands. There's far too much cheese and he has to cut these long elastic strands with a knife.

Francois talks with his mouth full again: "Gon."

"Like I said. We spoke about Trina."

"What'd she say?"

Joe takes a bite, chews and swallows, smiling all the while. "She said I'm better off."

"Because you didn't end up with Trina?"

"Because I had the experience. And it started the long chain of events that ended with me in Boston having dinner with her. If I hadn't met Trina, I wouldn't have met Anita."

"Strange logic, coming from a girl."

"Yeah. She also said it was good because it made me harder. She said you can only make it in life if you're hard. If you're soft, people will walk all over you."

"Sounds like a real tough nut. Corporate spy, doesn't believe in love, sleeps with her legs open, doesn't talk only about herself, leaves the bed before spooning. Are you sure she's not a dude?"

"Pretty sure."

"She hot?"

"Wouldn't a girl who is everything you just said be hot?"

Francois chews and nods. "Even if she wasn't, she would be. And she'd have some swagger, that's for sure. Let's pray you meet her again."

***

Xav comes from other direction, dressed preppy, a canary sweater over a pink shirt, big collar, stiff cuffs turned up, meaty watch on his wrist. He's got a couple of folders in his right hand. "You're late."

"Got held up."

Xav doesn't break stride. "No time. Jour fixe. And Supe's in a mood. What went down in Boston?"

"We lost it. What about my emails?"

"They'll have to wait."

He pivots and catches up to Xav.

"You all right?"

"People are so stupid."

"All six billion?"

"Close to it. Okay, not all of them."

"What happened?"

They enter the small meeting room and take their usual seats. Joe loops his leather satchel over his chair and removes his jacket. He takes a couple of deep breaths. "It'll take more than one sentence."

Supe bustles in, open notebook balanced on one hand, Bluetooth set lodged in his ear, like some trinket he picked up at a *Star Wars* convention. "Morning, troops."

No one replies.

"I hope you all had tremendous weekends."

He hooks up his notebook and switches the projector on. He gets the calendar, splotched with assorted colours and dates, coded according to importance; there's a lot of red on the screen. He turns to his team and claps his hands together.

"Update me."

Working clockwise, they go around the table, each team member outlining the current status of their various projects. Supe strokes his beard, asks some questions, states the obvious, gives a few superfluous orders.

"Thanks, Xavier. Joe?"

"Uh, Toronto was a success. There's the big conf in Barcelona in two weeks. And I'm off to Ottawa next week, to get some face time at the hospitals."

"You can't do that from here?"

"The CM's like personal contact. You send them an email and they don't always reply."

"Keep it short. Get up with the sun and make it a day trip. We're already over this quarter's expense budget. And Boston?"

"Uh, Enora, you want to field that?"

She sits up, leans forward, hands clasped together, almost in prayer. "Interesting project, bad developer. Dead in the water. I think we should leave it."

"Really?"

"Well, Joe pretty much killed it before we had a chance to make an offer."

"I did everything I could. I also did all the right research."

Supe raises a calming hand. "Joe, let's not make this personal."

"Natrofield was there right after us. They were always gonna go with them. Like they did with A-Plus. They just wanted leverage. And nicotine is one thing, but I think it's way too risky to get involved in diet supplements and sugar alternatives."

Xav taps a pen on the table. "I agree. We're a pharmaceutical company, not a beauty shop."

Supe smiles thinly, annoyed. "That's true, but we also have to respond to market trends. And you gotta fight harder, Joe. Really fight. Sounds like you gave up before you even went in. Take one for the team. We're all fighting for you."

"Yes, Miles."

"Now, I need you in Miami this week. Flight's Wednesday morning."

Joe looks at the room's one empty chair. "Where's Brett?"

Supe reaches into his coat pocket and pulls out a card. He flips it onto the table. "Falicia was induced last night. Sign this. I've had Marjorie organise some flowers."

The card does the rounds, each person pausing briefly – pen in mouth – for inspiration before scribbling something innocuous and barely legible. By the time it gets to Joe, the card is covered with "All the best" and "Good luck" and "Best wishes", everything emphasised with exclamation marks and smiley faces, and written at various angles.

He picks up a pen. A lot of things come to mind. Pay attention. Keep your eyes open. Watch out for others. Be aware of everything around you. Don't trust others with your life. Don't ride a bike with headphones on. One mistake and someone dies. Done. Over.

He writes and hands the card to Xav.

"'A marathon starts with the first step.'"

"Max used to say that."

Xav signs it and hands the card to Supe, who is wrestling with the projector cable. He yanks at it, hard, and it comes out.

"Joe, Miami is our D-Day. I want you to storm that beach and take no prisoners. I want you to network and I mean really network."

"I'll give everything, Miles."

"I got Marjorie to forward the ticket to your email. And I asked her to put some of Brett's business cards on your desk. Be sure to hand them out."

"All right."

"You look pale. Everything okay?"

"Yep. Fine."

"I want you here on time next Monday."

"Sorry. Bit of trouble on the road this morning. Bike trouble."

"Don't make it a habit."

Joe follows Xav out of the meeting room.

Xav whispers as they walk. "What do you think? Sexual frustration? Impotence? Shooting blanks?"

"I think this hell hole is all he has."

"If you're not gonna play, it's no fun."

"This isn't exactly a funhouse, Xav."

"Who stuck a carrot up your arse? Forget the meeting. Supe just needed someone to blame and you know Enora's never gonna get it."

"True."

"What happened this morning?"

They get to their cubicles.

Enora is already there, headset in place, tapping at the keyboard, sipping coffee, legs crossed, her knees jutting out from the hem of her pleated tweed skirt. "Yes, yes. That's a brilliant idea. Let me socialise that and get back to you."

Joe docks his notebook and fires it up. "I'll tell you at lunch."

He takes a deep breath. He digs a thumb into one eye and an index finger into the other, pushing hard, bringing up deep reds and purples, but still the vision remains. The guy's head and body at a sickening angle, blood spooling out from underneath his hair. His face frozen in shock, mouth formed in a perfect oval, nostrils flared as if still sensing danger. His blue eyes glisten and shine, then slowly fade as a thousand memories pass in a flash, or maybe just one or two, or maybe just a glimmer of what might have been, the experiences to come. There's a shadow of intrigue in his cheeks, a ripple of curiosity through one slightly raised eyebrow. One ear bud has come loose and is floating in the blood, the speaker pointing up. He is dying, somewhat appropriately, to The Fray's *How to Save a Life.*

The computer beeps. Joe punches in his ID and password. The email program starts automatically. He has 253 new messages. His phone rings.

***

They do sushi, setting a later lunch time by email and feigning work so Enora, whose stomach starts rumbling at precisely 12:27, doesn't tag along. In the restaurant, only a couple of groups and a few stragglers remain, suits like themselves, with folders and notebooks open under the pretext of doing work. Everyone's stretching lunch for all it's worth, killing time, so when they get back to the office, there's only four hours left instead of five.

Xav struggles with the chopsticks, grabbing the food as it passes only to drop it before getting it to his plate. He snatches up each dropped morsel quickly with his hands and looks around to see if anyone is watching.

"You're skilled. Why don't you just use a fork?"

"I'm getting better. I'll be catching flies with these things soon."

"That'll taste good."

Xav mocks Supe's take-charge tone: "Update me."

"From when? Boston? That was a waste of time. Enora pushed for that meeting, you know. The guy we met with hated her."

"So he should. From this morning."

"I had trouble getting started."

"Flat tire?"

Joe sips his tea and looks around the restaurant. The suits are slamming food into themselves, just like he and Xav are doing: wrestling with chopsticks, using their fingers, trying to look at ease and relaxed. The small clusters of groups, with their boisterous, chaffing laughter and pasty skin, give the restaurant the feel of a half-empty high school cafeteria.

"No."

"Your cat all right?"

Joe nods and chews a little. "What are we doing, Xav?"

"Having lunch."

"I mean here, this job, these clothes, this life. All these things that are supposed to be so important but are really not. Profit margins, sales targets, one tiny step up the career ladder. Who gives a fuck?"

"You thinking of quitting?"

"And do what? There'll just be another job like this waiting for me, sitting next to another Enora and dealing with another Supe."

"There's only one Xav. And that's why you can't quit. Because of me. I won't be able to face that place if you do."

"Thanks."

"I'm serious. After a week, I'd probably come to work with a shotgun and blow everyone away."

"Can't you just send a rude email instead?"

"I don't have your way with words. Look, I'll use a paint gun, how about that?"

"Deal."

"What's up, Joe? You have an accident? You gotta stop riding that bike. It's a death trap."

"I saw an accident. This morning. He died. Right in front of me. Everyone, just, watched. Just, stood there. One kid filmed it."

"Let it be a warning to you. Get a car already."

He takes another sip of tea and turns to watch the automatons chew, swallow and choke. It's graphic. "Do you think things happen for a reason, Xav? Or is life just this random collection of unrelated events? Just a bunch of stuff that happens and then we're dead, sooner or later."

"Sounds like that funeral you went to back home really got to you."

"It was a wedding."

"Oh, sorry. But to answer your question, I don't believe in destiny."

"I don't mean that. Like, take us. We met at Denny, but before that you were living in Calgary and I was in Sydney. Think of all the things that had to happen for us to be both working at the same company, in the same department and to be a desk apart. You telling me all that is just random? It's just...luck?"

"I never thought about it. But I see your point. You could go back further, say that our parents first had to meet each other for us even to be born, and for their parents to meet each other. And. My brain hurts."

"I know. I thought about this all the way back from Harbrook."

"Don't stress over things you can't control."

Joe drains his tea and looks at the scattering of leaves in the bottom. "Xav, I tell ya, I don't want this to be it. We get up, we go to work, we go home, we try to do things that interest us, when there's time. That's it?"

"Eventually we'll get married and raise families."

"Don't you think it's already too late for that?"

"No. I haven't even met the right girl yet."

"Think about it, Xav. If you had a kid tomorrow, you'd be nearly fifty when he or she learns to drive."

"So?"

"So there's too big an age gap. No matter what, you'll always be old to them."

"How old were you parents?"

"Uh, twenty-seven and twenty-three, I think. You?"

Xav shakes his head. "Let's just say they're retired, and have been for a while. And before you start flapping it in my face, yeah, I had trouble with them. They were from another era, and I mean black and white TV. My mum still can't use a computer. She was forty-five when she had Iris. Imagine how it was for her?"

"Hey, that means your parents..."

"Thanks, Joe. That's exactly the kind of image I want to carry around with me for the rest of the day."

"Everyone walks in on their parents at some point."

"God. I think they're still doing it. Every time I see a wheelbarrow, I'm reminded of them. Last Christmas, I asked my dad what he wanted and he said Liftomex."

Joe nearly falls off the stool.

"That's not funny."

"Yeah, it is."

"Old folks shouldn't be shagging. Can you imagine it?"

"You gotta assume they do. Liftomex is one of the biggest sellers on the market. Denny was built on it. It's always...on the rise."

Xav laughs. "Sales are going up and up."

"Max used to say that every generation thinks they invented fucking."

"He had some good things to say. Like that marathon bit. You should write some of it down."

"Yeah, I should."

Xav sighs and pushes his plate away. "How am I supposed to go back to work now? You've ruined me. You're totally right. This is it, and it's not much."

"What would you rather be doing?"

"Don't know. Skiing, going back-country out in Lake Louise."

"You miss home?"

"Just the wilderness, and only now when you remind me of it. Thanks, buddy."

"Sorry. Maybe work will help you forget."

"Work. It's what we define ourselves by. It's the first question anyone asks you. What do you do? And then all judgements are passed."

"You want Supe's job?"

"No."

"What then?"

"Honestly? No idea. When I finished high school, I was a ski instructor in Banff. Best winter of my life."

"You can't be a ski instructor forever."

"No, but there must be something like that. A combination of doing something you love that pays."

"Maybe you can go into the wheelbarrow business."

"Man. Stop that."

Joe laughs. "Whatever you do, it would be better than this."

"We're nothing but certified drug dealers. A production line for a few billion addicts. At least you get to do it under the Florida sun."

"You know I won't have a second of free time."

"But you'll be there. Can look out the window and imagine what you could be doing."

"Like you dreaming of black diamonds and ski bunnies."

"Stop it. You're killing me."

"But that's what I mean. I'm going to Miami and I could sit on the beach for a couple of days, but I'll be indoors the whole time, shaking hands and passing out Brett's business card. Everything I do, all of my time, is for the benefit of someone else. What about us? Who's doing stuff for us?"

"Sounds like you need a holiday, Joe."

"Yeah, from myself. From my life."

"What you need is to be self-employed. The technology makes that possible. Work from home. Like Francois."

"He can barely afford macaroni and cheese."

"He's in the wrong industry. You just need the right job. The right product."

Xav's phone rings.

"It's Supe. I better take this. Xavier Dowler speaking...Hi, Marjorie...Yep. Put him through...We're just finishing up, Miles. I was bringing Joe up to speed on Brett's key account list...Yes, over lunch... Okay. In ten."

Xav pockets the phone.

"It's a tracking device. He knows you're here."

"Don't be so paranoid. Enora probably told him. You wanna get the check today? I'll get it tomorrow."

"Sure."

Walking back to the office, Xav sets a brisk pace, weaving between the slower pedestrians. Above, the clouds threaten rain. Avenue Papineau is a hive of activity, even on a Monday afternoon, everything and everyone moving in fast motion. Quite a few are walking down the street engaged in loud, animated conversations with themselves. As they pass, he sees the earphone in place, the microphone held close to the mouth or clipped to a lapel, and gets snippets of conversations.

"Sara's pregnant? Is Lance the father?"

"I think you should sell. You're almost broke as it is."

"I can't tonight. I've got Pilates at nine."

"I don't have time to meet the principal. You'll have to go."

"Tell him tomorrow. My bunny costume's at the drycleaners."

"Her butt looks huge in those jeans. She always dresses like a whore."

"Where did it happen?"

"Huh?"

"The accident."

"On Pine. Near Laval. Narrow street, lots of traffic. Your typical Monday morning shit fight."

"Who's fault was it?"

"Nobody's. Everybody's."

"You've lost me."

"Xav, slow down."

"Try to keep up."

"The guy on the bike wasn't wearing a helmet, and he was listening to music. There should be a law against that. The girl was writing a text. The driver was talking on the phone. And in their heads, I think they were all somewhere else, just drifting through this moment and not part of it at all."

"And you?"

"I was wearing a helmet, watching the road, watching every parked car in case a door opened, watching every person in case they walked in front of me, watching every driver to see who I couldn't trust."

"That's some major multi-tasking."

"I was just concentrating on what I was doing."

"How did it go down?"

"The girl ducked between two parked SUVs. She was short so you couldn't see her. She walked straight in front of the biker. Didn't even look. She could've been hit by a bus. The biker swerved to miss her and got cleaned up by the car behind, which was going pretty fast. He went flying and landed on his head."

"He should've been wearing a helmet."

"I don't think even that would've saved him."

"You call the police?"

"An ambulance, first. I grabbed the girl's phone and used it. She thought I was trying to steal it and hit me with her handbag."

Xav laughs.

"She wasn't even really aware of what she'd done. The street jammed up real quick. There were already a bunch of delivery trucks and vans double-parked. When the ambulance finally came, it couldn't get through. It didn't matter."

"Was it, you know, messy?"

"No brains on the road, if that's what you mean, like a Tarantino bike crash. Blood mostly. The people, they just stared."

"Like people do at accidents."

"No one seemed shocked."

"Welcome to the desensitised century. And you? Were you shocked?"

"Not really. All I could think was that it could've been me."

They reach the Denoris entrance and swipe their security cards.

"I waited for the police. The girl and the driver tried to leave, but I made them stay. When the police came, they both said the biker had made a sudden swerve for no reason."

They get in the elevator.

"And?"

"And they said he wasn't wearing a helmet, and riding on the street, so what could they do."

"They being the police."

"They wrote down my name, but that was it."

"Awful, but they've got a point. And you should learn from it. I keep telling you, riding in this town is dangerous."

"He died because of someone else's mistake, not because he didn't have a helmet."

The elevator dings. They walk down the noisy hall.

"Either way, he's not coming back, is he?"

"No."

"And at the end of the day, it wasn't you."

"No."

At their cubicles, Supe is sitting in Xav's chair and chatting with Enora.

"Ah, there you are. And they say the two-hour lunch is dead."

***

He enters the apartment, dripping.

"Hey, Pops. Yeah, in a minute. Let me dump all this wet stuff."

He drops his satchel on the table and removes his jacket, shoes, pants and socks, draping it all over the radiator.

"It was tough getting home. You know how people walk in the rain. Heads down, umbrellas up. It was actually pretty funny. When it rained really hard, I stopped and waited. That's why I'm late. I watched them all struggling in the slosh, bumping into each other. How was it here?"

In the kitchen, he opens a can of cat food. Popov jumps up onto the counter.

"You're full of bounce when it's dinner time, aren't ya? Here. Don't you think people are fascinating? They don't seem to have any idea of all the stuff that's happening around them. When did it go like that? Pops, stop eating and tell me. What's the matter? Cat got your tongue?"

He leans his elbows on the counter, cups his chin in his hands and watches Popov eat.

"You got it so easy. You don't have to go out there. I like people, I do, but it seems a lot of them are walking through the world like they're royalty, like they're rock stars, and everyone has to get out of their way. Come on, Pops, give me something. You used to have the answer to everything."

Popov looks at him, cocking his head as he runs his long tongue through a couple of dextrous circles, then giving his jaw a yawning snap worthy of a well-fed lion.

"Hah. Feed your friends. That's something you used to say. That was a label on our fridge. Remember? Feed your friends. What does that mean? Bribery? Trying to win their love? Maybe it means take care of them, keep them whole, keep them going. Yeah. Feed them energy and support. And, and you have to know exactly who you should be feeding and if they're worthy of it. So, it means choose your friends, choose who you support. Feed your friends. That's good. I should write that down."

He goes to the table and flips open the damp satchel. The notebook is wrapped in a plastic bag. All dry, no damage. He empties the satchel.

"Colonel Mustard."

He picks up the Colonel and spins the dial. Click, whirr, click, whirr. F-E-E-D Y-O-U-R F-R-I-E-N-D-S. He lifts up the label and tears it off.

"Where should I put it, Pops? How about I stick it to your head. No, on the fridge. Like it was. That way, I'll always remember to feed you."

He sticks the label to the fridge.

"Looks good. Let's add to it. What else? Uh, only people will let you down."

Click, whirr, click, whirr.

"Control, Pops. That's what it's all about."

That label goes onto the fridge as well.

"I know, I know, it's a bit negative, but that's how I'm feeling tonight. I feel like everything's complicated. I need to simplify. That's right. Simplicity is the answer."

Click, whirr, click, whirr.

"But how do you simplify a world that's so dependent on technology? Huh, how? Don't look at me like that, Pops. I can't quit. Then we'd lose everything, including your good eats. Yeah, ma sold the house, but she kept all the money. All your work now funding their life in the sun. Fuck it. I really should give Len a chance. Shouldn't I?"

Click, whirr, click, whirr.

"Never trust a borrower. Yes, yes. They've gone to Naples, Pops. Florida, not Italy. Len would never be that adventurous. He's never been out of the country. I'll be down there on Wednesday. Miami. No, I'm not going to and I don't feel I have to. Anyway, I'll be too busy handing out Brett's card and free samples of laxatives. Shit looseners, dick hardeners, acid reducers, panic stoppers, head pills, heart pills, stomach pills, arse pills, mood pills, love pills, there's a fucking pill for every fucking thing. Don't try to fix your life or change anything. Just take a pill. Problem maintenance and not problem solving. That's another good one."

Click, whirr, click, whirr.

"Everything today is problem maintenance. No one is out there looking to solve a problem. It's easier to pop a pill. There's your solution. Or stick up a sign, transfer the problem to someone else, forward it to their email. Then it's not my problem anymore and I can focus again on me. But no pill can save you from being hit by a car."

The door buzzes. He quickly pulls on an old pair of jeans and opens it.

"Hey, Francois. Thanks for coming over."

"Your text sounded urgent, if a text can sound urgent."

"I was out the rain when I wrote it. You want a drink?"

Francois removes his jacket. "What are you having?"

"I was just about to make a pot of tea."

"Got anything stronger?"

"There's beer in the fridge."

"You call that strong?"

"It's all I got. I haven't had time to shop."

They move through the apartment. Francois reaches out for the handle of the fridge. He stops and reads.

"'Only people will let you down. Never trust a borrower. Simplicity is the answer. Feed your friends. Practice problem solving rather than problem maintenance.' What's this all about? Are these magnets?"

"Labels."

Francois tries to pull one off. "They're stuck."

"Permanent labels. Reminders for life. I forgot them for a while and now they're back."

"Like a little boy sticking his homework on the fridge."

"Yeah."

Francois takes a beer. "You want one? Fine. Stick with the hippy juice. I swear, if you drink any more of that stuff, your hair'll turn green."

Reminded, Joe puts the kettle on and starts preparing the tea, filling the filter with leaves and placing it in the centre of the pot.

"How was your day?"

"Crap. You?"

"Double crap. I'm on thin ice at work."

"So? You hate it there. Maybe your subconscious is trying to get you fired, to free you."

"Maybe."

"You're dying in that place. Xav too."

"Speaking of dying, you ever see someone die?"

"Just a high school buddy who wanted to be a stand-up comedian. God, that was awful. Open mic night. They needed one of those hooks to yank him off stage. You?"

"Yeah. I know it sounds stupid, but there really is this moment when the light goes out, you know, in the eyes. Like a microwave counting down to zero. Ding. Finished. The eyes turn to glass."

"What have been smoking?"

"On the way to work this morning."

"Yeah?"

"On Pine. This guy on a bike, he got cleaned up, a couple of metres in front of me. Two seconds later and it would've been me."

"But it wasn't."

"No."

Francois looks at the fridge again. "That's what this is about."

"This girl just walked right in front of him. Didn't look. And after I told her, she wasn't even guilty or sorry."

"You don't know that for sure. Maybe she's at home right now crying her eyes out. Maybe she's praying for him, for herself."

He pours water into the pot. "Maybe. I hope so."

"You never know. What people show in public is never the same as what happens when they close their door on the world. For all we know, the biggest musclehead might go home and play with a train set while listening to Mozart."

"We could just look through his window, film him and post it on Veedus. Then it wouldn't be private."

"Still, you get my point."

"Never assume."

"Right."

"Max said that. Don't make assumptions, because the human brain likes to turn assumptions into facts."

"Ah. This is all from him."

"Yeah. I tried to talk to Xav about it, but he didn't really get it."

"That's all too heavy for him. His phone is his universe. If it's not in there, it doesn't exist."

"Do you believe in God?"

Francois drinks and burps. "Is that a joke?"

"I'm serious. This guy on Pine. What happened to him? Did he float up to heaven? Or is he just a pile of dead skin and bone?"

"Well, I was raised a Catholic. Don't get me wrong. I think it's fine that people believe. My folks still go to church every Sunday. It's the only thing they do together, apart from doctor visits."

"They ask you to go?"

"They gave up on me years ago. I pretty much stopped believing when I found out masturbating was a sin. By then, I'd done it so many times, no amount of Our Fathers or Hail Marys would've saved me."

"Touched by the hand of God."

"Careful. There were stories of that in our neighbourhood. I think that turned me off as well. I told my folks I wanted to use Sundays to study. They accepted this. Of course, I used that free time at home to, you know, love myself."

"And now? What do you believe."

Francois takes a slow drink. "Not sure. Get me started."

"Me? I guess, uh, I don't want to believe that this is it. It would be nice to think there's another place beyond this, that's better. Where people are a bit nicer to each other. Where they care."

"They care here."

"When it matters to them."

"Maybe you're living in the wrong country. Or the wrong century."

"I've felt that everywhere I've been."

"That probably says more about you than about the world. And? Do you think there's a better place? A heaven beyond?"

Joe takes the tea pot and pours himself a cup. "No. I have a horrible feeling that this is it."

"Depressing."

"Yeah. You know, one minute you're riding a bike and the next you're dead. And this guy this morning, he had a weird look on his face."

"What kind of look?"

Joe sips. "Don't laugh. It changed. Shock, fear, anger. More annoyed than anything else, like it's all really unfair, that he of all people doesn't deserve this. But then, something happened and he became all peaceful and serene. Stop laughing."

"Sorry."

"Forget it."

"Joe, come on. He went all serene. Then what?"

"Well, just before the light went out, he looked, relieved."

"He crap his pants?"

"I'm serious. Maybe I just wanted to see it, but I thought there was a hint of him being glad it's over. I guess that's how I might react. I don't have to rush anymore, keep obligations, pay bills and go to work. I'm free of all that."

"Enlightenment right at the point of death. Terrible."

"Yeah, but imagine living every day like that. Care free. Worry free. Obligation free."

Francois looks into his beer. "Perfect. But totally unrealistic."

"Why? Sometimes I get it in the pool, when it's empty. I get so into what I'm doing, I completely lose touch with the world. I forget everything and just swim. Stroke, breathe, kick. One, two, three. That's it. No thoughts."

"You swim in a trance."

"But then I realise I'm not thinking and snap out of it."

"I get that sometimes when I'm shooting. I'm so focused on the shot, I don't even hear the telephone, or anybody talking to me."

"See? You know the feeling. Letting go of everything, if only for a moment. I'd hate to think we only have that feeling for good when we're just about to die."

"But at least you get that one moment of clarity."

"How's that beer, Francois? Half full."

"Almost empty. Can I have another?"

"Help yourself."

Francois opens the fridge. "You know what I like about you, Mr Solitus? You've got beer in bottles. Everyone else, it's cans. But you, bottles. And you drink leaf tea. You're doing it right."

"Thanks."

"But I know what you mean. My beer's now completely full. It comes down to perspective, doesn't it? That's what I learned on the first day of photography class. Perspective, point of view, framing. What's in and what's out. Hey, this would make a great retrospective."

"What, beer bottles?"

"Photos of people dying. Set up a sequence so the photos capture everything you just said. One photo for shock, the next for fear, the next for anger, and then the last for relief."

"Bit morbid. And I'm starting to think that's just how I wanted to see it. My perspective."

"Yeah, but you dodged the question. Do you believe in God?"

"Max called the church in Harbrook the Gestapo."

Francois laughs. "But that means you'd want to go. You know, kids always want the opposite of their parents. My folks go to church and I reject it. The pot-smoking, free-living parents raise a kid who wants to go."

"I was happy to follow Max."

"What was he again?"

"An architect. He started off as a carpenter and went to night school later."

"He built your house."

"Which ma sold."

"Oh, no."

"Sold everything. It's all gone. Gordie totalled the Volcano after his high school prom. Drunk as a skunk behind the wheel. But that was ma's. There's nothing left but Eddie and Colonel Mustard."

"Who?"

Joe holds up the label maker. "Max had a bunch of them. He

collected them. He used to leave labels all over the house. Sentences like these."

"Reminders for life."

"Yeah. Even most of them are gone. Someone scraped them off. Ma probably."

Francois looks at Colonel Mustard. He punches off a label, figures out how to tear it and then hands it to Joe.

"'The universe is trying to help.'"

Francois nods. "I thought about what you said last night, the girl in Boston, people meeting because they're supposed to. I woke up this morning with this sentence in my head, like someone had put it there."

"'The universe is trying to help.' Max would've loved that."

"There's your higher meaning. You don't have to believe in God or heaven or religion. Believe in the universe, that people will meet because they're supposed to, that things will happen and there'll be some kind of reason for it, if you think about it and look for it."

Joe grabs Colonel Mustard. "That reminds me."

He clicks off a label and sticks it to the fridge.

Francois watches. "'If you go looking for shit, that's what you'll find.' Again, perspective. That guy dies in front of you and you learn something. The universe is helping you, making you appreciate and understand the importance of living care free."

"Not possible. There are too many things to think about."

"True. Life, it doesn't let up, does it? There's always another email to answer, another problem to deal with, another project to do, another bill to pay, all these standards people expect."

"There's not even time to search for deeper meaning."

"Good thing we're not married with kids. Then we'd have all these other people to worry about and care for when we can't even care for ourselves. And what about us? Who's caring for us?"

"Yeah, Francois, what about us?"

"You wanna have kids?"

"I'm missing a vital ingredient for that."

"I mean later."

"Not sure. It all looks so, difficult and time consuming. Maybe I need the right girl."

"The corporate spy?"

"She doesn't want to have kids."

"She said that?"

"Yeah, right when I was fastening my, my raincoat."

Francois laughs. "How romantic. What was her argument?"

"It was interesting. She said if you were a kid and could have a look at the world before entering, would you want to be born?"

"Good question. Global warming, pollution, over-crowding, terrorism, wars on nearly every continent, unemployment, earthquakes, hurricanes, tsunamis, weapons of mass destruction. It's not such a great place to be a kid."

"That's what she said."

"She's got a very depressing point, but in the end, it's just her perspective. We can see things differently, if we want to."

Joe picks up the label Francois made and goes to the table. He peels the back paper off and sticks the label to the front of his satchel.

"I wanna carry this around with me. The universe is trying to help me and everyone else."

Francois comes in and they sit down at the table.

"Don't get hung up on the state of the world, Joe. There's a lot of problems that you can't fix. Sometimes it's better just to go to the pool and forget about it all."

"Work's pissing me off. Gordie got stuck into me about it."

"For being an office monkey?"

"No, about Denny. All these pills that we lived for thousands of years without, and tripling the prices when people need them. He thinks we've created an addicted world."

"Caffeine, sugar, nicotine, alcohol. That's what the world's addicted to. And money, and consuming."

"And technology."

"And connectivity."

Joe sips his tea. "I think people are addicted to themselves, to their own satisfaction."

"This is getting way too heavy for a Monday. Got any chips?"

"I think there's some nuts in the cupboard. Cashews, maybe."

"You need to go shopping."

"When? I gotta be in Miami on Wednesday."

Francois gets up and rummages through the cupboard. He finds the cashews and pops them open. He chews as he talks: "Before you ask, I can't feed Popov. I gotta job in Quebec City this week. Corporate snaps."

"Don't worry. I'll ask Mrs Bourget."

Conference substitution in Second-hand Spain

"Shoes, too."

"I'm gonna miss my flight."

"Then you shoulda got here earlier."

"I did. I spent half an hour standing in line."

Through gritted teeth: "Safety takes time. Anything in your pockets?"

"Nope."

"Shoes on the conveyor belt."

He walks into the full-body scanner and stands as directed, arms out, exposed. He feels like he's in a cloning machine, which wouldn't be so bad; then he could send the clone to Miami.

The guard motions him forward and goes over him with the hand scanner, jabbing him in the crotch along the way.

"Hey, that's a no fly zone."

"Excuse me."

"You know, this would all go a lot faster if the conveyor belts were longer. That way, each person wouldn't stand there for ten minutes getting their stuff in order."

"You got anything else to say?"

"I could say a lot about this machine."

"Like you'd be the first. Go home and blog about it."

He knows he's pushing it, but the whole procedure is just so annoying, so inefficient, so invasive.

"Would you prefer a full body pat down? A cavity search?"

"No. Sorry. It's just a bit too early for me, and I have to make this flight."

"You're clear."

"Thanks."

He puts on his shoes, belt and jacket, pockets his keys, phone and wallet, and slides his notebook back into his leather satchel. He closes the flap.

"The universe is trying to help. Then airports are outside the realm of the universe."

He shoulders the satchel and jogs to the gate. No boarding announcement yet, but even if there was, the speakers crackle and echo so much as to be completely incomprehensible.

At the gate, everyone is sitting around, jammed in shoulder-to-shoulder, back-to-back, not an empty seat, perhaps warming up for seven hours together in cattle class. They hide themselves behind newspapers, hunch over electronic devices, or sit back and close their eyes as music fills their ears. Some just stare blankly into space, brains already in transit. They are adults mostly, all within the airline's various target groups: upwardly mobile professionals with disposable income, business people pacing while talking on mobile phones, early retirees in flamboyant, seldom-worn holiday clothes.

The screen says the delay is twenty-five minutes, technical problems. At the counter near the turnstile, an attendant is fielding complaints from passengers waving boarding cards and wanting better seats, and from others just wanting to know what's taking so long.

He takes a seat in the lounge of the adjacent gate, which is completely empty. After standing in all the lines checking in and at security, the slow shuffling forward and the huffs of annoyed sighs blowing against his back, it's nice to have this moment of respite.

He turns on his notebook, certain the twenty-five minute delay will stretch into at least an hour.

He doesn't want to get on the plane, doesn't want to be in Miami, at another conference, again representing someone else. He's always pinch-hitting, coming off the bench to do the work of others.

"Supe's got it in for me."

He swallows a Dozoxin, hoping it will kick in just after the first meal. It seldom works like that, and he just ends up tired the rest of the day. Maybe this time it will go as planned, as it says on the box.

He takes care of his work email, mostly stuff he's been cc-ed into and only has to skim through. He checks the *Gazette* site for news about the biker and finds two bland, efficient paragraphs. No names are given. No pictures. He does a few other searches and happens upon a video titled "Roadkill on Pine" on Veedus. It's grainy, but he sees himself crouched over the biker, the pool of blood on the tarmac, the twisted wreck of the bike, the audience crowding around. It's disturbing, and real. A window to life, with no one aware they're being filmed, no one acting for the camera. He plays it again. Off to the side of the shot, the driver and the girl are talking to each other, heads bowed close, getting their stories straight, flirting almost. The girl makes a call and turns her back on the victim. The driver looks at his watch and lights a cigarette.

He watches the video a third time. Even though he can see himself, it's like the whole thing happened to someone else.

A few more searches reveal the biker's name. He goes to ceeville, but Henri Petit has built a wall around his city. He puts the name into Plasher and there are a few active ponds. He clicks on the most current. Opinion is mixed. Some are bitching about Henri, insulting him, with a minority trying to defend him. A few people are using this forum to air their grievances about cars and traffic in general, all of them mentioning global warming. It quickly degenerates into a shouting contest. The language is colourful, ugly and abusive, with the usual spelling mistakes. In the debate about cars and bikes, Henri himself gets left out. The car lovers form a mob and gang up on the few two-wheel advocates in the forum. A few trolls jump in to stir the shit.

"There's no way you'd say such things to someone's face."

"Ladies and gentlemen, our flight to Miami is now ready for boarding. We'll start with families with small children and will then take passengers in rows twenty to forty."

Everyone stands up. They crowd towards the lone flight attendant, forming a hasty line that resembles the short, fat neck of a bottle. They stand very close together, almost intimately, like a team huddling before kick-off. Hand luggage bangs against legs, elbows make contact with breasts, heads peer around shoulders, people basically stand on the heels of the person in front.

He watches, fascinated.

***

The bags take a while. All those who had been so eager to be the first off the plane, who stood up well before the seatbelt sign had been turned off, are now standing around with everyone else, waiting. People kill the time catching up on messages, texts and missed calls, frantically getting up to speed on everything they were disconnected from. Thumbs fly. There's a lot of buzzing and beeping, and repeated and echoing shouts of "Yeah, I'm at the airport." There's a lot of huffing and puffing, impatient sighing at the frozen carousel, and melodramatic watch looking. They line themselves up, arse to crotch, some with a foot on the carousel, human dominoes waiting to be pushed over.

He hangs back and rubs his eyes. He yawns. He tried everything: relaxation music, the most boring, unfunny rom-com on the film list, read every page of the tedious in-flight mag and even the safety instruction card in the hope it would lower his eyes. Nothing worked.

"It's probably a tic-tac."

The carousel whirrs and clunks to life, a gigantic magnet that draws everyone closer. They encroach on each others' space. No one seems to mind. In fact, they seem to enjoy the intimacy, the closeness. The bags spill out, the branded luggage of first class, followed by the bulky, bulging, generic wheelie cases of economy. The scramble begins: with people hustling to grab a suitcase only to realise it's not theirs, people trying to sling on a backpack while cradling a phone, people lifting bags carelessly so they bang it against someone's knee or shin.

He manages to get his bag and wheels it towards the exit. Outside, he bypasses the long row of taxis and finds the stop for the J bus. He gets on and starts playing with his phone.

By the time he looks up, they're already hurtling towards Miami Beach.

It's hot.

Miami looks like Spain; the south, where he went with Trina. That experience, that adventure, when he was so tuned into the moment. Forgot everything. Care free. All the way to Barcelona. The stained and cracked whitewash, the satellite dishes perched on windows and balconies, the wiring, antennas and aerials, the underwear, shirts and frilly nothings slung between buildings, the shouted conversations of the locals. But it's far from the same. There's none of those grubby, damp pensions they fucked in, no garbage trucks waiting to empty the dumpsters at midnight, no cafes and bars spilling out onto the streets and squares, no men just standing around and looking.

Miami is more spread out and expansive, duller and less inspiring. It doesn't lift the spirits, hint at the ancient or tempt exploration and discovery. There are no winding streets, old city walls or stone church towers. The skyline is more dominated by golden arches, over-sized food signs, gas stations, drive-thru everything, and enormous billboards that rotate in a clear purchasing order for the attainment of the American dream.

"Whatcha wanna do?"

"Hang."

"Yo, fa shizzle."

Joe laughs.

"You got a problem, bro?"

The two teenagers opposite him scowl and try to look mean. Oh, they're bad, real bad. They're both wearing baggy jeans, pure white sneakers straight out of the box, or mum's washing machine, and long wifebeaters their pale chests are too skinny to fill out. Thick silver chains dangle from their necks and they both have one white headphone in place; the other hangs in front like an accessory, as if to say, "Hey world, you've got half of my attention." Joe can hear the music, the same hip-hop but at a different point in the song; stereo, in delay, a badly mixed loop. They both have bored, disinterested sneers on their faces, like they're doing some kind of mirror acting exercise; bored with the bus, with Miami, the world, even each other.

"I wouldn't know where to start."

The one on the right makes a few rapper-like hand gestures. "What tha fuck you mean?"

"Nothing. Carry on...bro."

More gestures, fingers shaped like pistols. "Hey, fuck you, man."

"Are you asking me out?"

"Fucking faggot."

"Sorry. I just assumed you were a couple."

The two teenagers exchange an awkward look. The one providing greater pretence of toughness leans forward.

"Shut ya mouth or I'll fuck you up."

A woman stands next to Joe, shopping bags in hand. "Your language is awful. Who taught you to speak like that?"

Seeing the woman, Joe stands up to let her have the window seat. She puts her bags on that seat and then sits in the aisle seat. She stares straight ahead.

"You're welcome."

He goes to the middle of the bus and stands next to his suitcase. He can hear the two teenagers shouting at each other. The woman asks them to be quiet and one teenager tells her to fuck off. The GPS on his phone tells him he could get off at the next stop and walk the rest of the way, rather than get on another hot, stinking bus. It's 2.7 kilometres, about half an hour.

He gets off and heads down Sheridan.

It's good to have some space, to be in control. Big SUVs, pickups and family vans fill the driveways of the suburban caves along Sheridan. Other cars are parked on the verge, on front lawns, in the narrow gaps between trees and letterboxes, wherever there's space. There are tall palm trees on one side of the road, flapping in the afternoon breeze like the loose pages of a broadsheet left on the ground.

He wonders if it's hurricane season.

The breeze feels good. It dries the wet corners of his shirt and clears some of the fuzziness from his head.

Plenty of the smart, good-looking houses have for sale signs out front, with the smiling face of a trustworthy real estate agent. The GPS tells him the beach is half a kilometre east. He could swim in the Atlantic, ride Eddie all year round, not have to bear the grim Montreal winters. He could throw all his assorted pairs of gloves away, all his jackets. He could get Francois to move down as well, to split the costs and raise their quality of life.

The GPS now tells him that Naples is 185 kilometres to the west.

"Pass."

Sheridan Avenue gives way to the wide and wholly uninviting expanse of Pinetree Drive. Traffic is heavy. A car slows down next to him, the window lowers.

"The airport's thataway, dude."

The car speeds off, the driver laughing. The narrow, unloved sidewalk runs next to the road. The going is slow, the holes and cracks making him lift the case and carry it, and the cars pulling off and onto Pinetree force him to stop and wait. He puts his head down, into the diesel wind.

By the time he gets to Dade Boulevard, the whole enterprise of stretching his legs, clearing his head, being independent of transport and moving into a three-bed-two-bath house on Sheridan with Francois has become completely misguided. The salty taste of the possible hurricane blowing in from the Atlantic has been replaced by the sandy hue of fuel and the warm stench of sewage. It sticks to his tongue, like someone is scrubbing his mouth with an old gas station toilet brush.

Finally, he crosses the bridge of Convention Center Drive and heads for the entrance of Hall D. He's sweating, smelling, his eyes watering and surely looking like he's stoned. The suited and skirted automatons are spilling out onto the street to be swallowed up by taxis and minivans. It's barely worth going inside, but at least he can get his passes and set up the booth for tomorrow.

He wonders if Anita is here.

On the other side of the entrance, standing under the air-con vent, he scrolls through the numbers on his phone, finds hers, presses call, then cancels it.

***

He locates Miami Ice, a scratchy attempt at a cocktail bar on Ocean Drive, and takes a seat facing the Atlantic. He can just see the water, between the gaps in the passing cars. The noxious stream of honking and growling traffic out front is taking a lot away from the scene, giving the air a nasty taste, and ruining any chance of a pleasant ocean-side evening drink.

"Joe. You found it."

They hug, pulling back to take each other in, hands on shoulders.

"Good to see you, Declan."

"You too. When the hell are you gonna start looking old?"

"I've found a grey hair or two."

"Bullshit."

They sit.

"Jesus, Joe. How long's it been?"

"Three years. Your wedding, back home in Harbrook."

"I'm surprised you remember. You fell asleep on your motorbike, backwards, with your feet on the handlebars."

"I did?"

"Yep."

"Seems like ages ago."

"Did you go back for the ten year reunion?"

"High school? Nuh. You?"

Declan shakes his head. "Sounds like none of us went. Still, would've been good to get everyone together. You, me, Loius, Rex, Lanno. Last time was my wedding."

"The bachelor party was a blast. I remember that."

"When's yours?"

"Not for a while yet. Still single."

"Damn."

The waiter stands next to them. Joe orders a strawberry daiquiri, Declan a pina colada.

"Well, what do you think of my local?"

"The Icebergs it's not."

"What?"

"I studied in Sydney. UNSW. I sent you some postcards. I used to swim at the place there called the Bondi Icebergs. Salt water pool, right on the beach. Great view."

Declan points at the road and smiles. "Unlike here. Any sharks?"

"Not in the pool."

They both look in the general direction of the water. They're sitting right at street level. People walk in front, cars roar past, two people are shouting conversation at each other in Hispanic accents on the balcony directly above.

"How's Sara?"

Declan adjusts his glasses. "Good, good. She wants to move."

"Back home?"

"Out of the city. She doesn't want Jesse growing up around here. She wants a house, on a street where Jesse can play."

"Huh."

"She's got her heart set on some gated community out near the Everglades Parkway."

"Where's that?"

"Miles from here. Inland. I'd have to drive about an hour each way."

Their drinks arrive.

"Cheers, Dec."

"Cheers. Good to see you."

They both sip.

"Yep. Where's your school?"

"On Pinetree."

"I walked down there today, on the way to the Convention Center."

Declan looks at him incredulously. "You walked? From where?"

"Uh, the bus stop, on Forty-first, I think. Where the J from the airport stops. Got out and walked from there."

"Nobody walks in Miami. Why didn't you rent a car at the airport? Save yourself all that hassle? You're here on business."

"I don't like driving in a strange place. Too stressful."

"Take a taxi."

"It was good to walk, see some of the city."

"Not many sights out there."

"The area I went through was pretty nice. Lot of houses for sale."

"Bayshore. Expensive, even with the crunch. And Sara vetoed that. Too dangerous at night. When we move out to the sticks, I'll have to find a job out there too."

"What about Sara? She working?"

Declan sips and frowns. "She wants to have a girl first. She's got everything planned."

Joe sips as well. The ice makes his teeth hurt.

"We always said we'd never become like our parents, you know, gathering dust out in suburbia, completely disconnected from the pulse of the world. We said we'd stay in the city, still go out and do all the things we always did. But..."

"Kids change things."

Declan shakes his head. "It's not that. Jesse's great. I wouldn't want it any other way. It's just that there's a point in your life when it's just not fun anymore to go out and party. It's boring. You know? Or are you still passing out at weddings?"

"No, I'm with you. I think it's pathetic to see guys in their thirties and forties drinking and acting like teenagers. A work buddy is always trying to get me to go out with him on Fridays to after-work parties. I went a couple of times and it's shameful. All these focused paper shufflers hell bent on careers and after a couple of drinks it turns into a frat party. They're sober all week but come Friday, they drink themselves into oblivion, and do coke and ice and other stuff."

"Trying to forget their lives."

"Yeah."

"That's bleak."

"That's the working life, Dec. You wake up on Monday and suddenly it's Thursday. Another week is over and you gave all of it to some company. You only eat take-out, you have lunch in front of a screen, you battle and fight to please people you hate. You bust your butt to sell products the world doesn't need. Then, the weekend comes and you're too wrecked to enjoy it. Xav, my work buddy, spends his weekends either paralytic drunk or sleeping it off."

"You're making me feel very good about my life."

"When do you normally get home?"

"From school? Around five, unless there's a meeting or PTA stuff. You?"

"Seven, if I'm lucky. It depends how long our team leader stays. No one has the stones to leave before him. In the winter, I never see daylight."

"You should move down here."

"What?"

Declan shouts above the roar of passing delivery trucks. "You should move down here!"

"Yeah. I like it."

"What are you here for anyway? Your call came outta nowhere."

"Trade convention. I'm filling in for someone else. It was all very last minute."

"Don't you have clients to meet? Hands to shake, flesh to press?"

"That starts tomorrow."

"Right. Been back home lately?"

"Last weekend. Ma and Len got married."

"I know."

"Yeah, I spoke to your dad."

"He said you did a lot of coughing during the ceremony, like you were trying not to laugh."

"Gordie kept texting me."

"Where was he?"

"Sitting next to me."

"That's why your ma came over and separated you."

"You heard about that?"

"I think the whole of Harbrook knows."

"Len's a tool."

"Be happy for your ma. She's allowed to move on."

"Sure, but with Len? Sorry, I know your dad's friends with him."

Declan looks at him through the sides of his frames. "It's no secret how you feel about Len. Anyway. I'm sure there's more to it than you ever said."

"Not really."

They lapse into silence, both sipping.

"What happened to that girl you brought to our wedding?"

Joe squints at the traffic, struggling to put all those alcohol-fractured pieces back together. "Sharissa?"

"She was nice."

"We were done before we crossed the border. She didn't even hang onto me. Held the bars next to the seat."

Declan laughs. "What was she, eighteen?"

"Twenty-one, so she said. She was interning at Denoris. That was awkward for while. Everyone knew."

"I guess your bored colleagues need something to talk about."

"Everyone's fucking someone at work. There's no chance to meet other people. We spend the whole day there, with each other. The office is our social world. You should see the Christmas party, Dec. It's an orgy. They should hand out packets of condoms instead of bonuses."

"I am missing out."

"You're not. What about you? How's school?"

"What do you think?"

"Probably like it was for us in Harbrook. One long popularity contest you can never win."

"Bingo. But the path to popularity has changed."

"How?"

"What happens at school isn't nearly as important as what happens online."

"Ah, ceeville, Plasher."

"And the rest. Remember that MySpace story from a couple of years ago? The mum who faked being a boyfriend online to get revenge on a girl who tormented her daughter?"

"Ended in suicide, right?"

"We deal with stuff like that every day. Maybe not that extreme, but these kids are wired, and I mean constantly. There's no passing notes anymore. It's all texts and IMs. The worst punishment for these kids is confiscating their phones. But that's useless because they have two or three, or they use a friend's."

"Never thought of that."

"You ever hear of the-t-wall?"

"No."

"It's a new website. T-wall meaning toilet wall. Basically, you can write anything about anyone, and do it anonymously."

Joe pulls out his phone. He opens the site.

"That's it. Put my name in."

He does so. "Woah. 'Nettles takes it up the ass. Mr Nettles should have his eyeballs pulled out and roasted. D-Net, you're the best teacher at RAG.' That one's good."

"I wrote that."

Joe laughs.

"Trust me, Joe. Anything positive has been written by that person. Everything else is negative. And it's not just the teachers. All the students are writing about each other as well. You could write about your boss. Put your name in."

Joe taps at the screen. "I've got a profile. Kingstan says, 'Joe Solitus sleeps upside down wrapped in his own wings.' That's from Gordie. I used to call him Stan."

"I remember that. The Eminem song. Never in the history of nicknames has there been a more fitting nickname. He even had the short bleached hair and the trailer trash scowl."

Joe pockets the phone. "Do you think employers look at this? Before they call you for an interview?"

"With the internet, you can almost get a complete profile of someone just from all the sites they're part of, who they're friends with online, what photos and videos they've posted. Why wouldn't they look at the-t-wall, or ceeville?"

"You're scaring me, Dec."

"I didn't think you'd be so naive. Everything online is there forever and everyone can know it, if they want to. Sorry, but me and Sara have been fighting over exactly this point. She's an internet junkie, spends way too much time online and is more interested in a comment some dick in North Dakota made on her blog than in what happens at school. She doesn't seem to get that the internet is a lawless, public place."

"You guys all right?"

"Yeah. It'll pass. I think she's just bored. She needs to go back to work. Still, can you believe this world we live in? Anyone can say anything about anyone else. There's no responsibility or accountability. My kids at school, they don't know a world without the internet. They've grown up with screens. They think they have the right to comment about everything."

"You're making me feel old, Dec."

"We're worse than they are. The kids at school, they grew up with all this tech, but our generation has adapted. We use it more than they do. And we're the ones making crap like the-t-wall and ceeville. That facebook guy is our age."

"I should be designing websites instead of pushing pills."

Declan scoffs. "For every internet billionaire there's probably a million guys living in their parents' basement still getting pocket money. You're better off."

"Maybe."

"Look at you. You've got a fancy phone. You're wired in, all teched up."

Joe holds up his phone. "I hate this thing. Denoris makes me carry it, and it has to be turned on all the time, even when I'm on holiday. Give me the chance and I'll dump it."

"Sure you would."

"I'm serious, Dec. These things are dangerous. People don't pay any attention when they're using them. Car crashes, bike accidents, people bumping into each other in the street. They're more interested in the call than in anything else going on around them."

"Well, you hate phones and I hate the internet. What do we do now? Can't live without them."

Joe taps his phone. "Last year, car crashes caused by cell phones accounted for three hundred thousand injuries and three thousand deaths."

"Don't believe everything you read online. I tell my students that sourcing Wikipedia lowers their grade. But they still do it."

"It's easier than opening a book."

"You're way off. These kids don't even deal with books. The principal at RAG wants to shut down the library. No one uses it. For these kids, everything is just a quick copy and paste. And ebooks just make it easier."

"Little Jesse will be the same."

"Worse. Look at the world now and how it's changed in the last ten years. How's it gonna be ten years from now?"

"No idea. When we were kids, there was no way we could've predicted the world would turn out like this."

"You remember that? Growing up in Harbrook?"

Joe swirls his daiquiri. The ice has melted. It's more pleasant to sip, but tastes mostly of water. "It was great."

"We used to ride out to Squam Lake. No helmets, no cars around."

"Remember we tried to build that raft, with Louis, Rex and Lanno?"

Declan laughs. "It sank half way out. We had to swim back. You practically carried Lanno back to shore."

"How old were we?"

"Ten. Eleven."

"Eleven. That was the year Lanno got a Nintendo for Christmas. No more raft building for him after that."

"Or Rex."

Joe sighs. "Things were simpler."

"We still had all the same problems as kids today. It's just coming from a different medium now. What used to be locker and cafeteria gossip is now posted online. But it's all still gossip. Ah, enough about all that crap. How are you doing, Joe? Still swimming?"

"Rarely."

"But you did in Sydney. The place on the beach. Iceland."

"The Icebergs. Kind of ruined me. Once you swim in salt water, you can't go back to chlorine."

"I don't know how you did that. You used to stink at school. That's why no girls went out with you."

"Except the girls on the swim team."

"They liked the smell. They had it too."

Joe laughs. "My ma had to blow a trumpet to get me up in the mornings."

"You loved it. King of the school. Winning all those trophies. I can't believe you don't swim anymore."

"If I did, is there a pool around here?"

Declan points south. "A couple hundred yards that way. Of course, there's a massive one straight ahead, salt water too."

"Maybe I'll take a splash."

Declan checks his watch and drains his drink. "I better go. Sara thinks I'm at a school meeting. You need a ride?"

"My hotel's around the corner."

"Where?"

"On Washington. The Mayola."

"I'm going straight past. Come on."

"I'm good. I'm gonna grab a bite somewhere. I got your drink. Business expense."

"Thanks. Man, it was really good to see you. A bonus."

They stand and hug.

"You gonna visit your ma?"

"No time. I'm flying back on Sunday."

"It's like a three hour drive."

"The conference will take up all my time. There's no chance."

Declan walks to his people-mover and beeps it open. "Does she even know you're here?"

"No. Can we keep it that way?"

Declan climbs in. "Sure. If you write something nice about Mr Nettles on the-t-wall."

"Done. Say hi to Sara."

Declan nods. It takes a few minutes for him to get the people-mover out of its tight spot and then he has to wait for a break in the traffic. Joe stands there, watching.

***

The buzz of a thousand anxious conversations echoes in the hall. It blends into a droning hum like white noise, words filling the space. A lot of suits and skirts are dashing about, brochures and catalogues flapping from their hands, name tags swinging, Bluetooth sets in place, like kids playing an elaborate game of hide and seek; or some modern form of orienteering. The air is thick with the steamy breath of people speaking with self-imposed importance. Palms slap as verbal deals are struck, surely to be broken later with the arrival of a counter offer. Backs are patted and egos soothed. Phones ring, business cards snap, glasses fog up, coffee is thrown down like a shot, rolls are eaten in three bites and a muffin in two.

He's bored.

His feet hurt.

It's cold enough for him to keep his suit jacket on. A couple of times, he blows on his hands, momentarily confusing this air-conditioned hall in Miami with Rue Sherbrooke in January. Earlier, on his way to the bathroom, he passed Natrofield's booth – their installation – which includes a café with an espresso machine. He saw half a dozen Japanese men in golf clothes on some kind of sponsored junket and a bunch of salespeople in suits. All young, good-looking guys and girls, but there was no sign of Anita.

"Joe? Hey, Joe."

"Alfred. What's up?"

They shake hands. Joe feels Alfred's big pinky ring push against his hand, right on the bone. Alfred's dressed preppy: white shirt, yellow tie in a huge Windsor knot, tight, thin grey sweater, cuffs of his shirt folded once over the sweater's sleeves. But he's not lean enough to pull it off. He looks like a fat comedian doing a satirical bit on guys who dress preppy.

"Come on, Joe. It's me, Alfie. Think of all those nights out. You, me and Xav. The triple threat."

"How's it going? Still at Massobix?"

Alfie pulls down the v-neck of the sweater to reveal the Massobix logo stitched on his shirt, on the left pocket, which is bulging with a man boob. The stretchiness of the sweater makes Joe conclude it's more parts polyester than anything else.

"What's it like?"

"If you'd bothered to contact me, I would've told you. Two years, Joe. We were practically brothers at Denny. We interned together."

"I wasn't allowed to contact you."

"Supe strikes again. So, you're still there plugging away."

"Xav too."

"Going nowhere slowly, both of you."

"Should we join your crew of misfits instead?"

Alfie helps himself to the jug of coffee and pockets a couple of pens. He picks up a business card. "Who's Brett Townsend?"

"Your successor."

"Like anyone could replace me. He any good?"

"Supe's number one. Calls him B-Town."

"That's lame."

"Know what he called you after you left? A-Holl."

"I heard about that. Lame too. Shame Supe's not here. I could take him out to the parking lot and show him what a real asshole is by tearing him a new one."

"Disgusting."

Alfie sips his coffee. "What are you pushing?"

"Not a lot. The brand mostly."

"That'll get you far."

"You know how we work. Most of our new stuff came out at New Year. When everyone's interested in changing themselves, at least for a few weeks. You?"

"Nothing special. Hear about Natro's new doozie?"

"The sugar patch?"

"The what?"

"Nothing."

Alfie leans close. His aftershave smells minty, or it's his breath. "I'm nailing a chick from sales. Total milf. She let something slip about Release. Yeah, I think it's called Release, or maybe Relief. It was hard to understand her. She's not so good at talking with her mouth full."

"What a lovely image."

"True story."

Joe reaches out and pats Alfie's sizeable belly. "I guess you were relying more on the audio than the visual."

"Back off, Joe. I gave up smoking last year. I put on a few pounds. You know how it goes."

"Right, sorry. So, what is Release, or Relief, or whatever it's called?"

"Not exactly sure. She was pretty vague."

"Other things on her mind?"

"When did you turn into such a mean prick?"

"Oh, around the time you jumped ship and I got saddled with all your leftovers."

Alfie picks up the business card again. "What about B-Town?"

"He came on a year later. Supe redistributed your stuff, didn't hire anyone new."

"That's bad management."

"It is. Look, sorry, Alfie. As you can gather, I really, really don't want to be here."

"Who does?"

"What about Release?"

Alfie leans close again. "It's the delete pill."

"Huh?"

"You take it and forget."

"Forget what?"

"Whatever you want. You focus on what you want to forget, take the pill and the memory's gone."

"She say all that? Couldn't have had her mouth full for very long."

"Fuck you, Joe."

"There's no possible scientific basis that a pill could work like that."

"Joe, Joe, where have you been, Joe? There's already a couple of studies done on this. There's the science to back it up. The military got into it a couple of years back, for soldiers with PTSD."

"Yeah, I remember that."

"Danni said it'll be huge. Bad memories, anxieties, fears, habits, whatever. This'll cure it."

"It won't work. It's like hypnotherapy. Forgetting you're a smoker won't stop the body from craving nicotine."

Alfie snaps his fingers. "That's what I said. Like in that Jim Carrey film, with the chick from *Titanic*. You get stuck in a loop of remembering and forgetting."

"And wanting to remember and wanting to forget."

"Right."

"It'll never get approved."

"There's worse stuff out there, Joe. Even beer is about forgetting. Sailiun, painkillers, antidepressants, anything that numbs you to the world. There's a plethora of pills you could drop."

"You realise that if it works, it will make a lot of other stuff obsolete."

"That's why we're trying to stop it."

"How?"

"Sabotage. We've got couple of FDAers in our pocket. They're gonna blacklist it."

"You need more than one nark."

"Then get Denny on board as well. If we all move, we can stop it. Ask Supe."

"He'll just deny we have anyone on our books."

"Please. Every company has. You've seen the cars those FDA guys drive. Think about it, Joe. Danni says it's already in trial."

"Already?"

"Hey, what's that smell?"

"The beach. I took a swim this morning."

"You didn't shower?"

"I like the salt."

"Smells good. Should be a cologne."

"Kramer already had that idea. On *Seinfeld*."

Alfie looks at his watch. "I better get back. I'll leave to your thousands of clients. What are you doing for dinner?"

"Uh."

"Let's hit the town. Is Xav here?"

"Just me."

"The biggest convention in the south and they send you?"

"I guess management think the products speak for themselves."

Alfie pokes him on the shoulder. "They're decades behind. And that's why Denny is number six. You're not willing to put out. To spend. Now, Natrofield, they're putting out, you know what I mean."

"Don't leave me with more imagery of you and your Natro skank."
"Hah. Still the same old Joe. I'll swing by at six. We'll tear it up."
"Great."
"You're here till Sunday, right? Then we've got us a three day binge."
Joe watches Alfie waddle to the next booth.

Discussing karma with the Creative Primer and others

He's first off the 747 at the central station on Boulevard de Maisonneuve. He weaves between the clusters of students with notebooks under their arms and netbooks balanced on their palms. They squint at each other after spending much of the day in the Grande Bibliothèque. They hold on grimly to cardboard coffee cups and blow at the rims. He wonders how they can bend over books in some dusty reading room on such a beautiful Sunday afternoon. They could be out tossing the friz in Mont Royal or at the very least spouting old, second-hand and non-applicable-to-real-life philosophies in a cafe in the Vieux Port.

I did most of my studying at the Icebergs, he thinks.

He passes the bus stop, opting to go the rest of the way on foot. It's good to have the uncrowded sidewalk, the space, the silence. Every joint aches a little, feels rusty and stiff. He walks and creaks, stiff legged, elbows bent. C3PO. The tin man.

"'If I only had a heart.'"

Down Maisonneuve until it bends into President Kennedy, the garbage piled neatly in tightly tied bags, the recyclables separated. Nothing sifted through, nothing slashed open, no contents spilling onto the sidewalk like a run-over rabbit's insides.

Unlike Miami. All those dark, smelly alleys A-Holl dragged him down, into places having drug conventions of a different kind, the dealers with guns in their coat pockets instead of business cards and free pens.

He goes right at De Bleury, crosses Park, heads into the Oh The Pain. The smell of real food sharpens his senses. He joins the back of the line.

He waits.

He sends a text to Francois that he's back and will meet him at the pool at seven.

Francois replies immediately: "hungover. will be there. will drown."

A woman bumps his arm as she passes. She steps up to the counter and orders.

"Ah, excuse me, but, uh, as you can see there's a line."

She looks at him, annoyed that he's interrupting her ordering and curious as to why he would. "I'm sorry. I don't have time for this. I'm double-parked."

"And we do?"

She turns to him, one hand on the counter, digging her high heels in. "Look. I've got to pick up Tanora from soccer, finish a presentation for a big meeting tomorrow, go shopping, and do about a thousand other things, okay."

"Oh, I guess that makes it all right."

She raises her eyebrows at the three people in front of him, all ear-phoned and tuning out. Two heads are bopping, one girl whispering as she sings along. The girl in front of him is talking on a hands-free set and giving a running commentary of what is happening in the bakery, including this line standoff.

"They don't seem to mind. They appreciate my situation."

He turns to the bakery attendant. "Hey. Why are you serving her?"

The attendant shrugs and gives the woman her order. While waiting for her change, she puts her phone to her ear and turns her back on the line.

"I'm at the bakery. Yes, I got your blueberry muffin. I'll be there in fifteen."

She struggles with the bag of bagels, the muffin and her phone, and perhaps with the long contents of her to-do list. It all looks very difficult, very meaningful, and she's so absorbed in it all, she forgets her coffee on the counter.

"Madame?"

She swoops forward and nabs the cup, pivoting in her stiletto and swinging the bag of bagels so it hits the man now trying to order. He doesn't notice.

She passes Joe, phone cradled between neck and head, holding the steaming cup with her teeth. She can't get out of the bakery fast enough. But she stops again and turns to grab a couple of packets of Sweet'n'low. She tears these and drops the pellets in the cup, still held by her teeth, as she pushes backwards through the door, hitting the next person trying to come in. She climbs into her double-parked, white SUV and zooms off without checking the traffic.

"You sure showed her."

"Are you talking to me?"

"Who else?"

"I thought you were still on the phone."

She takes the hands-free set out of her ear, letting the cable dangle from where it's clipped to the strap of her shoulder bag.

"No. I'm waiting in line, like the regular polite people."

"Can you believe that? Some people think they're all alone in the world."

"She was in a hurry. We just did our good deed for the day, letting her in."

"I guess."

"Maybe we just saved her marriage. Her family."

"That's one way to look at it."

"However you look at it, she got what she wanted."

"Yeah, but karma will catch up to her."

She smiles. "Maybe it already did."

This comment nestles itself snugly in the middle of his brain, fills him with a joy he hasn't felt since Francois informed him that the universe is trying to help.

"People don't really understand that karma is important."

She looks at his case. "You new in town?"

"I live around the corner. I just flew back from Miami?"

"How is it down there?"

"Hot. Dirty. Fluorescent."

"You've got all the makings of great porn flick there. What's your name?"

"Joe."

She tilts her head slightly. "Joe Does Miami. Doesn't sound so good. Um, Hurricane Joe Blows Miami."

He laughs. "That's good, but not my team."

"Ah, a straight man. I didn't think there were any of you left in this town."

"They work too much. Never see the light of day."

"But they do see the fluorescent neon of Miami."

"Yeah. When they're lucky."

It's her turn to order. She steps up to the counter. "You wanna coffee?"

"Sure. Uh, a tea actually."

She gives him a strange, judging look. "You wanna sit?"

"Yeah. I do."

She orders in French. He wheels his suitcase to the side and drops his satchel on a chair near the front window, at the one vacant table. Then he goes back to help her carry. She's also ordered a couple of croissants.

They sit.

"Nice bag."

"Thanks."

"Can I have it?"

"No."

She picks up the satchel. "Looks old."

"It is, and it's mine."

"'The universe is trying to help.' Are you some kind of religious nut? I mean, you get people to stand in line, talk about karma. You're not gonna try to convert me, are you?"

"Very much the opposite. But I do believe in karma."

"It's important."

He gestures at one of the croissants. "Can I?"

"Go for it."

He takes a bite. "Oh. That tastes of everything good in the world."

"You didn't eat anything on the plane?"

"Airline food? No way. It's poison."

"I like it. Always makes me feel like I'm going some place I want to."

"Interesting perspective. Not a healthy one, but it puts a positive spin on something that's very, very negative."

"Thanks. So, Joe. What do you do?"

He sips his tea and takes another bite of the croissant.

"What?"

"Sorry. I'm not a fan of that typical line of questioning."

"Fine. I'll add to it. What do you do...for fun?"

"I like that. For fun? Lots of things. Outdoor stuff, things that don't require technology, things that remove you from the world, at least for a while."

She sings, badly: "'He's just a small town boy, living in lonely world.'"

"Not another Gleek."

"I don't watch that. A whole show based on covering the original. Badly. I heard that song on *Scrubs*."

"I remember that. Great show."

"It was."

"Yeah, small town, but not lonely. And I like cities. It's the technology I'm not big on. Phones and computers and everyone connected all of the time. Everyone tuning each other out."

"They have all that in small towns too."

"What about you? What's your fun zone?"

She slurps her coffee. "I like flying and travelling. But I don't do it as much as I'd like. Work, work, work."

"Doing what?"

"I thought you didn't like those questions."

"It's more that I don't like my answer."

"Say it."

"You first."

"I'm in advertising. Hey, by the way. The karma line. Can I have that?"

"What for?"

"A campaign I'm working on. Hair care products."

"What does karma have to do with hair?"

"You know, what goes around comes around. How you treat your hair is how it will look and feel, and that will make you feel better about yourself and change your life."

He touches his hair. "Not me."

"You're not the target group. Anyway, sounds like your karma's well in order."

"Hope so. Advertising, huh? I'm jealous."

"Don't be. We work, like, insane hours. And I'm just a copywriter. The most worthless, expendable part of the creative production line."

She reaches into her bag, digs around, and hands him a battered business card.

"'Cheryline Jackson. Creative Primer.' Is this for real?"

"The agency likes stupid job titles."

"This is the winner. You sound like an undercoat. For painting a post-modern house."

She laughs as she bites into a croissant, covering her mouth with long fingers that have the odd streak of black pen on them.

"That's good. You in advertising too? You've got a way with words. And you're feisty, stand up to people."

"No. Don't laugh, and don't hate me. I'm in pharmaceuticals."

"Another pillman. There's a lot of you in Montreal."

"I'm supposedly the good and friendly kind, but I'm no superhero."

"It worked for Roger Ramjet."

"Who?"

"Roger Ramjet. He popped a proton pill and got all the strength of American freedom behind him."

"They could use him in Iraq. And elsewhere."

"It's a cartoon from the sixties. The orifice is going through a retro phase. Everything's getting dug up. *The Monkees*, *HR Pufnstuf*, *The Brady Bunch*, all that cringe-worthy crap. Ever see the old *Batman*?"

"Oh, yeah. The purple tights. Pow! Bam! Who could forget?"

"I'm impressed. My orifice pals can't even remember Burton's *Batman*."

"I loved it. My dad said it was groundbreaking."

"Why?"

"The whole homoerotic fantasy. Batman and Robin were more than just a dynamic duo. The cave, the car, the pole, the lingering stares."

"Like the *Ambiguously Gay Duo*."

"That's hilarious. And you can bet the old *Batman* was the inspiration."

She sneaks a look at her watch. "You're a bit of a weird one. You're not part of such a duo, are you?"

"No."

"Give yourself free samples?"

"Nuh."

"You're not like other guys."

"What does that mean? You don't wanna see me again?"

Another glance at her watch. "Undecided. Look, I gotta get back to work. I'll make a deal with you. If my CD goes for the karma line, I'll buy you dinner."

"And when he doesn't?"

"I'll think about it. What's your last name?"

"Solitus."

She writes it down on the back of her right hand, in the same black pen her fingers are streaked with.

"Nice meeting you, Joe Solitus."

"You too."

They shake hands.

"I hope your CD goes for it."

"We'll see."

He watches her walk out of the bakery. Through the window, he sees her tapping at the screen of her phone and wonders if she's familiar with the-t-wall.

***

"Nice tan."

"Morning, Xav."

"You got some sun."

"At dawn and dusk."

"And? Successful?"

He puts the kettle on. "The conference? Boring with a big fat B-Town. You want some tea?"

Xav pumps a few coins into the coffee machine and bangs the side to get it working. "Fuckoffee first."

"I don't know how you drink that sludge."

"It fires me up."

"You do understand that what you put into your body is what you get out."

Xav shrugs. "By that logic, it's working. And it's better than the urine you drink."

The kettle slowly starts making more noise, reluctantly, bored almost, like a prostitute attempting to fake yet another orgasm.

Xav sips his little cup of coffee. "When did you get back?"

"Yesterday."

"How was the flight?"

"What do you think?"

"Bad seat. Bad service. Bad food. Screaming babies. Complaining adults. Security delays. Guys laughing at a scanned image of your package. Some stranger feeling you up."

"All of the above."

Xav raises his cup in toast. "The terrorists have won."

The kettle starts to heave and huff, straining to please and to reach a quick result.

"Any familiar sights at the conf?"

"You get one guess."

"Oh no. Really?"

"Yep. And he's still a first class A-Holl."

"You go drinking with him?"

"Had to. You know how he is, goes into full bully mode if you say no."

The kettle peaks and pants out steam from its spout. Joe pours the water into his cup. He dips the tea bag a few times and takes it out.

"Don't you have to leave it in for like five minutes or something?"

"Not with green tea. Two minutes, max."

"Like it makes any difference."

"It does."

"You're all show, Solitus."

They take their drinks into the small meeting room. The team is crowded around Brett and his phone, cooing at a picture on it.

"Got your eyes."

"And hairline, already."

A couple of people chuckle.

Xav peaks over Brett's shoulder. "She's a peach. What's her name?"

"Samuel."

"Oh. Sorry, Brett. It's always hard to tell."

Supe bustles in, Bluetooth set in place. "Okay. Get onto it, Marjorie. Asap. Morning, troops."

Everyone takes their usual seats. Supe leans across the table to shake Brett's hand.

"Congrats."

"Thanks, Miles. And thanks everyone for the flowers and the card."

"My idea, B-Town. Now. Update me."

They go around the circle, spinning a collective web of false productivity, attributing importance and necessity when there is none, creating haste and pressure when none is required, each person making it sound like they alone are keeping the company afloat. Supe goes through the motions of contributing, supervising, taking credit, thoughtful beard stroking, obvious stating.

"All right. Thanks for that. Go get em, team."

Chairs slide on the laminated wood as people stand up to rush to their cubicles.

"Joe. A moment."

"Sure."

Supe waits for everyone to leave, looking over his shoulder. "My office."

They walk through the open plan office, Joe following a fast-moving Supe. As they pass the cubicles, he sees a few people peer at them without turning from their screens.

"Come on, Marjorie. Think on your feet...Oh, do I have to do everything myself? Send him the presentation as a PDF. Or just print it out."

Joe fights the temptation to slightly kick one of Supe's feet so the toes of one foot would connect with the heel of the other and he would go sprawling to the floor, hopefully to land on his right ear and for the impact to lodge the Bluetooth set permanently into his head.

Supe turns to Joe. "Some of the dinosaurs on the board aren't computer literate. Can't even use PowerPoint."

Joe nods. "Huh."

They make it to Supe's office without Joe tripping and kicking the shit out of him. It's not a real office; it's a cubicle separated from the open floor by three head-high dividers plus the building wall. There's a window, which doesn't open, two desks pushed together, and a high-backed, fake leather chair. The desks are covered in files, folders, printouts and catalogues; Supe's continuing attempt to keep up his paper trail facade. So much paper, so many projects, so much importance, so little time.

"Take a seat."

There's a small chair next to the gap in the dividers, the "door" of the "office". He picks up the chair and puts it alongside the desk. He sits. Supe sits as well, leaning back and stroking his beard, then tilting the chair forward and resting his elbows on the desk. He mistimes it and his elbows land on the keyboard. The computer beeps. He quickly corrects himself, pushing the keyboard forward. Elbows in place, he puts the tips of his fingers together, making a large triangle, thumbs at the bottom. He looks through it, then bounces the tips of his fingers against his nose.

"How are you, Joe?"

"Uh, fine. Bit tired, from the trip. The conference was pretty draining."

"Long flight."

"Yeah."

Supe sits back and crosses his arms: casual, informal, personal. "There's so much extra hassle these days, isn't there? When I started, we just went to the airport and got on the plane. Times change."

"Yes."

"We have to move with the times. I'm a good Christian, Joe, and I don't believe in this evolution rubbish, but I do believe we have to adapt to changes. The best adapters are those who are masters of change management. Do you know what I mean when I say change management?"

"Replacing the dinosaurs on the board?"

Supe laughs heartily. "No, no. Ha-ha. You're way off. No, we need to monitor how we change, to make sure we do it in the right way and at the right time. Change, Joe, is all about timing."

"I'm with you now."

"Oh, you are, are you? I'd like to think that. I really would. But you, we, were the victim of bad timing, and you, we, weren't able to change fast enough. Do you see where I'm going?"

"It was bad timing for Brett's wife to schedule having her baby last week."

Supe slaps the desk. "That's why I hired you. You're sharp. Yes, very bad timing. I should have asked B-Town to postpone that until at least after Miami. Still, there's no going back now. We have to look forward."

"Change management."

"Now you're getting the idea. You pick up on the details, Joe, when you have to. A lot of the time you're just riding the coat tails of other people, more effective people, like Enora. You waste time, and the company's money, with superfluous trips to Toronto and Ottawa when you could do it over the phone. You struggle when the heat is really on. And sometimes you associate with the wrong people."

"Look, Miles, I went out with Alfred because he had a scoop about a new product from Natrofield."

Supe's eyes narrow. He tries to look inquisitive, cagey and domineering, but he looks like someone suppressing a fart. "Go on."

"It could be big and it could affect every company in the industry. He said Massobix is trying to stop it, along with the FDA."

"Stop what?"

"You don't know about this?"

"I want to hear you say it. I want to know what you know, first."

"It's something called Release, or Relief. Alfred didn't know exactly."

Supe looks contemplatively out the window. "I've heard about this."

"I thought so, but I still spoke with Alfred to get as much info as

I could. I didn't tell him anything about us, about what we're doing."

"Good. That would come back to you."

"Karma."

Supe waves a hand. "I don't believe any of that eastern nonsense. What do you know about Release, Joe? Let's compare notes."

"It sounds like a wonder drug. Makes you forget something specific. An addiction, a fear, a memory, maybe even someone who broke your heart."

"A mind enhancer."

"Right."

Supe swivels his chair from side to side, thinking. Or pretending to think. Joe wonders if Supe is just buying himself some time, playing out some leadership trick he learned at a weekend seminar in upstate New York. Joe waits for the trick to play out and looks around. There's a photograph blown up to the size of a poster tacked on the divider next to Supe. It's fuzzy and grey, but he can see Supe on a beach, bucket in hand, concerned look on his face, pouring water on a whale. Also on the divider are posters from Greenpeace, a few postcards, and lots of photos printed on normal white paper stuck on top of each other in a disorderly collage. On the desk, next to the enormous mobile flat-screen monitor, is a silver framed picture of Supe's weekend son and daughter. Next to that is a trophy with a brass golfer on top, in full swing.

"Natrofield. Where do they get such great stuff? We don't have the R&D they have, or the finances. I know what you're thinking, Joe. I should've told the team about Reveal sooner."

"Release."

"Right. Release. It was just a matter of time they'd take ADs to the next level. The inside word is the army's been using something like this for a while. CIA, James Bond stuff."

"Huh."

"I told the board to invest in it, but they couldn't get their old heads around it. They never thought it would get developed. Where are Natrofield at with it? Do you know?"

"Alfred said it's in trial."

Supe picks up a piece of paper. "And he said that when you were at the, uh, the Harem?"

"That was his idea. I didn't know it was a strip club. I thought the best thing for Denoris was for me to find out more about Release and bring that information to you. Alfred's got a loose tongue when he drinks, you know that."

Supe frowns. "Yes. I remember that. I was glad to see the end of him. But I'm not sure whether to say good job or you're fired. What do you think I should say?"

"I don't know, Miles. I felt we needed to know. But, as you already know about Release, I guess it was all for nothing."

"Again, no sense of change management. No feel. You're disappointing me, Joe. And your efforts come back to me. I'm the one who has to answer for it. For you. I'm the one who talks to the board. When you screw up, I take the heat. No big orders in Miami?"

"Most of the clients wanted to deal with Brett."

"And so they should. B-Town's flying at the moment. Got the whole south in his pocket. You could learn a lot from him. Stable family life, motivated worker, first in the office, last to leave. B-Town's destined for big things. What about you, Joe? Where do you see yourself in five years?"

He has a flash, of being in Supe's chair, surrounded by the facade of multi-tasking busy-ness, asking some hapless underling that exact question.

"Uh, well, I'd like to get into marketing. People are always telling me I have a way with words. And I think our marketing strategy could use a serious revamp."

"Do you? Well, bad news there, Joe, and try to keep this to yourself. The marketing department's on death row. I'm recommending to the board that marketing gets outsourced from January next year. But that's just between you and me."

Supe taps his nose a couple of times. It pushes a small booger out the side that nestles itself in his moustache.

"How many in that department?"

Supe picks up another piece of paper. It's blank. "Twenty-nine. But we'll take care of them. Some will get redeployed to other departments. Some we'll have to let go. So, you haven't answered my question. Five years."

"What about Australia? When are we opening the branch there?"

"It's on the drawing board."

"It has been since I was an intern."

"Change takes time, Joe. The board is pretty slow to move on things. But when it does, we'll need people we can trust to get it started. Do you see yourself as leadership material?"

"I'd like to think so, yes."

"No, no. A real leader would give a decisive answer. A real leader is not something you hope to think you are. You're either a leader or you're not."

"I am."

"You're good with people, Joe. Miami should've been your opportunity to step up, really show your abilities. Instead, you ended up at the Harem with A-Holl putting company dollars into some whore's g-string. I want you to focus on the upcoming conference in Barcelona, Joe. And I mean really focus on Barcelona. Think of this as your chance, your almost last, to prove yourself. Come back a winner, or we might end up back here having a more awkward discussion."

He wants to grab Supe by the hair and pound his face into the keyboard. "Okay, Miles."

"You've got potential, Joe. Some. But you've got to learn to focus that potential. You need to realise what's important, for Denoris, for your career. We're family here. A team. We support each and we don't let each other down."

Joe stands and puts the chair back in place. "I'll do my best."

"Do more than that. And I want a report about Release by the end of the day. Find out everything you can."

"Of course."

Supe smiles. The booger is set free and lands on the desk. "Good talk, Joe."

He squeezes through the gap in the dividers and then manoeuvres through the zig-zag of cubicles, making sure to walk with purpose and keep his head high. He even manages to swing his arms jauntily, but a little too much, like a novice model on the catwalk. He has the flash of temptation to slip out of his suit jacket and fling it over his shoulder with a finger hooked in the collar.

When he gets to his desk, Xav pushes his chair and rolls over to him.

"What was that all about?"

"Just a pep talk for Barcelona."

Enora turns, headset in place. "I'm going as well. I don't think Miles trusts you after your pathetic efforts in Boston and Miami."

"You killed Boston, Enora. I took the blame for it. You should be thanking me."

"You can remember it however you want. Miles knows the truth."

His phone rings. He's scared to turn on his computer and see all the unread messages, the emails he could have read at the airport yesterday when he was staring out the window at the slowly taxiing planes.

Enora smiles at him. "Are you gonna get that?"

***

"You were a good cook, Pops. You used to make really good stuff. All in one pot. Remember when we camped at Green Mountain and you made this soup on the fire? And all these people joined us and had a bowl. You fed like a dozen people. And they all hung around. Someone opened a bag of marshmallows. Another guy shared the beer from his cooler. Someone had a guitar and you played a few songs. Everyone sang along. And best of all, we went hiking the next day. It was Monday. You called my school and said I was sick. We were supposed to get up at dawn and ride back but you slept in. And then you said it was too nice a day to go to school, or to work. So we went for a hike, out to the reservoir. We had a swim and rode back in the afternoon. Ma was so pissed off. You took her out to dinner and I had to watch Gordie."

Popov jumps up onto the counter, right next to the cutting board.

"Hey, I'm trying to run a hygienic kitchen here, Pops. That kind of behaviour will get me condemned. Don't worry. It'll be our secret. What? No garlic? Come on. We don't have any girlfriends to kiss tonight."

He peels the garlic, cuts it and minces it with a fork.

"You taught me that. Ma used to complain because every cutting board smelt of garlic. And every fork. Ha. Remember she bought you a garlic press for Christmas? You used it to put banana on your toast. Never pressed any garlic with it."

The doorbell buzzes. He wipes his hands on a towel and goes through the apartment.

"Hey, Francois. Come on in."

"Ca va bien?"

"Yeah, all right."

"Is Xav here?"

"No. He's not coming."

"Who were you talking to?"

"Popov. We like to discuss the world sometimes."

"He got a lot to say?"

"Not much. But he's very expressive, and disagreeable, when he wants to be."

Popov comes down the hall. Francois bends over and scratches him behind the ears. Popov submits to this, with indifference, does a lazy figure eight of Francois's legs, tail high and arched, then walks into the bedroom.

"That's all you got say? I love you to, Popov. He's just like you. You take the love and you walk away."

"I learned it from him."

They move through the apartment and into the kitchen. Joe gets back to work with the steaming pots and bubbling pans.

"You wanna drink?"

"No tea."

"There's wine open on the table."

Francois hooks his jacket over a chair and helps himself. "Can I water you as well?"

"I'm good. I've been drinking while cooking. Adds to the atmosphere. I'm on my second glass."

Francois holds the bottle towards the light. "You mean your fourth."

"I opened it last night."

"Guests? I think I smell, above the smoke, the sweet scent of a woman. And coming from the bedroom."

"It's not. Believe me. But a girl was here."

Francois stands in the kitchen and watches Joe grate the cheese. "And?"

"You'll like this. I met her in the Oh The Pain on Park. Last Sunday. Shit, I can't believe the week's already over."

"What happened to yoga with Xav? And his weekly attempt to get into the pants of Swami Scully?"

"She ignores him. And I wasn't in the mood. He wanted to go to Smash after."

"Smashed at Smash. What a great way to end the week. Maybe he'll get his leg over."

"Maybe he'll get home in one piece. I'm so done with all that."

"That's where all you ants go on Fridays, isn't it?"

"Not me. I only went to please Xav."

"And take care of him."

Joe pours some of his wine into the sauce and stirs. "I worry about that guy."

"Don't. He's an adult. Even if he behaves like a teenager."

"It's your fault, Francois. You're the one who told him he's still in his youth. He's more frat boy than ever since you said that."

"Sorry."

"You're not."

"I'm not his biggest fan. Why are you friends with him anyway?"

"If we didn't work together, I probably wouldn't be. But at work, you need to have a group, be popular somewhere within the crowd."

"That's lame."

"That's how it is."

Francois sips. "What about this date? You got her back to your crib, but not into the boudoir."

Joe drains the pasta. "I don't think she was that impressed with me. Or maybe she picked up that I wasn't impressed with her."

"Either way, she only lasted a glass. This is good, by the way. Where's it from?"

"The Moselle. In Germany."

"I thought they only had whites. You know, super sweet, girly Rieslings."

"Actually, Moselle Rieslings are dry and a bit sour. This is Dornfelder. From the same area. Beautiful part of the world."

"Yeah, yeah. You've been everywhere. Wow. This girl, was she hot?"

"She's pretty, in an extroverted librarian kind of way, without the startling moment when the nerdy glasses are removed and her long hair is let down. She's like the cousin you always thought about committing a major family scandal with but she never fired your pistons as much as you wanted."

Francois laughs. "Been there."

"And she was a bit too sure of herself. Like she knew a lot about me and just asked the usual questions to double check the info, you know? She told me she searched me online, before the date."

"So? Everyone does that."

Joe serves the pasta in bowls and then scoops Bolognese on top. "Parmesan? It's fresh."

Francois takes his bowl and then sprinkles a liberal amount of grated parmesan over the top. "I didn't think anyone did this anymore. Grate their own cheese."

"I was in Parma once. Even visited the factory. After that, I couldn't eat the packaged stuff ever again. Especially that dried-out powdered stuff."

They take their bowls and glasses and sit down at the table. Francois hoes in.

"Ah, tasty. Thanks, Joe."

"A recipe from Max. Vegetarian Bolognese."

"You should be eating like this every night. I should be. So? What did she find about you on the net? There's not a sex tape somewhere you never told me about I hope."

"Not that I know of. When we met on Sunday, five minutes after she left, she asked to be a ceevillian. I accepted."

"Can't say no."

"It's like that, isn't it? You're forced to accept. Then we hooked up last night and she got stuck into me for having Alfred on my list of ceevillians."

"Who's Alfred?"

"A guy I used to work with. Complete tool. Anyway, she said she did a copywriting project for Denoris a couple of years ago. Freelance. B2B stuff. She's a copywriter, but her actual job title is, get this, Creative Primer."

Francois nearly drops his bowl. "So, what am I, an Image Maximiser?"

"You'll always be the Solo Snapper to me."

"Thanks."

"She worked with Alfred on the project. And he pretty much stalked her until she got a restraining order."

"It's incredible to think that sort of shit happens. What's wrong with this guy?"

"Alfred's a prick from another era."

"When they slapped women on the arse and called them sweetheart."

"Right. So I went through all the hoops of this date just for her to come back here and give me a total serve."

Francois shakes his head. "What do these women want?"

"From the looks of it, revenge."

"What? We're the ones who should be after that. She…What's her name?"

"Cheryline."

"God. She should be getting revenge on her parents. Cheryline, at some point in her life, broke some poor guy's heart, maybe more than one. And now she's out for revenge. That shit with Alfred was her karma catching up with her."

Joe laughs.

"What's so funny?"

"That's how we got talking. Karma."

Joe tells the story of what happened in the bakery.

"Man, some people are rude."

"Some are. Not all of them."

"And? Did she use the line?"

"Sort of. She said it didn't fit her project, but her CD wanted to use it for something else."

"And what do you get?"

"The fruits of Alfred's labour, and a free dinner."

Francois shakes his head before taking a sip of his wine. "You gonna see her again?"

"Don't think so. She blurted out the story, got real mad, drained her wine and left. It all came from nowhere. One minute we're having a fun evening, the next she's leaving red-faced and in tears."

"You know something, Joe. I don't think there's ever been a worse time to be single. A single man, I mean."

"Xav says it's never been easier. Just a couple of clicks."

"Can you imagine all the potential crazy that would open up? That photoshopped pic of Angelina Jolie actually turns out to be some thirteen year-old, or maybe a horny old grandma. Or worse, it's someone you know. People can be whatever and whoever they want online."

"Xav says it's like shooting fish in a barrel."

"He's an idiot. Those girls, if they are actually girls, will arrive at his door and ask him to do all kinds of weird shit. Like fuck in a teddy bear costume or pee on them, or stuff so weird I can't even imagine it. I'd never use that to find a date."

"A lot of people do."

"That's the problem, Joe. People are forgetting how to interact, beyond keyboards and screens. Even speed-dating's died."

"You ever try that?"

"Once. I went with my sister, as a favour. She didn't want to go on her own."

"And?"

"It was like having ten really fast job interviews."

Joe laughs.

"And I didn't get any offers."

"Maybe the free love of the sixties would've been better for you."

"All those dirty hippies? No way. Can you imagine the bevy of STDs floating around in the Woodstock mud?"

They finish their meals at the same time.

"You want some more?"

Francois holds up his bowl. "Please, sir. But only because it's so good. You really know your way around the kitchen. I never thought your oven even worked."

Joe goes into the kitchen, serves them both a portion, sprinkling the remaining parmesan on top. "I'm changing things up. No more take-out. I'm gonna shop and cook more."

"Good luck with that."

"What I need is more time."

Joe brings the bowls back in and sits down.

"Thanks. Where'd you learn to cook anyway?"

"Max. He knew how to do everything."

"Hey, did you meet that Natrofield spy in Miami?"

"No, but she'll be in Barcelona."

"How do you know that?"

Joe takes out his phone. "She texted me. Look."

"'get a in b.' I think I love this girl. Maybe you should marry her in Barcelona."

"Bad location for proposals."

Francois smiles. "Yeah. Trina. Sorry."

"Ten years, and it still hurts."

"And it always will. What happened to her, do you know?"

"I guess she went back to London and they got married. Maybe they're in Australia now and have a couple of brats. I don't know. I don't care."

"Yeah, you do."

"I don't, really."

Francois points his fork at Joe. "It could be worse. She could end up married to your best friend."

"That's awful. You have my sympathies."

Joe slides his spoon around the bowl, getting the last bit of sauce and a tiny ear of broccoli, then drops his bowl on the table. "Good."

Francois reaches out and picks up a card. "What's this?"

"An invitation. To a funeral."

"Who's Henri Petit?"

"The biker who got cleaned up last week, right in front of me."

"I thought you didn't know him."

Joe refills their glasses. "I don't."

"So how did you get the invite?"

"Maybe they got my name from the police."

"That roadkill video. You sent me the link."

"No names on it."

"Don't need them. Haven't you heard of idntphi?"

Joe shakes his head.

"You can get it for a phone, and a computer, I think. I-D-N-T-P-H-I. It's a face recognition site. You take a photo of someone and idntphi searches the web for a matching pic. Someone snapped you in this vid and matched it to ceeville or some other pic. And got your name."

"This tech crap's getting outta control."

"You gonna go?"

"Can't. I'm in Barcelona."

"You want me to feed Popov?"

"Yeah."

"And talk to him as well?"

"If you want. You can talk about me while I'm gone."

"And then you can feed me again when you're back."

"Sure."

"What's wrong?"

"It's just...what if the guy who found my name is Henri's brother or dad or someone close? They might try to get revenge."

"You tried to help. And I thought we decided only women are out for revenge."

"I don't mean me. I mean the driver, or the girl that walked in front."

"That's more likely."

Joe sips his wine. "This world. What's happened to privacy? Face recognition. Anonymous comments. People searching each other before their first date."

"And that's just the stuff we know about."

"I never knew about idntphi."

Francois looks into his glass. He swirls the liquid around. "That's what I mean. Imagine all the things you don't know about."

Broken hearted memories of Trenus Lagosius

It's early evening. They hoof it down the Rambla, the sea of heads sparked by the flashes of cameras, held out at arm's length. It's almost like the tourists are reaching their cameras out to the thieves leaning against the racks of newspapers and the skinny fridges full of bottled water. Here, take it, and all of my holiday photos as well.

They hold hands, arms swinging a little. The loose straps of his backpack brush the milling tourists and he has to be careful not to turn too quickly and take someone out. That's hard, because she's pointing in every direction, drawing his attention to every small detail that catches her eye. Everything is for sale: bags, shirts, postcards, posters, magazines, drinks, food, and probably small gypsy children, if you go down the right narrow street and know who to ask.

There's life on them streets, Jonah.

By life she means people, lots of them, out parading and looking at each other.

You sure you know where you're going?

She stops and opens the guidebook to where her fingers are placed. She points. Down here.

Street entertainers attract crowds that stop and stare, forming perfect half circles and creating jams on both sides of this middle part of the Rambla. The entertainers have small tin plates in front of their frozen positions: Miss Liberty, Elvis, Dracula, a man in a silver suit with a glittering cowboy hat. One person is dressed and painted in red and green, an elaborate dragon. He wonders how long it must take to put all that junk on, and get it off. And does he walk through the city like that, or put on the costume in his car around the corner?

The air smells of Vespa exhaust, bad breath and underarm sweat. It's very noisy.

She tugs at his arm and they take a right down Carrer de l'Hospital. The sidewalk is narrow. He walks behind her. Her backpack looks massive. It hangs half way down the back of her thighs. He watches each calf flex and tense as she executes that weird bouncy pigeon-toed walk of hers, in her running shoes. The only shoes she's got with her;

claims she doesn't even own any heels. She seems unreal.

She speaks over her shoulder. Hungry?

Very. You?

Always.

I'm still weak from that run last night.

You girl. We need to bust you into shape or I'll be calling you Johanna all the way to Italy.

I told you. I haven't run in a while.

You had good form, but no legs.

I'd swim you out of the water.

No way.

She stops in front of the sign; the blue triangle, the white house and tree.

Right again.

Shame on you, boy, for doubting. Let's dump our stuff and go out for some tapas.

You're the boss.

She leads the way inside. It looks clean, renovated. They hand over their cards and passports, fill out the forms, read the long list of rules.

He leans close and whispers. We should've booked a hotel.

No. No. A hotel is basically a mortuary for the living. Here, we can get to know some folks. Mingle a little with our travelling fraternity. Swap stories. Tell tales.

He smiles at this, even though she's said it in every village and town they've passed through since Lagos.

She scoops up both sets of keys from the counter and heads for the stairs. He follows. Their room is a narrow closet with a double bunk. Each bed has a folded blanket and a wafer thin pillow. He almost expects to see a grimy toilet in the corner, with no seat, but there's just a yellowing sink and a skinny mirror. A double locker is jammed between the bunk and the window. It's not easy for two people to move in the room, but they manage to shrug off their packs. She goes to the windows and sweeps them open like they're in the honeymoon suite of the Ritz, with a balcony overlooking the Med. The sounds of the street climb the three floors and enter the room: exuberant and impatient shouts in Spanish, a truck revving, a horn sounding long and repeatedly. She stretches, cat-like, little balled fists in the air and arms extended, up on her toes. Her t-shirt lifts a little and he can see the frilly white V of her panties poking above the waistline of her shorts. He goes to the window and stands behind her. They both look down at the street. A Vespa zips past, the rider and passenger engaged in a loud conversation. At the corner, a dying van belches and coughs. The driver gets out, scratches his head and lights a cigarette. A few other men come over and huddle around the driver, giving advice and gesturing wildly with their hands.

She turns and bites his neck.

Ow.

He's alive.

She shoves him down onto the bottom bunk. They have fast, physical sex, pushing through the wafts and odours of the day's journey and the pine scented floor cleaner; with the urban soundtrack of vehicles and voices, and what sounds a little like a cheering crowd on the street below. He's in. Olé!

They can hear you.

You prudish Americans.

I'm only half prudish.

We were fucking way before we came down from the trees, Jonah. Get over it. Plus. Oh, that's good. Plus, the book of Genesis is practically porn. Snakes, forbidden fruit, naked in the garden of love. How do you, hmm, how do you think Adam and Eve spent those long boring afternoons? They had no TV.

He laughs, feeling good all over, like his stinking toes are sending off sparks of joy and not vapours of fetidness.

After, they lie awkwardly on the single bed. He has one leg and a butt cheek hanging over the side. The metal of the bunk is cold against his skin and pinching a little. The noise of the street seems louder than before. More trucks, more people, more Vespas, even more impatient shouts. It's edging past ten and the city seems to be really coming alive. He closes his eyes, breathes in the disinfectant and diesel. It's numbing, distracting, and that's the best thing of all.

Up ya get. I need a feed.

She dresses quickly, pulling a plain white shirt over her flat runner's chest, no bra, and digs a fleece out of her backpack. She zips it up; it's covered with static, frizzy strands of her mousy hair. She has her running shoes on before he even sits up.

I'll meet you downstairs.

She bends over and kisses him. Don't dawdle, or I'll find another Jonah to go out with.

Do you think there's one here?

Probably. And he'll be better than this version.

Thanks.

Come on. Mush, mush.

She closes the door loudly. He rummages through the pack for a clean shirt. Everything is dirty, or half dirty; hand-washed in a hostel basin with shampoo and still smelling not quite clean. There's the old Hawaiian, but he can't wear that. He unfolds it and holds it up in front of the window, looking at the wood-panelled wagon, surfboards on top, the waves crashing in the background, the palm trees and yellow sand. It all looks so pleasant and simple. He sniffs the collar.

No.

He pulls on the shirt he wore on the train and closes the windows. The stairs strain his quads and calves. They went for over an hour and she barely worked up a sweat. But it was great, barefoot in the sand, and then falling in the ocean after. He wouldn't have run with anyone else.

He gingerly takes the last steps down to the reception area. She's standing in the middle of the floor. There's a guy in front of her, down on one knee.

~~~

He wakes. The glowing red of the alarm clock says it's 4:23. Light is slicing through the avocado curtains, making the familiar look vague, or the vague familiar. The beige desk with an avocado hotel folder on it. One beige closet with a safe, six hangers, a folded plastic laundry bag, a shoe horn and a sewing kit. Flatscreen TV on the wall that last night declared "Welcome, Mr Solitus" at maximum volume and then talked him through the range of porn films and pay-per-view blockbusters on offer. Plastic stand holding the TV remote and also advertising the available PPV.

4:24. Barcelona. Morning.

He sits, feeling groggy, sick. The avocado and beige of the room isn't helping. It feels like he's drowning in a bowl of rotting melon salad. This room, designed as an all purpose second home, could be anywhere. And that's the marketing strategy. Same sheets, same furnishings, same bathroom products, same six hangers, same smell, same porn.
~~~

He stumbles into the bathroom. He pees, swaying, smelling all the old urine that's sprayed over the side of the bowl, glad his own bathroom doesn't have that smell. Cheryline noticed. It was the only positive thing she had to say before she ranted and left.

He flushes. He tears open an avocado soap and washes his hands and face. The complementary mouthwash barely scours away the over-breathed air and pre-heated burps of the flight. He spits and coughs, drawing deep in his throat to get it all out, all that waste of others that's now lodged inside him. Another flight, another continent, but with all the same hassles, setbacks, delays and bodily consequences.

He shaves and washes again.

The Mayola towel is patchy and stiff, the ends just starting to fray. As he dabs it against his face, he wonders how many butts and balls this towel has touched. Best not to think about it, or the adventurous couples who played hide the remote while watching unlimited porn. What other juices and streaks and stains has this towel mopped up?

"Forget it."

He pads through the room naked. He falls into the stiff chair at the desk and pulls his notebook out of the satchel. As it boots, he plays with Colonel Mustard. He considers clicking off a label, something about over-reactions to minor problems, like the security guards at Dorval making him empty his satchel at gunpoint, because the Colonel had set off the scanner's alarm.

Click, whirr, click, whirr.

He pulls the back off the label and sticks it to his satchel.

"Yes. 'Don't panic.' The best advice ever. And the universe is trying to help."

He catches up on all the texts he missed while in transit and sends off a couple of short replies. Nothing is pressing, but people expect some sort of response, however meaningless and empty.

The computer fired up, it takes an hour to clear his almost twenty-four hour lag of work email. A lot of cc stuff he has to read through, some final demands from Supe, with Enora in cc.

"I'm not sitting next to her on the way back."

He reads, writes and sends. It's now 5:45. Noises are coming from Via Laietana below. Traffic, people, a dawn busker drunkenly singing a cappella opera, and it all must be loud to climb the six floors and sneak through the two centimetre crack of the open window.

He goes to the *Gazette* website, reads through the latest news. A multi-car pile-up on the 15 across the river in Brossard reminds him of Henri Petit and the funeral that took place while he was over the Atlantic, while he was receiving behavioural briefings from Enora. He goes to ceeville. Someone has set up a dedication city for Henri, but it only has nineteen ceevillians, all listed as cyclists. He flips to his own city. Cheryline has written on his private billboard.

"SORRY for the outburst. Karma IS important!!! It was bad for my karma to take all that Alfred crap out on you. Can I by you a croissant to restore balance in the universe?"

He replies: "In Barcelona. Happy to break French bread with you when I'm back next week."

He reads through the other billboards of his ceevillians, looks at photos, clicks on a few links, watches some videos, one thing leading to another in an endless search for nothing.

It's now 7:03.

He dresses, opting for his most conservative suit. It's grey and so dull he wonders if anyone will actually notice him. White shirt, light blue tie with the yellow D in the middle. He thinks about a grey vest, but opts against the preppy look he considers pretentious. He checks himself in the mirror, flattening and spiking his hair a little. His hopes the blonde will help him travel like a local.

Downstairs, the lobby restaurant is getting set up for breakfast. Two small round women, both with beige aprons over avocado shirts, looking like wine barrels on legs, are hard at work. It smells good, but Denoris doesn't cover breakfasts.

It's 7:20. There's no sign of Enora.

He steps outside. The air is fresh and warm. The streets are wet. White suds cover the sidewalks and foam gathers in frothy puddles over the steel drains. Women are doing the cleaning, spilling dirty mop water from shop doorways. Men ride the back of garbage trucks and sit in the cabs of vans. Traffic moves with urgency. Conversations cross streets, are shouted from one balcony to another, reach from an ajar shop door to a bathroom window three floors above. Everything echoes and the noises multiply, and the volume increases with each person who exits a building or bus and joins the fray.

His phone tells him to take Carrer de la Princesa. He complies. A sign points to the Picasso Museum, where he had stood in line for hours, staring at his feet, trying not to cry. And finally inside where all those cubic, straight-cornered, flat-chested women had reminded him of her. The only solution had been to get out: of the museum, of the hostel, of the country.

She had said it was over, had been for months, was happy to be single.

He grimaces as he steps around the garbage bags, but then stops. A smallish doorway opens into a sweet, warm-smelling bakery. He buys half a dozen Magdalenas, straight out of the oven, and manages to mime that he wants tea, not coffee. The woman holds up a green box of menta and that will have to do.

"Si, si. Menta."

He walks, eats, sips, ignores the directions his phone gives and heads towards the green expanse of the Parc de la Ciutadella. He takes a bench by the pond and points his face to the sun, already above the lines of the buildings and stinging with warmth. He can smell the zoo. The Magdalenas and mint tea make him feel like his stomach is glowing, like a healer is holding a hand against his belly.

A few people jog through the park, some struggling, some enjoying it, some stopping to stretch, some deep in conversation with themselves. They have assorted technology strapped to their arms or clipped to their shorts. He manages to pick out one runner, a middle-aged man, not wearing earphones.

He yawns, feeling like he could sit there all day.

Buzz, buzz.

"Hola, Enora."

"How can you be so cheerful?"

"Look out the window. The Spanish gods have given us a beautiful day and we get to spend all of it indoors."

"Where are you? The meet was in the lobby."

"You weren't there. I started already. I'm at the CCIB."

"The what?"

He stands and starts walking to the park's exit. "The convention centre."

"Well, you are out to please. Get my accreditation while you're there. That'll save me some time."

"I told you not to drink on the flight."

"I'm fine. It was cheap wine, something wrong with it."

"Sure. It was the quality, not the quantity."

"That's right. And I had some work to do first. I want to be fully prepared."

"Sure, sure."

"I'll be at the entrance at half past eight."

His phone directs him down Passeig du Pujades and across the broad tarmac of Carrer de la Marina. While he lounged in the park, it seems the whole city spilled onto the streets: cars, scooters, bikes, trucks, vans, guys with push-carts, an old man with a pack mule. Everyone and everything on the move. The wind funnels down de la Marina, bringing the smell of salt with it. His every inclination is to walk south, straight to the beach. But he crosses the street and then cuts down de Llull, zigzagging a few blocks, defying the phone, until he lands on Carrer del Taulat. This will take him all the way to the CCIB, hopefully before Enora arrives in a taxi. White paint is flaking from some of the buildings and the day's construction work is well underway. He remembers that, all the building, the cranes, the empty bags of cement pressed flat against the street by the cement trucks and left there. It's still like that. The dust and sand hangs in the air. The jackhammers and mobile generators make it impossible to talk, even to think, yet the locals hurry past with phones pressed to their heads and fingers in their other ears. Every step is made with purpose, with intent, and no one veers or alters their walking path to prevent collisions. He's the perpetual loser in this game of sidewalk chicken.

He stops to buy a bottle of water, two bananas and an apple. He sucks the bottle dry before Carrer del Taulat becomes Passeig del Taulat. It's not an attractive walk, despite this neighbourhood being just a few blocks from the beach. It's rundown, unloved, over-used. He's astounded by the amount of activity for 8:02. The Vespas duck between the cars and line up at the traffic lights, soaring off just before the lights turn green. Delivery trucks double park and block the narrow streets. Guys unload vans with cigarettes dangling from the corners of their mouths and lean on their stack trolleys and pallet jacks to discuss the news of the day. The traffic backs up behind them and horns sound out a frustrated chorus. The unbelievable level of noise makes Sherbrooke at peak hour seem like a village.

It's not nice being back here. He's not getting closure, like he hoped. He doesn't have the new perspective that sweeps away the hurt, makes him feel good about his life's journey so far, brings him full circle. None of that. She put the ring on her finger, turned to him and shrugged, and walked straight out the door. The length of the Spanish coast, together, and it meant nothing. Was forgotten, straight away. And when she left, the incredible diversion that she was, all the crap came back, that nightmarish demon he couldn't outrun. But he tried. Running as fast as he could. East, travelling like mad, trying to outrun himself.

Waiting at a red light, he turns. A waif of a boy takes his hand off the shoulder strap of Joe's satchel and grins innocently.

"You want woman?"

"No."

"Man?"

He crosses the street and gets to the CCIB. The suits and skirts are milling about out front, shaking hands, talking excitedly on phones, pacing with importance. He gets in amongst them. Teeth glint in the morning sun. It seems everyone has forgotten their sunglasses. They all squint against the morning light, shielding their eyes with folders and printouts. He sees a few familiar faces from Miami, nods at them, exchanges thin smiles, and turns his back on an approaching A-Holl. Inside, Enora's waiting, her accreditation pinned to her heavy flannel suit.

"Where were you?"

"Caught by the vultures outside. Got some interesting leads. I was networking, Enora, and I mean really networking."

"You sound like Miles."

"Really? That's good, isn't it? I want to be just like him."

"Sure."

"You look hot, and I don't mean in the sexy sense."

She fans herself with a catalogue. "It's so warm here."

"You should swap that winter suit for something more fitting to the conditions."

"And now you're a fashion expert too. Shall we?"

"I don't have my pass yet."

He weaves through the assembled mass of fawning and pawing sales people. They're gathered in tight clumps, blocking access to the registration table, talking loudly and unaware of the people they're holding up. He pushes through a group and gets to the desk.

"It's already been picked up."

"Huh. Thanks."

The mosh pit impedes his progress, but he gets back to Enora, who's dangling the pass from her fingers.

"Looking for this?"

He reaches for it, but she pulls it back.

"Not such a good start, Joe."

"Is my every movement going to be reported?"

"I'm here to help, not hinder."

She leads the way into the main hall, shimmying through the crowd, waving to people she knows and probably to plenty she doesn't. She calls out names, tries to greet people in different languages.

"This is how it's done, Joe. Watch and learn."

"You know, if you really want so badly to get ahead, shake those hips of yours for someone from Natrofield. Find out about Release."

"About what?"

"Come on. I know Miles briefed you, but he only found it out from me."

"I'll leave the dirty work to you. Sounds like you could use a win. Do it for the team."

"I thought the easiest way to get a promotion is not to do it for the team but to do it with the team leader. Am I right?"

"You're full of it, Joe."

"You went from being Supe's assistant to having all the key accounts in sales, all within a couple of months."

"Unlike you, I'm good at my job. I earned everything I got."

"Yeah."

Enora stops at a small, half assembled booth. "This can't be us."

Joe laughs. "Supe's budgeting strikes again. I hope you paid for that taxi from your own pocket, or I'm telling."

***

They enter the lobby and walk to the elevator.

Enora presses the button. "I am sooo finished. I think I'm still jetlagged."

"We've been here three days already."

"I don't like this city. Too hectic. I'll be happy to go home."

"It's not so bad going back in time."

"Excuse me?"

"The jetlag. It's not as bad going backwards. The body seems to prefer gaining time rather than losing it."

"That makes no sense at all, Joe."

"That's been my experience."

The elevator doors open. Enora steps in.

"Are you coming?"

"Pass. I can't face that nasty room yet. I'm gonna have a cup of tea in the lobby."

"I'll talk to Miles when we're back. This hotel doesn't make the kind of impression Denoris should be making. We can't bring clients back here."

The elevator doors close.

"But we can bring back some busboy named Jose for a wrestle between the Spanish sheets."

It's a relief to be alone, to be done with the hand shaking, arse kissing, business card swapping and false promising. No more snivelling meet and greets, pretending to be interested in some company no one's ever heard of located in a town no one would ever visit. And no more lunches, dinners and drinks that drag on and end with nothing except a large bill. And no more trying to muster enthusiasm for something he could not give a crap about. Sell more pills? Why? How does that bring us further as human beings?

The night receptionist is also responsible for the small bar. He orders a tea, sits down and flips open his notebook. He doesn't want to, but Supe has been sending a steady stream of messages and he has to reply, even with the time difference. The only problem is, he's got nothing positive to say.

He punches in his company ID and password. "Goodbye job."

The tea arrives. He lifts the bag out and slides the saucer over the top of the cup.

He has 159 unread messages. He skims the ones he's on cc, files away all the contact confirmations from the people he's met at the conference so far, and replies to Supe's mails, updating the day's activities and, yes, promising to bring back a couple of bottles of Rioja.

"He probably found that online. Searched Spanish wine and that was the first thing that came up. Doesn't know where the stuff actually comes from."

He stops and looks out the window, trying to ignore his reflection and see the street. Hot day in late August. Rented bikes clunking and squeaking as they head north from Almeria along a dusty, dangerous highway. The day trip was her idea. Lunch in Rioja; the wrong Rioja. Not a vineyard in sight. Trina was way wrong, and laughed about it. Drinking too much wine anyway. Getting lost. Stopping at a supermarket on the way back to ask for directions. Sharing a two litre bottle of water in one hit. Trina sucking it dry. Finding the way, weaving down narrow farm paths with stone walls built half a millennium ago. The goats cheering. Trina never getting tired, never shutting up, always with some comment to offer. Skirting Almeria on the way back. The brutal head wind as they neared the coast. Clambering down the rocks for a swim outside of Castell del Rey. Trina dumping the bike, chain side first, into the sand and dancing out of her clothes. Trina all taught and sinewy, like an under-aged communist gymnast, narrow-hipped and flat-chested. The oily water. The line of cigarette butts and water bottles left by the tide. Trina comparing everything to Perth, with nothing even remotely measuring up. Sitting on the beach. Trina telling him about Jordan, about what had gone wrong and what she had missed and how she was now so much better off to be rid of him. Trina saying she didn't want to be in another relationship and just wanted to stay travel buddies. And him thinking this was totally fine, as long as they kept moving and she kept talking and it kept his mind off all that shit he didn't want to think about.

"You watch any longer you'll get square eyes."

"Huh?"

She's dispensed with the blue suit he saw her in earlier, when she slipped into a huge black Mercedes with a couple of men who looked Russian, or Slavic. Somewhere east. Now, she's wearing a daring wrap-around dress, splashed and streaked with red and yellow and black. It's outlandish but somehow suitable, like it was made in some tiny boutique workshop around the corner.

"You look fantastic."

"Thanks."

She sits down, pulling the hem of her dress up a little, revealing bare shins the colour of soft butter.

"But you're not blending in so well with the Mayola colour scheme."

She looks around. "This place is hideous. Half the people staying here should be on suicide watch. How can you stand it?"

"No choice."

"There's always a choice."

"Not for us."

"Catching up on busy work?"

"Just working at looking busy. Anna, right?"

"Don't pull that, Joe."

"Anita Rudolph. How could I forget? That red nose sniffing in my satchel."

She laughs, seems a little drunk, pleased with herself. "Like you've got anything we'd want."

"You should stop at our section for a look."

"I must've blinked when I passed it. I guess for you guys, size doesn't count."

"We're going for quality, not quantity. Niche markets, specialist products."

"That old line. Did that idiot Miles brainwash that into you?"

"You know him?"

"Of course. We know everything about Denoris, and Massobix, and everyone else."

"What about who killed JFK? And did we really go to the moon, or was that all some Hollywood ruse?"

"We don't know that just yet, but give us time."

"What do you know about Denoris, apart from the morons in management?"

She looks around with distaste. "They always put you in Mayola. That's why I knew I'd find you here. I think that's just keeping the brand alive. How's the room?"

"Like all the others. You wake up and have no idea where you are."

"Charming. Padded walls?"

"Almost. You wanna see it?"

"That's rather forward."

"Just so you know where we sleep. That's all."

"No. I'm thirsty. Can I tempt you with something harder?"

"Sure."

He finishes the tea and packs away his notebook. Outside, she leads the way down Laietana. Her heels clack against the sidewalk, the sound of someone who knows where she's going. He sees a few people stare at her as they pass, not because she's particularly beautiful, but because the dress demands attention, a second, lingering look from a craning neck, from women mostly.

It's nearing midnight, but there are plenty of people on the streets, still rushing about. Buses, taxis, cars, bikes, scooters, skateboards, roller blades, even a pair of earphoned runners shouting conversation at each other. A whole city on the move when they should be pulling on pyjamas and climbing into bed.

She turns to him. "Are you banging the *Mad Men* fan?"

"Enora? No way. Not if she was the only girl in the Garden of Eden and God put a gun to my head and said procreate or else."

"She's been hanging around our area a lot, trying to spy, but she's terrible at it."

"She's on a mission."

"What kind?"

"Your kind."

"That's good to know. But I already told everyone to stay away from her."

"Good luck. She has ADD."

"That won't help with her spying. And isn't she a bit too old for that?"

"She's got the reverse. Her disorder is that she doesn't get enough attention. She has all these little habits that force you to look at her."

Anita laughs.

"I bet she was even there with her name tag on."

"She was. But I never bothered to look at it. I like her fashion style though."

"Again. ADD. Trying to get attention. A bit like you with this dress."

"This was a gift. I had to wear it tonight, to show the giver what it means to me."

"Who's that?"

"Moscow friends. Investors."

"I thought they were only interested in buying soccer teams."

"Russia is a potentially huge new market."

"I know."

They take a right down a narrow side street. It's very crowded, too noisy to talk. People gather in tight groups in front of a building with extravagant columns, arches and gilded balconies. A large statue juts out like the bow of a ship.

"What is this?"

She walks through the crowd, doesn't break stride, doesn't look back. He sees the back of her dress disappear down another narrow street and rushes to catch up with her.

"Hey, Anita. What was that?"

"The Music Palace."

"It's beautiful."

"Yes."

"Aren't we heading back towards the hotel?"

"I know a nice bar around the corner. I just wanted to show you the palace."

"It was the most breathtaking three seconds of my life."

"Be grateful. You wouldn't have seen it at all without me."

"I must've missed it last time."

"You've been here before?"

"You don't remember?"

"Help me. This way."

They take a left, going deeper into the labyrinth of the Barri Gotic.

"Boston. My heart. Under twenty-three."

"That was a great story."

"You didn't believe it?"

"Sounds like you did."

He stops. "It really happened."

"I thought it was your bit. You trying hard to show your sensitive side and impress me. I mean, come on. You meet this beautiful girl in, where was it?"

"Lagos."

"And you click from the first instance and travel together along the coast. She's free-spirited and funny and eccentric and wild, and you get all the way to Barcelona only for her old boyfriend to already be there and he proposes to her right in front of you. That sounds to me like a really bad romantic comedy. Banging the Bride, or something like that. Things don't happen that way in real life."

She starts walking again. He follows.

"What then?"

"Nothing that romantic, or that sad. People marry someone they meet at work. Or a friend sets you up. You don't meet the love of your life in some shabby pension in Portugal. And guys don't get down on one knee anymore. Guys only want to get married to prevent them from being dateless and lonely forever."

"It happened. You liked it when I told you in Boston. You went on about how people are supposed to meet, and that included me and Trina. And you said I was better off for having had the experience. You said it made me harder."

"Did you record our conversation?"

"I listened."

"Yeah? I didn't think guys did that anymore either. They're all on their phones, texting, emailing, surfing, always somewhere else in their heads. But you listen and pay attention."

"Not for everyone."

"Oh, I should be flattered."

"Yes. And you should believe me about Trina."

"You're telling it with even less conviction than last time. Here. This is it."

She leads him into a small bar. There's a handful of tables, all empty. They look like old school tables, small, square-legged and wooden. Three people are squeezed onto the sofa near a shelf of books. Sixties-era illustrated magazines are stuck to the walls; toothy, big-haired housewives aglow in tan and orange, holding cakes and finished meals towards the camera. Four glass cases have hand-made jewellery on display, and there's a round glass cooler with three different cakes inside. They take the largest table, in the middle, and sit at one corner. Under the table, their knees touch. He expects her to move but she doesn't. She even smiles at him.

The waitress comes over, looking bored, and seeming to wonder why they've come in. Anita orders in Spanish.

"A coffee? What happened to having something stronger?"

"I think I've had enough. Russians, they toast everything. And if you're going to listen so intently to my every word, I better stay sharp."

He orders green tea, with honey, and a piece of chocolate cake. The waitress drifts away.

"I gotta know, Joe. What's with the tea? You had that in Boston too."

"I like it."

She points at him. "That's what was in your bag."

"You did go through my stuff."

"I thought it was some weird Canadian grass. I was wondering how you got it across the border."

"My emergency stash."

"What's the deal with that?"

"It's good for the circulation. A litre a day."

"I drink double that in coffee."

"You don't drink tea?"

"Not since my grandma died. She always made it. Black tea, with two tea bags."

"The thing with green tea is that it can't brew for longer than two minutes. That's very important."

"Grandma let it sit forever. It was like drinking motor oil."

"And bitter, I bet."

She shrugs. "Everyone's got some quirk. Yours is tea."

"What's yours?"

The waitress puts the drinks on the table, along with a jar of honey. She puts the piece of cake between them. Joe picks up the honey.

"The real stuff. I like that."

Anita takes the long coffee spoon out of the glass, licks off the milk froth and attacks the piece of cake.

"Feel free."

"Hmm. Tasty. You don't mind?"

"No."

"I had a boyfriend who hated it when I ate from his plate. I kept doing it until he broke up with me. It took a while. I gained ten pounds in the process. He was weak."

"Can we not do that?"

"What?"

"Talk about each others' boyfriends and girlfriends."

She has another spoonful of cake. "You started it, with your star-crossed Spanish fable."

"You forced it out of me. The only other person who knows is Francois."

"I'm honoured that you told me."

"Well, no more."

"Joe, everyone has baggage."

He sips his tea. "Yeah, we've all got baggage, but it shouldn't make such a difference."

"It makes all the difference. Every relationship you ever had, every date, the girl who wouldn't kiss you in the second grade, even what your parents taught you, it all influences what happens when you meet someone. Let's take you. Heart broken in Barcelona, picking up strange girls in Boston, riding around on that manly motorbike. Who knows how many girls you've been through."

"Not that many, and not for very long."

"You never had a girlfriend? I don't believe you."

"I had girlfriends. It just didn't last."

"Your tea quirk annoy them?"

"Maybe. Something did. Or there was something about them that I couldn't stand."

"Such as?"

He uses the fork to get a morsel of cake. "That's good. I like this place."

"Keep it a secret. It would be awful to have half the conference in here."

"True."

"So? What killed your relationships?"

"I thought we weren't gonna discuss this."

"You started it. Again. You wanna know what I think? It can be big, it can be small, but if it bothers you enough, why not end the relationship. I had a boyfriend who pissed standing up, even when I told him over and over not to. He told me he didn't, but the whole bathroom stank."

"My dad taught me to sit."

"That's good parenting."

"Yeah, he taught me a lot of good stuff."

"Like how to avoid answering a question."

He sips his tea, has another fork load of cake. It's disappearing quickly, getting attacked from both sides. Fork and coffee spoon are set to clash in the middle.

"Fine. I'll give you the most recent example. It was our, sixth date, I think, and she kept answering the phone during dinner."

"So?"

"So we're eating, talking, whatever, and she's phoning and texting and always looking at the fucking screen."

"I'm sure you've done that, Joe."

"Not on a date, and never during dinner. There has to be some moments when you're free from your tech. I think it's rude to talk on a phone in public, especially when there are lots of people around. Why do we all have to listen to your conversation? What makes you so important?"

"If we can't be contactable, what's the point of having a cell?"

"People should be more discrete, that's all, respect others. Go into a telephone box, or speak more quietly. Don't stand next to me and shout, 'Yeah, Bob, I'm at the bar. Where are you?' Or worse, more personal stuff that I just don't wanna hear."

"But you have one."

"Have to. For work. I wouldn't have it otherwise. And it's always on silent."

She smiles. "You'd have one even if you were unemployed. Everyone has a cell. It's part of life."

"Not mine, if I had a choice. We lived a long time without them and I could do that again. Easily."

"We lived a long time without electricity too. Could you live without that? And aeroplanes, and television."

"And cars. I'm not big on cars."

"Why?"

"Too many reasons to list."

"Name two, and don't use the eco card."

"They create apathy and selfishness. They're the height of laziness."

"You've answered that before. I could taste the venom. What about flying?"

"Hate that too."

"The internet?"

"With a passion."

"Television?"

"That I like, but not reality TV."

"Then you're living a contradiction. You can't have one technology and then dismiss all the others."

"I know. But there's still a big difference between using technology and abusing it. Take these people with their hands-free sets, walking down the streets looking like they're having intense conversations with themselves. And we all have to listen."

"Stop listening then. If people want to be connected, let them."

He scoops up some more cake. "You grew up in Kansas, right? In the city?"

"Lawrence. College town. Not too big."

"When you were a little girl in Lawrence, Kansas, there were no cell phones. There was no internet. You remember?"

"We had all that in high school."

"Yeah, but before that. How did you contact your friends?"

"We phoned. We went over to each others' house. We met at the mall. At the park. Me and Gem, we had this ongoing thing where we wrote to each other in a diary. We both had a key. I would write something and then drop it in her letterbox or give it to her, and then she'd write something. And on and on until the diary was full.

Then we'd start again. I guess it was a very primitive and slow form of chatting."

"Or not-so-instant messaging."

"Gem's still got them all. She lives in Dallas now. Married. Two boys. Husband's a douchebag. I was in big D last year and visited her. We went through all the old diaries. My oh my, the things we thought were important then."

"You think girls still do that today?"

"Why would they? They can text and IM. Quicker and easier, more their thing."

"Yeah, but in twenty years..."

"I'm not that old."

"Figure of speech. In twenty years those girls won't be scrolling through old chat rooms or reading old emails. It'll all be gone."

She reaches forward, takes the last morsel of cake and leans back, the spoon upside down in her mouth.

"Now you see what I mean."

She takes out the spoon. "Maybe it's better that way. Some of the stuff in those diaries, it was embarrassing. I was so in love with Mr Palmer, the ninth grade art teacher. He's probably in his sixties now. But I'll say one thing. My handwriting was beautiful. I wrote everything in yellow and it was impossible to read, but only because of the colour. I seem to have lost that skill."

"Nothing's written down anymore."

She holds the spoon in her right hand like it's a pen. "I can't even read the handwriting of my assistant."

"How old is she?"

"He. Eighteen, I think."

"Do you recruit your assistants from kindergarten?"

"He's interning. A lot of the mid and lower level assistants are interns. Saves money."

"And you can treat them like dirt."

"Yes, but I don't."

"You do. Work them like slaves and then release them into the working world all jaded and ruined. And speaking of release, what is it, Anita?"

She looks into the bottom of her glass and spoons out the froth. "What's what?"

"Release."

"A teenage boy learning for the first time how to handle himself?"

"I'll tell you then."

"Go for it. It'll be news to me."

"It's the delete pill. Perfect for sufferers of anxiety and mental disorders, and for addicts."

"Sounds like it would be good for poor boys who had their hearts broken in Spain."

"It's probably just a tic-tac and it works because the package and marketing says it does."

"Oh, it's much more complicated than that."

"So, you do know."

"You need to get out of your microscopic booth, Joe. Everyone at the conf is talking about it. Rumour marketing."

Joe leans back. "Does it even exist?"

"Does it matter? Everyone is talking about Natrofield. That's the important point."

"But if there is no such thing, that'll really damage your company's image. No one'll ever believe anything you talk about."

"Well, right now, everyone wants to know what we're doing."

"But is it real or not?"

"You tell me."

"It would never get approved."

"The FDA? They don't look at half the stuff they stamp."

"You realise that such a pill would make a lot of other medicine redundant?"

She smiles. "That's why a pill like that would cost a lot of money."

"A vanity drug for the rich and famous."

"Or just for the military. If there was such a thing called Release. Still, it's good to be reassured that Denoris is nowhere near such innovation. I thought you'd be more interested in our progress with X-en?"

"With what?"

"The meeting you bombed in Boston. Sweet-Aid. We've rebranded it X-en. X dash E N. But pronounced like zen."

"And that will be the marketing strategy. Finding inner peace, getting in touch with yourself."

"You don't look it, but you're smart. There'll be a different name for kids. We're working on it. But, yes, X-en will be aimed at self-help. Lose weight, get control, empowerment, feel good about yourself."

"You've got a major market for that in your own backyard. America the obese."

She nods, then picks up the empty plate. "Shall we have another piece of cake?"

***

She rolls off him. "Multi-tasker."

"Huh?"

"You have sex with me and think about other things."

"I do not."

"I can see it in your eyes. It was the same in Boston. I'm just about there and you're putting together a to-do list. Milk, butter, eggs, feed the cat, water the plants, call grandma."

He laughs.

"It's not funny. It's a major turn-off. Did one of your exes dump you for that?"

"Maybe."

"Then, stop it."

"It's a trick."

"Sex is not about tricks."

"Let me tell you something, Anita. For men, it's all about tricks. The more smoke and mirrors the better."

She lifts the beige sheet and looks at his body. "You're not that small. Not huge either. Just above average."

"Why do girls think guys are insecure about their size?"

"It's important."

"It's not the length of the rope, it's how you swing it."

"Said the man with the small dick."

"I'm fine with how I am. It sounds like you were too."

"Not anymore. I'm not interested in tricks. I'm interested in you. You should be focused on me, and not doing your taxes or whatever."

"That's not my fault."

"Your dad teach you this trick?"

"I learned this myself, from trial and error. You don't understand what it's like for men. We're all expected to be absolute studs, you know, who can go on for hours and get the girl screaming for God in under a minute. And if we don't deliver, we'll be kicked out of the bedroom."

"You lasted pretty long."

"That's the trick."

She nods slowly. "Ah, distraction. You get your brain off the fact you're enjoying yourself to keep from coming too soon. You shouldn't have told me that."

"Too late."

"Must be awful being a dude."

"Only these days."

"How do you guys go through life with those things? Must be such a nuisance."

"Every guy has some kind of trick. If he doesn't, he'll blow his load in under a minute, like nature intended."

Buzz, buzz.

"That's yours."

He closes his eyes. "Forget it. It can wait till morning. Technically, I'm already asleep."

"You're really not a fan of that thing."

"My life would be so much better without it. The world would be better."

"How do you feel about the drugs you push?"

"Don't ask."

"You know, I'm having trouble predicting your responses, Joe. I normally know exactly what a guy is going to say."

"I'll take that as a compliment."

"Don't. If you want to be successful in life, you've got to be predictable, dependable, reliable."

"Like everyone else."

"Exactly. Only better."

"Sounds pretty boring. All these people out there striving to be the same as the next guy."

"I'm a realist. That's how it is."

"How do you feel about technology?"

"I like phones, and I love the internet."

He yawns. "That's like loving a cordless drill or a hairdryer. The internet's a tool. Sometimes useful, most of the time not."

"It has incredible power. You can mobilise an army in the blink of an eye, when it's used right. Start a revolution."

"It's a massive time waster. You sit down, check your email, and stand up three hours later and a few hundred dollars poorer. And probably less of a human being."

"If you don't like it, don't use it."

"I try not to, but I have to. Our whole life is communication. I couldn't work without the internet, or the phone."

"You need a different job then."

"When a company brings out a pill that helps people forget, then I'm definitely in the wrong business."

"Come work for us."

"Same shit, different pile."

"But more money, better products."

"Sorry, Anita. Evil doesn't course through my veins."

"Is this your bed banter? Sex tricks and complaining about the world? God, you Canadians are weird."

"I'm American, and half Australian."

"Yeah, a bit of everything. Someone who hates technology, but not all of it."

He looks at the glowing red of the alarm clock. "We better go to sleep."

She stands up, taking the beige bed sheet and wrapping it around her. "I'm not sleeping in this rat hole."

She goes into the bathroom. Joe pulls on his briefs and lies back down on the bed. She comes out, underwear on, toilet singing, and throws the bed sheet at him.

"You're fun. I like the whole strange bit you do."

"Thanks."

"That was from the heart. I don't say it to everyone. I hate most guys. They only want one thing?"

"Sex?"

She pulls that extravagant dress over her head and twists into it. "Commitment."

"What? For one night?"

She ties the dress at the side. "Let me tell you something about men, Joe. Once you're out of college, or even high school, you're looking for a mate for life. Always trying to find someone to replace your mother. The older you get, the more desperate your search becomes. And needy is not sexy."

"Maybe that's just been your experience. You're the catch of the century."

Her face drops. "Oh, don't you start with me. We've got a great thing going here. It's fun, it's easy, there's no pressure. I haven't felt at any point that you need me."

"I don't."

"Keep it that way."

"Huh. You don't believe in love and you don't want commitment. I'm sorry to tell you this, but you sound like nearly every guy I've ever known."

"I believe in love."

"That's not what you said in Boston. You said love was all about convenience."

She snaps her fingers. "Communist love. I told that to my friends. They loved it. Well, Joe, if I'm too much of a man for you, say so."

"I'm up to it, as long as you let me keep my tricks."

"I want to see you again."

"Tomorrow night?"

"Busy."

"I'm flying back on Saturday."

"Too bad."

"Yeah."

She comes around to his side of the bed and sits down. "Feeling adventurous?"

"Not at this very moment."

"Let's take a vacation together."

"I'm not going with you to Lagos."

"Oregon."

"My brother lives in Portland."

"You can visit him, after."

"I don't know, Anita. Maybe we should get to know each other first."

"Not so adventurous."

"I went from Europe to Australia almost entirely by land, when I was eighteen."

She shrugs. "Might be more of an adventure to spend a week with me in Oregon. Look, Joe, the best way to get to know someone is to take a trip together."

"I've had some bad experiences."

"More girls phoning during dinner?"

"Just bad choices. Ending up far from home stuck with someone I didn't like."

"You like me?"
"Yeah."
"Well, this is Oregon, not Spain. If it all goes bad, you can leave and go to Portland."
"When?"
"In three weeks. Can you swing it?"
"I think so. I've still got holidays owed from last year."
She stands up. "I'll send you the details."
"Where are we going exactly?"
"A surprise. But you'll love it, I guarantee it."
"I hate it when people say that."

In the wilds of Oregon with Stan, Miss Untouchable and Flower Power

He sits at the edge of the pool, feet dangling in the water. He wants that place, moving through the water, thinking just about the next stroke, the next breath, the next flip turn. Meditative swimming. In the groove. He thinks that if he gets to that place, he'll forget about Supe's suggested order that he treat his one week holiday as a company imposed suspension; and about Enora regurgitating the report he wrote on Release three weeks ago – sent only to Supe – in the Barcelona wash-up meeting; and about Supe and Enora's mocking laughter in response to his off-hand remark that Release could all be just an elaborate publicity stunt; and about Supe's bullying sarcasm that Joe went to Barcelona and all he came back with was the demand for a week off.

He could forget all that if he gets in the water and starts swimming. Just focus on the movement. One, two, three, breathe. That's it. That's the only thing that's important.

He puts in his ear plugs, shutting out the echoed shouts of the pool attendant, the kids yelling as they throw rings in and dive for them, the old ducks in floral caps talking as they breaststroke so slowly they're basically treading water. All muffled. He hears his heart, feels it. His swim cap is stuck together. He carefully pulls it apart and snaps it on, pushing the back of his hair underneath. The band of his goggles is starting to whither, just slightly, and will need replacing soon. He spits in them and rubs the lenses with his thumbs.

Supe, he thinks. Denoris. Natrofield. Oregon. Anita. Cheryline. Gordie. Ma. Len. Max. Joe.

He gives his head a shake. "Stop it. Swim."

He puts his goggles on, pressing them in place and drops into the water. He farts, giggling as the bubbles hit the surface, getting the warm flash of seven twelve year-olds crammed into the end of the lane and all farting at once to give the illusion of a Jacuzzi. Scott had to get out because he crapped his pants, and ran to the bathrooms with both hands on his arse.

He laughs. "Still funny."

The fast lane is empty. There are a few heads bobbing up and down in the pool, a couple of strugglers beating their arms and legs madly and getting nowhere, but no one good enough for the fast lane. It's his.

He pushes off from the wall and dolphin kicks underwater, his arms extended and hands clasped together. He reaches the surface and begins his stroke, long and slow, letting his body ease into the motion. Picking apples, climbing ladders, reaching for the cookie jar, sweeping the arms in an S, like they're canoe paddles. All those things he can't remember being taught but will never forget; movements that are programmed into his body. The best way forward is simply to focus on the stroke and let the rhythm take over. Don't try, don't force, don't struggle. Go through the water, because the water is your friend.

He thinks about work: Enora getting all the credit for Barcelona, himself on death row, the others in the team ganging up on him to get some good accounts and projects from Supe, even Xav using him to score some points.

He hits the wall, flips, dolphin kicks and heads back. One.

He thinks about the flight back from Barcelona: the scunge, grime and sourness of the journey; the sneer of check-in attendants blithely announcing delays and hidden costs; the suspicious, profiling glares of security personnel, convinced no pocket is empty; the sticky seats and abandoned newspaper of the departure lounges; ten euros for a bottle of water and a sandwich made and packaged half a world away; the smell of feet and acidic breath on the plane; half the people freezing and the other half sweating and opening vents for cold air; the post-meal gatherings around the tiny bathrooms, people sticking their butts in your face; the punishment of sitting next to Enora, watching her pound white wine and Dozoxin and then listening to her snore; and every single person standing up before the seatbelt light is turned off and reaching for their phone.

He hits the wall and flips. Two.

From Barcelona to Frankfurt to Montreal, with empty seats only in business and first, travelling back in time; from the spacious flights, stand-by tickets and hassle-free airports of his late teenage, pre-9/11 odyssey to today's cramped, line-infested world of annoyance, impatience, selfishness and sweaty fear. All these people travelling together – somehow able to afford it in times of financial crisis – but not quite willing to accommodate each other. Exit row seats, extra leg room, three carry-on bags, longer bathroom times, controlling the arm rests, these have become things worth fighting for.

It's a week ago, but still all fresh. Let it go. Just swim.

He sees the black T on the bottom of the pool and prepares to flip. But there's a man standing in the middle of the wall, his legs spread, filling the lane, making it impossible to execute a turn. Joe's forced to grab the small section of wall next to the lane rope and turn the old-fashioned way. The plastic discs of the lane rope scratch against his back as he spins his legs underwater. But the man pushes off from the wall at the same time, puffing and snapping in a wild breaststroke, his legs kicking wide enough for his toes to nearly touch both lane ropes. He shakes his head as he goes, just keeping it above the water, and breathing so loudly Joe can hear him through his plugs.

There's no possible way around and he's forced to trail behind, just kicking. The only chance is the wall, or the guy drowning. Better, he thinks, and more likely, is that the guy only has one lap in him. It certainly looks that way. As they near the wall, the guy's legs sink with each kick, so he's swimming almost vertically.

Joe moves to left side to get around, but the guy slaps the wall with both hands, like he's in a race, and pushes off again. They almost collide.

"Outta the way!"

Joe reaches into the water and grabs one duck-kicking foot. The guy struggles to free himself, kicking madly like a trapped animal. He splashes water at Joe.

"What the fuck? Lemme go."

"'Fast swimmers first. Those are the rules."

The guy kicks free. "I don't see no sign. Pass me if you're so freaking fast."

He takes off again, fighting the water, even slower than before, head shaking, filling every inch of the lane. Joe slips under the lane rope and goes back to the wall.

"Idiot."

He pushes off, dolphin kicks again and breathes only on one side until he passes the guy. He flies past the old woman breaststroking, almost swimming over her she's so slow. He gets to the wall and flips.

He manages five laps until a hand reaches into the water in front of the wall and stops him. He looks up. The attendant thumbs towards the next lane. The old woman is standing next to him, smiling victoriously and so shrivelled and wrinkled she looks like she's been in the pool all day. A white prune held together by a lavender one-piece.

"Fast lane."

"Get that incredibly slow guy outta there and I will."

"He's fast enough."

"Is that a joke? You'll have to rescue him in a minute."

"Fast lane or get out."

Joe goes under the rope. "If he even touches me, I'm suing."

"Yeah, right."

He sets off again, swimming angry, making himself tired, and going slower because of it. There's no chance to get a rhythm. He constantly has to look out for the other guy, who gurgles and chokes through maybe ten laps. Passing him means basically swimming under the lane rope. When he passes, he feels the force of the water the guy's killing himself to move. It even seems like the guy is trying to kick him.

When he sees Francois at the wall, he stops.

"Hola."

"Hey, Francois."

"How's the water?"

"Forget it. This guy's fucked the whole thing up. I hate breaststrokers."

"What guy?"

He looks down the empty lane. To the side of the pool, he sees the paunchy guy waddling towards the showers, hands on hips, blowing out breaths, proud of himself, strutting even.

"Sorry, I'm late."

"Well, you're here now."

Francois smiles. "Let's swim out that stress."

"Yep. Remember, straight arm, reach as far as you can, from the shoulder."

"Righto, coach. What are we in for?"

"Five hundred free, hundred kick. Then, we'll do some medleys."

"You mean you will. I'll stick with plan A."

***

Francois drives and Joe gives everything to beat him. He arrives just as Francois gets out of his car.

"You're quick."

Joe opens the door to his building. "Lot of traffic tonight. Slowed you down."

"Yeah."

"You've given up riding already?"

"Too dangerous, especially during Sunday evening rush hour."

Joe puts his bike over his shoulder and hauls it up the stairs.

Francois follows. "I hope you've got some beer."

"Went shopping yesterday. And I bought some nachos, just for you."

"Good man."

Joe opens the door to his apartment. He leaves the bike in the hallway and quickly hangs up his swimming stuff in the bathroom. When he comes out, Francois has two beers open on the table, with a few nachos spilling out of the bag.

They sit.

"Cheers, Joe."

"To soft landings."

"And meets meant to be."

"You like that."

They drink.

"It's given life a whole new purpose. I'm looking at everything differently. Finding connections everywhere."

"Not all of them positive."

Francois takes a handful of nachos, cupping them in his right hand and eating with his left. "Did you hook up with her?"

"I got A in B."

"Hah. And?"

"We only had one night together. The conf was all-consuming."

"Still got a job?"

"For now. I scored a big contract with a German distributor. On the last day. Enora tried to take credit for it, but my name's all over it. And they only want to deal with me."

"Congrats."

"Yeah? I think getting fired would be the best thing that could happen to me right now."

"Careful."

"Why?"

"The universe might swing it to make that happen. What'll you do then?"

"No idea. Anita said I could work for Natrofield."

"The dark side."

"Yeah, in Boston."

"No way. I don't do long distance relationships. And you're under contract as my swimming coach."

"You're getting better. Technique's really improving."

"I can't do those medleys you do."

"I could teach you."

"Man, freestyle's hard enough. But it's so weird. The harder I try, the slower I am."

"And the more tired you get. You look at the great swimmers and it looks like they're coasting through the water."

"The Aussie in the evil Spiderman suit?"

"Ian Thorpe."

"That's him."

"There's a better example."

Joe flips open his notebook and turns it on.

Francois sits back, still feeding himself nachos. "So? Anita. Sounds like she's trying to get you to move to her hood."

"Maybe. We're going away together first."

"Uh-oh. Where?"

"Some place in Oregon."

"You sound very excited."

"Yeah, well, I gotta confess, it's not what it should be. I like her, but I feel like I should really like her."

Francois sips his beer. "She's everything you could possibly want, but you're not feeling it."

"Yep."

"Damn."

"Yep."

"Are still gonna go away with her?"

Joe taps at the keyboard and manipulates the track pad. "Yep."

"To Oregon."

"Not sure where exactly. She said it's a surprise."

"Oh, she's spontaneous too. It's an absolute shame you feel nothing for this girl."

"Maybe the holiday will change that."

"I don't think so."

Joe turns his notebook towards Francois. "Here. The Russian."

The video is grainy, the sound bad.

"When was this?"

"Perth. End of the nineties, I think. The hundred final. That's him in lane five. Look at him. No cap, just a pair of Speedos."

"Face cut from the square Russian mould."

"Watch."

"He doesn't even look like he's trying."

"Look at all the water the other guys are splashing. And this wasn't long after he was stabbed. The guy was a freak. All technique."

"Is he the reason you started swimming?"

"Ma was a swimmer. She got offered a scholarship, but her father wouldn't let her take it."

"Bastard."

"Yeah, he was. Real old school. Republican too. He died when I was in Sydney. Ma said I didn't have to come back for the funeral."

"How's she doing?"

Joe reaches across the table and hands Francois a postcard. "Read it. There's nothing remotely personal in it."

"She wants you to visit."

"Good thing she doesn't know I was down there a couple of weeks ago."

"If the universe wants her to find out, she will."

Joe laughs. "Now you're stretching it."

"Click on the other Popov video. The training one."

Joe does so.

They kill a couple of hours watching various videos.

***

Buzz. Buzz.

He reaches out and turns off the phone's alarm. He rolls back and stares at the ceiling, tracing the copper pipes to the doorway. Popov jumps up onto the bed.

"Morning."

He strokes the cat. Popov purrs.

"Can you call in sick for me?"

He staggers into the bathroom. He shits, shaves and showers, savouring all the comforts of the familiar: the grooves of the toilet seat, the inconsistent hot water, the towel that has only ever touched his butt and balls. He pads into the kitchen with that towel tied around his waist. He turns on the kettle, waits, and makes a pot of tea. He takes this and a bowl of muesli to the table and flips open the notebook. Someone named Anastasia Rudanski has asked to be a ceevillian and has written on his billboard, if he's willing to accept her citizenship. He does.

"'Gigi's Coffee House, Ashland, next Sunday, 2pm, come alone.'"

He opens a map of Oregon, locates Ashland down near the border with California, clicks away a bunch of pop-ups advertising hotels, rental cars and single girls in Oregon, and finds Gigi's on Will Dodge Way. He reads a couple of reviews, clicks away more pop-ups, then goes back to the map, zooming out to see the 101 he rode from Los Angeles to Port Angeles.

He books a flight to Portland and finds a company out near the airport that rents motorbikes. He gets all the confirmations sent to his phone. No printouts, no tickets, no paper, no sitting in travel agents. All done in five minutes.

He finishes the muesli and refills his tea cup. On Plasher, he starts a pond: "I hate breaststrokers."

He writes: "You take up space, get nowhere slowly, swim like you're alone. GET OUT OF THE POOL."

He sits back, sips his tea and watches all the anonymous people from all over the world join the pond. Opinion is divided. Some agree with him and others shout him down and abuse him. Each person is using all of the eighty-eight characters allowed, sometimes carrying sentences over from one plash to the next. Arguments ensue, playful and cheeky at first, but soon resorting to the usual invective, bullying and insults.

He turns his computer off and dresses, stuffing a tie in his pocket. He does his hair, finds his sunglasses and packs his notebook into his satchel, along with some fruit. He oils the bike chain, shoulders the satchel and, with a sigh, locks his apartment door.

***

"Fuck me swinging."

Gordie initiates their one-hand-clasp-forearm-against-shoulder-rap-mogul hug.

"What the hell, bro?"

"I'm here to surprise you."

"Fucking straight. I'm officially surprised. Come in, come in."

Joe edges into the apartment. It's a mess, but no more so than the last time he was here. He thinks the apartment is exactly like the inside of Gordie's head: chaotic, indulgent, selfish, careless, unsatisfied, juvenile. The list could go on with an adjective for every item he steps over, every shoe and toy, every chewed straw.

"Where's Richie?"

"Fuck knows. Class."

"It's Saturday."

"Maybe he's snoozing in the library."

"Beautiful day for it."

"Yeah?"

Joe drops his backpack on the floor and puts his helmet on top. He leans his satchel against the pack and takes out his stash of tea.

"What's with the hard hat? You bang Eddie all the way here?"

"I rented a bike out near the airport."

"Style. What you get?"

"A plastic Suzushi."

"I wanna take it for a tear."

"Get your own."

"You're never gonna let that go, are ya?"

"You nearly killed her, Gordie."

"She's half mine."

"I'll buy you out."

"It's not about the fucking money."

"You could use it to get a cleaning lady. How do you live in this dump?"

"It beats that sterile ICU you live in. Where every little thing has its place and can't be moved."

Joe goes into the kitchen. "You could use it to buy a dishwasher."

"That's Richie's fault. He always cooks."

"What do you do?"

Gordie leans against the kitchen doorway, crosses his arms. "Take out."

"That's good for you. You want some tea?"

"Fuck no."

Joe locates the kettle behind three dirty pots stacked on top of each other and a pile of greasy pizza boxes. "Got a tea strainer?"

"A what?"

"Something to strain tea."

"Maybe Richie's got something like that."

Joe eyes the shelf as he rinses and fills the kettle. The shelf is sagging in the middle: cans of soup, instant macaroni and cheese, a massive bag of rice. Next to the coffee machine he finds a box of coffee filters. He puts some leaves in a filter and then tears the ends and ties them together.

"What're you doing here, bro?"

"I'm here to see you. On vacation."

"You need it. You were one stressed out dude in H-brook. I even slipped a little something in your drink to loosen you up."

"What?"

"It worked. Only problem was it wore off."

Joe rinses a cup in the sink, just getting it under the tap. The sink is piled high with dirty plates, bowls and cutlery. It's been there so long, it's all stuck together, and alive.

"That's the last time I give you any free samples."

"You should be thanking me. You were the biggest downer at the wedding."

"Len had that covered."

"What do you do in Montreal that stresses you out so much?"

"That's life, Gordie. You'll learn soon enough."

"No way."

Joe drops the filter in the cup and, with the kettle boiled, fills the cup with water. A few leaves escape, but it does the trick. "I better take you shopping."

"I know how to shop."

"You mean you know how to pick up the phone and order."

"Fuck, Joe. Can't you check all that stress at the door? Don't pollute my crib with it, aight."

Joe takes out the filter and drops it in the garbage. "Actually, I feel really relaxed. I think you're the stressed one and you're reflecting it all onto me. You all right?"

Gordie rubs his eyes and bends the visor of his purple Lakers cap.

"Yeah. Under a bit of pressure."

"From?"

"The semester's nearly dusted. One year left."

Joe sips. "So?"

"What the fuck am I gonna do?"

"What do you wanna do?"

Gordie rubs his nose with the palm of his hand and sniffs. "What would you do?"

"Me?"

"Why'd you go into the pill game?"

Joe shrugs. "I wanted to live in Montreal, so I applied to companies there. I got lucky."

"Fucking lame."

"I didn't wanna work, but I figured that if I had to, I should at least work in a place that interests me."

"Boring, but logical. But it doesn't matter where you live, you still get up and go slave for someone else."

Joe sips and nods. "I think it matters where you live. It makes everything else bareable."

"I can't involve myself in all that crap. Suits, meetings, deadlines, profit margins. What's the fucking point? I see the dicks downtown and I don't wanna be like them."

"Is this what they're teaching at college these days?"

"My prof says I should do an MBA. He said I need to. Ma said she and Len can bankroll it."

Joe talks into his cup. "With the house that dad built."

"What?"

"Nothing. Do the MBA."

"Fuck that. Look what dicks with MBAs have done to the world. Anyway, everyone's got one, so they're worthless."

"You like it here?"

"Nuh."

"What about your friends?"

"They're moving away. You know, planning their careers, lining up summer internships, doing MB fucking As. What a waste of time. They'll end up like you, stressed out and working twelve hours a day."

"What about Australia?"

Gordie shakes his head. "Never interested me."

"Huh. How come you didn't say any of this at ma's wedding?"

"You looked like your brain was fried enough. I wasn't gonna add to it."

"I'm listening now."

"For how long?"

"I gotta be in Ashland tomorrow."

"Ah, great. I'm just your fucking stopover before you hook up with some ho in Ashland."

Gordie walks out of the kitchen. Joe finishes his tea, waits, then follows. He finds Gordie on the small balcony. The wire railing is rusted and broken. Gordie is slouched in one of the battered fold-out chairs. He pulls the visor of his cap over his face. Below, South West Pine is snarled with traffic. Joe can hear a consistent hum coming from the nearby Naito Parkway.

"Look, Gordie, I organised this trip so I could see you. We could've gone anywhere, but I said Oregon."

"Fucking straight."

"I mean it. It's always good to see you."

Joe sits down in the other fold-out chair. They look at the building opposite. Through one window, he sees two kids jumping and swinging their arms as they play a computer game with wireless controls. It looks like bowling, or maybe tennis. He wonders why they don't go outside and actually play tennis.

"Ashland's a cool place. Going to Crater Lake?"

"That's the plan. I hope the weather stays like this."

Gordie flips the lid off the cooler box next to him. He pulls out two cans of beer and hands one to Joe. They click them open.

"Who's the chick?"

***

He starts early, leaving Gordie asleep in that festering mess. Richie stumbled in at some point during the night, turned on all the lights and put on music in the living room, waking him. He apologised drunkenly, but then went into the kitchen to fill the apartment with the smell of fried onions and eggs, singing as he cooked and ate.

It's an easy out, south on the Naito Parkway and then straight onto I-5. There's little traffic. The Suzushi's full of zip, even if it feels like there's nothing between his legs: no character, no personality, no weight, no temperament. It's just a machine, one of a million off an automated assembly line. He can ride it with one hand.

Highway 101 is definitely more picturesque, but he doesn't have time for winding detours, or to stop in Salem, Albany, Eugene, or any of the other towns that come up as names on a sign.

The miles tick over. His back hurts. He misses Eddie.

He stops for gas in Grants Pass, wanting a full tank, unsure of what will happen in Ashland. Will she even be there? He's made good time from Portland and so dawdles over lunch at Maude's Riverside Cafe. He sits outside, facing the sun, and thumbs through the Saturday edition of the *Daily Courier*. The SUVs, pick-ups and trucks roar over the nearby bridge. The other diners look like they're in church clothes. He works his way through a salad with smoked turkey breast, a pot of green tea, a piece of homemade cheesecake with blueberries on top, and the *Courier*, even glancing at the want ads and thinking about Gordie.

"Just don't move to Naples, Stan."

Back on the I-5, he decides that Gordie has a point. He's been trying to rationalise it the last few months, and that's kept him going, but he wants to quit. It's time for a change, for radical change. Time to get control.

He wonders what the hell he could do other than take a job with another pill company.

The Ashland exit takes him down Main Street. There are tree-covered hills to the south and plenty of trees on Main. Banners hanging from streetlights advertise the Oregon Shakespeare Festival. Down the side streets, he gets glimpses of nice houses with compact, manageable gardens. It's clean and pleasant, an ideal place to be newly-wed or nearly dead, as Max would say.

He regrets not having come here three years ago, and wonders what other sights and towns he missed by sticking to the 101.

He takes a left on Pioneer and then a right on Will Dodge. He finds Gigi's. It's closed.

He gets off the bike, shrugs off his backpack and satchel and all the other gear, and stretches.

"They're renovating."

He turns around. "Hey. So, it wasn't all some crazy set up."

"You thought I wouldn't show?"

"Maybe you're out for some twisted revenge against the male population."

She takes off her sunglasses and smiles. "After all these years of being tricked. I think I could come up with something more punishing than Gigi's in Ashland. Shame they're closed. Great muffins."

He feels he should kiss her hello, but for some reason doesn't think it appropriate. That big hat she's wearing also makes it difficult to get close to her face. He keeps his distance.

"You got the vacation time."

"I did. It's been retooled as a quasi suspension. I've got a week to get my act together."

"You don't sound very motivated."

"I'm not."

She comes towards him and takes off her hat. She kisses him on both cheeks.

"You smell like an old exhaust pipe. How long did it take from Montreal?"

"I flew to Portland and rode from there."

"But it's the same bike."

"Eddie would be very insulted to hear that. How did you get here?"

"Flew to Medford, via San Fran. Taxi here."

It's then he sees the carry-on suitcase on the sidewalk, a large handbag looped over the handle.

She perches the hat on top. "We should have communicated better. I thought you'd rent a car."

"I've got the bike. But we won't get all that stuff on it. And I don't have another helmet."

"So?"

"I don't know what the law is here."

"I had a boyfriend in high school who took me to Kansas City on his bike. We went up and down State Line Drive, no helmet on one side and a helmet on the other. He thought it was hilarious."

"The simple folks of Kansas. Forget *Jersey Shore*. Lawrence is the reality show people would watch."

"I hate *Jersey Shore*."

"Me too."

"I thought you loved TV."

"Not all of it. And not reality crap."

She puts her sunglasses back on. "Do you have a phone?"

"You don't?"

"Give me yours."

He hands it to her. She takes a piece of paper from her handbag and dials. "Hi, this is Anita Rudolph. I've got a booking for two cabins for a week...That's right...Look, we've got a problem. We're stuck in Ashland. Is there a pick up van or a courtesy bus?...Okay...Thanks."

She hands back the phone.

"And?"

"Not very helpful. She said there's a public bus, but only one or two on a Sunday."

"How far is it?"

"About an hour."

"Hitch-hike."

"Are you joking?"

"I'll wait with you, and I'll follow right behind you when you get a ride."

"No way. I think I'll rent a car. I'll have to get back anyway."

Joe shakes his head. "Not so adventurous."

"There's adventure, and then there's stupidity."

"I saw some rental chains on the way into town."

"I'll get a taxi. You follow."

"I hope they're open."

***

They take Dead Indian Mountain Road. It winds through a landscape he had forgotten existed. Forests and hills untouched by humans, or touched long ago and then left alone. He saw a lot of this in Australia. Not this green, but more unspoilt, more wild and desolate; land that hadn't been ruined by the endless search for profit, or marked out and claimed as prized territory and then bled dry.

There's nothing on the road. No towns, no houses, no traffic. A few signs point down narrow roads, promising a village or a campground, but they don't look appealing. They look like the roads from a B-grade horror film, when the car breaks down and the characters wander into the woods looking for help only to be sliced in half by a chainsaw wielding hick or hung on meat hooks by a man who sleeps with his mother.

Anita drives fast, accelerating out of the corners, pushing the Floptima to its limit. Trailing close behind, he smells the burning clutch. The Suzushi is more than a match, but he lets her get ahead, to make her feel she's a fast driver and he's struggling to keep up.

She sticks to Dead Indian. Signs point to Howard Prairie Lake, then to Lake of the Woods. The water looks enticing. He wants to stop, shrug off all this gear and jump in. But the Floptima hugs the next corner and whirrs away, as Dead Indian becomes Falls Highway. Finally, she takes a left down a narrow track. There's no sign. Because of the dust, he has to keep his distance. The track winds down towards a blue lake and a scattering of cabins. Cars are parked around what looks like the main building. Anita slides the Floptima between two tanks, the hybrid filling of an SUV sandwich. He brings the Suzushi to a halt and gets off. It's a joy to take off the backpack, satchel and helmet. He stretches and groans.

"We should've put your stuff in the car."

"Yeah, well, too late now. Where are we?"

"In the wilds of Oregon."

Joe runs his hands through his helmet-flattened hair and tries to spike up the fringe. "Sounds like the title of a fantasy book."

"I always wanted to write a book."

"Everyone's got a story, but not everyone can tell it."

She leads the way towards the building. He picks up his stuff, then holds the door open for her.

"I could tell it. A young girl goes to New York to become an actress and after a series of setbacks she finally makes it only to fall in love with her high school sweetheart and move back home."

"Still sticking close to the truth?"

She rings the bell at the counter. "I just need a catchy title."

"In the Wilds of Manhattan."

"Lame."

"Okay, then. How about Broadway Wilderness."

She nods and smiles. "I like that. Clever."

"Good afternoon. Can I help you?"

Anita turns to the receptionist. "Hi. We're booked until Saturday. Here's the confirmation."

"Welcome to Rusticity. Did you find us all right?"

"I've been here before."

"You called from Ashland. We're glad you made it in the end."

"I rented a car."

"That means you can do some touring. There's a bunch of parks that are worth visiting. Here's a map."

Joe unfolds it. He traces the route they took from Ashland, gets an idea of where they are. "Is this us here?"

"Yes."

"Can you swim in the lake?"

"I've seen a few people going in. There's a polar bears swim at dawn, if you're game. That's five dollars for the map."

He pays.

"Here are your keys. We'll need your phones, computers and any other technology you have with you."

"Excuse me?"

The receptionist holds out her hand. "Rusticity is a tech-free zone. Your phone, please. And computer, if you brought one. Music players, video games, pocket radios. Anything you've got."

He turns to Anita. "Why didn't you say anything?"

"And ruin the surprise?"

He puts his phone on the counter and takes his notebook out of the satchel. "What happens to it?"

"It's safe here at reception. You get it back when you leave. That's why you're here, isn't it? To disconnect to reconnect?"

Anita picks up the keys. "That's why we're here."

"Enjoy your stay. The restaurant opens at six."

He follows Anita down the path towards the cabins. The lake shimmers between the trees.

"What is this place?"

"A retreat."

"No phones, no tech. What's that about?"

"There's nothing in the cabin either. No TV."

"What'll we do the whole week?"

She stops and looks at him through her massive sunglasses. "Get to know each other. Here. I'm gonna take a bath. See you for dinner at seven."

She drops a key in his palm and continues down the path.

"Where are you going?"

"To my cabin. This is a retreat, Joe, not a resort."

"More like a monastery."

He unlocks the door and edges inside. It's cold and dark, the cabin cast in the shadows of the surrounding trees. There's a thermostat near the door, with a small remote control attached to it. He turns the heat on.

"That counts as technology."

The cabin is just one long room, like a trailer. There's a large single bed in the middle and an armchair facing the window. The only lights are lamps, with two flanking the bed and another on the small table next to the armchair. He turns them on. Everything is made of wood, even the lamps. No pictures on the walls, no decorations. A door to the right opens into the bathroom, which, he's surprised to see, has a large bathtub, raised from the floor on old-fashioned feet.

"What does that cost?"

It's then he starts to tally up the furnishings and accoutrements: the plush towels hanging from the heated rack, the row of branded toiletries, the three vanity mirrors. He does some accounting in the main room as well: the thick down cover, the four plump pillows, the carved wooden arm-rests of the armchair, the rolled up yoga mat leaning against the wall, the large basket of fresh tropical fruit. They haven't talked finances yet, but he's sure he's paying his own way. Hers too?

He unpacks, gets organised and uses the bathroom. He puts his swim gear in his satchel, along with a towel, a banana and a plump Clementine. Outside, he hears the clack-clack of a woodpecker beating against a trunk. Above the canopy of trees, he sees a few birds gliding in circles and figure eights.

He breathes in and out.

The twigs and sticks on the path rustle underfoot as he heads down to the lake. The other cabins all look unoccupied, or their occupants are out enjoying the day.

It's very quiet.

At the lake, he can hear the two fishermen talking with their backs to each other in a dinghy about 200 metres from shore. He rolls up his jeans, kicks off his shoes and walks into the water. It's warm in the shallows, but drops a few degrees with each step he takes.

"Maybe there's a pool."

He sits down on a bench. The wood is varnished and untouched: no graffiti, no carvings of undying love.

He wonders where all the people are. Maybe they can't handle being tech-free for a week.

He wonders how Supe will react when he's not always contactable as agreed. This suspension has become solitary confinement.

"Good."

He wonders what all this is going to cost him. His most expensive holiday yet and he'll go home to no more pay checks.

He wonders how to tell Anita he's not that into her. No tricks needed now.

He wonders how many calls, messages and emails he'll miss in a week. It's not what he's missing that bothers him; it's the time it will take to go through everything in a week from now.

He bites into the banana and chews.

He wonders where the banana is from. It's delicious, actually tastes like a banana.

The sun slices through the trees and warms the back of his neck. He closes his eyes and breathes. The air tastes of nothing. No smog, no exhaust, no urgency, no over-breathed air, no recycled air. Nothing. He hears the two fishermen celebrate a catch.

The sounds of footsteps make him turn and look. A group of runners pass, various body types in various states of disarray and struggle. Only their leader, a small, wiry girl, is bouncing with energy, running around and between the other runners to get them going.

"Iris?"

She turns and waves. "Hi, there."

She continues running.

***

They face each other, sitting opposite at the one long table. Other people are sitting alone or in twos, scattered up and down the table. Conversations are hushed. The background music is whale song.

She sips her red wine. "What do you think?"

"I like it."

"Really? You look a little jumpy. Restless."

"I'm just worried about my job. I have to be contactable during vacations."

"What kind of a vacation is that? You might as well be at work."

"That's how it is for us. Weekends too."

"That's awful. You never get any distance."

The waitress appears. They both order the trout. Joe also orders a green salad, with no dressing.

"We can both pick from it."

Anita nods and leans forward, elbows on the table, chin resting on her hands. "Who are you, Joseph Solitus."

"To start with, I'm not Joseph Solitus. I'm Jonah Solitus."

"Oh, I just assumed..."

"Everyone does."

"You Jewish?"

"No."

"But you're snipped."

"Yes."

"That must really hurt."

"Fortunately, I don't remember."

"Maybe there's some deep trauma buried inside your subconscious. You look like someone who carries around a big hurt."

He leans across the table, feeling he's come this far he might as well play the game, or at least look like he's playing. "What's your preference?"

She raises her eyebrows, then turns and looks out the window. Joe looks too. Outside, the forest is slowly darkening to a liquid green. The wind makes the branches ripple like the waters of a mountain river.

"I don't like cover ups. You know, like there's something to hide. Besides, it looks better. Neat, trimmed, ready for presentation."

"Maybe you should write your book about that. You sound like an expert."

She whispers: "Foreskin Wilderness."

"The sequel to *Brokeback Mountain*."

She laughs. "But back to you. You're not Jewish, but you're called Jonah. Isn't there something in the Bible about him?"

"There's the Book of Jonah, but everyone remembers the whale."

"He got swallowed."

"And we've got the right soundtrack for it."

"Maybe they're singing about it. Maybe it was the greatest moment in whale history."

Their meals arrive. The waitress puts the salad next to Joe's plate, but he moves it into the middle of the table. He dresses it with olive oil and balsamic vinegar.

"That was fast. Looks like they've got everything prepared."

"And for you the roles are reversed. Jonah swallows the fish."

"Can we stick with Joe?"

"Why?"

"Only two people have called me Jonah."

She points at him with her fork. "The Spanish tramp. And the other?"

"How's your trout?"

"You should know."

"Every fish tastes a little different. Mine is really fresh. I think I was watching the guys catching it earlier. Here."

She takes the flesh of his fork. "Tastes the same. Try mine."

"Pass."

"Come on. I'm disease free, I promise."

"You put lemon on it."

"So?"

"I'm allergic, remember? Homemade lemonade. With honey, not sugar. Something I've missed out on."

"Ah. I didn't believe you."

"Why would I lie?"

"I don't know. To be interesting. To be different from everyone else."

"Trust me. I can't have lemon, and Spain happened."

"I learned the hard way not take everything men say as the truth."

"That's a great attitude. That makes us all liars."

"Until proven otherwise. You men, you're always stretching the truth."

"Everyone does. You did."

"I'll give you that. So, who else called you Jonah?"

He chews some trout and swallows. "Max. My dad."

"He live in Montreal too?"

"No."

"Where then?"

He takes a sip of wine, forcing it down. "He's dead."

"I'm sorry. What happened?"

"Heart attack. You want some more wine?"

She holds up her glass. "You gotta love California plonk. Woah, that's enough. Trying to get me drunk?"

"You don't need my help for that. What about your parents?"

"Split. After Mandee was born. My kid sister."

"How old were you?"

"Seven."

"Huh. Crap."

"It happened to all my friends. Sara Tomlinson, her parents stayed together and we all thought she was a freak. But she had God on her side and that didn't help her quest for popularity."

"You miss it?"

"What, school?"

"Lawrence. Your family."

"No. Okay, sometimes. It's, you know, simpler there. And I don't mean that people are backward and stupid and sitting on the porch cradling shotguns and drinking moonshine. The life, it's simpler. They all don't seem to have that much to worry about. What?"

"I'm with you. I also grew up in a small town. It was great. I couldn't imagine being a kid in Montreal."

"Or Boston."

"Or Barcelona. That place was mad. I needed ear plugs to sleep."

"All the demons in the Mayola keeping you awake. All those Denoris employees who OD-ed."

"The ghosts of conferences past."

They both eat some more. He looks around. The remaining diners are all sitting alone. Some are reading books, one has a newspaper, another is writing madly on a yellow legal pad. One girl is just staring out the window, knife and fork poised over her plate. He thinks they all have the hairstyles, clothes and demeanour of city-dwelling professionals. There's no sign of Iris.

"Is that why you come here?"

She nods. "At least once a year, to recharge."

"Why don't you just go home?"

"There's more stress there. I've been gone too long. They're so used to me not being around that they don't know what to do with me when I'm there."

"Who's they?"

"Mom and Mandee. She's at KU."

"Studying?"

"Working. In admin. We didn't have the money for college, and me and Mandee weren't smart enough to get scholarships. My dad never paid for anything. His alimony checks bounced like basketballs."

"Bastard."

She shakes her head. "No, he's not. I like him. We keep in touch. And I don't blame him. My mom, she's, difficult. Says she's manic-depressive, but you and I both know that just helps to get more powerful prescription drugs. I'm too scared to ask her if Mandee got her name subconsciously or as testimony to mom's suffering."

He laughs.

"In the end, I ran away from her and I can completely understand that he did too."

"But he ran away from you as well."

"It was hard for him, so he says. He lives in Tuscon, don't laugh, in a trailer."

"You visit?"

"Couple of times."

"What about your sister?"

"Not even once. No contact. She's too much like mom. Thinks her name is her excuse as well."

"You their dealer?"

"I keep telling them that all the drugs they take won't help. They need to change their lives and their attitudes, not their prescriptions."

"Placebos with massive marketing budgets."

"See? You know how it is. But they're hooked. When I saw my dad, I realised I was a lot like him. How is it with you? I'm gonna guess that you're more like your mom."

"Wrong. I'm just like Max. Gordie's like ma, but the interesting thing is he's nothing like Max."

The waitress comes up to them. "Would you folks care for dessert?"

Joe nods. "I'm on vacation. Why not? Did I see waffles on the menu earlier?"

"You did. With cherries and cream."

"Sold. With a cup of tea."

Anita smiles. "I'll have a bite of his, and an espresso."

The waitress takes their plates away.

"Won't that keep you up?"

"I hope so. But back to you. How old was Gordie when your dad died?"

"Uh, ten."

"There's your answer."

"Maybe, but he doesn't look like him. He's already losing his hair."

"You will too, one day."

"I hope not. Max had a full head of hair."

"Why do you call him Max?"

"I always did. Ma said it was my first word."

"I think kids shouldn't call their parents by their names."

"Suddenly you're an old-fashioned girl."

"It doesn't sound right."

"I liked it. I always thought of Max more as my older brother. I think he liked that too."

"Were you close?"
He nods.
"Must've been hard."
"As it was when your dad left. All kids suffer somehow. Even Sara whats-her-name whose praying parents stayed together."
The hot drinks and waffles arrive. The heat of the waffles melts the cream and the cherries ooze between the squares.
"Thanks."
Anita watches the waitress walk away. "Bless her soul for bringing two forks."
He takes a mouthful. "Hmm, it's really good. Fresh. Not powder plus milk. Made from scratch and right off the grill. I think the chef knew we were coming."
"You fancy yourself a bit of a connoisseur, am I right?"
"What I don't like is food that's not fresh, and stuff that's fake. Like the salmon in Boston. Wasn't fresh."
She gets a red, yellow and white fork full. "Good waffles in Montreal?"
"Probably. The best I had was in Germany."
"Eating away your heartache."
"Spain was after."
She sips her espresso. "You like Germany?"
"Sure. Why not?"
"Because of the history. All those bad guys, none of them snipped."
"All the Germans I met were really nice. Genuinely nice and not superficially nice like us Americans."
"Why Germany?"
"It was the only flight I could get. It was all spontaneous. I went to Logan, bought the ticket and got on the plane."
"Very adventurous."
"Also pretty stupid. I just wanted to get away."
"Was that after Max died?"
He chews, the cream suddenly tasting bitter. "Yep. Whew, that didn't last long. Shall we have another round?"
"Better not."
"I saw a group of runners this afternoon. I might tag along tomorrow."
"Go for it. I'm going to just do yoga, read, eat and sleep."
"Are there classes?"

"You do it?"

"Sure. For years."

"There's a program on the desk in your cabin. All the activities on offer. The first class is at eight, I think. It was last time."

"Pre-breakfast yoga. Great."

"There's a mat in your cabin."

"I saw it already."

She smiles. "So you listen and pay attention. I think I'm starting to find out just who Jonah Solitus is."

"Joe."

"Aw, can't I join that elite club?"

"It's very tough to get in."

"Well, Joe, maybe I can earn my stripes by kissing better the scars of an earlier wound."

***

The birds are making a racket, calling from tree to tree, trying to outdo each other. He opens his eyes and blinks. Silver slithers of morning light are coming through the gaps in the curtains, cutting swathes like lasers at a rave. When it hits the furnishings, the tan wood gleams. He reaches for the bedside table and feels the cold metal of his watch.

"Oh, crap."

He sits up too fast. A pair of evil hands yank at either side of his spine. He manages to get to his feet, groans, and straightens himself out.

"A swim would sort that out."

He opens the curtains. There's dew on the grass, and a few of the lower branches drip with moisture as well, making him wonder if it rained last night. If it did, he didn't hear it; dead to the world in a dreamless sleep. The sun is out, but still low, and through the gaps in the trees he sees blue sky so pale it's almost white.

Colonel Mustard is lying on the desk, on top of the activities program, the black tongue of a label poking out.

"'Love your tricks, Jonah. See you for yoga.'"

He cuts the label and drops it in the small trash can under the desk.

The wooden floor is warm underfoot. He takes the wrong door to the bathroom and discovers a small pantry kitchen. There's a coffee machine and a miniature microwave.

"More technology."

He takes the pot into the bathroom, swills it a few times and fills it with water. He pours it into the coffee machine's reservoir and turns it on. The water immediately starts to gurgle. In the bathroom, he pees, long and strong, flushes, and splashes cold water on his face. The plush towel catches at the hairs of his three-day growth, leaving small bits of cotton he brushes away with his hands.

In the main room, he sits at the desk and eats a banana, listening to the birds and the gurgle of the coffee machine. The machine starts to win, filling the cabin with the noise of a cheap motor boat fighting the current. He retrieves his stash from his satchel and fashions a coffee filter into a tea bag. He drops this in the pot and watches the sencha leaves slowly tinge the water a reddish green. There's one cup, not much bigger than an espresso cup, a matching saucer, a tiny spoon, various sugar options, and a few small packets of ground coffee. He uses the spoon to fish out the filter and takes pot and cup to the desk. He pours, sips, and pours again.

He looks at the activities program. On the top it says "Exercise your soul."

"That's good. That's what we're here for. No tech, no contact with the outside world, and probably no job when we get back."

He picks up the Colonel.

Click, whirr, click, whirr.

He cuts the label, peels off the back and sticks it to the front of his satchel. He drains the cup, pours another, and drains that. Two gulps and it's gone. He pulls on the one pair of shorts he brought, slips on a t-shirt and opts for sneakers with black dress socks. He looks in the mirror and smiles.

"Unprepared."

He unfolds the map, sips, pours and sips. The next town that's more than just a blip on the map is Klamath Falls, twenty-odd clicks south-east.

The tea finished, he tucks the yoga mat under his arm and closes the door behind him. Outside, a few other people are carrying mats towards the annex of the main building. One man with a Tintin haircut joins from an adjacent path and they end up walking together.

"Morning."

"Morning."

"You off to yoga as well?"
"No, I'm going to hold up a liquor store with this."
Joe laughs. "I'm bear hunting."
"Haven't seen you around."
"Just arrived. Yesterday. You?"
"Been here a week."
"And?"
The man chews his gum sourly. "I'm going crazy. No internet, no TV, no phones, not even a freaking radio. The dull capital of the world."
"Why are you here then?"
"Boss sent me. A couple of my deals went sour."
"What do you do?"
"Financial analyst."
"For who?"
"Can't say. One of the big ones."
"So greed isn't good?"
"Keep your money out of the market. Guys like me will cost you all your hard earned."
"What was the damage?"
"A bigger amount than you could imagine. So many zeros it'd make you freaking dizzy to look at."
"You're in exile. Laying low."
"Very low. See the guy behind us?"
Joe turns. A block-headed man in a tracksuit and sunglasses is following about twenty metres behind.
"My minder. Preventing escape."
"That bad. He do yoga too?"
"He does everything I do. He even takes a dump at the same time."
"I'm Joe."
"Dylan."
Joe takes his right hand out of his pocket, but Dylan continues carrying his mat with both hands, to the side a little, like it's a rifle and he's on the hunt.
"What are you in for, Joe?"
"I was brought by someone else. I had no idea what I was getting into."
"But you're free to leave."
"Yeah."
"Do it. Cut out before the boredom makes you homicidal."

They enter the building. Dylan leads the way through the small gym and into an all-purpose studio, which already has half a dozen people in various poses on their mats. They all look sleepy and check the mirrors with sideways glances, patting down hair and adjusting clothing. Conversation is hushed, if spoken at all. The soft sounds of waves crashing and gulls squawking come from the speakers. There's a few spinning bikes pushed against the wall and a punching bag hanging from the ceiling in the corner.

Joe unrolls his mat and sits on it. Dylan takes the space next to him and lies down, knees bent. The minder gives the punching bag a solid one-two and also takes his place on the floor. A few more people come in and the room starts to feel full.

Joe holds up a hand. "I'm sorry. I'm saving this place for someone. She'll be here in a minute."

The girl unfurls her mat and sweeps it into the air like she's laying a picnic blanket.

"Uh, excuse me. It's taken."

She sits down cross-legged and pulls her hair back into a severe ponytail. "Yes. By me."

Dylan laughs and sits up. "What's your name?"

The girl turns away from them and starts stretching, bending and flexing, but never holding the stretch like you're supposed to.

Joe mumbles to Dylan: "Serene Bitch. That's her name."

The instructor enters and takes his place at the front of the room. "Okay. Let's find our centres."

***

"Does he talk?"

"He hasn't said a word to me all week. Ask him?"

"Do you talk?"

"No, I'm a moron."

Dylan laughs. "See? There's the problem. I don't speak moron."

"I'm Joe."

"Marcus."

They shake hands across the table.

"So, that's your name."

"You guys spent a week together and you didn't even ask his name?"

Dylan shrugs. "He never told me."
"You never asked."
"Well, excuse the fuck outta me. How do you engage in simple pleasantries with someone who's guarding you?"
"You're free to leave whenever you want."
Joe sips his tea. "Ah, I get it. If you leave, you're out of a job."
Dylan nods.
"Well, you might as well enjoy it. It's really nice here."
Dylan spreads jam on his toast. "And do what?"
"Take a hike."
"Did it."
"Join the running group."
"Running's for overweight secretaries."
"Sit in the sun and read."
"Didn't bring anything."
"I'm going to Klamath Falls today. I could you bring something back."
Dylan turns to Marcus. "Is that all right?"
"Sure. I would've gone too, if you'd asked."
"You tell me this now?"
Marcus smiles into his bowl of fruit and yoghurt. "Again, you never asked."
"So, we could've had a drink together, gone bowling, caught a film."
Joe laughs.
Dylan pulls out his money clip. He takes off a hundred. "I want all the *Wall Street Journals* from the last week. A couple of tit mags, some hard core stuff. I've been beating it to *Town & Country*. And a book, I guess. And something strong to drink. Cognac, maybe. And a couple of good cigars."
"What kind of book?"
"I don't care. Whatever everyone's reading."
"You want anything, Marcus?"
"I'm all set, Joe. But thanks for asking. It's really nice to have someone around who's polite enough to ask, and to talk."
Dylan holds up his hands. "I didn't know communication was allowed."
"You guys are like a couple."
Marcus shakes his head. "He's not my type. Too greedy and selfish."
"You're pushing it, man. You don't scare me."

"Are you sure about that?"

"When I'm back in my groove, I could ruin your life with one phone call."

Joe drains his tea. "Well, I'll leave you guys to enjoy your new found communication. I'll bring the stuff by your cabin later."

"It's lucky number eight. If you bring a bomb, he's in unlucky number nine."

Joe stands up. "See you later."

"Later."

He takes the narrow path back to the cabin, the crushed brick crunching underfoot. A woman shuffles past, Nordic walking sticks digging into the path with intent. He sees Serene Bitch meditating under a large tree. The wind swishes her ponytail and blows her bangs forward. She swiftly tucks these behind her ears, keeping her eyes closed.

He knocks on the door to Anita's cabin, but there's no reply.

***

The town feels like a movie set, with only the fronts of buildings and everything built in haste to be easily torn down and removed. Even the activity on the street – the greetings locals give each, the waving from lowered windows, an apron-wearing guy sweeping his storefront with an old-fashioned straw broom – seems contrived and scripted, and reminds him of all the actors populating Seahaven in *The Truman Show*.

"Your favourite film."

The Suzushi is out of place among the pickups, SUVs and dirt bikes. It even sounds foreign. People stop and watch him as he passes, a modern day outlaw cruising into town on a Japanese horse.

He has a cup of tea and a piece of apple pie in Mabel's on Main. Mabel herself, her name badge yellow and faded, her wrinkled right claw permanently attached to the coffee pot and constantly swilling it, tells him there's a big sports store out on Midland Highway, owned by Jerry.

"Books? Try Bob's in Altamont. He'll be in there somewhere."

"Thanks."

"You're welcome, honey. Some coffee?"

So he gets his running shoes and some sporting attire, and with the directional help of a few sceptical and suspicious locals, he finds Bob's. Inside, the books are stacked to the ceiling in a disorderly fashion, making it impossible to look through them quickly or grab at one that interests. He decides on a copy of *City Boy* for Dylan. The first twenty or so pages are ruffled and dog-eared, but that's as far as the reader got. He asks Bob if he's got any older stuff.

"How far back? Homer?"

"No, no. Graham Greene or Hemingway."

Bob eyes the book Joe's holding. "Sure that's your kind of stuff?"

"Just because it's older, doesn't mean it's not good."

Dusty Bob, his face brown with age, like the pages of a book left open in the rain and sun, cracks a smile. "This way."

They go into the back of the shop, sometimes having to slide sideways between the stacks of books, which are teetering precariously, set to fall with the slightest shove.

"I put the new stuff out front. That's what everyone wants, you see. Like that trash you've got in your hands. Those who still read, that is."

"This's for someone else."

"I hope so. I always say, a good guide for choosing a book is if it's got the word bestseller on it, avoid it like the plague."

"I prefer the older stuff."

Bob stops at a low shelf. "Here."

"Thanks."

"Take your time."

Bob shuffles back towards the front of the shop.

He's read most of them, and smiles as he recalls the varied joys the books brought: the warm sand of Bondi Beach where he did the reading, the hours wasted perusing fleamarkets and secondhand bookshops. Good memories, but sad too, all those days and nights in lonely Simple Sydney, from the shared house in Clovelly to university to Bondi, like he was a ghost, invisible, undetected.

He settles on a tattered, stitched hard cover of *The Razor's Edge*.

At the counter, Bob picks up the book and gently opens the cover. "Did you ever read his short stories?"

He nods. "My dad had them all. He used to read them to me before bed."

"Better than *The Cat in the Hat*. Can you believe Maugham? He went to the South Seas when they were still eating people. Imagine."

"What's the damage?"

"Nineteen fifty."

He pays, drops the change in the jar for the Altamont Little League and wishes Bob a good day. He rides back along Sixth to Klamath Falls, stopping to buy a current issue of the *Journal* and some porn for Dylan. There's a computer in the shop.

He points at it. "That got internet?"

"No. We're living in the dark ages. Sure. High speed."

"How much?"

"Five an hour, but let me go out back and start pedalling first."

He considers it, wonders what he's missing and fears for his job. The bigger problem is his phone, but he could send an email to Supe and explain the situation. And he could clear his other emails, check up on ceeville, and then there's the breaststrokers pond he started on Plasher.

"Wanna use it or not? No porn. I've got that blocked. Anyways, you've got enough here to last a year."

"That's not for me. It's for a friend."

"Yeah, it always is."

"Look, uh, I'll come back tomorrow."

"Suit yourself."

He gets a few supplies from the supermarket next door and rides back along Falls Highway in bright sunshine, the straps of his backpack pulling at his shoulders.

Close to Rusticity, he takes off his helmet, while riding, and lets the wind blow through his hair as he roars the Suzushi over the hundred mile an hour mark.

***

He works his way to the front of the group.

"Iris?"

"That's what the name tag says."

"I'm Joe. Solitus."

"You're not very fit, Joe Solitus."

"I haven't run in ages."

"It looks like that."

He strains to keep up with her. "I work with, with your brother."

"Which one?"

"Xavier. In Montreal."

She looks at him. "We know each other?"
"Yeah, from Xav's birthday party last year."
"You the swimmer?
"Yep."
"I thought swimmers had lungs of steel."
"Lungs, yes, but, but not legs."
"And your shoes are right out of the box. I bet they're hurting."
Reminded, he feels the blisters on his little toes. "They are."
She runs to the front of the group and then turns and jogs on the spot. "Come on, people. The turnaround is just up ahead."
She waits for the runners to pass. Dylan is tripping over his feet and pounding the ground to match it with Serene Bitch, who prances like a ballet dancer, lifting her knees high and only using the front of her feet, as if she's leaping over fallen logs or tiny streams. It appears she learned how to run while doing the ribbon routine of rhythmic gymnastics. Dylan's face is red and he runs like he's about to fall head-first onto the ground.
"This is killing me, man."
"Keep chasing that carrot."
Joe lets Dylan get ahead. Marcus passes as well, looking relaxed, barely breaking a sweat. Joe and Iris run side by side at the back of the group. Blessedly, she slows her pace.
"You know him?"
"Who? Dylan? We met this morning on the yoga mat."
"He's been hitting on me all week."
"Looks like he's found another tail to chase."
"I guess I should feel lucky."
"Yep."
"What did we talk about at Xav's party?"
"Sports. Uni. Life. You were pretty bored so I tried to amuse you by, by making up nicknames for everyone at the party."
"Hah. That was hilarious. Do it again."
"I've already got a few. The girl with the ponytail, that's Serene Bitch. Tennessee Tintin is chasing her."
"Is that where he's from?"
"He had a bourbon and coke for breakfast."
"What about the girl with the monstrous chest up front."
"No-carb Supporter. I thought of that while we were stretching."
"Everyone was looking at her, but I don't get it."

"She looks like someone who goes in for strange diets. Like, like no-carb or raw food or all juice. And you saw her rack."

"What do you think that cost her?"

"More than her self-esteem is worth."

"You'd think with that kind of money she could buy herself a sports bra."

"Right. No garb. No clothing. No carb, no garb, and in desperate need of all kinds of support."

"Ha. Cool."

They catch up to the group at the bridge. Dylan is on the ground, lying on his back, knees bent, his chest pumping up and down. A few others are hunched over with hands on knees. Serene Bitch is facing the water, one hand on her belly and the other just below her throat; still trying to find her centre.

Iris calls them together and leads them through a few stretches. Joe helps Dylan up.

"Forget it."

"What?"

"Her. Irene."

"Iris."

Dylan puts a hand on Joe's shoulder as he stretches a quad. "A canucklehead."

"You don't like her because she's Canadian?"

"Cold as their winters, eeehhh."

Joe tilts his head towards Serene Bitch. "She warmer?"

"She just needs the right incentive. Girls like her, they pretend to be in complete control, like to think they are. No, they don't need men, and they don't want our attention. But offer her the right incentive, the right prize, and her legs will part like the Dead Sea."

"The Red Sea."

"What?"

"Moses parted the Red Sea."

"Nuh. Dead Sea."

"You wanna bet?"

Dylan licks his lips. "You sound sure of yourself, Bible boy. Better not. I think I'm still running an unlucky streak. Anyway, there's no way to find out."

"Maybe Serene Bitch is a church goer. That could be a way to start a conversation."

"Yeah. Might also give me a hint at her incentive. Maybe Jesus is what she needs."

"I don't think so."

"Me neither. I smell career. She's probably some lowly team assistant with no chance of promotion. Had a fling with someone in the office, someone higher up, trying to fuck her way to the top, but it didn't work out. She just got used. And she quit and came up here to get away from everyone and strategise her next move."

"She say all that on the run?"

"Doesn't have to say anything. All the signs are there."

"What'll you do, offer her a job?"

"More analysis is required."

"If you can keep up."

Iris claps her hands together. "Right. It's all downhill from here. Let's go."

The round of groans makes her laugh.

"Come on. Just think about how good it will feel when you're back."

She leads the way down another path, this one taking them into the forest and away from the lake they had followed from the start. It's cooler under the shade of all the trees.

With difficulty, Joe works his way to the front. "I thought you were at UVic?"

"I was."

"What happened?"

"Taking a break."

"Xav never said anything about that."

"He doesn't know. And it's going to stay that way, right?"

The force of her glare almost knocks him off his stride. "Sure."

"Xav doesn't know the first thing about me. He thinks he does, but he's way off."

"He doesn't know much about me either. He's mostly focused on himself."

"He never listens."

"Unless you call him on the phone."

"You got a name for him?"

"It's a bit mean."

A couple of people from the group pass, running single file. Iris keeps to Joe's pace.

"Let's have it. I'm sure it's deserving."

"The Multi-tasking Procrastinator."

She laughs. "Oh, that's good. That's right on. Doing all these things and getting nothing done. Getting nowhere. Like a hamster in a treadmill. And dreaming of tomorrow. I can't wait to call him that."

"No, you can't. He doesn't know, and it's going to stay that way, right?"

"I'll say I made it up."

"He'll know it's from me."

"So he does know something about you."

"Yeah."

They run for a while in silence.

"What are you in for, Joe? Nervous breakdown?"

"I was brought here by someone else."

"A female?"

"Yeah."

"She's not running."

"Haven't seen her all day."

"Maybe she left. A lot of people don't make it to the second day. They miss the tech too much."

"Really?"

"It's pathetic. They think the world can't possibly go on without them."

"Maybe they've got obligations. Maybe they don't want to be left out."

"Whatever. Popularity requires full attention."

"Huh?"

"That's what it's all about, isn't it? Being popular. Being liked. And getting popular and staying that way takes work and commitment and time. Especially online popularity."

They reach a clearing. The cabins start to appear in the gaps between the trees. A few more runners pass. Serene Bitch is putting on a burst of balletic speed, intent on getting there first: knees high, elbows pumping, prancing like an uncoordinated gazelle trying to outrun a lion. Joe looks behind. There's no sign of Dylan.

"So, you don't care about being popular?"

"I have my friends. That's enough."

"You don't miss the tech, being here?"

"I've got my phone."

"How come?"

"Us employees can have as much tech as we want. You're the ones trying to get away from it."

"Can I use it?"

"No."

"Forget it. I don't need it. I was in Klamath Falls this morning, saw a computer and didn't even use it."

"But you thought about it."

"Hard not to."

"Stay here, then. The feeling will pass."

"I'm going to."

"How long are you booked in?"

"Till Saturday."

"Your girlfriend too?"

"She's not my girlfriend, but yeah."

They reach the grass area near the annex. A trolley has been set up with water bottles, towels and a bowl of green apples the size of softballs. The runners crowd around it, taking a bottle and towel and drinking right next to the trolley, preventing others from getting close. Serene Bitch is walking in tiny circles, breathing heavily, now trying to create a centre after failing to find her own.

Iris stands in the middle and claps. "Great run. You've earned an afternoon sitting by the pool. Same time tomorrow."

The other runners slowly start to disperse. Joe sees Dylan walking across the grass, his arm around Marcus's shoulder and being supported by him.

Joe smiles. "I swear. They're gonna fall in love before the week's over."

Iris comes up to him. "Wanna take a swim?"

"Lake or pool?"

"Pool."

"How big is it?"

"I don't know. Maybe ten metres."

"All right."

"You can show me your form."

"I'll sink to the bottom."

"Don't worry. I'll dive in and rescue you."

Joe takes a towel and two bottles of water from the trolley. He hands a bottle to Iris.

"Thanks. You did that at the party too."

"What?"

"Got me a drink. And some food."

"Xav told me to look after you. Because you didn't know anyone."

They take the path around the annex, Joe walking gingerly.

"You look like you're suffering."

"I am. Baby feet."

"Xav told you to take care of me? I think he just didn't want to be responsible for me. Typical Xav."

"He means well."

"He only cares about himself."

"He cares about you."

"When it matters to him. He hasn't called me in ages."

"Call him."

"That's not how it works in my family. You can't just call to say hi. There has to be an ulterior motive. There has to be something you want from the other person."

They get to the pool. Anita is lying on a sun chair, looking fetching in a black and yellow bikini, her face hidden by her enormous hat and sunglasses.

She lowers her book. "I knew I'd find you here eventually. Who's this?"

"Iris. She leads the running group. Iris, this is Anita."

"How's it going?"

"I've found my happy place."

"Well, I'm gonna take a swim. You in for the run tomorrow, Joe?"

He looks at Anita. "Not sure. My feet and legs are screaming no. We wanna hit some of the parks too."

Iris pulls off her running shorts and shirt and kicks off her shoes. "Crater Lake's a must."

Joe sits down on the sun chair next to Anita. He groans.

Iris dives into the pool, pops her head up and freestyles to the other end.

"She can swim."

Anita holds her book in front of her face. "I'm jealous."

"Don't be. We know each other already."

"Small world. I guess you've left old flames burning in lots of places."

"Way wrong. She's the sister of one of my colleagues."

"Sounds believable."

"Why don't you ever believe what I say?"

"You give me selective truths, and selective lies. It's difficult to decide which is which. I'm erring on the side of caution."

"We should get married. Then you can passive-aggressively torture me like this for the rest of my life."

"Not into commitment. Where have you been all day?"

He takes a long drink and starts untying his shoelaces. "Yoga. Breakfast. I went into Klamath Falls to do some shopping. I knocked on your door at various times this morning, but there was no answer."

"I slept till noon. Then I managed to get myself to the pool. Nice, isn't it? You can do some swimming."

He watches Iris get out. She's very skinny, but not in an unhealthy way. She wraps a towel around herself, picks up her clothes and heads for the annex. She doesn't look in his direction.

"It's too small."

"Pool's a pool."

He gets one shoe off. "Ow. What are you reading?"

She holds the cover towards him.

"Oh God, not you too. That's required reading for anyone without a Y chromosome, isn't it?"

"So you should read it too."

"How is it?"

"Fun to read, total mommy porn, but it sets feminism back about a hundred years."

"Back to the grey ages."

"Ha."

He gets the other shoe off and manages to peel his socks from his feet. Both pinkies are red and his heels are raw. "How did Max do this?"

"What?"

"Nothing. I'm gonna take a swim."

He takes off his shirt and jumps in. He does a couple of lazy laps, without even swimming. It's enough to do a flip turn and then dolphin kick underwater to the other end. The shorts make him feel like he's swimming in a tent. He stops and hangs his elbows over the edge of the pool. He sees Dylan sit down next to Anita.

"What's your name?"

***

"Hey, you decided to join us again."

"I needed a few days for my feet to recover."

"Haven't seen you around, day or night."

"Do you prowl the grounds at night?"

"Sometimes. Sleep trouble."

"Huh."

She pushes against the wall to stretch her calves. "The animals were out last night, especially in cabin eight."

"Tennessee Tintin figured out her price."

"What?"

"Serene Bitch. Dylan's being trying to nail her since Monday. I guess he worked out what she wanted."

"Why should she want anything from him?"

"There must be more to it. Dylan's not exactly an attractive man."

She crosses one leg in front of the other, bends forward, her hands flat against the ground. She's lean, taught and sinewy. "Are they coming?"

He wants to pull at those tendons above her knee, strum them like a guitar. "Probably not."

She talks to the ground as she stretches her very flexible hamstrings. "What did you do the last few days?"

"Had a look around. Crater Lake, Wildlife Refuge, a few other places. I borrowed a bicycle helmet from reception."

"Great. Where is your...travelling buddy?"

"She left. This morning."

Iris straightens. "Just like that?"

"Yep."

"She leave a note?"

"A label."

"A what?"

"I've got this old label maker, you know, with a dial that's got letters and numbers on it. You make labels to stick on things."

"What did it say?"

"Two words. 'Natro calls.'"

She pulls a foot behind her to stretch a quad. "You've lost me."

"I guess she had to go back to Boston for work."

"Which means she was contactable, somehow. Maybe she kept her phone in her car. A lot of guests do that, when they know what they're getting into."

"Doesn't that defeat the purpose of being here?"

"Very much so. Are you gonna stretch?"

He starts copying her, calves, quads, hamstrings.

"How's it been so far? Be honest."

"I struggled the first couple of days, but now, I could live like this forever. I'm gonna have a thousand mails when I get back, and probably no job, but at least right now I'm not a slave to technology."

"So don't go back."

"It's not that easy."

"Sure it is. Stay here, get a job. Easy, eh?"

"Doing what?"

"Dishwasher."

"Pass."

She snaps her fingers. "Swimming instructor. Summer's coming. You could be responsible for water sports."

"It's a great idea, but I'd still have to go back first, to sort everything out."

"You don't wanna stay."

"But I am gonna keep this going in Montreal."

"Running?"

"Yeah, and the digital diet."

"You won't last a day, unless you completely withdraw from society and go live in a hut somewhere. The world won't let you go no tech, not even low tech. You'll have emails for work, your friends will send texts, and you'll use the internet without even thinking about it. You'll go straight back to where you were before. You're hardwired, programmed."

"Maybe so, but I can control my own use. I'm not gonna waste time on ceeville or Plasher or watching stupid videos. From now on, the internet will be a tool, and not something I spend half the night on."

"What about the phone?"

"That's no big deal. I never use it much anyway. I hate them."

She starts swinging her arms from side to side. "I'd like to know how you progress."

"I'll send you updates."

She gives him a cheeky grin. "How?"

"By post, telegram, carrier pigeon. I'll figure something out. Maybe I'll pick up the phone in my apartment, my old land line, and call you."

"Do people still do that?"

"It's easier to text, isn't it?"

"See? There's your problem. You can't disconnect because everyone around you is connected. You're stuck."

"You're not helping."

She checks her watch. "Looks like it's just you and me."

"Where is everyone?"

"A lot of people leave on Friday. Their companies only pay for the working week."

"Huh. Everyone here on a paid vacation?"

"Sure. Remember what I asked you on day one?"

"If I'd had a nervous breakdown."

"That's how most people end up here. The high powered execs flip out from working hundred hour weeks and get sent here to cool off. They stay four or five days, sneak into Klamath Falls to use the internet, make calls from their cars, and then leave to be back at work on Monday. I'm guessing your Boston skank was here on company funds as well."

He laughs. "Boston skank. Sounds like a disease."

"The whole no tech thing here, it's just a gimmick. A hook."

"A USP for the marketing department."

"Right. It's just a resort. The no tech thing gives it an angle that separates it from the competition. All the guys that come here are just Dylans at various ages and with various weight and health issues. The girls are like what's-her-face, Serene Bitch. All of them getting away in order to get back."

"I guess that includes me as well."

"I don't think you were as bad as all them when you got here. You're already way ahead."

"Thanks, Iris. I'd like to believe that."

"You're on the digital diet. Keep it that way. Prove everyone wrong. Easy, eh?"

He looks around. "Sounds like it."

"What are you up for? The punishing route or the brutal track?"

"Is there a third option?"

"Traumatising terrain."

"I think I'll take brutal. It sounds the least damaging."

She claps her hands together. "Follow me. And try to keep up."

They run past the deserted pool, then take the winding path down to the lake. She sets a fast pace. He's breathing heavily by the time they reach the water.

It's a warm morning. She takes off her shirt, tucks the ends into the back of her shorts and runs in just a white bikini top. He feels a pang, something old pulling at him inside. That surfboard chest with the sternum jutting out like a diving board. The flat stomach that makes him feel chubby. The ease with which she moves across the ground, lightly, effortlessly, like her feet weigh nothing, running pigeon-toed.

"Didn't your mother teach you it's not polite to stare?"

"Sorry. You look like someone I used to know."

"A good connection, I hope."

They follow the water, keeping the lake on the left. The path is wide enough for them to run side by side. They run for a while in silence.

"All right?"

"Yep. Is this the brutal part?"

"Not even close."

"How can you be so fit?"

"I play hockey at UVic."

"Ice hockey?"

"Both. Field in summer, ice in winter. I'm the only one on both teams."

"I'm impressed."

"Don't be."

"You miss it?"

"The competition, yeah. But not the training, or the injuries. People give girls sports such a bad rap. They have no idea how tough it is. We train against guys and no one leaves anything in the bag during games."

"I think I'll stick to swimming."

"For fun or do you race?"

"Used to. I didn't like the training either. Six in the morning before school, every morning."

"Harsh. But you gotta want it."

"I used to have rings around my eyes until lunch. They called me Lemmy."

"Why?"

"Cause I looked like a lemur."

"What a great nickname. Lemmy."

"Like the guy from Motörhead."

"Is that your biker gang?"

"It's a band."

"Never heard of them. BC or AC?"

"Huh?"

"Before Cobain or after?"

"Before, and after. They're still around. Lemmy looks like something rock'n'roll chewed up and spat out. My dad had a couple of their records."

"CDs."

"No, records. LPs."

"Is your dad, like, a hundred?"

"He never bought any CDs. We used to go record shopping in Boston."

He feels another pang, something else pulling inside him. Flipping through albums at fleamarkets, the dusty smell of boxes left in basements, Max forever able to pull a diamond out of the rough and bargain well for it. Then Gordie telling him so blithely he'd sold all the records on eBay; the ones he hadn't sampled and scratched into oblivion.

"They take up too much space. So do books."

"I like books. And I like records. The covers were fantastic. And Max always took his time putting the records on, you know, wiping the dust away and telling something about the band. It was great."

"Who's Max?"

"My dad."

"Sounds like he's from another century."

"He was. And so was the music. It sounded incredible. Before everything went digital and you could make a CD with just a computer and some talentless waif. The Rolling Stones, the Beatles, Led Zeppelin, Otis Redding, Bob Dylan, Bowie, Jethro Tull. Fantastic stuff, and it sounds so, so real."

"Never listen to that old stuff."

"You should. Especially the Beatles. They changed the world. And it all still stands up. Do you really think we'll be listening to Lady Gaga and Justin Bieber in fifty years?"

"Probably not, but that's not the point."

"Most people can't remember who won *Idol* last year."

"This way."

They take a short hill, leaving the lake. He runs behind her, watching her tight arse pull and flex the spandex. The tendons running from her hamstrings to her knees are thick and perfectly straight. *Parallel Lines*, Blondie. He sees that she's not wearing socks, but there are traces of white powder around her heels. *Cocaine Blues*, Johnny Cash.

"Were you any good?"

"At music?"

"In the pool."

"I think I didn't have the necessary killer instinct. There were other guys who looked like they needed to win more than me. You know, their parents screaming from the stands."

"You just let them win?"

"Sometimes, yeah."

"Weird."

"I got offered a scholarship, but I didn't take it."

"Why not?"

"It wasn't right. And I was sick of swimming. I went to Australia instead, studied there."

"Nice. I'm gonna go there after I'm finished. Working holiday."

It's cooler under the shade of the trees, but they soon come down the other side of the hill and get onto a road leading back down to the water. There's a small bay scattered with tiny islands. The water glistens in the sunshine. He thinks of Spain, of running barefoot along the beach.

"Beautiful day."

"Sure is."

"The weather always like this?"

"Don't know. It's my first spring."

"When did you get here?"

"November."

"People come in winter?"

"They come all year, when the company pays. There's plenty of stuff to do. Cross-country skiing, snow-shoeing, stuff like that. There's more wildlife, too."

They run on the road that follows the water, skirting the bay and taking a stretch of land that extends out into the lake, like a finger. A dog comes from nowhere and chases them for about a hundred metres, barking and snapping at their heels. Iris manoeuvres herself so that Joe is always between her and the dog.

"Can we take a break?"

She quickens her pace to lose the dog. "In a minute. We're nearly there."

"Where?"

"Brutal Beach."

"I'm not sure I wanna get there."

"Yeah, you do."

The road becomes a path and then that narrows to nothing. She picks her way between the trees, again very light on her feet, following what look like animal tracks. She skips ahead, until she's just a flash of skin and white among the trees. She stops at a clearing, beckons to him, then disappears down the side. When he gets there, she's standing on a small beach, shorts and shoes off. She looks like a cross-dressing twelve year old boy.

"Coming in?"

"Definitely."

He scampers down the short, steep hill, and falls once. She laughs.

"You'd be hopeless on skates."

"You wait till we're in the water."

But she already is, diving in and then freestyling away from the beach. Her kick sends the water high into the air. He takes off his sweaty shirt and spreads it on a rock to dry. His feet hurt, but the grassy sand feels good between his toes. He thinks about taking off his shorts, to jump in naked like he used to with Max in Squam Lake, but decides against it. He runs for the water and dives in.

His lungs shrink.

"Fuck me! It's freezing."

"It should be. It was ice a couple of months ago."

He floats on his back. "The surface is all right, but a metre below, man."

She floats on her stomach and edges towards him. Their hands touch.

"Sorry."

"I should've brought my wet suit."

"Are you that keen?"

"Open water swimming beats the hell out of being in the pool. There was a lake near where I grew up."

"Where?"

"New Hampshire. I think I told you that at the party."

"You probably did. But I deleted most of that night from my memory. I was hitting on you and you never picked up on it."

"You were not."

"You go back home a lot?"

"There's nothing to go back to. Ma moved away. Gordie's in Portland. Friends are spread over the country."

"What about your dad, Matt?"

"Max."

"Where's he?"

"He's dead."

"Sorry."

"Me too."

"Now Montreal's home."

"Guess it is. It doesn't really feel like that though. I've been there five years and it still feels like it's only temporary."

"You got a skank there too?"

"No."

"Be honest."

"There's just me and Popov."

"Russian skank."

"That would make her Popova."

"Ha. Your Russian booty call then."

"My cat. Popov and I, we live together, but that's it."

"Cats are cool. Dogs are not."

"Agreed. We'll have to fight off that mutt on the way back as well."

"We'll take another way."

"Then there'll be another dog."

"No."

"A shortcut, I hope."

"So, no girls? Not even any dates?"

"A few, but there's not really any time to meet someone. And I refuse to date anyone I work with."

"Everyone's single online."

"Xav does that. He's crazy."

"He really needs a girlfriend."

"He won't find one that way. But he's got the same problem as me. No time. We work all week, travel a lot. And everyone we meet is either already seeing someone or coming off the rebound and not wanting to get hurt again."

She treads water next to him. "Everyone's got issues."

"Yeah. Here's mine. I get up, I go to work and I come home finished. I just wanna sit in the corner and put a bag on my head. A day becomes a week, a week a month, and then it's October and

I'm complaining about the year passing so fast."

"Time moves slowly here. Every day is just a day."

"Yeah, but you'll get it soon enough. When you finish college and get a job. It doesn't matter where you live or what you do. Everyone still gets up and goes to work."

"Grim."

"It's too cold for me. I'm getting out."

He swims for the beach, ploughing through the water with long, easy strokes. His quads and calves hurt, and he wonders how he's going to make it back. Out of the water, he sits on a rock in the sun and watches Iris breaststroke towards the beach.

"I don't hate her breaststroke."

Her tanned body shines when she stands, and once more something yanks inside him. She's got no hips and no breasts, and is all flexing and unflexing sinews, ligaments and tendons. She sees him staring and stops.

"What?"

"You have a boyfriend?"

"Guys don't normally go for me."

"Get out."

"You didn't."

"I mustn't have been paying attention that night."

"I'm not the right type. Never was. Guys, they want big tits, a J-Lo butt, a chick like you see in hip-hop videos."

"They've got it way wrong. They're victims of porn. Popular culture dictating to them what's sexy."

She sits down on the rock next to him. Their shoulders touch. Her skin is cool and surprising soft. They both look at the water. There's not a breath of wind.

"I asked my parents for implants for my sixteenth. They said no."

"Good. That would've ruined you. Then you would've given in to everyone's expectations."

"You think I'm hot?"

"I once fell, very badly, for a girl who looked a lot like you."

"And?"

"We spent three fabulous weeks together, then she ripped out my heart, beat it with a tenderiser, boiled it, made some gravy, and feed it all to me with a silver spoon."

She laughs. "I'm sure you deserved it."

"Karma caught up with me."

"You believe in that?"

He nods. "There's connectivity in everything we do."

"Careful. That sounds like illusory correlation. Or maybe apophenia. Finding connections only because you want to. That's Intro to Psychology, first class. Anyway, I thought the plan was to disconnect?"

"Only the tech."

"But you're going back to it all tomorrow."

"Yeah, but I'm not gonna use it."

"Your skank left, but you stayed."

"I like it here. And I'm glad she left. She kept talking about work. That's the last thing I wanna think about. I can't believe I'll have to face that place again on Monday. Sit down at my desk. Deal with those people. Everything there, it's so important, but it's really not. We're all just ants in a massive hole."

"So quit."

"It's not that simple."

"Sure it is. You walk in and tell your boss he can stick the job up his butt and rotate. Easy, eh?"

"Yeah. What about you? When are you heading back?"

"September, maybe."

"You'll miss a whole year."

"Your math skills are incredible."

"What happened?"

"What do you mean?"

"How did you end up here? Look, Iris, if you wanna talk, go for it. I'll listen and I won't make any jokes."

"Is that your line?"

"Huh?"

"The line you give girls, to show that you care and aren't just trying to get into my pants."

"I don't have any lines. I don't have any success. And I don't try to figure out a girl's price like Dylan. You just look like you wanna talk, that's all. To connect with someone."

"Why don't you talk."

"About what?"

"Your life. What you wanna do. You wanna get married and have kids?"

He looks at the water. "If I can't sort out my own life, how can I be responsible for someone else's?"

"Good question. More wannabe parents should ask themselves that."

"Look at the world, Iris. Would you wanna be a kid today?"

"Absolutely. There's so much to like about it. So many beautiful things. You just need to ignore the news and everyone's bad attitude."

"I wish I had your take. My dad used to say, if you go looking for shit, that's what you'll find."

"And that means the opposite's true."

"Yin and yang."

She shakes her head. "Poor Joe. Spent his whole life looking for shit when he could've been looking for beauty."

He feels a hand on his back, a finger tracing up and down. "That tickles."

"You have a sexy back. Not like the freakish triangle the pros have. All shoulders and lats like they're trying to grow wings. You've got good definition, good shape."

"Thanks."

She leans behind him. Her tongue slides between the groves of his spine. She works her way up and bites him on the neck.

"Ow."

"I knew it. The sensitive type."

She kisses him.

"What are you doing?"

"Recon. Seeing what's out there."

"'The truth is out there.'"

"What?"

"From a TV show."

She kisses him on the mouth. He puts a hand on her flank, thinking it will go straight through her, but his thumb pushes against the tight skin between her ribs.

"Do you eat?"

"Like a horse."

"Have dinner with me tonight."

She climbs on top of him. "Not allowed."

"That's why you brought me out here."

"Wasn't planned. But we went looking for beauty and that's what we found."

He kisses her skinny neck. "Not exactly brutal."
"It will be."

***

"Joe. Wait up."

Dylan runs towards him in that teetering style of his, but with a bit more energy in his step.

"Morning."

"Hey, Joe. Where you going with that mat in your hands?"

"Let's write a song."

"I bet you get that *Hey Joe* thing a lot."

"Not really. No one listens to Hendrix anymore. If someone covers it, then I'll be in trouble. Let's hope it doesn't get butchered on *Glee*."

"I love the classics. Deep Purple, Black Sabbath. Great fucking music."

"Morning, Marcus."

"Top of it to you, Joe."

"What are you so happy about?"

"'Start spreading the news, we're leaving today.'"

"You guys are turning this place into a musical."

Dylan dances a little, stirring the porridge with his yoga mat. "Grand finale song and dance number. We're outta here."

"Me too. What about, uh, what's-her-name?"

"Lolita."

"Her name's Lolita?"

"Yeah. So?"

"Nabokov ring a bell?"

"Wasn't he a bad guy in a Bond flick?"

"Forget it."

"She's coming back with me. Changed her flight."

"I gotta know. What got her?"

Dylan flashes a toothy, smarmy grin, like he spent his teenage years copying Tom Cruise in the mirror. "Found out she lives just across the Hudson. A Jersey girl."

"You offered her a job."

"I'm giving her an opportunity. Life changing."

"As your assistant?"

"In research. Analytics. We always need sharp people, and girls are useful for providing balance in the team. Now, she can make something of herself. Thanks to me."

"She thank you for that?"

Dylan leans close and whispers. "I could've saved all that cash I blew on freaking porn."

They walk through the gym and into the empty studio.

Dylan drops his mat on the floor. "Where is everyone?"

"Gone. Where's Lolita?"

"Sleeping it off. Dude, she likes it rough."

"I heard."

Marcus gives the punching bag a one-two. "The whole state heard."

Joe spreads his mat on the floor. "That must be some salary you offered. Still, it was interesting that she was calling out God's name and not yours. I guess she's more thankful to him."

"You're just bitter cause your score dumped you and left. I had her price figured too."

Joe yawns. "You think so?"

"Yep."

"Let's hear it."

"She's an opportunist. She's looking for something big to latch onto. A rich old guy or a prince in disguise. She'd be the first to blow the Messiah on his second coming. Ha-ha. Or his third."

"You can't offer her any of that."

"That's not the point. Knowing what a woman's price is means you can lead her in the direction she wants to go. And she'll follow. They always do."

Iris enters. "Marcel sends his apologies. He's a bit under the weather, which is a weird thing to be on such a beautiful day."

Joe whispers to Dylan: "You never figured her price."

"Who'd want to?"

She puts on some music and takes them through some rigorous warm-ups. Joe feels every inch of his legs. His hips hurt too, right at the point where she gripped him with her knees, like she was trying to crack his pelvis. Brutal.

It's more stretching than yoga, and she goes to each of them and pushes them a little more. They do as they're told, and grunt, groan and protest. Dylan can't hold a pose for longer than a couple of seconds, and even Marcus starts to work up a sweat, a gritty grin on his face.

"Come on. Go a little further. Push yourself to be better than when you walked in here this morning."

Joe struggles, his body rebelling, his mind in a thousand other places. He goes through the movements, holding, breathing and releasing, but his eyes keep falling on her. She's got the same shorts on as yesterday, but with a loose t-shirt over the top, tied at one corner to fit. Incredibly, on the front of the shirt is the elaborate black and white artwork of the *Revolver* album; drawn by Klaus someone who knew the Beatles in Hamburg and was the boyfriend of Astrid someone who then hooked up with fifth Beatle Stu Sutcliffe who left the band and died in Hamburg before they were famous. And Klaus went on to play bass in Lennon's seventies band. Max knew everything.

He wants to pull the shirt over her head, run his thumbs in the grooves between her ribs and touch the tip of her sternum with his tongue.

"Feel the beauty inside you. Look for it. You'll find it. That's it. Hold, and release."

She's very flexible, and seems eager to show it. When she reaches for her toes, her stomach touches her thighs. Not even lithe Marcel could match that. He marvels that she even does yoga athletically, attacking it like it's a competition and there can be only one winner. She fucks the same way, in battle, eager to prove her strength and endurance, grabbing the sword with both hands to pull it from the stone.

It was all so right. The beach, the stiffness of the rock she pinned him against, her constant movement, her show of power and control. He let her win, felt that she needed it, and tried to respond with as much physicality. But he kept thinking that some nice Christian family would drift past in a boat, or appear at the top of the clearing, the children's mouths agape, the mother putting a hand over their eyes and the kids pulling the fingers apart.

"Yes. Yes. Breathe in the good, breathe out the bad. And relax. Okay, that's it for today."

The three of them clap.

"Thanks, but come on. It's yoga, not brain surgery."

Dylan groans as he rolls up his mat. "That was some workout. Coming for breakfast, Joe?"

"In a minute."

"Gotta wake Lolita. Later gator."

Marcus follows, flicking the sweat of his forehead with an index finger.

Iris sidles up to him. "How's the bod?"

"Sore. I need a swim."

"Bring your wet suit next time."

"You want me to come back?"

"Sure. Montreal's half a world away."

"You could visit."

"You wouldn't have any time for me."

He smiles. He wants to reach out and grab her, throw her down on the yoga mat and wrestle her. He's struck by the thought that she wants to do the exact same thing, with a referee, best two out of three.

"I'd make time. I know Popov would like to meet you."

"Would he? When are you starting?"

"After breakfast."

"Already packed?"

"Yeah, but I can't get that fantastic bathtub in my backpack."

She laughs.

"Look, Iris..."

"Don't go there, Joe. Make all those stupid promises you'll never keep."

"I was gonna ask if you wanna take a walk down to the lake."

"I'm hungry."

"I'll grab some breakfast and meet you by the pool. How's that?"

"Done."

In the restaurant, he sees Dylan talking with Lolita. He wonders what her parents were thinking when they named her that. Maybe they didn't know. She and Dylan look happy with themselves, keen to get back and get started. New opportunities, new phases in old lives, people anxious to be going forward, going somewhere, but never really aware of where they actually are; this moment, this place.

He grabs two apples, two bananas, two yoghurts and two spoons. He finds Iris lounging on a sun chair by the pool. She's dripping and glistening.

"I wish I had a camera."

"To brag to your friends back home?"

"For me. Nice shirt, by the way. The one you had on earlier."

"Cool, huh? It's Rocco's. The chef. He's into old school music, like you. He played me some Beatles on his guitar last night."

Jealousy, old and new, ripples through him. Suddenly, he hates her, and he strips away all the layers of need and want he'd gathered since Brutal Beach. He wants to put down his yoghurt and spoon and leave.

"Told you it was good. Here."

"Thanks."

She peels a banana, dips the end in the yoghurt and puts the whole thing in her mouth.

"You normally have to pay to see a girl to do something like that."

"Stick around and you'll see it for free."

He bites into an apple, chooses his words, decides to go for it. "Iris, can I tell you something?"

"As long as it's not heavy. Can't handle that today."

"You can take it as you want. It's not really about you. Yesterday, that was one of the best days of my life. Not just from what happened and how it happened, but how I felt, from the moment I woke up to when I went to sleep."

"You found some beauty."

"I didn't think about anything. Didn't care about anything. Even when I was telling you about work, I didn't care about it."

"I knocked on your door last night but you didn't answer."

"Sorry. I was asleep. At nine, I think."

"Shame."

"You were prowling the grounds again. How come?"

"You know how it is. You lie down, really tired, and then you think about something, and then something else, and one thought leads to another until there's so many thoughts you can't turn your brain off, and all you want is to go to sleep and start again tomorrow. During the day, I'm all right. I can keep myself occupied. But at night, it all comes down on me."

"Have you tried taking something?"

"I'm not putting that crap in my body. I know what goes into it."

"From Xav. That's smart. There's a pill for everything. There could soon be a pill that'll help you forget something."

"Like what?"

"Anything you want."

The banana finished, she spoons yoghurt into her mouth. "What would you choose?"

"Lots of things."

"Take the one from the top of the list."

He takes another bite, chews and swallows. "The girl who looked like you."

"No way. If you forgot her then you wouldn't like me."

"I'd still like you."

"Cool."

"Your turn."

"That's easy, eh? The whole last six months. Press the delete button. Make it gone."

"The same stuff keeping you awake?"

She puts the empty yoghurt tub on the ground, spoon inside. It falls over. "Are you happy, Joe?"

"Yesterday I was."

"Let me change that. I hate the word happy. Are you satisfied?"

He shakes his head.

"What's missing?"

"A decent, consistent amount of the first question."

"Happiness and satisfaction aren't the same."

"But one leads to the other."

She smiles admonishingly. "Stop being so clever."

"Are you happy, or satisfied?"

She lies back and stares at the sky. "What I don't get is how someone can have everything and still not be satisfied."

"Well, even the happiest person might actually be really hurting on the inside and the smile is all show."

"Do you do that? You smile a lot."

"It stops people from asking questions. If you just smile, everyone thinks you're okay. Of course, if they come up to you and say something like, you look sad, then they're the one who's sad."

"Reflecting your personality. That's some pretty cheap psychology, Joe."

"I read about it once. You know, books that take up so much space."

She gives him a playful push. "Bizarre."

"What's bizarre is going into someone's apartment. You used to be able to know something about the person by the books they had and the CDs on the rack. You know, you can tell a lot about someone from what they like. Now, there's nothing. Anyway, are we talking about you, having everything and not being satisfied?"

"Look at me, Joe. I don't have everything."

"You look great. If other people don't think so then that's their problem."

Her slightly embarrassed smile makes him think she doesn't get complimented often. Trina was the same; she liked the compliments, but always received them with embarrassment and scepticism, like she didn't deserve them. He sees deep insecurities entwined in Iris's taught sinews and tendons, the hurt of boys who didn't return her love. And like Trina, it could be those very insecurities that have defined her physique.

"Everyone always told Alexa how hot she was."

"Who's that?"

"My roommate. We were on the hockey team together?"

"Field or ice?"

"Ice. She was really good too. On a half scholarship, you know, able to go shopping in certain places for free, and go to a couple of bars and restaurants without paying. She got given a list every semester."

"I know how it works."

"She didn't have to train little kids like I did, and her parents had money. She always had her picture in the paper. The face of the team. I was so jealous of her."

He looks at the pool, not wanting to go there, but feeling she needs to. "Why are you talking about her in the past?"

"Jack was on the basketball team. Really excellent guy. They were gonna get married after graduation. She was gonna be a lawyer. And all that wasn't enough. Don't you think that's, like, totally unfair? What does that mean for the rest of us?"

"Maybe she saw that you were happy and she was jealous of you?"

"Fuck that psycho-babble crap."

"What happened to her?"

"We had practice. I was late, flirting with some guy after class. He just wanted my lecture notes. I thought she'd already left, but all her gear was in the closet. We keep our hockey stuff in the closet near the door. If you put it in the room, it stinks the whole place up. I knocked on her door and opened it. Jack had put this bar in the corner so she could do chins ups and hang upside down and do crunches. She had a great body. Stacked and curved, what all the guys want. There she was. Hanging there."

"Fuck."

"And the thing was, she...she looked happy."

"I know that look."

"How do you know, Joe? You ever walk in on someone who hanged themselves?"

"No, but I've seen people die. The last expression on their faces, they were all pretty similar. They looked relieved. It was over and they were glad about it."

"That's so stupid. And selfish."

"I know what I saw, Iris. Maybe I saw just what I wanted to see, but think about it. There's nothing left to fight for, no more appearances to keep up, obligations to meet, lies to keep track of, people to impress. Why wouldn't you feel relieved? I would."

"So we should all go and hang ourselves?"

"No. But what would be good is to have that final sensation all the time. I had a bit of it yesterday. Iris, have you ever had a game when you were so focused, so into it, that the whole world disappeared? All you had was the stick in your hand and the puck in front of you. And there was nothing else."

She smiles thinly. "I once scored four goals. The puck was the size of a basketball. The net looked like the Grand Canyon, with an ant as the goalie. It was incredible. In the zone."

"I had it a few times swimming. The only thing that's important is the movement. You forget everything else. You don't think. You just feel."

"You can't walk around like that. There's too much to think about."

He nods. "I know. I know. Can I ask you something about Alexa?"

"Yeah."

"Stop me if I go too far. But. What did she use? Did she have a rope, or a belt, or something from her closet?"

"What's that got to do with anything?"

"It makes a difference if she prepared it or not. Went to the shop and bought a rope because she wanted to do it. If she used something in her room, then it was spontaneous, and she had a day when she couldn't take it anymore."

"She used her black karate belt."

"Then she had one really dark day, when it was all too much. Everyone has days like that. The truly weak give into them. The rest of us refocus our thoughts and try to get on with it. I'm really sorry, Iris. This would keep me awake at night as well. It does, sometimes."

"At the start, it's her. I miss her. But then I think about why she might've done it. And I can't come up with a reason. If she had no reason to live, how can the rest of have a reason? How can I?"

"But that's from your point of view. You thought she had everything. She obviously didn't think so. Maybe because she never had to fight or struggle for anything, she never built her character. Like you did. Everything comes easy to you and you end up weak and insecure as a result."

"It's still unfair."

"It sucks that you found her. Still, maybe the universe was trying to help."

"Don't go religious on me, Joe. That's one of the reasons I left. I never believed any of that shit."

"What do you believe?"

"Now? Nothing."

"What happened to Alexa?"

"They buried her. That's it. She's gone."

"Look, it's got nothing to do with God. Think about what the experience has taught you. Out of all of it, you learned some really important things."

"Like?"

"Like you're stronger than Alexa, and you can handle the tough things that life will throw at you. That no matter what happens, you'll stand up and keep going. And being beautiful and popular is not everything. You and I both know you'll go back to UVic and finish and make something of your life."

"I can't go back."

He points at her with his half-eaten apple, already browning around the bite marks. "But it all happened and you came here, where we got to meet each other again. Think of all the events that took place for you and me to be sitting by this pool, at this retreat, having this conversation."

"Your universe helping?"

"I can't believe that it's all random."

"Illusory correlation."

"That's not what I mean."

"Alexa kills herself so we can fuck on a beach in Oregon? That's how the universe helps? No way."

He puts the apple on the ground and peels the top off the yoghurt. He spoons some into his mouth. It's warm. "I guess I don't ever want to think something's for nothing. Especially something bad. Like you said yesterday. If you go looking for beauty, that's what you'll find. I like that. You've changed me."

"You've gone soft."

"Yeah, still no killer instinct."

"That's not funny."

"It is, a little bit."

She sits up and hugs him. "Thanks, Joe."

"Good to talk?"

She pulls back and nods.

"What happened to Jack?"

"Dropped out. Went home to Tofino. I had a massive crush on him. It was always...awkward. I could hear them through the wall."

"You should contact him. Maybe he needs to talk too."

"Guys aren't good at that kind of stuff."

"Garbage. The whole tough guy thing is a Hollywood attitude. Guys like to cry just as much as girls, and they need to. We were just taught not to."

"Who did you see die?"

"Couple of people. No one close."

"You're lying. You deliberately made a point of making eye contact."

"You learn that at college or from TV?"

"Was it your dad?"

The yoghurt tastes like it's going bad in his mouth. He wants to spit it out, but somehow swallows.

"And there it is, tough guy."

"There what is?"

"The crap you smile through. You think no one notices, but they do. That's probably why girls are attracted to you, like you're some wounded puppy they can care for."

"I'm a cat person."

"Whatever. Come on. I told you my bad stuff, now you can tell me yours."

"This is a conversation, not a negotiation."

She stands up and throws the *Revolver* shirt on. It goes halfway down her thighs, the sleeves over her elbows. "Fine. Be a man. Lock it all up inside."

He grabs her hand as she passes, stops her. "Iris, I haven't told anyone. Ever."

"Not even my lookalike?"

"Especially her. I met her just after it happened."

"What happened?"

He shakes his head. "I can't."

"So, it's not good to talk. It's actually really simple. You open your mouth and all the words fall out. Easy, eh?"

"No."

"Okay. Have a good trip back. It's been almost real."

"Iris, wait. Look, I'll make a deal with you."

"I thought this wasn't a negotiation."

He smiles. "Everything is. Life is about making deals and compromises. I need more time to think about it. It's been so long, I can't really tell anymore what actually happened and what I've dreamt in between."

"So?"

"I wanna see you again. Somehow. Here, in Montreal, wherever. We could meet half way in Saskatchewan."

"Maybe you can sit around and wait for your universe to help. Or you could get proactive and fly to Victoria."

"You're gonna go back?"

"Sure, why not?"

"Good. Then I promise that whenever we meet again, I'll tell you everything."

"Pinky swear."

"What?"

"Pinky swear on it."

"How old are you?"

She holds out her right pinky. "Twenty-one."

He takes it. She squeezes his pinky and shakes it a little.

"Say it."

"I swear on these pinkies to tell you about my dad the next time we meet."

She lets go. "Done. Now what?"

He looks at his watch. "I better get started."

"All that and now you just ride off?"

"I can't stay here. I gotta work on Monday."

"Do yourself a massive favour, Joe. Give up your day job."

"And do what?"

"Whatever you want. Become a waiter in Victoria."

"Tempting."

"Of course, you could just wait for your universe to take care of everything for you."

"Now you're making fun of me."

She kisses him. "I think you can handle it."

"So? How do we say goodbye?"

"How about, I'll see you again when the planets align for us to meet again. Easy, eh?"

***

"Where the fuck have you been?"

"Hey, Gordie. No brotherly hug?"

"You ignore all my texts and now show up uninvited."

"Can I come in?"

"Explain yourself first."

"Let me in, Gordie, or I'll go to a hotel. There's a perfectly reasonable explanation for all of this, if you're willing to hear it."

Gordie moves out of the doorway and backs into the apartment. "I'm on the balcony."

Joe drops all his gear in the living room and helps himself to a glass of water in the kitchen. Out on the balcony, he finds Gordie slumped in a fold-out chair, notebook on his knees, headset on, chewing a green straw. Gordie taps at the keyboard, stares at the screen intently, then pumps his right fist.

"Yes. Fucking straight."

Joe sits down. "Turn it off."

"I'm listening."

"Not a word until you turn it off."

"I'm up three grand."

"You're what?"

Gordie folds the notebook shut and rips off the headset. "Nothun."

"Put the phone away too."

"Can't. I'm waiting on a very important text. Flash party today. I'm getting the location texted to me and we have to be there in fifteen minutes to get in."

"We? I'm not going."

"Yeah, you are. The chicks are unbelievable at these parties. My stressed out bro needs a good time."

Joe sips his water, tasting the diesel and fumes of Highway 97 on his lips. "You're the one who's stressed."

"Let's hear your excuses for non-contact."

"I ended up at a resort that had no tech."

"What? No hot water or electricity? Or a resort for the cult of less?"

"They took my phone and computer when I checked in. And there was no phone in the room, and no TV."

"A prison."

"It's a retreat. To get away from it all. To disconnect."

"Sounds like hell. Can't possibly be real."

"Believe what you want. Look it up. They've got a site."

Gordie scoops up his notebook and flips it open. "Does this fantasy camp have a name?"

"Rusticity."

Gordie laughs. "That's the best you could come up with in a week? Wait. I've got it. Okay. It's for real. You shack up there with that Boston babe?"

"She left after a couple of days."

"Couldn't get it up? Don't you have those pills that help limp old men like you?"

"She had to go back to work."

"But you stayed."

"It was great living with no tech."

"While the rest of us think you're lying in a crumpled mess on the side of road."

"Bad example."

"Get over it."

He stands up.

"Jesus, Joe, will you calm the fuck down."

"I'm completely calm. You're the one who's off the chart."

"Sit. Come on, it's me. You wanna beer? How about a cup of tea? Man, you are one unhappy dude."

"Reflecting your personality."

"What?"

Joe sits again. "Forget it."

With his notebook open, Gordie starts playing with it again. "What's up with the chick? You guys serious?"

"She lives in Boston."

"So? You can sext each other. And vid phone. I got that going with half a dozen girls."

"Yeah, and you never actually touch any of them. It sounds like too much work for no result."

"My bro, he knows what to do with women. How did you spend seven days disconnected from the world? Must've been mega boring."

"It was the best week of my life. Had nothing to care about. Did some yoga, slept, ran, ate, met some nice people, did some touring. Crater Lake's nice."

"Yeah, I hear it's good."

"You haven't been there?"

"Nuh, but I checked Richie's pics on ceeville."

"Go down and see it for yourself."

"Don't need to. And I got no time. Under the hammer. Exams, papers."

"I thought you just cut and paste everything."

"You still have to change it a bit so the profs don't notice. That's the real work. Can't use full sentences because they come up on scans."

"Sounds like cheating is more work than writing something original."

Gordie takes out his phone and looks at the screen.

"I'm not coming."

"That's not it. But we'll take your bike. Richie's got a helmet."

"No."

"It's the only way we'll get there in time."

"What about all your work?"

Gordie looks at him incredulously. "It's Saturday."

"Love your priorities."

"Speak for yourself, Captain Uptight. What did you bring me?"

"They didn't have souvenirs. But I do have something."

He gets up, retrieves a book from his satchel and goes back out onto the balcony. He hands the book to Gordie.

"*The Razor's Edge*. Porn, I hope."

"Read it."

"It looks about a thousand years old."

"It's about a guy who searches for a higher meaning in life while everyone around him is just interested in consumerism and status and getting ahead. None of them understand his choices."

"Sounds like you need to read it, not me."

"I did. Twice."

Gordie types, slides his index finger on the track pad. "It's an album by AC/DC."

"The book came first."

"Who reads books? Keep it."

"It's for you."

Gordie continues working the notebook. "Already got it. Downloaded to my e-reader. For nothing."

"I don't know how you can read off that thing."

"I don't know why you lug around books. Your apartment's full of them too. I've got a thousand books in one. Any book ever written if I want it."

"You read any of them?"

Gordie's phone buzzes. "That's it. North Basin. Let's rock."

Joe drinks his water.

Gordie gets up and drops his notebook on the sofa. "Move, Joe."

"I'm not going."

"This is not a choice."

"I'm not gonna spend the afternoon with a bunch of zombied kids."

Gordie comes back to the balcony, wearing a different cap. "Gimme the keys."

"Forget it, Stan."

"This is important."

"You have a very strange sense of what's important. But everyone does."

"Gimme the fucking keys, Joe. Or..."

"Or what? You'll write something nasty about me on the-t-wall?"

"I didn't write that."

"Another Stan. Look, I'll take you there, but that's it."

"Let's fly."

Joe picks up his helmet and follows Gordie down the stairs.

"Faster, bro. We got twelve minutes to get to North Basin."

"You know where that is?"

"Last party was out there. It rocked."

Outside, Gordie already has his helmet on. It's a scooter helmet, too small for his head, and he holds his green Celtics cap in one hand.

"What happens at these parties?"

"People show up, dance, have a good time. There's music, booze, food, whatever you want."

"Drugs?"

"You'll love it."

"I'm not sticking around."

Joe puts on his helmet and fires up the Suzushi. Gordie directs him down the Naito Parkway and over Freemont Bridge, egging him on the whole way, slapping his shoulder. Traffic is heavy, but he edges the bike between the cars, zipping in and out of lanes. Gordie whoops with delight and points to the North Basin exit.

"Gun it, bro."

He can't help himself. The road through the industrial area is clear. He gives the Suzushi all it's got. They fly down the road until Gordie points towards a mess of parked and abandoned cars, to where kids are running from all directions.

"Down there."

The dirt road next to the rusted brown railroad tracks is narrow and bumpy. They pass a lot of people running and Gordie shouts at them to get out of the way. Joe gets glimpses of the people they pass; kids mostly, teenagers running with bottles of water and phones in their hands. Some of the girls are running barefoot, with a stiletto in each hand, or with a pair sticking out of their shoulder bags. The Suzushi struggles in the dirt, hopping and digging in. Gordie whoops again.

The main gate is crowded. The thump and shudder of drum and bass is coming from the warehouse beyond the gate.

Gordie pushes Joe's shoulder. "I know the guy at the gate. Go right through."

Joe edges the bike forward, revving it loudly so the kids part a little. They stare at Joe, perhaps thinking him a celebrity of sorts. One girl tries to grab Gordie's arm to get on the bike, but he shakes her off. She goes sprawling to the ground, legs in the air. People laugh and point at her. Joe sees in the mirror that no one tries to help her up and the crowd closes in on top of her.

"Yo, Brodie."

"Gordowski. You made it. Nice ride."

Brodie lets them in, slapping and fist-bumping Gordie's hand. The gate closes behind them.

"Ha. You're stuck now, bro."

Joe steers the bike towards the other handful parked to the right of the warehouse. Gordie jumps off.

"Fucking straight."

Joe takes off his helmet. "Gimme your apartment keys."

Gordie puts his ear to Joe's mouth. "What?"

"Your keys! I'm going back!"

Gordie shakes his head. "No way. It's all happening right here. Loosen up, bro."

Joe looks at the crowded gate. The number of people trying to get in has doubled from a few minutes ago. They're starting to push against the fence. A few are trying to climb it, only to be pulled down by burly guys in black shirts. That fence goes right around the warehouse. No escape. He clicks the straps of both helmets to the Suzushi and follows Gordie towards the one steel door. Gordie dances as he walks, baseball cap backwards, jeans hanging below his flat arse, underwear showing, phone in hand. He puts it to his ear.

"What? WHAT?! Yeah! Okay. The bar. THE BAR!"

The door opens. The drum and bass seems to flood out, making the pebbles and broken glass on the ground vibrate and jump. Then they're inside, swallowed up by the mass of people.

It's dark, except for all the camera flashes, and anything glittery that catches the silver and yellow lasers as they slice through the air. White shirts glow incandescent purple, as do teeth. There are spotlights pointing to the ceiling, placed underneath massive banners advertising vodka, perfume, cars, other nightclubs, online poker and the next season of *True Blood*. People bump into him as they dance, not with reckless abandon, but with the serious intent of people determined to have a good time, and to show it. They dance as they think adults do, as they've seen in music videos, as they've practiced in front of the bedroom mirror or playing wireless dance games. Bodies pulse, arms pump and faces pout. Eyebrows are arched and teeth gritted. Everyone trying really hard. For all its improvisation and spontaneity, its youth and drugs and alcohol, there is an overwhelming seriousness, with the feel of a competition, that every single person is judging and being judged. All the self-expression that will follow – the blogs, texts, plashes and ceeville billboards – is more important than the event itself.

He follows Gordie's green baseball cap through the crowd; he's a head higher than all the girls. And they're all girls, dancing in tight groups, crotch to arse, running hands through their hair, shaking their hips, bending into crouch positions like strippers. Give them a pole and they'd try to swing from it. It's hard to tell their ages in the glimmering darkness, and impossible to think with the deafening noise. It feels like the Blue Man Group are trying to beat their way out from inside his skull. He looks for the DJ, thinking if he could get to the mixing desk, he could yank out the cords and bring silence to the warehouse. But there is no DJ. There's not even music. It's just a continual rhythm overlaid with snippets of songs he's heard before.

Two girls are exchanging tongues, being filmed by an older guy who is nodding and grinning at the small screen of his phone.

Another guy is weaving through the crowd, phone camera raised in front of him and getting girls to flash their breasts, which they willingly do. Sometimes, tissue paper falls to the ground, glowing purple.

A reed of a man in a huge overcoat, with a goatee and sunglasses low on his nose, is selling drugs in a concealed and shifty way, like there are undercover agents watching him.

On large steel barrels, stood upright as tables, empty bottles surround bowls filled with condoms. The girls grab these, blow them up and tie them like balloons. They float into the air, glowing purple and revealing familiar brands and logos.

Girls grab at his shirt as he passes. Hands touch him, pull at his arms, run across his back and shoulders, squeeze his butt. There's nothing remotely sexual about it. He feels like a puppy brought to school for show and tell.

Gordie's mouth moves in front of him. Then Gordie shouts in his ear. Still nothing. Gordie points at the dull lights of the bar off to the right side. They manage to get there. Gordie slaps hands and shoulder hugs the barman and comes back with two drinks in plastic cups raised high in the air. Joe takes the cup offered to him and Gordie drops a tablet inside both, which quickly dissolves. Gordie raises his cup in toast, but Joe hands him the cup and tries to walk away.

He feels dizzy, from the toxic haze, the sweaty air, the continual flash of cameras and from the inhumane, torturous beat of drum and bass. Worse, he knows that outside, it's a sunny Saturday afternoon in one of America's most beautiful cities and all these kids have chosen to come in here. And all so they can have bragging rights online.

He gets around to the side of the crowd and finds a wall of the warehouse. He sees light coming from an adjacent room, from the slither left by the rug nailed over the doorway. He lifts a side of the rug, hoping to see daylight. A girl is being fucked from behind by one guy and is blowing another. She's awkwardly keeping her balance on the mattress that's laid on the ground. She doesn't even seem to know what she's doing. She's naked, but the guys are both fully clothed, jeans open, belts loose. The guys high-five above her and she spins around, almost toppling over. To the side, two other guys are whacking off, impatiently waiting their turns and filming it all with their free hands.

He lets the rug fall and then pushes back into the crowd. The girls seem to get in his way, crowding in front like he's got something for them. They grab his arms and try to get him to dance. One girl reaches up and kisses him. She tastes vile. Then she pulls back, pouts like a model and sneers at him when she sees he doesn't have a camera or anything else in his hands. He pushes her aside, pushes more groping girls aside, all those hands clutching at the darkness, looking for something to grab onto. He's polite at first, but soon starts shoving them with force.

He gets back to the bar. Or is it a different one? He finds another wall, another slither of yellow light, another rug nailed to doorway. He doesn't want to, but he lifts it. Six guys, all in baseball caps at various angles, sit shoulder to shoulder around a green table covered in ruffled notes. Each guy has a stack of notes in front of him and two cards, face down. In a corner, another group are crouched over a dice game, with notes spread in a pile on a flattened cardboard box.

He lets the rug fall and looks out over the crowd. There are more guys, heads taller, looking down at the girls and trying to dance with them. They carry drinks above their heads and look from girl to girl, deciding who to offer them to.

Cameras flash, lasers slice through the air, the beat punches his intestines. Girls kiss and then kiss someone else. Vodka cocktails in plastic cups chase down small pills. Inflated condoms float up to the ceiling. A guy has a girl pinned to a steel barrel, fucking, or dancing, or both. Maybe she's trying to fight him off. The music loops and loops like it will never end, like it never started. The air stinks of basement mould and the gym socks of a benchwarmer. It has the heavy humidity of a guy's bedroom after he was up all night scheming towards popularity. Bulimic vomit on the floor of a junior high toilet, a cheese sandwich forgotten at the bottom of a locker, cheap air freshener sprayed to cover the smell of dope, aftershave on guys too young to shave, shop-lifted perfume.

A hand grips his shoulder. He turns to take a swing. It's Gordie. His mouth moves and he gestures for Joe to relax, pressing the air down with his hands. Here, have the rest of this drink.

Joe pushes Gordie's hand away. The drink falls to the ground. He goes into the crowd, shoving girls aside, breaking through tight circles and splitting couples apart. He sees a flash of daylight come from the opened steel door and heads for it. Hands grab at him, fondling, scratching, even reaching into his pockets. One hand gets his wallet, but he slaps it away. A wave of people is surging in and he fights against it. The bodies are jammed close together and still they're all trying to dance, with even more seriousness than before. Heads rub against shoulders and they sweat and move as one. He sees daylight again, the door opening as more people come in. He manages to get to the side, to where other banners are hanging. He takes out his keys and tears a hole through a canvas vodka bottle, large enough to squeeze through. Shapes move in the shadows. One guy is sitting with his back against the wall, his jeans around his ankles. A girl is squatting backwards on top of him, moving up and down. Her face grimaces with pain, then she licks her lips and reaches for Joe's belt. He shoves her hand away and she laughs soundlessly, the fillings in her teeth catching the light of a laser. He follows the wall, tripping over a few passed out people, and gets to the door just as it closes again. He tries the handle, but it just moves in his hands. The crowd presses him against the door, so when it opens again he falls out.

He squints at the sunlight, getting to the side of the crowd outside and then rubbing his eyes. The noise is not as bad, but the drum and bass seem to echo inside of him, vibrating through every cell, nerve, muscle and vein. He feels dirty, ashamed. Pissed off. He walks around the crowd and gets to the Suzushi. Two teenage boys are leaning against it, heads bowed over their phones. One kid is self-consciously smoking a cigarette, while the other has a massive cigar and is holding it in his fist, like he doesn't quite know what to do with it. A bottle of champagne with a fancy label is being passed between them.

"Get off."

"Cool ride."

"Thanks, now get the fuck off."

"It's a free country."

"Get off now or I'll ram that cigar down your throat."

The kid reaches behind him and pulls out a gun. "How bout I blow your motherfucking head off."

"Hey, look, I just wanna leave."

"Get us in."

"You don't wanna go in there."

The kid raises the gun again. His skinny arms don't look strong enough to hold it up. "You want your bike, get us in."

Suddenly, the crowd in front of the door starts to disperse. People surge out of the warehouse, flowing like liquid. They stream towards the gate.

The kid shoves the gun into the back of his jeans and throws the cigar away. "Fuck. It's a raid."

The boys join the throng sprinting for the gate, this river of humanity gushing towards the dirt path for North Basin and spilling over the sides as people run through the trees, along the railroad tracks and jump fences to other warehouses and parking lots. Guys run tightening their belts. A few girls carry frilly bras in their hands, and others their high heels. A lot of people are whooping and cheering, like this was the part they were waiting for. Some are texting as they run.

There's no sign of the police. Joe hears no sirens.

Gordie runs over to him and puts on his small scooter helmet, tucking his cap into his jeans in the process.

"Hit it, bro. We're blown."

"Stan, you fucking idiot."

Gordie throws the helmet at Joe. "Move. This is some illegal shit."

Joe puts the helmet on and fires up the Suzushi. People are still streaming out of the warehouse, raising their hands to the sunlight and staggering a little. There's no way through. Like the other guys on bikes, they have to trail behind the crowd.

Gordie shouts to Brodie at the door. "Later, Big B."

Brodie throws out a couple of dazed looking girls clutching shirts to their naked chests and then slams the door. The girls rub their eyes, pull their shirts on and try to run. One falls. The other tries to pick her up. When she just stays sitting on the ground, the girl runs.

"We can't leave her there."

"Yeah, we can. Go. Go."

Joe stops the bike next to her. "Get her."

Gordie bangs his fist against Joe's shoulder. "You fucking mad? Gun it for the gate. Five-O will be here any minute. Oh, for fuck's sake, Joe."

Gordie complies, picking the girl up and putting her on the bike between them. She's so small, she nearly disappears. Joe feels her head against his back and wonders if she was just the meat in another two-guy sandwich.

There are only a few stragglers on the path, those too out of it to run; those who stop to stare intently at tree trunks or pick up leaves from the ground and hold them up towards the sky. Joe weaves between them, the Suzushi ripping at the dirt. On North Basin, kids are jumping into moving cars, with legs hanging out back windows. Others are running while a few are on skateboards and bicycles. Joe takes a right. Coming from the other direction is a police car, its lights not flashing.

***

He waits for the guy in the turban to get hand-scanned, then patted down, again hand-scanned and then taken aside for a full pat down. He yawns, waits for his cue, then does his time in the scanner. The security guard hands him his satchel.

"'Exercise your soul.' How do you do that exactly?"

Another guard looks at the bag. "Mental push-ups. Brain strains."

"Ha, yeah, and if something hurts, don't panic. The universe will come and help."

They both laugh. Joe tries to smile, but it's too early for cheer, too early to be fumbling with little bottles of liquids in a sealable plastic bag, too early to have some stranger staring at your naked image. He shoulders his satchel and backpack. It's also too early to be wondering why your kid brother is such a tool, and too early for the airport to be this busy.

"Where are all these people going?"

He buys an expensive cup of tea from a mobile cart. At the departure gate next to his, he finds a row of empty seats, sits down and sips. It's noisy, and growing louder as people raise their voices above the noise. A kid's soft crying develops into a wail in order to be heard, a solemn goodbye turns into the shouts of promises and sorrow, and two departing lovers scream at each other as if from the bottom of a tower to the top. There's also the cluttering noise of movement and routine: the squeaks of wheeled suitcases, the spoken earnestness of "Yeah, Brad, I'm at the airport," the extended sighs in response to delays, the inaudible crackle of the PA, the thump of butts hitting plastic seats, the drone of the floor cleaner, and the whiz and whir of golf carts ferrying people to their gates. He watches and listens, fascinated. As a way of counteracting all the noise, everyone is tuning each other out, attempting to put themselves into the centre of their own universe. They text while walking, listen to music while sleeping, write emails with a phone cradled between head and shoulder, dig their hand into a bag of potato chips while taking a photo of their plane. No one seems to notice anything apart from what they're doing, their own problems and concerns. And even with that, their level of awareness seems low. People bump into each other, walk directly in front of another's path, take the seat next to someone so their shoulders touch, wheel their suitcases over people's feet. Again, he's fascinated. All these people sharing this space, and all somewhere else in their heads; a blip on their own screen with the whole world moving around them.

The tea is bitter and cheap, too long left in water that's been kept hot for over a day. He drinks it anyway, grimacing as it goes down.

It's tempting to turn on the computer and the phone, to get wired and tune out, like everyone else. But instead, he drops the cup in the trash and walks over to the one pay phone next to the line of four credit card-operated computers. He pumps in some coins. The phone rings and rings.

"Salut."

"Hey, it's Joe."

"He's alive. He's alive. Where've you been?"

"In the wilds of Oregon."

"What number is this? I almost didn't pick up."

"It's a pay phone."

"You calling from last century? I didn't think those things existed anymore."

"They do. At airports."

"Which one are you at?"

"Portland."

"You think you'll make it back in time?"

"There's a one hour delay. But yeah, I should. I'll go straight from Dorval."

"You want me to pick you up?"

"I'll take the bus. Did you try to contact me last week?"

"I sent a bunch of texts, but when you didn't reply, I guessed you had better things to do. I know how you feel about phones."

"I had no phone. I was staying at a place that was tech free."

"Sounds like paradise."

"It was."
"Do they take out a guy's pacemaker when he checks in?"
"Almost."
Francois laughs. "That's why you're using the pay phone. You're scared to turn your phone on."
"I'm scared it'll overload and smoke will come out. Could be I don't even have a job to go to tomorrow."
"The world will keep spinning if you don't. What time is it there?"
"Almost eight."
"Gordie with you?"
"No. He took me to the party from hell yesterday and then he spent the rest of the night discussing and bragging about it online."
"I thought college kids were all career focused. They still party?"
"These were more like high schoolers. Junior high schoolers."
"I hope you didn't."
"No, but others did. The display was stunning. It was like walking through a porn theme park for teenagers."
"I bet there's lots to tell. Let's go for a bite after the pool."
"You remember Iris? Xav's sister?"
"What about her?"
"She's working at Rusticity."
"Where?"
"Rusticity. That's where I stayed. No phones, no computers, no TV. I sent you a postcard."
"Hasn't arrived yet. But I like the sound of the place."
"It was one of the best weeks of my life. I'm a changed man."
"And Iris was there."
"Yeah."
"What a coincidence."
"You think? No one knows she's there. Not even Xav."
"Ah, a meet meant to be. You all right, Joe? You sound, I don't know, distant, or is it just the old-fashioned phone?"
"Hang on. That's my boarding call. Talk to you tonight."
"See you in the pool."

Treasure hunting with the Simplicity Disciples

Each step downhill is a pleasant reminder of the morning ride out to Chateauguay and back. He got wet, stopped for tea and cake, and came home with the wind at his back.

"Gotta do that more."

Rue Sherbrooke is a sea of heads, the sidewalks a slalom course for those on the move. The going is slow. Families are strolling, with parents trying to keep their children from running away. There are packs of teenagers, walking close together in long lines, sometimes arm in arm, like protestors. Girls his age and older move in groups of four: a blonde, a brunette, a red head, and an older looking woman who's meant to be sexier and more adventurous than the other three combined. Large shopping bags swing from wrists that hold phones to ears. Some people spin around trying to locate friends and acquaintances. They talk on their phones, stop in the middle of the sidewalk to search and bring a dozen walkers behind them to a halt, causing a jam that has people jumping onto the streets to get around. Drivers blow their horns at these people and "Get off the road" is shouted from lowered windows, in English and French. The lines stretching from ATMs and food service windows jut out and make short barricades on the sidewalks.

He should've known better, Saturday afternoon on Sherbrooke, like Saturday afternoon in any city anywhere in the world. He ducks down onto Metcalfe, where there's more sidewalk to be had and he can walk without having to watch out for everyone else. Metcalfe bends into Cathedrale and he slows his pace.

It's a beautiful afternoon, nippy, but with enough sun to prickle the senses that summer is coming.

There are buses parked in front of the basilica, but no tourists. The bus drivers stand in a loose circle smoking cigarettes; one has a small silver flask which he passes to the others.

He stops to stare at the basilica, at its green roof and cubic front.

"Jesus was in advertising."

He feels the sudden urge to boo the church, to cup his hands around his mouth for amplification and let out a long jeer. And he could, because there are no cars here to drown it out, no people to warn him that God is watching, no one brandishing self-printed pamphlets to come up and offer a better, improved God.

He keeps walking, booing internally, letting it echo inside him, the unfairness of it all. But, he thinks, not even God, if He exists, is paying attention anymore.

Down Cathedrale, onto Notre Dame, then weaving between the traffic to get on Saint Paul. There's nothing beatific about the streets, despite their names: Saint Henri, Saint Pierre, Nicolas, Sulpice, and just about every other saint imaginable. He wonders where the saints are today. Delivering wisdom online perhaps, curing leprosy with mouse clicks, turning water into vodka on Second Life. Or sitting in boardrooms and voting to outsource production to Taiwan and Bangladesh, to set up call centres in Mumbai, to rebrand, remarket, relaunch and resell; saints constantly in search of target groups, core business, key markets and consumer profiles.

"No. Stop it."

He likes Montreal's Vieux Port, and dawdles in a few of the galleries.

The café on Saint Duzier is a hole-in-the-wall, no-name place, down a narrow alley that the tourists don't even give a first look, a place people would walk straight past unless they knew the street number. It has a half a dozen small round tables, each with only two chairs, and the backs of the chairs hit other backs of chairs. Three of the tables are occupied; men hunched over notebooks. Behind the makeshift counter, which is a piece of board on two wooden horses, there's a pale green art deco cappuccino machine. The lone waitress has this gurgling and frothing, the coffees spewing into tall glasses, three-quarters milk. There are paintings on the walls, for sale, and they could be the crayon scratchings of a six year-old who gets juggled between parents in different cities, or the laboured masterpieces of the waitress herself.

He's on time and takes a seat at the table that's pushed up against the front window. There's nothing to look at except the bare, naked alley of Saint Duzier, the cobblestones shining with wear from another era; before the Vieux Port became a tourist trap of souvenir shops and renovated hotels. Back when the streets were crowded with thousands just trying to get by, where Stevedore families lived all in one room as those with money headed out of the city for the safety and nuclear standards of the suburbs.

He recalls the exhibition Francois took him to last year – or the year before – of black and white photographs of the Vieux Port between the wars: the smiling faces tinged with charcoal, even in summer; the little kids with scabbed knees huddling together, with one kid cradling a ragged, home-made looking ball under one arm; the simple fare laid out on tables which probably doubled as beds; the ships crowding the docks and the hopeful immigrants hauling massive trunks down the gangways, en route to a better life; the dockworkers standing proudly in front of barrels and cranes; the mournful faces as the depression takes hold; the unemployment lines, the empty bakery shelves, the boarded up shops, and the bearded men holding up pleading signs, their eyes already seeing a future that didn't include them.

He looks at his watch. She's ten minutes late. He smiles, thinking of Siobahn the Baggage Handler and her impatience rant. There's a copy of the *Gazette* hanging from the coat rack. The entire Saturday paper has been crammed onto this one wooden stick, making the pages impossible to turn. All he can do is read the front page and the back, and then get glimpses of what's inside.

"Look, babe, we've both changed. I'm looking to start a new phase in my life. We're going in different directions."

He turns and eyes the man, can see over his shoulder the static video image of a girl.

The waitress stands beside him. "What would you like?"

"Maybe you can tell him to take his private conversation elsewhere?"

She shrugs and wipes her hands on her apron. "Just ignore him."

"A green tea, please, with honey."

She moves behind the counter and puts the kettle on.

Ignore him, he thinks. Not possible. And that's the whole point. No one wants to be ignored. Everyone's aching for attention. Look at me, hear me, notice me, because I'm the centre of the universe. He recalls what Iris said about popularity. That's what it's all about these days. And it takes work and commitment. Iris. Miss her.

"Hi, Joe."

She bustles in, kisses him hello on both cheeks and flops down in the chair.

"How's it going?"

"You found it."
"Yep."
"You just get here?"
"The patrons have been entertaining me for about fifteen minutes."
"What? Why?"
"Because we agreed to meet here at three."
"But I texted you that I'd be late."
He holds up his hands. "No phone."
"You lose it?"
"No."
"Stolen?"
"No."
"It fell in the toilet, right? I read that's the number one reason for phone repairs. Everyone playing *Angry Birds* on the can."
The waitress puts Joe's tea on the table. He goes to work on it.
"Hi, Cheryline."
"Hey, Randi. Black coffee, in a bucket if you've got it."
"You wanna a blueberry muffin too? I saved you one."
"No. Yes."
Joe sips his tea. He wonders why it's never as good as the tea he makes at home.
"What's going on, Joe?"
"I'm on a diet."
"Me too. You know nothing about the muffin."
"A digital diet. Did you see my billboard on ceeville?"
"I don't read those. Who cares if Jackie in LA is getting her nails done, but can't decide between ruby red and strawberry pink."
"Or if Buddy in Vancouver just farted."
"And all those music videos and links. Who's got the time for that crap? Or the quotes, like they've run out of anything original to say."
"Except, I farted."
She laughs. "You're fun. Sorry for last time. I'm glad we get to see each other again. I'm paying, by the way."
"Karma doesn't know what money is."
"Yeah, but I still want to restore balance."
"It's forgotten."
"I thought you'd bury me in your cemetery."
"Creative Primers are in short demand in my city."
"Hah. So, what's with the diet? You look like you're in great shape."

"It's not that kind of diet."

Randi slides a huge glass of black coffee onto the table, along with a blueberry muffin and a few packets of Sweet'n'low. She squeezes Cheryline's shoulder as she passes.

"You come here a lot?"

"I work around the corner. Randi was in graphics until she opened this place. That's her stuff on the wall. Good, isn't it?"

He nods and sips, thinking again about how a cup of tea is the biggest scam in the beverage industry. Hot water and a two cent tea bag, and it costs as much as a coffee made with an expensive machine and ground beans.

"What's wrong?"

"Nothing. It's just...I guess no one orders tea here."

"Why would they?"

"Because it's better for you than that sludge."

"Ah, you're on a coffee diet."

"My whole life. Never touched the stuff."

She takes a bite of the muffin and rips open two packs of fake sugar at once. She drops the pellets inside and stirs. "How do you get through the day without coffee? I'd be asleep at lunchtime. Hell, I wouldn't even wake up in the morning."

"Your body's used to the caffeine. Mine isn't. I don't wake up craving it."

She sips. "Aah. It gets my creative juices flowing."

"Are you working? On a Saturday?"

"Yep. Monday deadline."

"For what?"

"Can't say. Non-disclosure. And we never used the karma line in the end. You can have it back."

"What'll I do with it?"

"Save it for a rainy day."

"What was wrong with it?"

"CD said it alienated the JTG."

Joe stares at her.

"The Jesus target group. So, what happened to your phone?"

"That's part of my diet. I've gone low tech."

"How's that going? Still got any friends?"

"It's great. Went for a bike ride this morning. Not a care in the world. Haven't felt this good in ages."

"But you didn't get my text that I was late."

"I can wait. I read the paper."

"I wonder what else you've missed. Don't you wanna know?"

"Probably lots of things. Maybe nothing. Certainly nothing important. If it is important, I'll find out eventually. We don't have to know everything the minute it happens. And think about it. If you'd known I had no phone, you would've tried to get here on time."

She takes another bite and shakes her head. "Wrong."

"You just sent a text and expected everything to be fine. The phone is like a safety switch, an instant excuse. Before everyone had a phone, no one was late like they are these days."

"That's crap. People have always been late."

The guy on the video phone turns to face them. "Can you two keep it down. I'm on the phone here."

"This is a cafe, buddy, not a telephone booth."

The man picks up his notebook and goes to the corner. "Some joker arguing with his girlfriend. No, that's not how it was between us..."

Joe laughs. "I'm so glad that's not me."

"You're bizarro, Joe."

"Thanks."

"What other digital things are you cutting down on?"

"Internet time. Email. I unplugged my wireless box. I'm also done with doing any work-related stuff on weekends or after hours."

She sips her coffee and talks over the rim of her glass. "And?"

"And what?"

"You still got a job?"

"Sure."

"We'll see how long that lasts."

"I already talked it over with my boss. We made a compromise."

She raises her eyebrows.

"No bonus for me this year. And I gave him a great idea that he presented to the team as his own."

"You're killing your career."

"Maybe. But I least I got my weekends and evenings back. I can separate work from my private life and I can turn the phone off."

"You won't get promoted either. Something bad will happen and you'll get fired."

"I'll do something else then. How did you get into advertising?"

She sips, considering this. "Luck. An alignment of the stars."
"How so?"
"It's not that interesting. I had a boyfriend who was a CD at another agency. They were shorthanded and he got me to come in. It was just fact checking, putting bullet points in order and making sure there were registered trademarks where they should be. It all went well and they brought me in for other stuff. Pretty soon I was a copywriter. And now I'm a Creative Primer, but still freelance."
"You didn't have any training?"
"Once you learn the tricks, it's easy. You do a couple of projects and they all become pretty much the same. The CDs and the graphics people, they're the creative ones. Us copywriters just rewrite what the client gives us or rehash what was done before. The clients know what they want to say, but don't know how to say it."
"I could do that."
"Not unless you're willing to work weekends. And your digital diet will get you nowhere in this business."
"Probably not. I'd still like to do something different. Now that I've got control of my life back, I'm seeing opportunities everywhere. Things I just walked straight past before. Have you ever stopped to see how beautiful Montreal is?"
"I never see it in daylight."
"You're missing out. You need to get back control of your life."
"Great. Another man who wants to tell me what to do."
"Sorry. It's just that...I've had a great couple of weeks. I've completely simplified my life. Making decisions is a lot easier with all the noise turned off. Internet, email, texts, phone calls, time wasting. It all stopped me from choosing what's really important. Now, I go home and I have the whole evening to do what I want. I've simplified my choices. Life is easy."
"How are you spending the evenings? In front of the box, I bet."
"I went to the pool one night. Had dinner with my friend Francois. Did two yoga classes. Last night I went to the cinema. I haven't done that in ages."
"What did you see?"
"There was a sci-fi festival at Cinema du Parc. You know it? It's around the corner from where I live. They were showing *Mad Max*."
"The one with Tina Turner?"
"That was later. This was the original, before Mel Gibson was

anyone. Post-apocalyptic Australia, cars out in the desert. It's brilliant. Looks like it cost about a thousand dollars to make. No computers, no digital technology, no special effects. Just a bunch of people having fun making a very weird film."

"I'll find it online and have a look. I like sci-fi."

"It's better on the big screen."

"What did you say a minute ago, about simplifying and decision making?"

"Simplify your choices."

She sits back and drains her coffee. There's some grainy sludge at the bottom and she downs this too. "Simplify your choices. Yeah. How did you get to this point? I mean, how did the diet start?"

"I took a holiday at a place in Oregon where no tech was allowed. They confiscate your phone and computer when you check in. It's very corporate, all business people recovering from breakdowns, but I loved it. I decided to take that attitude and apply it to my life here."

"You don't feel disconnected?"

"No. I'm simplifying. Everything's easier."

"Yeah, simplify your choices. That's it."

"What is?"

"The slogan. They're consolidating their products, less is more, that kind of thing. Simplify choice. That's it. Gotta go. Thanks, Joe. I'll text you."

***

"You know what you should do?"

Joe leans back in his chair. "I have a feeling you're going to tell me."

"Start a ceeville page, with that theme."

Francois laughs. "The point is to go low tech, Xav."

"I wanna know how many people out there would be into this. Don't you?"

"The internet's not an accurate measure of popularity."

"You don't know what you're talking about, Francois. It totally is."

Joe pulls his notebook out of his satchel. "I think you're missing the point. It's a digital diet."

"That everyone will want to be on. Start a page."

"What would we call it?"

"What was the name of that place you went to?"

"Rusticity."

"Use that."

Joe boots up the notebook. "I think we need to come up with something original."

"You think Supe will go there?"

"Probably not. He'll send Enora to make the deal."

"But it was your idea."

Francois looks at Joe. "What was?"

Xav interrupts. "Supe went ballistic when Joe didn't answer any emails, texts or calls. But then Joe bribed him with a brilliant idea."

"Which was? Joe, please speak for yourself."

"A line of vanity medicine for retreats like Rusticity, and spa resorts. You know, downers, weight-loss pills, relaxers, wonder pills with small amounts of HGH, stuff like that."

"HGH? I'm not down with your pill lingo."

"Human growth hormone. The elixir of youth."

Xav interrupts again. "Yeah, but packaged and marketed as supplements and not as medicine. It'll open up a whole new market for us. And you let Supe take all the credit for it."

"Why? Xav, will you let Joe talk."

"Calm down, man. Go for it, Joe. The floor's yours."

"It was a bargaining chip, so I could go low tech outside of work hours. That reminds me. I better turn the wireless box on."

He gets up and plugs it in.

"You're gonna have a ton of email at work tomorrow."

"Yeah, but at least I got my life back, Xav."

"It won't last."

"We'll see. Right. I'm on ceeville. What'll we call this city?"

Francois leans over Joe's shoulder to look at the screen. "What did the Creative Primer steal from you?"

"Karma is important."

"Creative whater?"

Francois runs his hands through his hair. "Karma, karma, karma."

"Karma chameleon?"

"Karmaland?"

Xav snaps his fingers. "I got it. Karmaville."

Joe shakes his head. "Going low tech isn't really about karma. It's gotta be more simple than that."

"Easytown."

"Sounds like a porn city."

Xav laughs. "Come...in Easytown. Ha."

Francois picks up the wine and empties the bottle into his glass. "No more wine for you. The key word, Joe, is simple."

All three stare at the screen. Joe's fingers are poised over the keyboard. He types.

"Simplicity. That's brilliant."

"And incredibly, it's not taken."

Xav sips his wine and then looks curiously at the empty glass. "That's because everyone uses their own name."

"Well, it's mine now. The mayor of Simplicity is Joe Solitus. Should I use my real name?"

"Why not?"

"This is the internet. Once it's there, it's there forever."

Francois shakes his head. "Too late. You already signed in with your own name."

"It's just a test."

Joe types as he talks. "I've made it a farming village. Anyone who joins up has to have a trade. I've just sent it to all my ceevillians to join up."

Xav pulls out his phone. "I'm in. I'm a blacksmith. I'll forward it to all my ceevillians too."

Francois does the same with his phone. "'Welcome to Simplicity, the low tech town. Only farmers, handworkers, artists and craftspeople are wanted. Become a ceevillian if you want to reduce your dependence on technology. Here, simplicity is the answer.' That's good, Joe."

"Thanks."

"So, I think I'll be a shepherd."

Joe looks at the screen. "Ten people have already joined up. A carpenter, another shepherd, a shearer, a milkmaid."

"That's gotta be a girl."

"It's Cheryline."

"Who?"

"The Creative Primer. She's in advertising, when she's not wasting time on ceeville. Holy crap. There's now twenty. Twenty-four. Twenty-nine. Fuck this. I'm turning it off."

"Wait, Joe. Write something for your ceevillians."

"Like what?"

Xav looks around the apartment. He gets up and goes to the fridge.

"One of these labels. Here. This one. 'Practice problem solving and not problem maintenance.'"

"That's not the best label, but it fits. What do you think, Francois?"

"Try it. Maybe twist it to include simplifying, somehow."

Joe taps at the keyboard. Xav and Francois look over his shoulder.

Xav reads: "'Simplicity rule number thirteen. Practice problem solving rather than problem maintenance.'"

"Not bad, Joe."

He clicks send and then shuts down the computer.

"What are you doing?"

"Digital diet, Xav."

"Don't you want to read the comments?"

"No, not really."

Xav taps at his phone. "There's now forty-seven ceevillians. I knew it. This is gonna be huge. You could organise tech-free days, when all the ceevillians turn their phones off and stay offline. We could organise events, picnics, barbeques. This is important. Major."

Joe slides his notebook back into the satchel. "No, it isn't. It just shows how many people are bored at home with nothing better to do on a Sunday night than play with their computers and phones. And they all probably just joined up because they feel they have to. Now, both of you get out. I'm going to bed."

Francois stands up. "Good idea. Thanks for dinner, Joe."

Xav drinks from his glass, even though there's nothing in it. "We'll discuss this tomorrow at lunch."

"Hopefully I'll get lunch. I might spend the whole day reading and answering pointless emails, like I did last Monday."

"Do it now."

"Good night, Xav."

Francois smiles from the doorway. "Don't worry. I'll make sure he gets in a cab."

***

"Update me."

They go around the circle.

"I'm really doing this well..."

"I'm doing just great with that..."

"I've got this project totally under control..."

Potential, negotiations, key accounts, critical meetings, core business, profit, cliché, cliché, cliché.

"Thanks, Xavier. Joe?"

"Uh, well, uh. You know what, Miles. I'm not going to dress up my projects as if I'm saving the company, and the world, or just talk smoke and mirrors about nothing and waste everyone's time. Last week, I contacted a bunch of CMs in Ottawa. I heard back from a couple and I haven't heard back from the rest yet. Three deals are finalised."

Enora leans forward and raises her finger. She has a greedy look on her face, a retro goose sitting on a golden egg. "Actually, if I may. I got an email from the chief of medicine of Ottawa Civic. He wanted to make a deal, but no one answered his email. I followed it up over the weekend."

Supe slaps the table. "That's the kind of commitment we need. It's a good thing you work next to her, Joe. You can learn just by watching."

"Wait a minute. How did you get his contact? Did you hack into my email?"

Enora bristles. "Of course not. When you didn't reply, he sent an email to our info address. It got forwarded to me on Saturday morning."

"That's what I want. Commitment, round the clock. Keep it up, Enora. You're setting a standard we all can follow. Now, go get em, team."

They all stand up.

"Not you, Joe."

Joe sits back down. Enora purses her lips into a smile as she leaves, her tight tweed pants ruffling as she walks.

"Look, Miles, I would've seen that email this morning and I would've taken care of it, you know that. Enora just wanted the win."

"Don't make this personal, Joe. Enora's on top of things. She's thorough, and she's a team player. But you, Joe, you try to put I in team. The question is, what do we do about it?"

"I think my work speaks for itself."

Supe pouts, disagreeing. "We're not all about bottom lines and profit margins at Denoris. Our main focus is best business practice. Streamlining processes and getting the most out of our staff. And part of that includes being contactable all the time. Think about it, if you had been online on Saturday, you would have solved this problem without having to depend on Enora's incredible attention to detail."

"Where are you going with this, Miles?"

"Phone and computer always on. When that phone rings, you answer. When the emails come in, you reply, and I mean really reply. You've got to be ready to react."

"What about our deal?"

"It'll have to be off. For now."

"This was just one time."

Supe shakes a finger. "That's how it always starts. If this happened once a week for a year, you'd have fifty-two examples of missed opportunities and lost deals. Is that what you want? If you were in my position, would you be willing to let that happen?"

"I guess not."

"You forget that everything that happens in this team comes back to me. It all comes back to me. That's why I have such a vested interest in your performance."

"Where does that leave us?"

Supe stands up. "Like I just said, always contactable. Good talk, Joe. I love the ceeville page, by the way. I'm a fruit picker. Maybe you should practice what you preach. Problem solving and not problem maintenance. Yep. 'Simplicity is the answer.' I like that."

Down the hall, he lets Supe get ahead and then stops at the kitchenette to make a cup of tea. He rinses the grey sludge out of the bottom of the kettle, fills it and turns it on. Xav comes up and pumps some coins into the coffee machine.

"How did that go?"

"My tech embargo has been lifted."

"I told you it wouldn't last. What're you gonna do?"

He takes his University of NSW mug from the shelf and drops a tea bag inside. "Not sure. Maybe it's time to show Supe the pics."

"No way. That's our last resort."

"We could show them to the board. Get them both fired."

"Supe will just twist it, call it a team building exercise."

"Or just deny everything and say the photos were doctored."

"They're for emergencies only."

Joe pours water into his mug. He lifts the tea bag up and down. "Max used to say, it's better to be fired than to quit."

"There's nothing wrong with quitting. You're just not allowed to. You can't leave me here."

"Don't worry, Xav. I'm not gonna quit. Not unless I've got

something else to go to. But I'm also not gonna check email or answer the phone out of work hours."

"Come on. You do it once in the morning and once in the evening. Simple. Takes half an hour."

He lifts the tea bag out and drops it in the trash. "That's not the point. Even if it takes five minutes, I'm not doing it. I'm sick of work being my whole life. Last weekend, I didn't think about this place at all."

"Yeah, and look what happened."

"That was Corporate Hipster's fault."

"Bitch."

"I don't hold it against her. I feel sorry for her. She was just doing her job. She's got more...commitment than me. Can you imagine how pathetic her life must be? Getting up at six on Saturday morning to sift through the info email for potential wins."

"Meeting Supe in hourly hotel rooms."

Joe shakes his head. "They're not fucking. The copy room was a one off, fuelled by eggnog and rum and Enora's desire to get ahead."

They take their cups back to their desks. With his free hand, Xav pulls out his phone.

"Have you checked your page?"

"No."

Xav shows him the screen. "Nearly two hundred ceevillians. This little self-sufficient farming village is growing fast. Even my little sister joined up."

"Let me see."

He stops walking and takes the phone. Gordie, Dylan, Marcus, Enora, Iris, Anastasia, Louis, Declan, as well as lots of other names he doesn't recognise.

"They all want to live low tech, like you. I'm telling you, Joe. This is something."

"It's just a bunch of people who clicked on a link out of obligation. That means nothing in the real world."

"Then let's bring it into the real world."

"How?"

"An event. A meet-up. A lot of these people are in Montreal. I know someone at McGill. We could do it there."

"What would I say?"

"You could talk about simplicity. Quote some of the labels on your fridge. Cut and paste them into a speech."

He hands back the phone and starts walking again. "No one would come."

"Yeah, they would. They're really into it. And you should give them an update."

"Maybe tonight. After my run."

"You run? Since when?"

Joe sits down at his desk. He jiggles his mouse and his screen pops up. He logs on. He has 437 unread messages.

"Hey, Enora. Thanks for covering for me on the weekend."

"You're welcome, Joe. Some of us know how to work."

"Tell you what. You're so good at it, how about you take my computer and do all my work for me. I mean, you obviously don't have a life. This way, you can let me have mine."

"Your life isn't worth having."

Xav laughs.

***

"We're missing yoga."

"So?"

"What about Swami Scully?"

Xav shakes his head. "She never showed up again."

"Maybe she was just visiting. In town on business."

"Maybe. You nervous?"

"No. No one's gonna show up. People have got better things to do on Friday night. Anyway, shouldn't you be at Smash?"

"This is better than after-work drinks with a bunch of dudes. Have you checked your page? Over five hundred ceevillians, last time I checked, and a lot of them are girls. This thing is fast turning into a cult. They want simplicity in their lives. You read the responses to your billboards?"

"Some."

"That one you wrote about looking for beauty. That was brilliant."

"It's from...it's not original."

"Is anything?"

Francois enters the room and walks down the stairs, a huge camera swinging from his neck. "I can't find the Super. You'll have to speak without a mike."

"It doesn't matter. No one's coming."

"I think you should take a look outside."

Joe heads up the stairs and out of the small lecture theatre. Through the glass doors of the McGill Arts Building, he sees about fifty people congregating on the steps. Some are leaning against the columns. Those who know each other are talking together, while those who are alone are hunched over their phones. They look like students, even those who aren't. He sees Cheryline standing with a group of scruffy, trendy people, creative primers and graphics designers, maybe. Other faces look familiar; people he met at parties or sat next to at a wedding. Their names escape him. Friends of friends of friends, all seemingly glad to have something different to do on a Friday night.

Xav sidles up next to him. "I told you. We're not all gonna fit in that room, especially if more show up."

Francois points. "We could do it on the grass. It's a nice evening for it."

Xav claps his hands together. "More fitting too."

Joe looks at the crowd. "Maybe they're here for something else?"

Xav goes through the door. "Can I have everyone's attention. Thanks. The room's too small. We're gonna meet over there on the grass."

The people begin to move, following each other. Joe, Xav and Francois wait and then head for the grass as well. It's a little wet underfoot. People put down their jackets to sit on, or spread out plastic bags, or sit on the front flaps of their shoulder bags. Some stand, off to the side, looking like they want a quick getaway.

Francois whispers to Joe: "You ready for this?"

"What am I supposed to say?"

"What do you think? The speech you wrote. Where did you get all that good stuff?"

"I did some research. At the library. A lot of it's from Max, but I've got the Quakers to thank for the best parts."

"You'll have to shout. Move through the crowd. Don't just stand in front. Move around. Let them all see and hear you."

Joe feels his stomach tighten. It's hard to swallow. "I didn't expect this."

"Too late now. But hold that pose."

Francois raises his camera and clicks it. He checks the LCD. "That's an expression you don't see every day. Man about to be hit by bus."

Joe looks at the crowd. "What do all these people want?"

"The same as you. Low tech. To simplify their lives."

"There's got to be more to it than that."

"Maybe you should ask them. Incorporate questions into the speech."

Joe looks up at the sky. It's tinged pink and yellow, with slithers of dark blue. He likes this time of year, when the days are long and summer's about to begin. The world seems alive with activity and opportunity; he feels more awake and in tune with the world. It's a beautiful evening, in a beautiful city, and somehow he's got these strangers on the McGill lawn waiting to hear him talk. He asks himself what would Max do in this situation. He was a great public speaker, and always took the floor at council sessions, PTA meetings and at the dinner table at home. He spoke slowly, self-assuredly, pausing for effect. He smiled a lot, but also looked pained sometimes, like the words weren't coming that easily and it was difficult to get out what he really wanted to say.

Xav goes to the front of the group. "Welcome, everyone, to the first ever simplicity event. Let me introduce you to the man behind simplicity. Joe Solitus."

The people clap and cheer. As he walks among them, weaving through the crowd, they greet him. He gives Cheryline a smile as he passes.

He's nervous.

Xav grabs his shoulder and whispers: "Just imagine they're all in bondage outfits. That's what I do."

"I haven't spoken in front of group this big since high school graduation."

"How did that go?"

"Max told me to try to sound like everyone else. When you speak in front of people, all they want is to hear bits of themselves. I nailed it."

"Do that now. You've got good material. Say it in a way they want to hear."

"Here goes nothing."

He moves around to face the group and holds his hands up to show the applause is undeserved, unnecessary, that they're all equals here. The clapping dies down.

"Thanks. And thanks everyone for coming out."

"Louder."

He raises his voice. “Thanks for coming out. My name’s Joe. Right, uh, you’re probably all members of simplicity so you’ve got a fair idea what this is all about. Thanks a lot for being part of the ceeville page and for all the billboards and comments you posted. It’s great to find people who have similar ideas about technology and how the world is at the moment. So, thanks to all of you for being involved and for making simplicity happen.”

The crowd claps. Joe smiles and nods, feeling good as he recognises the sound of self-applause.

“Let me say this right at the start. I’m a fan of the internet. I think it’s a fantastic tool and I can’t imagine a world without it. What I don’t like is that we’ve become completely dependent on it. By limiting my internet use, I’ve got back control of my life. It’s as simple as that. I went offline and outside. And best of all, I’ve now got more time.”

He steps forward and starts weaving through the crowd.

“I used to think, ahem, that there wasn’t enough time in the day to get everything done. I was rushing through the life, living at hyper-speed, always behind. I spent a lot of my free time on the internet. And you know how that goes. You sit down to quickly check your email and stand up three hours later wondering where the time went. The internet is informative, useful and entertaining, but there’s no beauty, no true friendship, no personal contact. Look at this. A fabulous evening, in a great city, with a bunch of like-minded people. You can actually reach out and touch the person next to you. They’re real. We’re not all sitting in our own rooms interacting over screens. I think this is great.”

He continues to move, making eye contact, smiling, but then trying to look pained and momentarily lost. He rubs his chin, softly hits his fist against his lips.

“Do you know Occam’s Razor? It’s a theory that says the simplest explanation is often the correct one. We’ve made our lives more complicated. Technology has complicated our lives. We’re slaves to it. So turn it off. Disconnect from the tech and reconnect with the world. Just like tonight. This is an important gathering, much more than a bunch of people commenting on Plasher. That’s the problem with the internet. We think it’s a social, interactive place, but there are no real people to hold on to. It’s an anonymous, lonely place, where people are never really themselves with their real names. But here, here, you have real friends, real experiences, real life.”

The crowd claps solemnly.

"The internet isn't a lifestyle or a social network. We've made this technology part of our lives, so we can also turn that around. Like cigarettes. If you start smoking, you're also the one who can stop smoking. You are in control. Turn it all off. Simple."

Someone shouts: "But I need it, to communicate and work."

"Sure, but we don't need all the time. All this communication, all these emails and texts, most of them aren't even necessary. Simplify it. Focus on what's important. Hell, sit down and write a letter to someone. Email is the blandest, most unromantic form of communication. Take the time to write a letter and show how much you care about someone."

"I don't have time to write letters."

"You would if you turned all your tech off."

"The post takes too long."

"We've forgotten how to be patient. We're programmed for instant gratification. We expect everything now, when we want it."

"Email's fast and free."

Everyone starts to talk at once. Joe raises his hands.

"Okay. OKAY! Look, there's nothing wrong with writing emails. Spending a whole day writing stupid emails with links to videos or making endless comments on Plasher, I think that's a waste of time. If you're doing that, you've lost control of your life. Look, you've all come out here tonight because you believe in simplicity. You feel it has something to offer you, but I know we can't go from a hundred percent to zero overnight. A good way to get started would be for all of us to have one tech-free day a week. Then you'll see how it is to free yourself from the internet and other technology. One day with no internet, no phones, no music players, no games."

"Which day?"

"Let's say, Sundays."

"And do what instead?"

"Whatever you want. Sit in the park. Read a book. Meet friends. Sleep until noon. Write a long letter to your parents and thank them for all the things you never thanked them for. Search for records at a fleamarket. Play golf. Visit grandma. Ride a bike out to the forest, sit under a tree and stare at the world. It's up to you. We could all meet in the park and throw the frisbee around."

"This Sunday?"

Joe shrugs. "That's a great idea. Are you in? I'm in. We could meet across the street from the angel statue in Mont Royal. Where all the drummers hang out. At around two. Yeah? I guess we'll all see each other then. The evening is young and the city is alive. Get out and enjoy it."

With that, the crowd claps and starts to disperse. A few people crowd around Joe, wanting more, wanting him to know their names and hear their stories. They seem desperate for advice, for direction. He tells them to simplify, repeating some of the key points of his speech. He promises to post the entire speech on the ceeville page.

When nearly everyone is gone, Cheryline comes up to Joe. "Great speech. I never thought you had something like that in you."

"Me neither. Cheryline, this Francois and Xav."

They shake hands.

"Are you the collective brains behind this boy? Which one of you wrote the speech?"

"I wrote it myself."

"It was awesome. There were about a dozen lines in there that would make great slogans. And the guys and gals were hanging on your every word."

Francois takes a photo of Cheryline. "They left pretty quick."

Joe looks down at the scattering of plastic bags, newspaper, water bottles and food wrappers. "And they left their mark. Come on. Let's clean some of this up."

Xav groans. "Someone else will do it."

"It'll take five minutes, Xav, if we all do it. And I'll buy you the cocktail of your choice if you help."

Cheryline picks up some trash. "Does that go for me too?"

"Yep."

Francois takes some photos of them cleaning up and then helps as well. "I don't know, Joe. I got a feeling we should be buying you drinks."

***

He wakes suddenly.

Popov jumps up onto the bed, stretches his back and claws at the blanket a little.

"Stop that. Yeah. I'll feed you in a minute."

The doorbell rings, long and loud. Popov turns his head.

"So, that did wake me. It wasn't a dream. You expecting someone?"

He throws off the covers and pulls on his jeans from last night. They're still slightly wet. He vaguely remembers walking through the rain after leaving Okey Karaokey, with Francois and Cheryline doing a very drunk a capella version of *Fairytale in New York*, dancing around traffic lights and getting all the lyrics mixed up, with Francois doing a French accent instead of Irish. There's even a distorted memory of himself singing *Locomotive Breath* in the bar. Oh God, did he really try to whistle the flute solo?

His head hurts. It's difficult to keep his eyes open. Popov follows him to the door.

"It must be for you, Pops. No friend of mine would come this early."

He misses the lock on the first attempt, gets it on the second. He clicks it, unhooks the chain and fumbles with the door handle.

"Anita?"

She charges into the apartment.

***

They walk up Avenue du Parc. After a rainy Saturday, today it's a cold and clear.

Anita breaks the silence between them. "I take full credit for this."

"You do?"

"I took you to Rusticity. I got you on this digital diet. I got this whole thing started."

"You can have it."

"Why aren't you proud of this?"

"Like I told you yesterday, I don't think it's really anything."

"Are you for real? This almost qualifies as an underground movement. All those ceevillians. Your videos have been viewed, like, hundreds of times. They're great by the way. You were great."

"You can stop saying that."

She pulls out her phone. "Here. Take a look for yourself."

"Can't. It's tech-free Sunday."

"Where did you steal all that good stuff from? It was gold. Especially Gollum's Razor. The masses gobbled it up."

"Occam's Razor."

"Right. You linked it perfectly. Sold the gospel according to Joe."

"Now you're stretching it."

The drums get louder as they near the angel statue. It's crowded, with drummers and viewers. Some people are dancing, many are just watching. When they see Joe, the news passes through the crowd and they turn in his direction. They try to cross the street against the traffic. Horns blare. People whoop and laugh.

Anita watches. "Did you get this many on Friday?"

But Joe is already backing away from the street, onto the grass and towards the playing fields. He walks quickly and looks behind him to see Anita following, and a few hundred people rushing after her. He sees Xav work his way to the front, struggling with a big backpack and two large plastic bags. He's wearing a plain white shirt with "Simplicity is the answer" written on it.

"Joe. JOE!"

He gets close to the fence of the soccer field. Stuck. Cornered. The crowd closes in on him. Xav tries to keep them back. Joe sees smiling faces, young and eager, people he's never seen before. He raises his free hand to get their attention and quieten them down. In response, nearly every second person points a phone camera at him.

"Welcome to our first ever tech-free Sunday."

Loud cheering and clapping.

"Right. Okay. Let's do this as simply as possible. Frisbee throwers over there. Pot smokers over there. Cloud watchers here next to the fence. Musicians over there. Readers, under those trees. Everyone else, do whatever you want. It's a beautiful day to be outside. Enjoy it and leave only your footprints."

The people attempt to organise themselves, but everyone seems to want to go in a different direction. Joe sees them pushing and shoving, arms raised as they point, phones pinned to their ears as they try to locate friends. A lot of people are crowding around Xav, who is selling t-shirts from his open backpack. They wave ten dollar bills in the air and slip on the shirts as soon as they buy them. Always green lettering on white.

"'Simplicity is the answer.'"

"'If you go looking for beauty, that's what you'll find.'"

"'Practice problem solving rather than problem maintenance.'"

And shorter versions.

"'Simplicity rocks.'"

"'"Problem solver."'"

"'"Searching for beauty."'"

Joe watches from the fence. The people have spread out on the grass in small groups, encroaching on the space of others who were already there, parents with small children who are now forced to move. They throw Frisbees and kick soccer balls. As equipment is in short supply, a dozen people have got an elaborate game of tag going. There are several tight circles of pot smokers, interlocking like the Olympic rings, and already immersed in a greyish-green fog. The creaky plinks of out-of-tune guitars get picked up by the wind, then dropped again. A few people are trying to sing along and others are trying to dance. All the cloud watchers have gathered around Joe. They stare at him, awaiting direction.

Anita looks up at him. "Do something."

"What?"

"Tell them what to do. They all listen to you."

He turns to the crowd. "Okay. Everyone lie down."

They do so, with some using their bags as pillows and half of them already wearing simplicity shirts. They point at the sky, talking about what they can see. Some laugh, some talk on phones, some try to photograph the clouds.

Anita shakes her. "I'm glad I came for this."

"Not just a spontaneous visit."

"Look at this, Joe. Look what you've started. What I started."

"I got two hundred bored kids to come out on a Sunday. Wow."

"Joe. Hey, Joe. You won't believe it. All the shirts, sold."

"Xav, this is Anita. A friend of mine from Boston."

"How's it going?"

They shake hands.

Xav's eyes narrow. "Do we know each other?"

"I don't think so."

"Can you believe this, Joe? I should've made a thousand shirts."

"Why? There aren't a thousand people here."

"For next time. Or an online shop."

"Why did you do that without telling me?"

"I sent you a text yesterday. I figured if you didn't want me to do it, you would've texted my back saying so."

"Fantastic logic. No phone, remember?"

"We need to stay in better contact. I made a stack of cash."

"Maybe you can use that money to buy everyone here an ice cream."

"No way. I've got my own overheads to cover."

Anita looks in the empty backpack. "Which shirt was the most popular?"

"The one with the slogan. 'Simplicity is the answer.' They all wanted that."

"Hey, Joe."

"Cheryline, hi."

"Sorry, I'm late. I miss anything?"

"Just the shirts."

She looks down at the cloud watchers, at those wearing the shirts. "Cool. Can I have one?"

Xav holds up the empty backpack. "Sold out. Next time, I guarantee it."

Joe does the introductions. "Anita, this is Cheryline. She steals my lines for her ad copy. And while we're at it, the guy over there taking photos is Francois."

"The man with the broken heart rule."

"That's him."

Cheryline looks at the crowd. "They all here for simplicity? There's gotta be twice as many as Friday. More. You were awesome, Joe. Those vids are great."

"I think I better have a look at them tomorrow."

Xav is incredulous. "You haven't seen them?"

"Digital diet. All of us are supposed to be tech-free today."

Anita laughs. "You might have to push that a little harder. All these kids are wired."

"Well, at least they're outside. They could be sitting alone in a dark room in front of a screen."

"That's true. Congratulations."

Joe points at a vacant expanse of grass at the end of the soccer field. "Let's sit over there. Get away from the crowd."

They leave the cloud watchers, get thankfully upwind from the pot and cigarette smokers, and out of earshot of the whooping and laughing tag players and frisbee throwers. Joe sits down with his back against the fence. The others gather round him.

"Bad news, Joe. My CD didn't go for the simplify choice line. You can have it back."

Xav snaps his fingers. "Simplify choice. That's going straight onto a t-shirt."

Joe smiles. "Why stop there? Baseball caps, coffee cups, flags, little bobble-head dolls."

Anita uses her phone to take a photo of Joe. "Better than that. Go on tour."

"We're not a rock band. And we're not that popular. And we don't actually do anything. What would we tour with? What's the show?"

"A lecture tour. Hit the college circuit. Have events like this one. Get the kids outside, like you want to."

"No one would show up."

Xav scoffs. "You said that on Friday and looked what happened."

"We were lucky."

"I guess you haven't checked the page since."

"Digital diet, Xav. How are you not getting that? And put the phone away. It's tech-free Sunday."

"Simplicity is getting bigger each day. And the page is full of comments and billboards. You can't keep up with it all."

"Everyone's got something to say, but that doesn't mean they're involved."

Anita thumbs towards the crowd. "These people are. It was the videos, Joe. They're great."

"And not just the ones me and Francois shot, but other people filmed and posted as well. Some guy even wrote a song about it and recorded himself playing it."

"You're joking."

Xav takes out his phone. "Look for yourself."

"Not today. God."

"Do it later then. And someone set up a rival city. Complexity."

Cheryline taps her phone. "Only eleven ceevillians. We're winning."

Anita looks towards the crowd. "You've really started something, Joe. I started something."

"You? This was me and Joe and Francois. I organised the event on Friday and I sold the t-shirts."

Joe holds up his hands. "Everyone is involved, Xav. Let's not get possessive. We don't even know what we've done yet."

Anita smiles. "That's simple. We've created a target group."

***

"This is all Colonel Mustard's fault."

"What?"

"Actually, it's Max's fault. No, Anita's. And Xav with those fucking shirts."

"A lot of people to blame. But who is Colonel Mustard?"

"The label maker."

Francois throws down his shot of tequila. "Ah. It always tastes so good after swimming. How is it with Anita? She staying with you?"

"Yeah. It's awkward. We toured the Vieux Port on Saturday. I thought that day would never end. She's flying back tomorrow."

"You tell her about Iris?"

"What do you think?"

"Girls love honesty."

Joe throws down his shot. "Phwoar. Not that kind."

"She could handle it."

"Yeah, but I don't wanna have that conversation."

"She's a tough one. I like her."

"You're free to steal her from me. Or are you keen on Cheryline?"

Francois sips his Corona. "I think she likes you."

"There's nothing going on between us. Believe me. I think I just made a friend. A good one too."

"So, Anita and Cheryline won't fight over you?"

"Nuh."

"Still, what a great day."

"Any day that ends in the pool is a great day."

"I mean the afternoon in the park. I made some great contacts."

"For work?"

"Yep. Could you believe the crowd? How many do you think were there?"

"I don't know. Two or three hundred."

"Good turnout for an underground anti-internet movement."

"Where are they all coming from, Francois? What do they want?"

"They need direction."

"So do I. Everyone does."

"Joe, modesty doesn't become you."

"What does that mean?"

"Come on. It's me."

"I have no idea what you're on about."

"You do."

"You think...you think I'm enjoying this? This was all Xav's idea, remember? He got it all going."

"And he's trying very hard to take credit for it. But the digital diet, simplifying, the labels, the speech on Friday, the delivery. That's all you, Joe. Xav doesn't have the charisma or the smarts to pull that kind of stuff off. It's all you."

"I just told them what they wanted to hear."

"And did it brilliantly. I think you better go home and look at the videos."

"I hate seeing myself on camera."

"There's probably a bunch from today that have already been uploaded, but you need to see the ones I made on Friday."

"That's the last ever tech-free Sunday. Did you see them all? On their phones, music players in their ears, everything. I even saw people with notebooks. They were blogging and plashing between frisbee throws."

Francois laughs. "Tech-free is never gonna happen. You know that."

"They're all missing the point."

"They don't have to do it exactly like you, but at least they're thinking about the tech in a new way and are reassessing what it means to their lives."

"That's not the same as switching it all off."

"No, but you can't expect them to do that. Maybe it needs more time. More motivational talks from the king of simplicity."

Joe rubs his eyes, feels the grooves left by the goggles. "Did you hear Xav and Anita?"

"Yeah, Simplicity Incorporated. SINC. Sounds like they've got big plans."

"They just wanna make money."

"Is that so bad? You should probably do it before someone steals the concept. You could quit Denoris and become independent. Hell, we could all get rich."

"What would be your part in all this?"

"Image Maximiser."

Joe laughs. "So, in a perfect world, Anita and Xav fall in love, you get together with Cheryline, Iris moves to Montreal, and SINC is bigger than Christianity."

"Cheryline's not my type. And she likes you. I thought she and

Anita might have a cat fight. That would've been worth filming. Still, what would be the offspring of an Image Maximiser and a Creative Primer?"

"A Creative Maximiser."

"Or an Image Primer. No, it's not a perfect world. Those couples are not going to form. Maybe you and Iris, but she's still on the other side of the continent. Anita and Xav don't have a chance. She'd eat him alive, spit out his bones in a neat pile and set them on fire. But SINC. I don't know, Joe. That could be something, if only as a clothing label. Simplify choice. That's cool."

"So the clothing line would be just one shirt for everybody?"

"Why not? Keep it simple. White shirts, different slogans on them. For all of Xav's idiocy, he really got it right. Especially the colours. I never thought he'd know about that sort of stuff. Green and white. Hope and purity. An army of eco angels."

"I was thinking more about blank envy."

"That too. It's always good if others want what you have. Good for sales, I mean."

"So, we all just quit our jobs and start SINC?"

Francois offers a thin smile. "I know your attitude to quitting. Maybe the universe will help. In the meantime, go home and look at the vids. You really were great."

"I just copied Max?"

"What?"

"I copied Max."

"It worked. Keep doing it."

***

"You're fired."

"Excuse me?"

Supe moves the papers on his desk, avoiding eye contact, looking busy. "Your out-of-office activities are compromising Denoris. The board has asked that you be dismissed."

"The board?"

"Yes."

"The board of dinosaurs who are suddenly wired into the latest online trends?"

"It was my recommendation."

"But you're a ceevillian of simplicity."

Supe's beard scrunches up as he grins. "Not under my real name."

"Ray Smiley. No one will ever know that's you. How about I go up to the board and tell them?"

"I can deny everything. There's no proof. Anyway, they don't even know what ceeville is. Half of them don't know what the internet is. Walt thinks it's our own internal computer network. The whole of the world wide web, in here."

"Huh."

"You don't look very disappointed."

"I'm trying to decide whether to sue you or not. I don't see how my personal life is grounds for dismissal."

"Then you need to read your contract. I guess you never read it in the first place. Details, Joe. That's your problem. You skip all the important details. You can't ever compromise the company, and that includes what you do outside the office."

"What about inside the office? Say, in the copy room?"

"Are you the one who's been stealing paper?"

Joe shakes his head. "No. Where, uh, what happens now?"

"You pack up your things and go home. Immediately. You leave your notebook and phone on your desk."

"Gladly."

"And you're not allowed to work for competitors or in the industry for six months."

"What?"

Supe raises a long index finger. "Read your contact. But seeing as you never did, I'll tell you now the six months is unpaid. You'll get this month and whatever holiday pay is owed to you and that's it. Now, get out of my office."

"Your cubicle."

"Pardon?"

Joe stands up. He slides his hands into his pockets and looks at the Greenpeace poster. "Is this really you?"

"Yes."

"It looks like you cut and pasted yourself into the picture."

"It's real. I was there."

"Where?"

"The Coromandel. New Zealand."

"Nice place. You went all the way there to save the whales?"

"I was on holiday. With my family. We saw the whales and I got involved."

"I'm impressed."

"You should be."

"I just want to be clear, so I don't make the same mistake again. This is the kind of out-of-office activity that's all right. If I save a whale in New Zealand, that won't get me fired?"

"It's the kind of proactive community action that would get you promoted."

"Ah, that's why you did it. But making an innocent page on ceeville that motivates people to go outside and maybe save whales or help others, that's bad?"

"You're simplifying the situation."

Joe laughs.

"What I mean is, what I really mean is that you're not looking deep enough. Your thought processes are too superficial, Joe, that's your problem. You never look at the bigger picture."

"Yeah, no big picture. No details. No change management. No whale saving."

"Now you're starting to get it."

"What about Xav? He's in this too."

"Also not under his real name. Besides, he's got the best sales results of anyone in the team this quarter."

"Maybe if he blows one of the dinosaurs on the board, he'll have your job soon."

"I beg your pardon?"

Joe looks closer at the poster, at a fuzzy-looking Supe with a yellow raincoat and matching hat. His pale legs are sticking out from his shorts, his white feet in brown, sand-covered sandals. Behind the whale, two blurred kids are playing in the sand. Supe's weekend son and daughter, then his full-time kids.

"I want six months full pay."

"That's funny. Didn't you hear anything I just said?"

"Six months full pay or I'll sue you for wrongful dismissal. You're just using simplicity as an excuse to get rid of me."

"Go for it. You'll lose and have a mountain of legal bills to show for your stupidity."

"This is ceeville, Miles, not child pornography."

"Keep your voice down. It doesn't matter. You compromised the company. You breached your contract. You're screwed. Now, get out."

"Fine. Six months full pay, plus my bonus, plus holiday, and all of it up front in one payment. Or I show the pics of you and Enora to the board."

Supe's hands are poised over the keyboard. Finally, he looks up and makes eye contact. "What pics?"

"Copy room, Christmas party, eighteen months ago. Remarkably, just a week before, out of nowhere, Enora was promoted from your lowly assistant to the sales team even though she had no qualifications or experience. And was then given all the key accounts."

"Nice try. I know what you can do on Photoshop."

Joe looks at the poster again. "You sure do. But what about videos? I've got that too. I could show it all to the board or I could just post it online, for the whole world to see. That might, and correct me if I'm wrong, but that might compromise the company."

***

He takes his time, pushing his bike along the sidewalk, looking in shop windows. He goes into a supermarket, buys the most expensive cat food they've got and a pile of fresh fruit and vegetables. The day feels long and full of possibility. It's even all right to stand in line and wonder how so many people can have free time at ten on a Monday morning. He's happy for them, because now he's one of them.

He loops a bulging plastic bag over each brake lever and wheels the bike home, his hands steadying the handle bars. There's no computer in his satchel, no phone. He's relieved of a massive pair of burdens.

He smiles at everyone. Some smile back, some look at him like he's crazy, most don't even notice him.

Who cares?

He gets to his building and lugs it all upstairs, the bike too. He opens the door.

"Joe?"

His heart sinks a little. He finds her in the living room, sitting at his dining table, notebook open in front of her, two phones next to her right hand.

"What happened?"

"I'm happy to see you too."

"You know how it is when you say goodbye to someone. It's a bit of shock to see them again unexpectedly."

"I changed my flight."

"I thought you had to work today."

"Home office."

"They let you do that?"

She stands up and walks over to him. "Sometimes. What are you doing here? And what's with all the produce?"

"You won't believe what happened."

"Neither will you."

"A busy morning all round."

"You first."

He goes into the kitchen and starts unpacking the bags. "I got fired."

"Just like that?"

"Yep. Walked in this morning and had to go into my boss's office before the first meeting. There was a little post-it note on my desk giving me the order. And when I got there, he fired me."

She comes into the kitchen, leans against the counter and crosses her arms. "What for?"

"This has been coming for a few months. I think he just wanted an excuse, a way to get rid of me without any consequences or pay outs. He said simplicity was compromising the company. My private activities putting Denoris's reputation at risk."

"Denoris's reputation is already in the toilet. But he's right. Simplicity is compromising the company. I'm sorry, Joe."

"Don't be."

"You need a hug?"

"This is the best thing that could've happened. I walked out of that place and felt like a million dollars. The nausea's gone, the tightness in my neck, the feeling like I couldn't swallow. It's all gone. They're all problems that belonged to another Joe Solitus."

"You're happy?"

"Absolutely."

"And this is how you celebrate? With vegetables?"

"I also bought some premium cat food for Popov. I thought I'd invite Xav and Francois and Cheryline over for dinner. You're welcome to stay."

"That sounds meaningful."

"Look, Anita..."

She holds up her hands. "Stop, Joe. You don't need to. Let's just let it go. It was fun, but I know you're not feeling what you're supposed to. Neither am I. And that's good because I don't sleep with people I work with."

"I'm not joining Natrofield. I can't do anything for six months. And I'm sorry. I had a really great time with you in Barcelona, and at Rusticity."

"So did I."

"Until you left."

"I had a work emergency."

He starts putting vegetables in the fridge. There's not enough room. "Where was your phone?"

"In the glove compartment of the rental car."

"You'd been there before."

He closes the fridge and looks at all the labels stuck to the door. He picks up the Colonel and quickly bangs off "Simplify choice". He sticks this to the door.

"That's a good one. Two words that say so much."

"Yeah. So, why are you still here?"

"I didn't change my flight because of you."

"You fall for Popov's charms?"

"Yes, but that's not the reason."

"Well?"

She points at the fridge. "That."

The phone rings.

"And that."

He stares at the phone.

"Aren't you gonna answer it?"

He picks up the kitchen extension. "Hello."

"Is this Joe Solitus?"

"Yes."

"We'd like to talk to you about simplicity."

"Yeah?"

"Can you give us some quotes? I can email you a list of questions."

"Check the ceeville page. It's all there."

He puts the phone down.

"I was just about the leave for the airport and your phone rang."

"You answered it?"

“It was a computer magazine. *Wired*, I think. Or *Weird*. I can’t remember. They wanted some quotes from you for a piece on the simplicity craze sweeping the web.”

“What craze? We got a few kids at the park yesterday. Big deal.”

She gestures with her hand and heads back to the dining table. “It’s viral, but small time viral. Underground, cultish. Still means something.”

He looks at the screen of Anita’s notebook. “I don’t believe it.”

“I’ve been sitting here all morning watching it happen. People uploading videos, people commenting on the simplicity page, people posting photos of themselves in simplicity shirts. I registered all the domains I could think off, and I registered simplicity as a trademark, all lower case letters. And your phone has rung a lot.”

On cue, the phone rings again.

“Hello?”

“Bro, I got ya. Finally.”

“Hey, Gordie.”

“Why the fuck aren’t you answering your cell?”

“Calm down. Work took it from me.”

“Is that really you in the vids?”

“Yeah.”

“...”

“Gordie? He hung up.”

“Maybe he lost his signal.”

Joe sits down at the table. “Have people been calling for interviews?”

“Some. Most of them just wanted to confirm that you actually exist. There were a few crazy people too, but they were the most entertaining.”

“How’d they get the number?”

“The internet knows a lot more about you than you think, Joe.”

The phone rings again.

“Gordie?”

“Joe, it’s me.”

“Oh, hey, Xav.”

“Is it true?”

“Yeah. Supe did it this morning, just before the jour fixe, while you were all in the meeting room waiting.”

“Bastard. He dumped all your stuff on me.”

“Come over for dinner tonight. I’ll tell you everything then.”

"Deal."
"Okay. Get back to work."
"Later."
Joe hangs up the phone.
"What did he say?"
"Supe gave all of my accounts to him. He's swimming in all my old shit, poor guy."
"When all he really wants is to sell more t-shirts."
"Is that what you wanna do?"
"I'm thinking bigger than that."
"Yeah, registering domains and trademarks."
"And more."
He rubs his forehead. "I need to clear my head. I think I'll hit the pool. Wanna come?"
"No, thanks. I've got work to do."
"Home office."
"Right. I'll be here when you get back."
The phone rings. He looks at it and then pulls the cord out of the wall. "So it doesn't distract you. There's an extra set of keys in the kitchen drawer if you wanna go out."
"I'm all right."
"I'll be back for dinner."
"Are you planning to swim for the next seven hours?"
He goes into the bathroom to retrieve his Speedos, towel, goggles, ear plugs and cap. "I'll probably stop and have a cup of tea somewhere. Maybe a piece of cake. Read the paper."
"You sure know how to entertain your guests."
He puts all his stuff in his satchel. "Yesterday wasn't enough?"
"That was...enlightening."
"Maybe it'll last a week. Then another craze will take over."
"I completely disagree, but it still cost you your job."
"I'm fine with that. I'm better off. And I got six months pay. And I can go to the pool on a Monday afternoon."
Popov jumps up onto her lap. She strokes him. "You're the world's most beautiful cat, do you know that?"
"Don't give him an ego."
"We can't hear him, can we Popov? Oh, if only I could take you home and keep you forever."
He loops the satchel over his shoulder and picks up his bike. "No

cat-napping. I'll see you later."

She waves. "Say goodbye, Popov."

***

He doesn't have enough chairs. Francois and Cheryline are sitting on his two kitchen stools, their knees as high as the dining table. They eat from plates held in their hands and flirt a little. Joe notices they're both left-handed.

Xav puts down his finished plate, having eaten twice as fast as everyone else. "I still can't believe they fired you."

"And with six months pay."

"What? Oh, no. Tell me you didn't."

"Sorry, Xav. I had to."

"It was for an emergency."

"I think this counts. Anyway, I didn't show any of them or give him a CD. The threat was enough. You could still use it too."

"It won't have the same punch."

"Look, it was wrongful dismissal. Supe knew that. I got what I deserved."

"I'm gonna quit too. I typed up my resignation this morning."

Francois smirks. "Going into the t-shirt business?"

"I was thinking more like a clothing label. Nothing fancy. Simple, minimalist designs. Sweaters, shirts, caps, socks, everything. Imagine it. Simplify choice on a pair of boxers."

Cheryline gestures with her fork. "Maybe for underwear you could use the searching for beauty line."

"Good idea. Can I have some more, Joe?"

"Help yourself. The kitchen's that way."

Francois puts down his plate and picks up his bottle of beer. "What are you gonna do, Joe?"

"Don't know. I was thinking today about the times I've been the most happy. When I felt like I was really in control of my life."

"And?"

"I had that when I was travelling. When I was out on my own and didn't have anyone to answer to, or any obligations to keep, or any work to do that was solely for someone else's end. I'm thinking of hitting the road."

"Where?"

"Maybe out west. Alberta. British Columbia. Vancouver Island. Always wanted to go there. I'd like to go back down under too. Maybe New Zealand, Indonesia."

"I wanna come."

Cheryline raises her hand. "Me too."

Xav comes out of the kitchen. "Me three. Where are we going?"

"None of us are going anywhere."

They all look at Anita as she sips her wine.

She puts the glass on the table. "We've got work to do. All of us."

Joe shakes his head. "Not me. I'm unemployable pretty much until Christmas."

"Only for drug companies. You could flip burgers at Mickey D's if you wanted to."

Xav talks with his mouth full. "We could start a business, Joe. SINC Clothing."

"You've already got a job."

"I'm serious. You saw what happened yesterday. This is a brand people want."

Joe points at Xav. "Use that word again and I'm throwing you out."

"It's got massive potential. And not just here in Montreal. I'm talking global."

Francois scoffs. "Don't stop there. Mars, Venus, Saturn. The whole galaxy awaits."

"Man, you of all people should really want this to happen. How many pictures you sell today?"

"Of Joe? None, but plenty were stolen. People took stills from my videos as well."

"At least you're getting great exposure."

"Exposure doesn't pay the rent, Xav."

"Well, you could be the snapper for the first SINC catalogue."

"Can I get an up-front payment?"

Cheryline gestures with her fork again. A slither of carrot hits the floor. She doesn't notice. "Can I write the copy?"

Xav smiles and nods at Cheryline. Then he looks at Francois, Anita and finally Joe. "Hey. We've got everything right here. In this room. We could start, like, now."

Joe sips his wine. "Start what?"

"SINC, Joe. SINC."

"I swim."

They all laugh.

"We already know simplicity's got a target group. We have to tap it."

"With t-shirts, Xav?"

"For starters, yeah. To get the brand going."

"Okay. Last warning."

Anita stands up. She goes to the sofa and retrieves her notebook.

Xav again talks while he eats. "But we could do lots of things. Diversify into music, tours, films, TV. Whatever we want. We could even apply simplicity to businesses, as grand per hour consultants."

Francois points at Xav with his beer bottle. "Don't forget God. He could use our help too."

Joe and Cheryline laugh.

"Francois, you should be behind this all the way. This is your chance to make something of yourself."

"Slow down, you pill-pushing office monkey. I've already done a lot more in my life that's worthwhile than you, even if you live to be a hundred. If I'd been born twenty years earlier, I'd be living in a penthouse in Manhattan."

"Whatever."

Anita spins her notebook so the screen faces them all. "We could argue all night, or we could actually get something done. Here. I made a business plan."

Xav claps his hands. "Now that's what I'm talking about. Marry me, Anna."

"Anita."

Joe, Francois and Cheryline laugh.

She gets some PowerPoint slides on the screen. "As I see it, SINC should have three business channels. Products, multimedia and events. Products would be clothing, merchandise, maybe even accessories like jewellery and fragrances, easily accessible stuff and not expensive. Xav is right. The designs should be minimalist and simple. Multimedia includes music, film, books and a fully interactive web presence. Events would be Joe giving lectures and talks, and meet-ups like we had yesterday. The events would offer profitable avenues for cross-brand advertising."

Xav holds his hands in the air, palms up, and looks at the ceiling. "Thank you. The angel has spoken. It's brilliant. I'm in. I wanna be head of products."

"It's all theoretical at the moment. We don't have any capital, unless you sold a million shirts today. And none of this can go ahead without Joe. He's the key to the whole thing."

They all look at him.

"What do you want me to say?"

Xav is incredulous. "Yes. Say, yes."

"Are you asking me to marry you as well?"

"If you get off your butt and get involved, then I just might."

"You're still employed, Xav. You can't just become head of SINC products tomorrow."

"End of the month then."

Anita shakes her head. "I think that's too late. This is happening now or not at all. Simplicity is just starting to build serious momentum. Like a lot of fads, there's a good chance it will go from underground to mainstream very fast. Or it will die. But I don't think it's going to go away, so we need to start asap."

Joe turns to her. "Can you?"

"I handed in my resignation this morning."

"What?"

"I'm all yours."

Cheryline stands up. "Me too. I'm a freelancer. If it all turns to mud, I'll just go back to freelancing."

Francois nods. "This is a winning horse. I'm getting on it."

"Wait, wait. You can't all start without me. I was the one who had the t-shirts made. I set up the event on Friday."

Joe sips his wine. "Calm down, Xav. Nothing's started yet. And we're all making decisions without really thinking them through. It might all be over tomorrow."

Anita shakes her head. "That's where I think you're way wrong, Joe. This's just going to get bigger and bigger. I knew that this morning. If we can get five hundred fans behind us in Montreal, why can't we get the same number in every North American city? Or more. And even if it stays relatively small, it's still a target group, one with buying power. We have to respond to that. The opportunity is now. The faster we get SINC out there, the more promotion we do, the more actual face time, the bigger it will get."

Xav slaps the table. "That's what I've been trying to say. Next time, I'll be the one with the PowerPoint presentation. Then you'll all listen to me."

"What about capital? How much is everyone willing to invest?"

Anita clicks through a few charts. “Here. I did a cost analysis. We can do everything at the bare minimum and try to cover our costs selling merchandise like Xav did yesterday. We’ll have a virtual office, do everything on the move. As it gets more popular, we can charge for live events.”

Xav nods eagerly. “What about online?”

“There’s no money in the internet, unless you’re getting revenue from ads or selling something. We could do that with products. But if we want to make big money, we need to get out in the real world. To have something that people will pay for, something that becomes part of them and not something that’s theoretically part of them. It has to be much more than just clicking on the link to the ceeville page.”

Joe looks at the estimates, projections and cost analyses. They look healthy and optimistic. “You did all this today?”

“Unlike you, I didn’t waste the day splashing in the pool and drinking tea.”

Francois laughs. “You went to the pool again?”

“I needed to clear my head. Get my thoughts in order.”

“How was it? I’ve never been on a Monday.”

“Chlurine.”

Cheryline clucks her tongue. “Pronounciation, Joe. Chlorine. Say it.”

“Chlurine. There were school kids in one half of the pool. Trust me. The water was as much urine as chlorine. So, chlurine.”

“Ew.”

“Yeah, but get this. On my way there, I saw a couple of people in simplicity t-shirts.”

Francois grins. “The universe trying to help, or at least, send you a message.”

“Maybe.”

Xaz slaps the table again. “That’s it. I’m ordering a thousand shirts tomorrow. I’ll sell them on street corners if I have to. Or next Sunday.”

Joe shakes his head. “We’re not doing that again.”

“Why not?”

“Because no one was tech-free. What’s the point?”

“The point is that there’ll be ten times as many people as yesterday, and they’ll all be willing to spend ten bucks for a shirt. Maybe twenty.”

Joe scoffs. “Maybe they’ll spend ten bucks just to be part of it.”

Anita nods. “Now you’re starting to get it, Joe.”

“Huh?”

"It's not about them seeing you. It's not even really about going low tech. It's about them being part of the event. Being there. That's what they'll pay for. Seeing Lady Gaga in concert is not nearly as important as being able to tell people you were there. And to blog about it and post videos and write a review and start a pond on Plasher and blah, blah, blah. What all these people need is something to talk about. Something big they can put their small little insignificant selves in the centre of. Their own lives are pretty boring and inconsequential, until they're part of something extraordinary. Even if they're just one face in a crowd, they can put themselves in the middle of it. Being at a SINC event would give them something relevant to say about themselves."

Joe saws the back of his neck with his hand. "Make them popular."

"Right."

"That's what it's all about. Popularity. Being part of the latest fad before everyone else knows about it. Having a funky t-shirt that gets attention. Being part of the coolest movement of the moment. All that increases your own popularity."

Anita smiles at him. "Keep going."

"You gotta make it something special. Something that hasn't been done before. Not just a weekly meet-up in a park. It has to be an event that people would really want to be part of. They would fight each other to be there, because being there is more important than actually doing anything there."

"And they'd pay to get in."

"Yeah."

Cheryline raises a hand. "I got it. Flash event. Spontaneous. Location given a few minutes before it starts. Public place, so others will see it. Limited number of people can get in."

"I went to something like that in Portland. It was insane. Kids came from everywhere. But it was disgusting inside, out of control. If we do this, can we at least make it porn-free?"

"I thought simplicity was tech-free."

"It is, but I don't want our events degenerating into a teenage orgy."

Xav laughs. "What the hell kind of party did you go to?"

"The wrong one. Gordie took me."

"Let's test it. This weekend. We put on the page that there'll be an event and post the location just before it starts. Ten bucks to get in. Simple."

"Don't get ahead of yourself, Xav. We haven't agreed to do anything yet."

"Should we vote?"

"Let's make the event free."

"Five bucks then."

Anita puts a hand between Joe and Xav. "We'll do it for...what do you call your two dollar coins?"

Xav, Francois, Cheryline and Joe all speak at once: "Toonies."

"Ha. That was cool. We're already a team. Right. A toonie to get in. That way, people won't even think twice about it. And they'll have the coin in their pockets ready. We'll need a location. With a secure entry so we can get that toonie from everyone, and stamp their hand or something."

Xav snaps his fingers. "With a simplicity stamp. I'll organise it. And I'll sell shirts at the entry too. I got a lot to do. Better call in sick tomorrow."

Anita puts her notebook away. "If you're serious about this, you should quit. That's what I've done. The rest of us are willing to commit and so should you."

The doorbell buzzes.

Joe looks down the hall, then at Anita. "You think they know where I live?"

"Who's they?"

Joe goes to the front door and edges it open. "Gordie?"

He tumbles into the apartment, chewing a red straw, backpack straps dangling, notebook tucked under his arm, one white earphone hanging loose.

"Don't you answer your fucking phone, bro?"

"You hung up on me."

Gordie drops his backpack. "I called you, like, a thousand times."

"I unplugged the landline. Work took my cell."

"Excuses, excuses. The only way to talk to you is the old-fashioned way, in person."

"You flew here to do that?"

Gordie moves down the hall, sees everyone gathered around the dining table. "I hope I'm interrupting."

"I have a feeling you're just in time."

On Revelation Road with the Sincophants

"Nervous?"

"Only when you ask me that."

"I would be. This chick's got pull."

"Xav, it's cable TV. Public access."

"Still. Big fan base. All over the world."

Anita comes up to them, Bluetooth set in place. "Joe, don't refer to her as a chick. Stick with Nova."

"You're the boss."

Xav waggles a finger. "Oh no she's not. We're all in this together, regardless of what job titles we've given ourselves. Be sure to say that, Joe. That we're all friends, all equals. A team. Remember, I organised the first public event, and I was the one who made the t-shirts. And it was my idea to start the ceeville page."

Joe laughs. "Sounds like a team effort."

Xav points at his chest. "It's coming from us. All of us. We've put SINC out there. Make sure you say that."

There's a knock on the door. Gordie puts his notebook aside and gets up to open it. A stagehand wearing an enormous headset and brandishing a clipboard like a knight's shield enters.

"Mr Solitus, we're ready for you."

Joe stands. He removes the make-up bib and checks himself in the mirror. He still doesn't like the short, clean-cut hairstyle they gave him as part of the makeover last month, but he can't deny the impact it's had. He does look more believable, more normal, more able to slip into a crowd unnoticed; someone who looks like everyone else. That had been Anita's goal. The everyman Joe, only slightly better than the rest. The clothing's part of that: suits only in black or blue, no designer labels or ultra expensive stuff, no ties, open collar shirt to present tolerance and openness, polo shirts for casual occasions. And with a smile consultant's help, he had added an ingratiating, modest yet confident half-smile to his limited range of facial expressions.

He practices the smile in the mirror.

"You look good, bro. Make sure you drop hints about our event tomorrow. It's gonna be be-he-he-he-hig."

Anita walks up to Gordie. "Have you got security organised this time? I don't want another scene like we had in San Fran. That was terrible publicity."

"Wrong. That was awesome publicity. The web was full of it. We even made the front page of the *LA Times*. All for free."

Joe turns to Anita. "Should I mention our next move?"

"No. Keep the spontaneity alive. We don't want people knowing where we're going next."

"Okay."

Anita turns to the group. "Can we all please keep our mouths shut about our movements. It's killing part of the cool vibe of simplicity."

Xav looks up from his phone. "The airlines have been giving us up."

"Or someone in this room has."

They all start to talk at once, defending themselves, shouting a little. Joe raises his hands.

"Hey. HEY! Everyone calm down. Let's just be more discrete. Like not wearing simplicity shirts on the plane, Xav."

"You should be wearing one now."

"That's a little obvious."

Anita nods. "Joe's right. We have to tone it down a bit. Things are going great. We don't need to do more than we're already doing. Our fans will take care of that. Let's scale it back. And that goes for the events, Gordie. Not every event has to outdo the last."

"That's the guys and girls involved. They want that."

Joe opens the door. "Here goes nothing."

They chorus, with varying amounts of enthusiasm: "Keep it simple, Joe."

He goes with the stagehand, who walks briskly down the narrow hall. All the doors are closed and unmarked. Brett Dennen is behind one of them. He really should say hello and try to get him to commit to the music festival. Maybe Anita will cover that.

The stagehand talks into his headset. "We're on the way."

"Any last advice?"

The stagehand covers the receiver with his hand. "Please don't ask about Nova's relationships or background."

"You said that already. Twice."

"Don't mention any product names and brands. Except those on the list I gave you. And don't move until you hear someone shout 'Clear'. Okay?"

"Got it."

"Good."

"She knows my family's off limits too."

"Nova goes wherever she wants. It's her show. If she asks something too personal, try to change the subject. Or better, answer the question. How does the microphone feel?"

He looks down at the massive mole on his lapel. "It's fine."

"Talk normally. Don't mumble, don't whisper and don't sigh heavily."

"I know. I've done this before."

"Even the biggest stars forget."

They stand in front of the curtain. Through the gap, he can see the bulbous silhouette of Nova. It's a small studio, two cameras, the audience sitting on fold-out chairs. He wonders how Nova comes out every day and manages to speak with such enthusiasm about celebrities and Hollywood. She's standing next to her purple sofa and reading from the teleprompter.

"You know, I've been wondering for a while if anything good has ever come out of Canada. Well, a bunch of folks from Montreal are attempting to change that. What started as an internet page among friends has grown into a movement that a lot of people are talking about, if not exactly participating in. *Wired* magazine named it the 'Summer of simplicity'. Well, we're happy to have with us today the man behind simplicity, Joe Solitus. Let's bring him out."

Mild applause. Nova looks behind her to the curtain. Joe feels a hand in his back. It gives him a push.

He walks slowly to the sofa, just getting around it without tripping, but stumbling a little to show his nervousness, that he's just a normal person like them and is nervous being on TV – even cable TV – as they would be. Nova steps forward, almost to catch him. She laughs at this, as does he. He takes her hand and kisses her on the right cheek, keeping her face camera side, as the contract stipulated.

They sit. Nova places her body at an angle, perching herself on the edge of the sofa. Joe takes a corner and eases one leg over the other. He sees a few people in the crowd wearing SINC shirts.

"Welcome to the sofa, Joe."

"Thanks for having me. Great to be here."

"'Simplicity is the answer.'"

"It is. So far."

"And you've brought that message to LA. How are you finding it here?"

"Great. Love LA."

"You coping with the heat? It's a record summer, off the chart."

"I like it. The sun shines in Montreal too, just not the whole year. And I lived in Australia, so I know what it's like. Seeing the sun is a great way to start the day."

"Absolutely. Ain't that right, folks? LA's the place to be."

Clapping and whooping. A lot more noise than such a small crowd can make.

Nova leans back, keeping her forty-five degree angle, half to Joe and half to the camera. "So tell us. How did simplicity become the answer? How did it all start?"

He works his mouth and face into that half-smile. "Well, it all happened really fast. Should I start at the start or work backwards from today?"

"Whatever you want. We're listening."

"It's pretty simple. A couple of months ago, I was at a retreat that's tech-free. No internet, no phones, no television."

"I wouldn't last a day."

"I thought that too. It was fantastic. Really. I didn't miss any of it. I got back to Montreal and tried to apply it to my life. A digital diet."

"How did that go? Bad, I bet."

"Right, not so well. But it showed me how dependent I was on cell phones and the internet. I've never been a fan of cell phones so giving that up was easy. The internet was harder. Plus, I pretty much got cut off from all my friends and social groups. Well, not from my closest friends, but from all the people I knew loosely. I was out of the loop and they forgot about me."

"So, simplicity is all about going tech-free?"

"Not entirely. We can't live without it completely and we're not saying you have to. It's about moderation. I still use the internet, just not nearly as much as I did before. All the tech is a major distraction. Once you turn off all the noise, all those distractions, an interesting thing happens."

"Tell us. Tell us."

"All this noise, all these emails and websites and i...music players and texting. All of it takes us away from the one voice we should be hearing."

"The voice inside ourselves. You turned it all off and heard yourself."

Joe turns to the audience. "See. Nova knows."

Loud applause. Nova attempts to look surprised, embarrassed even.

"That's exactly what happened. I had that internal narrator back in my head, like when I was a kid. You know? The voice in your head that narrates your life to you? I heard it again."

"What did he say? Is it a man's voice?"

"It's a woman's voice, actually. In an Australian accent. I know that sounds weird, but that's what she sounds like. She told me to focus on what's important for me. And that's what simplicity is all about. Getting back to basics, getting back inside your own head to listen to yourself."

Nova furrows her brow into a thoughtful expression, puts her hands together and points them like an arrow at Joe. "Not easy these days. There's a lot of noise. And the world is changing so fast. Kids today, they're all about technology. My daughter's wired into everything."

"How old is she?"

"Old enough to know better."

"What's interesting is that teenagers are the ones who come to our events. Teenagers and college kids."

"Generation S."

"Right. I think they love the tech, but they hate it too. They've grown up in a world completely different to us and I think they feel they've missed out on something."

"At least you're getting some of them outside. Nova says move, America."

"That's part of it, yeah. We wanted the events to be social and active, people getting together in the real world. So many of us sit in our rooms and interact with strangers, make friends and contacts with people we'll never see or share important moments with. Meeting people in person is so much more worthwhile and meaningful than doing it online."

"But these events sometimes get a little out of control. Like what happened in San Francisco two days ago."

"That was unfortunate, and not our fault."

"I saw the photos online. You practically trashed Golden Gate Park."

"The police were very helpful and cooperative. We're looking into exactly what happened. We think some negative elements got into the crowd and tried to use the event for their own purposes. It was a good lesson for us. We're going to have tighter security for our event in LA."

"Tell us more about that."

"That's top secret, Nova. We'll only announce it half an hour before it starts."

"How?"

"We used to do it on our cee...we used to do it online. Now, people sign up to our website. They have to register with a username and a password, and give a cell phone number. A text gets sent to them. Are you signed up?"

"Not yet. I'm not ready for the madness of one of your out of control events. I think I'll read your book first. What's it called and when's that coming out?"

"It's called *Simplicity Rules* and you can get it as an ebook on Monday."

"No print version?"

"We wanted something anyone anywhere in the world could buy. We don't think of ourselves as a Canadian company, or even North American. We're global. We want everyone to have the chance to get involved. Plus, an ebook reduces impact on the environment. Part of our business practice is to simplify, to do things in an easy, uncomplicated way."

"More companies should be doing that. I read that you don't even have an office. Is that right?"

"We do everything on the move. Our headquarters is virtual."

"You've been all over the country. Don't you miss Montreal?"

"I miss my cat."

"Aww. Where is she?"

"Popov's a he. And he's currently in a pet hotel in Montreal. Executive suite. He hasn't sent me a postcard yet, but I think he likes it there."

"Popov. Where does that name come from? Is your cat Russian?"

"I named him after my hero growing up. Alexander Popov. The swimmer."

Nova's eyes dart to the teleprompter and back. "Yes, you were a swimmer. You won some events in...in New Hampshire. Is that where you grew up?"

"Yep. Small town, New Hampshire."

Nova turns to the audience and shakes her head. "Sorry, folks. Still nothing big out of Canada. This movement has actually been started by an American."

"I'm half American. My dad's Australian."

"Now that you say that, you do have a funny accent. I thought it was your strange Canadian twang. Is your dad here? Let's bring him out."

Joe shifts in the sofa. He feels sweat running down his back. "No, no. He's not here."

"Still in New Hampshire. He must be proud of you."

"I was lucky to grow up there, to have all that space and the outdoors. We're trying to put that kind of lifestyle into our events."

"That's why you're always in the parks."

"We did that first in Montreal. A park encourages activity and makes it easier for people to move around and socialise. People can bring their dogs and other friends and there's space enough for everyone."

"And all of that is better than sitting at home in front of a screen."

"We like to think of simplicity as a community. Technology has taken us away from communal activities. And it seems to have removed any notions of social responsibility. We're trying to recreate a community, get people out and meeting each other. I got an email from a couple in Vancouver who said they met at our event there and fell in love."

"How romantic."

"Yeah, and they never would've met if they hadn't gone to the event. I ask myself how many other stories there must be like that. People who fell in love or became friends at one of our events. This big crowd and they found each other. I think that's great. We're not out to make money. Even if just two people in Vancouver meet and fall in love. That's enough for me."

Appreciative applause.

"When did it all start?"

"At the end of May."

"And now it's July and simplicity has cult status."

"No one is more amazed about that than me."

"It's almost like some people were waiting for it. Generation S, but the S is now for simplicity and not for screen."

"We like it when they get involved too, bring something to the event. Like in Calgary when a bunch of yoga instructors got everyone doing yoga at the same time."

"I saw that video. Amazing."

"Yeah, a thousand people all on one leg in the tree position."

"And a lot of them in white simplicity shirts."

"That was really great."

"And all this started in your living room in Montreal?"

"At the start, it was more about us, me and my friends. We wanted to reduce our dependence on tech and take control. All the tech means people don't notice each other. They walk through the world completely tuned out, with their heads down, not listening. That was us and we wanted to change. We want people to socialise face to face, to acknowledge each other and expand their worlds a little. If you'll pardon the pun, we want them all to get in sync with each other."

Nova laughs without making a sound. "How many employees does your roaming company have now?"

"Seven, including me. It's great fun travelling with them all. I get to go to work each day with colleagues who are my friends. And we're all doing something we feel really strongly about. It's not even work."

Nova turns to the camera. "Don't go away. We'll be right back to continue talking with the head of simplicity, Joe Solitus."

Clapping, background music.

"Clear."

People suddenly surround the sofa. Joe gets his face touched up, is handed a glass of very cold water.

The stagehand goes up to Nova and holds two fingers in the air. "Two minutes."

Nova's face is perfectly still as she gets doused with make-up. Her mouth barely moves. "You got anything more to say?"

"We could talk more about the book, or the music festival."

An assistant holds up a bottle and Nova drinks through a straw. "What music festival?"

"It's still in the planning stages. A live festival in my home town in New Hampshire, in September."

The people do some more work on Nova and then clear off just as quickly as they came.

A voice counts down. "Five, four, three."

Clapping, music.

"Welcome back to *Supa Nova*. We've got Joe Solitus on the sofa. Joe is the man behind simplicity, the cult low-tech movement that's coming to a park near you. So, Joe, you've got the book coming out and everybody seems to be wearing simplicity shirts. What's next?"

"Well, we're in the process of organising a music festival. A couple of indie bands have already signed on, but their names won't be released until the festival's about to start. It'll be in New Hampshire in September. We plan to hold it every year in a different location, with the proceeds going to local charities."

"Sounds great, but we're just about out of time. Are we? Yes. Care to tell us where tomorrow's event will be?"

Joe offers that half-smile again. "LA confidential."

"Give us a hint."

"Hmm. Okay. *The Hitch-hiker's Guide to the Galaxy*."

"Excuse me?"

"The book by Douglas Adams. On the front cover is 'Don't Panic'. The best advice I ever got growing up."

"What has that go to do with the event?"

"In the book, there's an item no inter-galactic traveller can do without. You'll need that item tomorrow. To sit on, perhaps."

"Okay. You've lost me, Joe, and probably much of America too. But thanks for joining us on the sofa."

Clapping and cheering.

"Up next, we'll be talking to musician Brett Dennen. And if we're lucky, he might just play us a song. Stick around. You're watching *Supa Nova*."

Applause

"Clear."

Again, people rush to the sofa. The stagehand gestures for Joe to stand up and follow him. Joe turns to shake Nova's hand, but she's already walking away, her back turned to him. He follows the stagehand behind the curtain and back down the hallway.

"Where is it?"

"What?"

"The event tomorrow."

"Are you signed up?"

"Yeah."

"Then you'll get a text tomorrow like everyone else."

"Or you could just tell me. Simple as that."

"Sorry. I can't."

"I don't get the clue."

"Read the book."

"Maybe I'll watch the movie instead."

"Why not search it online and get a million answers in a tenth of a second."

The stagehand frowns. "Brilliant idea. Or you could just tell me."

They get to the door. Joe goes inside. Everyone looks up from their notebooks and phones to cheer and clap. A champagne cork pops.

***

What's it like?

What?

Australia.

He takes a sheet of sandpaper and wraps it around a block of wood. Probably best I don't say anything, because that'll ruin the experience for you when you go. But think about what you already know. You've heard the music, seen some films and TV shows. You've got a sense of what it's like.

What about where you're from?

He focuses on sanding the legs of the chair. Hand me that file, would you? No, the other one. Thanks. There's not a lot to say about it. Farming towns. Nothing much happens there. The only thing people can talk about is what's screwing them over. The weather, the government, the foreigners, God. They don't know much about the world and they don't really get it if you want to know. Their worlds are so small.

Is that why you left?

Yeah, Jonah. And some day you'll have the same feeling. That this little world in Harbrook is too small and you'll want to see what else is out there. Hah. I grew up in Australia and ended up here. You're growing up here and might end up in there. It goes around, it comes around. Karma, Jonah, is important. Don't forget that. Always keep that in mind whenever you do something. Everything you do will come back to you, somehow. And everything that happens to you is leading you somewhere, whether you want to go to that place or not.

When I think of my life, of all the things that happened, it's amazing I ended up meeting your ma and having you and Gordie, and I get to live in this fantastic part of the world. I'm lucky. They call Australia the lucky country, but I'm the lucky one.

I wanna go there.

There's some amazing stuff to see.

Can't we go for a holiday?

Your ma hates to fly. So do I. And you can't go to Australia for just a couple of weeks. It's a huge place. You can't believe the distances. The empty highways. The miles and miles of nothing. Go when you're old enough to enjoy it, when you've got time to get out and explore it. Maybe you should study there. Keep that in mind. You've got about another ten years to think about it. But you'll get there one day. I'm sure of it.

~~~

He wakes. The room is incredibly bright. His watch says it's just after nine. In the morning. But it feels much earlier than that.

He sits up and rubs his face. In the adjacent bed, a mask-wearing Xav snores on, sleeping on his stomach, one arm tucked underneath the thin pillow, the other hanging off the side of the bed with his knuckles on the ground like a gorilla.

On his feet, he manages to get into the bathroom. He feels – and looks – like he's been sucked up and blown out by an industrial-sized air conditioning unit. Inhaled on one hemisphere and exhaled on the other. The toilet seat is up and the room stinks of urine. He pees sitting down, flushes, then splashes cold water on his face. He takes a towel and dries his face.

"I'm a man who knows where his towel is. Most of the time."

Everyone had got the clue, towels and intergalactic travel, had run to Venice Beach waving them in the air. But how many had actually read the book, or had even heard of it?

In the kitchen, he puts the kettle on and gets some tea from his satchel.

It's good to have this moment of peace and solitude.

The water starts to boil. He turns it off before it peaks so it doesn't wake anyone. He pours the water, dips the filter a couple of times and drops it in the sink.
~~~

Out on the balcony, the morning sun is painful, like a torture lamp shined right in the eyes. It seems to bounce off every window and car roof just to hit him in the face, all these spotlights urging him to confess, or perhaps burst into song. He has to shield his eyes with his hand to look at the water, and squint too. An early easterly has chopped up Coogee Bay, the white caps curling around the crooked crevices of Wedding Cake Island and slithering towards the beach. A lone swimmer plugs away far from shore, heading for the northern tip of the bay. His form is good, his stroke languid and easy, like he does it every day.

"Shark bait."

He sips.

A machine the size of a combine harvester is churning the sand over for another day, spinning anew the unhealthy concoction of cigarette butts, old band aids, broken glass and busted thongs, and probably the odd syringe and used condom. One man runs in the soft stuff in shoes, following the tire tracks of the plough. A few others are pounding the hard sand close to the water. But the beach really isn't long enough for running and he wonders why they bother.

"Mornin, bro."

"Hey. You look like hell."

Gordie lowers the visor of his SINC cap. He has sunglasses hooked in the collar of his t-shirt. He lifts then out and slides them on. "Fucking straight. I feel, like, totally upside down. Like my head is where my butt is."

"That's good, because your face looks like an arse."

"Fuck you."

"You'll get used it. It takes a couple of days. Good thing we've got today off."

Gordie takes a seat in a wire chair. He rubs his mouth with the back of his hand and yawns. "How's it feel, being back here?"

"Don't know yet. I still don't feel like I'm completely here. I think my soul grabbed a parachute and jumped out of the plane somewhere over Tahiti."

"You live around here? It's semi-nice."

He points. "Further up Arden Street. Near Clovelly."

"Aight."

"It was great being near the beach, but it was expensive. Five hundred a month, just for a room in a house with three others. I wonder if they're still there."

"Don't try to find out. They'll probably just want something from us. Like everyone else."

"It was Koby's house. He's probably still there. I didn't like him much. Bit of a prick."

"I thought all the Aussies were friendly. G'day mate, shrimp on the barbie and all that crap."

Joe sips. "He had that going on. But I thought he was a bit of complainer. A whinger, as the locals would say. I called him the Incredible Sulk."

Gordie laughs to himself. "You were always good at that."

"What?"

"Labelling people."

"It's just a joke."

"Yeah. No harm done."

Joe sips his tea some more.

"Where are we?"

"Coogee. This is where all the backpackers hang out. The English beer sponges."

"Thank the lord we're not staying in a hostel. Like we did in Toronto."

"The apartment's nice. Cost effective too. Two apartments and we're all in. And it beats the hell out of some shabby, generic hotel. Jesus, all those Mayolas I stayed in."

"Fucking straight."

"I've seen enough of them for one life. I can't believe that was me a few months ago. I'm so glad that's over."

The balcony door slides open.

"Gentlemen."

Joe smiles. "Morning, stud."

"Is it?"

"You better have a look in the mirror."

"Why?"

"You hair is completely flat on one side. You could land a plane on it."

Francois checks his reflection in the window. He tries to pat his hair down, but it just springs back up. "Cheryline's monopolising the bathroom. Again. Is there any coffee?"

"I've got some tea if you want it."

"That's not gonna be anywhere near strong enough."

"There's probably some instant. But you'll have to go down to Coogee Bay Road if you want something real. There's a bunch of shops down there."

Francois leans on the railing and looks down. "This is exactly how I imagined it would be. Except for the empty beach."

"It's winter."

"But it's as hot as it was in LA."

"Not quite. Anyway, the locals don't go to the beach in winter."

"It's warm enough."

Joe points down at the busy intersection of Arden Street and Coogee Bay Road. "Look, they're all wearing jackets. That woman, down there waiting at the traffic light, she's got gloves on."

Gordie and Francois both look. They stare at the streets below, at the honking cars and the tail-riding trucks and vans.

Francois turns to Joe. "Looks like Montreal. The hustle, I mean. I thought all the Aussies were laid back and slow."

"You told me that too, bro. These guys look even more stressed than P-landers."

"I guess I didn't pick up on that because I was at uni all day. And I biked everywhere, on the back roads, so the traffic never got to me. Come to think of it, the students were pretty stressed out, right from the first day of semester. A lot of them just couldn't get their planning sorted and had to write ten papers in the last week. By the way, Gordie, I'm still really pissed with you that you dropped out."

"Sabbatical. For now. In a couple of years, they'll give me an honorary degree. There'll be a statue of me on the lawn in front of Shattuck Hall."

"You're going back in September."

"I still say we should open SINC University. The college that focuses on each person's unique abilities and skills. We could turn Harbrook into a college town."

Francois rubs his eyes and pats at his hair. "What's the plan for today?"

Joe sips and shrugs. "Anita's probably got some kind of schedule for us. Nothing heavy. We should focus on feeling like we're here. All the work can start tomorrow."

"More interviews?"

"I think so. Some local current affairs show wants to do something on us. They wanna come to the event too. Make that part of the story. You guys should go and see the sights."

"What's there to see? Where are all the koala bears and kangaroos?"

"At the zoo, or out in the wild. Sydney's a city, Gordie. About five million people. It's huge."

"Is this the centre?"

"That's miles away. But you guys should go downtown, see the bridge, the Opera House, the Rocks. Check out the bats hanging from the trees in the Botanic Gardens. Maybe Anita's got a sightseeing trip planned."

"I'm sick of all her schedules. She's such a pushy bitch. Thinks she's the CEO. The boss of all of us."

Francois smiles. "You don't like strong women, do you, Gordie? She said something about a tour on the plane. I couldn't understand her because I kept my headphones on the whole time so Xav wouldn't talk to me."

Gordie slouches back into the wire chair. "Next time, we're going first class."

"If you're willing to pay for it."

"Come on, bro. Spread the wealth. Let's bling this thing, aight."

"I'm with you. I hate economy."

Francois shakes his head. "Does it make any difference? It's still a fourteen hour flight."

Gordie sniffs. "It's what we deserve."

"You ever fly first class, Stan?"

"Don't call me that."

"That's a no."

"Anything's better than cattle class. We gotta do things in style."

"That's not exactly simplifying, is it?"

"That's your excuse for everything. If I was running the show, things would be mega different."

"Yeah, we'd be living like rappers. Gold chains around our necks with SINC in diamonds. The S a dollar sign. Half naked girls hanging onto us like leeches. Thousand dollar bottles of champagne."

"Fa shizzle. Now you're getting it."

Francois laughs. "Gordie, I know Joe's angry you dropped out of school to join us, but I'm glad you're here. Juste pour rire."

"At least someone appreciates me."

"I appreciate you too, Gordie. It just when ma finds out, she's gonna come down on me. Len too. Like a Pentecostal sledgehammer."

Francois smiles. "What are you gonna do today, Joe?"

"Did you bring your swimming gear?"
"Yeah."
"Then I'm gonna take you to the Icebergs. It'll change your life."
"Where is it?"
"We can walk. Around the headland. It'll take a while, but it's a really nice walk. We'll bus it back."
"I'm in, but with all that airline junk in me, I think I'll sink to the bottom."
"You won't. It's salt water."
"Are you swimming again, bro?"
"Only in the Icebergs, Gordie. After being in there, I couldn't swim in chlorine ever again."
"Whatever. I'm going back to bed."
Gordie slides the balcony door open and heads for his room.
"He snores."
"I know."
"It's like someone slowly butchering a live pig. I could hear him through my plugs."
"We'll swap tonight. Xav snores too, so they should bunk together."
"Maybe they'll harmonise."
"Maybe they'll have a two-cowboys-in-a-tent moment."
This makes Francois laugh. "That would freak Xav out. Gordie doesn't lean that way, does he?"
"No, but ever since he went off to college I had this feeling his was keeping something from me."
"Doesn't have to be that. You just want a little gay in your life."
"To piss Len off. He's firmly of the belief that man love is a sin."
"He's living in the Stone Age."
"You know he called me last week in San Fran and asked me to invest in some property deal in Florida. I said no, but then he got on to telling me to use the events to put a little Jesus into everyone's lives. 'Those young ruffians need Him,' he said."
"No way."
"I told him and his fairy godfather to shove it."
"I bet that went down well."
"You ready? We can get some breakfast on the way. And we can have lunch at the Icebergs after."
"Just let me use the facilities first."
"Grab one of Gordie's caps too."

"I've got a SINC cap in my bag."

"Can we not be part of this, for a few hours?"

He watches Francois go through the living room. Cheryline comes from the other direction, a towel wrapped around her body and another looped around her head. Francois playfully grabs at the towel, but she evades him. She comes out onto the balcony.

"You're looking fresh."

"I had a swim this morning. Can we stay here forever?"

"Better ask Anita about that. Maybe we can come back for a vacation once we've hit all the other states."

"That'd be sweet."

She goes into the living room, then comes back out onto the balcony.

"By the way. The book's a hit."

"Already?"

"Yep. Lots of downloads, on all the big book sites."

"I didn't expect that."

"Well, on the flight from LA to Sydney, you became a best-selling author."

"You mean you became a best-selling author."

"It's your name on the cover."

Francois comes out on the balcony, his hair stuffed under a purple Lakers cap. He whistles at Cheryline. "Foxy lady."

"Keep dreaming."

"I need a towel. Can I have that one?"

Cheryline unwraps the towel from her head. "Here."

"Hmm, peachy. But that's not the one I meant. You all set, Joe?"

"Where you guys going?"

"For a walk."

"Take a phone, Francois. Just in case."

With a saucy shake of her hips, she goes back into the living room, walking on her toes to give herself a few more inches, to lend her soft calves some shape.

"Are you still into her?"

Francois shakes his head. "Just teasing. I think Gordie likes her. And Xav is very warm for Anita's form."

"He's got no chance."

"Well, there's no guessing who Jana wants to pair up with."

"Don't remind me. That's getting awkward."

"She's more groupie than personal assistant."

"She's Anita's assistant, not mine. God, I really hope this isn't gonna degenerate into some movie where we all end up conveniently paired off before the credits roll."

"We can't. We're an odd number. We need one more girl."

"Iris."

"You hear from her?"

"I thought she might come to the event in Portland, or San Fran. I guess she's still at Rusticity."

"Write to her."

"I did."

"Maybe there's a stack of letters at your apartment."

"I don't think so."

"Well, you're very much in the public eye, Joe. She's definitely gonna know where you are. Give it time."

"That leaves us and the Icebergs."

"Lead the way."

***

Francois turns his chair so he faces the water. He sips his beer and sighs. "This has got to be the greatest pool on the face of the earth."

"It is."

"But now I'm screwed. Can't go back to chlorine."

"To the Aquadump?"

"Nuh. It's over."

"I warned you."

"Did you come here a lot?"

"Every day. I was in great shape. Could swim in my sleep. A few people asked me if I was a pro. A member of the Aussie swim team. All the sun and salt turned my hair almost white."

"So you looked like a local. Would you move back?"

Joe shakes his head. "The world's greatest pool isn't quite enough to build a whole life around."

"It's a good start."

"Sure, but I never made any friends here like I did at the Aquadome."

"You know, you never talk much about your time here."

"Not much to say."

"Now's your chance. You were here, what, three years."

"Four."

"Why aren't you visiting people? Following up old friends and drinking buddies."

"There is no one. My whole Australia experience was pretty disappointing. Except for the swimming."

Francois gestures at the Pacific. "This was disappointing?"

"I didn't expect it to be that way. I thought I'd get off the plane and make friends right away. It didn't happen. I guess it was my fault, my state of mind. I didn't meet anyone. They had their little cliques and it was impossible to infiltrate them."

"What about girls?"

Joe sips his tea. It's tepid and bitter. "Uni here, it was like high school. They all gathered in groups. If there was a girl you liked, you could never talk to her alone. She'd have this wall of friends around her. I went to a couple of parties, but never really felt welcome, and they all drank too much for me. Boat races and sculling contests. And they didn't get all jovial and wanting to link arms and sing. They got a bit nasty."

"Interesting."

"That was my take. Others probably saw it differently."

"Maybe."

"Now that I look back on it, while I was here, it was a really lonely time."

"Ah, it's all bullshit."

"Huh?"

"It was the girl. What's-her-name."

"Trina."

"She ruined you. Ruined the whole country for you. I bet every girl you met, your eyes were glowing with revenge. I'm gonna seduce this girl and break her fucking heart. You scared them all off."

Joe laughs. "That's a good theory, but I didn't find a single girl who I thought was attractive. And no one worthy of revenge."

Francois looks around the dining area and then down at the pool. He lowers his voice. "They are a little big. Weird, when you think about it. All the sunshine, all these outdoor possibilities, but they look like Americans."

"I think Trina was a one-off."

"Stop idolising her. It'll make you crazy. She's way gone."

"But she left her mark."

"I wish you had a picture."

"You'd probably find one online. She was a triathlete when we met. There might be a photo of her in a race somewhere."

Francois pulls out his phone. "Full name?"

"Don't. I don't wanna know."

"You don't have to look. Name."

"Catrina Sanders. Unless she married that bald dick and took his name."

Francois taps the screen. "There's a pic here of her riding a fancy bike with a pointy helmet on."

"Is there a date?"

"Eight years ago. You think she still races?"

"Who the hell cares?"

"You do."

"I don't. Now, put the phone away and enjoy the view."

Francois does as he's told. "Poor old Joe in lonesome Sydney. What did you do with yourself?"

"Not a lot. Came here, studied, read, went for long bike rides. I worked construction for cash. I used to go down to Coogee Oval and watch sport. Cricket in summer, rugby in winter. I took trips when there was free time. Blue Mountains, Melbourne, Brisbane, up and down the coast, out west. The Christmases were tough."

"You didn't go home?"

"Too far. And I couldn't face everyone in Harbrook. Especially Len. And Gordie. All those fucking questions."

"That reminds me. Why does he think you don't swim?"

Joe looks out the window. The morning easterly has dropped and the water is flat and calm. A consistent set of waves is pushing towards South Bondi. He can see small specks of surfers rolling up and down, jostling for position as they wait for the right set.

"Long story."

"Give me the short version."

"Huh. Well, I was a swimmer at high school, got offered a scholarship in Vermont, but I turned it down."

"Because of Max?"

"I told ma and Gordie I didn't get the scholarship. Then I packed my stuff and went to Europe. While I was travelling, I applied for UNSW."

"Why did you lie?"

"It was easier. With the scholarship, I would've had a reason to stay. I lied so I could leave without being questioned. And I've kept the lie going ever since."

"Must've been hard."

"Lying's easy if you believe it's the truth."

"I mean leaving."

"It was simple. I packed my bags and left. Running away is the easy part. Dealing with everything is another thing."

Buzz, buzz.

"It's Anita."

"Better answer it."

Francois puts the phone to his ear, adopting a passable Australian accent. "G'day, Anita...We're in...Where are we, Joe?"

"Bondi."

"We're in Bondi...Yeah, we'll be there...Bye. Meeting at four in the apartment. We'll take a taxi back."

"Bus."

"Sorry. A bus. I didn't know there were any. I didn't see a single bus when we drove from the airport yesterday."

"Nothing but cars."

"And vans. I've never seen so many vans."

"Tradesmen."

The waitress comes up to their table. "Anything else?"

Joe turns to her. "Can we have the check, please?"

She calculates it on the spot with the little machine attached to her belt. "Look, I don't wanna intrude, but are you Joe Solitus?"

"Yes."

"Ohmigod. I saw you on *Supa Nova*."

"Is that on here?"

"Online stream. You were awesome. I love simplicity. Just love it. It's exactly what my life needs at the moment."

"Great."

"Can I have your autograph?"

"Sure."

She takes a notepad out of her back pocket and hands it to him. "I started your book. It's fantastic. The whole world should read it."

"Thanks."

"Is there gonna be an event?"

He hands her the pad. "What's the damage?"

She tells him. Francois pays, pocketing the receipt the little machine prints out.

"Let's go, Joe."

"Where will it be?"

Joe shoulders his satchel. "Are you signed up?"

"I never thought it would happen here."

"Sign up and you'll get a text, if there is an event."

She nods eagerly. "Have a great day. Thanks for this."

Joe and Francois head for the door. Joe looks back once and sees the waitress talking excitedly on her phone, untying her apron in the process.

Outside, the afternoon is warm. The air smells of salt and seagulls. They saunter down the hill to Campbell Parade.

"Maybe you should wear one of Gordie's caps. Big sunglasses too."

"And a fake moustache? Pass. Anyway, that was just bad luck. This is Australia. No one knows us here."

"She did."

The bus stop is empty. Joe checks the schedule. At street level, the smell of salt has been replaced by petrol fumes and garbage.

"Let's take a taxi, Joe."

"No cars. You know the rules."

"Are you telling me you haven't been in a car for ten years?"

"Only when there was no other option."

"So?"

"Now there's an option. Cars are the absolute height of laziness. The Aussies would look less like Americans if they walked and biked instead of driving everywhere."

Francois points back towards the Icebergs. "Check it out."

The waitress is barrelling down the hill, two other girls with her. They get to the bottom, see Joe at the bus stop and then try to cross the busy street, getting in, between and around the cars on Campbell Parade.

"What the...?"

Joe looks towards the beach, to the car park of South Bondi where a dozen teenagers are running in their direction. They also try to cross the street. Brakes screech, drivers curse, kids laugh, a few bonnets get slapped. The faster boys get ahead and sprint for the bus stop.

"I think we better get a taxi, Joe."

"Here comes the bus. It's going to Bondi Junction. That's good enough."

The bus stops and they jump on. It's empty. Two boys just manage to get on before the back door closes. They're shirtless, tanned and skinny, both wearing huge aviators, both with phones in their hands. They come up to Joe and Francois, put their pimply faces up close.

"Fuck me swinging."

"Are you really Joe Solitus?"

"Nah, mate, nah. It's a case of mistaken identity."

"Fuck no. They said it was you."

Joe tries to thicken his accent. "It's happened before, mate."

One kid takes out his phone. He taps at the screen and looks at it. He shows it to his friend.

"Fuck off. It is you."

"Why'd you lie? That's not fucking fair, mate."

They're suddenly very aggressive.

"Look, guys, sorry for that. We're trying to keep this low key. Top secret, you know? No one in Australia knows we're here."

One kid slaps the other's bare shoulder. "There's gonna be an event. Fuck yeah."

"When and where?"

"Yeah, where?"

"Nothing's planned yet. That's how it works."

"You can tell us."

"We'll keep it secret."

Joe shakes his head. "Sorry."

They both raise their phones and make photographs, taking turns to lean close to Joe for quick snaps. They smell of sunscreen and sweat.

"Where ya goin?"

"We can show you round."

Francois stands up and presses the bell. "We're getting off here."

"Us too."

They all crowd around the back door. The kids are pushy and jumpy.

"Where youse staying?"

"In the city. Darling Harbour."

"Noice."

"What's with the accent? You fakin it?"

"My dad's Australian."

"Fuck off."

"No fucking way."

"Ya one of us."

The door opens. Francois sees a taxi on the opposite side of the street and jumps out to hail it. It cuts across the traffic and stops in front of them. They get in. The two kids try to get in as well.

The driver turns and scowls. "Oi, no shirt, no ride."

"Wait a sec."

The two kids take the shirts hanging from the back of their boardshorts and try to put them on. They grapple with them, the phones in their hands making it difficult.

Francois shuts the door. "Go. They're not with us."

The taxi pulls away from the curb. Through the back window, Joe sees the two kids give them the finger. One kid even turns around and drops his shorts, pointing a very white and flat arse at them. The other kid is talking on his phone and gesturing wildly with his hands.

The driver looks in the mirror. "Bloody teenagers. Where to, fellas?"

Francois elbows Joe. "You all right?"

"Yeah."

"Where are we staying?"

"Opposite the Coogee Bay Hotel."

The driver nods. "Righto."

***

They have the meeting in the living room, with the two sofas pushed together so they can sit in a long line. Anita stands in front and addresses them all. Joe sits in the middle, flanked by Francois and Xav. He quickly thumbs through the schedule. He's the only one with a printed copy. Everyone else has a notebook or tablet in front of them.

Anita's heels click as she paces the floor. "I hope everyone's feeling adjusted. It's going to be a busy couple of weeks here. As you can see, Canberra, Melbourne, Adelaide, Perth, back to Brisbane, and then over to Auckland for the New Zealand leg."

Xav raises his hand. "Is it really necessary to go all the way to Perth? Holy crap, it's a six hour flight. How big is this country?"

"I know you're all a bit sick of the travelling. I am, too. But if you check the schedule, we have ten days in Perth. Think of it as a vacation. We've booked a couple of apartments on the beach."

Cheryline claps like a little girl at a puppet show. "Excellent."

"Now, for Sydney, Gordie and I spoke about it and we're going to do two events. One at Bondi and one in Centennial Park. Gordie, do you want to take it from here?"

Gordie puts his notebook aside and stands. He adjusts his cap, seems nervous. "It's all set. We scooped the park, sorry, scoped the park, and the beach this afternoon. Plenty of space. Minimum security."

"Do you think that's enough?"

"Relax, Anita. This is Australia. The people I saw on the streets today were so laid back they're practically walking around in a daze."

Joe whispers to Xav. "Maybe they put Sailiun in the water."

They both laugh.

Anita stares at them. "Can we stay focused, please? Or do I have to separate you two again? Activities, Gordie."

"The beach is a no-brainer. We'll bring some Frisbees and a few soccer balls for the park. I had the idea to spell simplicity in letters made of people. We write the letters in the sand so people know where to sit. Simple."

Xav shakes his head. "It'll never work. How do we do that at a crowded beach?"

"It's good, Gordie. The beach is empty this time of year. It always is."

Anita walks up to Gordie. "Joe's right. Let's make it happen. One of us could go in the banner plane and film it. Francois?"

"Okay. Pics too?"

"Yes."

"Could we stream it live to our website? Would be cool if everyone in the world could see that. A bunch of people spelling simplicity on the beach in Sydney."

"Done. Francois, you're in the banner plane. The rest of us are on the beach. We spell out simplicity at the start, then get on with the event."

"What's with the banner plane?"

"Cross advertising, Joe. Cheryline's got a couple of local companies interested in sponsoring the events."

"Advertising? Since when?"

"Why are you so shocked? You started it."

"Me? How?"

Cheryline leans forward to talk to him. "By plugging that hiking book on *Supa Nova*."

"That was a clue to the event."

"And some people went out and bought the book."

"Cheryline and I talked about it on the flight. Our brand has the potential to cross over into other products and streams, when it's used right. Our fans listen to you, Joe. You're now the spokesperson for our target market. A publisher and an author somewhere made a massive amount of money from you mentioning that book. We're not going to do that for free anymore. Don't promote any products without talking to me or Cheryline first. That goes for everyone. And don't tell people who you work for, ever. Or say where we're headed next."

Joe stands. "Wait a minute. When did this become about advertising? This is about simplifying, going low-tech."

"I thought you wanted to do that, Joe. Don't tell me you improvised that whole bit on *Supa Nova*?"

"I did."

"Even that part about the inner narrative with the girl's voice? I thought you were dropping a hint that we were going to Australia."

"I made it all up on the spot."

Anita offers him a thin, deprecating smile. "Another trick? It looked rehearsed. We all thought that in the green room. We were impressed too. So, moving on. Gordie, Cheryline. I want you two to follow up these potential advertisers. Today. They're on the list at the bottom of the schedule."

Gordie grunts. "So much for a day off."

Joe leans across Xav's notebook. "Let me see that. Fanta, Toyota, Qantas, Dell. What the hell is this?"

Anita stands in front of him. "Cross brand marketing. They pay us to be part of the event. When their brand is at our event, then our fans know we support them and will act accordingly. Everybody wins."

"That's not what this is about."

Xav smiles at Joe. "It's brilliant. Great work, Mr Solitus. You've done it again. Walked out of a room with a pile of sand in your hands and come back with a handful of diamonds."

"It wasn't planned."

"Yeah, sure."

Anita clicks towards the balcony. "It doesn't matter how it started, we've got to profit from it. We should bring out our own line of green tea as well. Simplicitea. What is that noise?"

She opens the sliding doors, making the cheering louder. Joe follows Anita out onto the balcony. He looks down over the railing. The small crowd shouts and cheers.

They chant: "Aussie, Aussie, Aussie, Joe, Joe, Joe."

Anita turns to Joe. "Looks like our cover's blown."

Joe feels shoulders bump against him as the others come onto the balcony. They wave and people in the crowd wave back, that is, all those hands not holding phones. Joe sees the two shirtless kids from earlier standing in front of the assembled mass. One of them has a megaphone and is leading the "Aussie Joe" chant.

Xav grabs Joe's arm. "Wave."

"Jesus."

"We're bigger than him. Getting there anyway."

Xav lifts Joe's arm and shakes it from side to side. Joe fights himself loose.

"Let me go."

Anita checks her watch. "Come on, Joe. Your interview starts in a few minutes. Go and make yourself look like everyone else. You know what do. Gordie, I think you better plan for a big turnout tomorrow, and in Centennial Park."

"Got it. We'll make the front page in Mongolia."

Anita and Joe go into the living room. The door buzzes. She goes to answer it.

"That's them. I'll stall them while you get prepared. Wear the polo shirt. Show the locals you're relaxed and outdoorsy like they are."

She looks through the peep hole and opens the door. Joe watches from the bathroom, holding the door almost closed. A reporter and two cameramen bustle in.

"I'm Anita Rudolph. Come on in."

"Chris Haynes. This is Warren and Dave."

"Nice to meet you. This way. We'll do it in the dining room. The living room's a bit chaotic."

"Like the scene on the street."

Joe hears chairs scrape on the tiled floor and closes the door. He splashes water on his face and dries it. Hanging from the shower rail is one of his blue suits. There's a folded green polo on the counter. He dresses, applies some moisturiser, practices his smile a few times, takes a few deep breaths and counts to three. He wishes he was back at the Icebergs swimming, when for about half of his sixty laps, he completely forgot about the world and his place in it.

He sighs and opens the door. They stand as he enters the dining room.

"Hi, I'm Joe."

He shakes hands with Chris, Warren and Dave.

Chris is all smiles. "Thanks for taking the time to talk to us. It's an exclusive, right?"

Anita nods. "Absolutely. That's what you paid for."

"Warren, can you set Joe up?"

The cameramen place their tripods with one camera facing Joe and the other facing Chris. Warren clips a microphone to Joe's lapel.

"Everything you say can and will be used against you."

Chris lays a hand on Joe's shoulder. "He's just joking. We'll edit out any bad stuff or stuttering. We won't make you look like an idiot, or cut and paste it together to make you say what we want you to like they do on other networks."

"Thanks. That's reassuring."

Warren taps the microphone. "Don't cough, don't whisper, don't sneeze."

"I've done this before."

"Say something. A tongue twister. Peter Pecker or something."

"Fischers Fritze fischt frische Fische."

"What does that mean?"

"It's German. I learned that getting drunk on apple wine in Frankfurt. Back when dinosaurs roamed the earth. I can't believe I remember it."

"Well, I'm impressed."

Chris claps her hands together. "You ready, Joe?"

"Yeah, look, how long's this gonna take?"

"Half an hour. Max. We're gonna do a follow-up at the event tomorrow, when you tell us where it is."

Anita sits down at the table, out of camera shot. "You might need a helicopter, if you've got one."

"Why?"

"Can't say. But I'd organise it if I were you."

Joe sees Dave and Warren share a bored glance. Warren even looks at his watch and then mimes a drinky-drinky motion with his hand. Dave nods.

Chris fixes her hair. "I'll have to ask the network. So. Let's get started, shall we? Ready? Warren, on me in three, two, one. Joe Solitus, welcome to Australia."

"Thank you."
"How does it feel to be home?"
"Uh, this isn't my home."
"But your father's Australian and you lived in Sydney."
"How do you know that?"
"Research. Okay. Let's start again. Three, two, one. Joe Solitus, welcome to Australia."
"Thanks. It's great to be here."
"How does it feel to be back home?"
"Well, I guess Sydney is kind of my second home. I studied at UNSW."
"And your father's Australian. It must really feel like coming home."
"A bit, yeah. But my home's in Montreal."
"Tell me about your father."
"He, well, he's the inspiration behind it all. He's the one who told me simplicity is the answer. SINC started in Montreal. Me and my friends just wanted to reconnect with each other and not over screens. We never thought it would turn out like this."
"And now you've brought it to Australia. Did you feel you needed to come here, to give something back to your country of origin?"
"I was born in America. In New Hampshire."
"But you have an Australian passport."
"We, ahem, we saw that SINC was growing in popularity here. We got emails from our supporters asking when there would be an event here. It was their support that made us decide to come."
"How does it feel to be back?"
"It's a nice place."
"You lived not far from here, is that right?"
"In Clovelly."
"We spoke to your former landlord. He had only good things to say about you."
"I enjoyed my time here."
"And now the prodigal returns."
"I wouldn't go that far. But it's nice to be here and we're amazed by the support."
"Yes, there's a crowd of your fans outside. What was going through your mind when you saw all the people gathered to see you?"
"I wondered how so many people could have the afternoon free on a Tuesday."

"It's school holidays at the moment."
"That explains it."
Chris turns to Warren. "Let's go out on the balcony. We're not really getting anything in here. There's no atmosphere. The room's dead."
Warren and Dave gather up their gear.
Anita goes out first. Joe walks with her. She whispers to him. "Stop being so defensive."
"Why do they think I'm Australian?"
"When was the last time something big came out of this country? They want to claim you as their own."
The living room is empty.
"Where is everyone?"
"I sent them to work in the other apartment."
Warren and Dave set up on the balcony. The crowd has grown. There's now a few hundred people gathered in front of the apartment building. Two policemen are trying to keep Arden Street clear, but one side of the street is clogged with traffic. Confused passersby stop to watch. Heads lean out of open car windows.
Chris looks below. "There's twice as many as when we were down there filming."
"At least they're outside enjoying the sun."
Chris raises her voice above the noise. "Warren. Three, two, one. A crowd has gathered in front of the building where Joe Solitus and his simplicity team are staying. Joe, how does it feel to be the head of such a popular movement?"
He gives that everyman half-smile. "It's great. All those people down there are sharing this moment together. That's what we want. Turn off the computer, put the phone away, get rid of all the distractions and experience the real world. That's what they're doing."
"Why do you believe the internet should be shut down?"
"What? I never said anything close to that. I like the internet."
"But you just said people should turn their computers off."
"That's not the same thing. We want people to cut back on their use of technology, to get out and talk to strangers and see the beauty of the world. You can still use the internet, just not for twenty-four hours a day and not to the point that it controls your life."
"That's the gimmick. Disconnecting."
"There's no gimmick. Look, simplicity isn't about wanting to be someone else, a wizard or a sexy vampire or a superhero, or an avatar

on a screen. It's about being yourself, letting people into your lives and opening yourself up to possibility and opportunity. You are the centre of your world."

"That's why people love simplicity. It puts them in the centre."

He leans over the railing and waves to the crowd. "Exactly."

***

The hands slap against the windows of the shuttle bus, which is more like a minivan with too many seats. The driver tries to edge the minivan forward, but the people get in front of it, putting their faces right up against the windscreen. The driver presses his hand hard against the horn. The minivan starts to rock, amid laughter and cheering.

Anita turns from the front seat. "Joe, do something."

"Me?"

"They'll listen to you. Tell them to back off."

He looks out the window, between the heads and arms and hands. "There's only a handful of them. Drive through them."

The driver shouts: "Are you bloody insane?"

Joe looks at the group. "Who leaked our travel plans?"

A chorus of denials.

His eyes fall on Gordie, who's filming the crowd with his phone and grinning at the screen.

"Stan?"

"Sorry, bro. Wrong again. But you gotta admit, great publicity. It's an event without even organising one."

Francois stands up. "It doesn't matter who told. We gotta do something now."

Joe looks around, all the Sincophants staring at him, waiting for him to take control, for him to lead so they can follow. He sees the minivan has a sun roof. He goes to the driver, who's still got his hand pressed against the horn.

"Does that open?"

"What?"

"The sun roof. Open it."

The driver hits a switch and sun roof slides open, letting in a slither of bright daylight like an angelic shaft from heaven. Joe sticks his upper body out. The crowd cheers, all thirty or so of them, mostly boys. They hold phone cameras in his direction. There's also a TV cameraman. Over near the terminal, the onlookers appear to be wondering what the hell is going on.

He looks down at all the teenagers, nearly all of them in white simplicity shirts. "Thanks, guys. That's a really great welcome. We hope you'll all be coming tomorrow."

The small crowd roars its approval. Self-celebration. The home team scoring a goal.

He holds up his hands to quieten them down. "But for that event to happen, we've got a lot of work to do. We really need to get to our hotel. We want to make the event here in Perth the best ever. Remember, we're here for you guys. You have to let us through so we can get it all organised."

He signals with his hands for the people in front of the minivan to part, and they do so, responding to the movement of his arms, edging backwards on both sides just enough for the minivan to move forward. Some of the boys at the front take it upon themselves to hold the others back, spreading out their arms and pushing people. Hands now slap the windows and panels in support. As the minivan starts to gain speed, Joe sees many in the crowd run for the car park to begin the chase. He waves to the kids running alongside. One boy tries to grab at the driver's door, but trips and falls to the ground. No one stops to help him up and the others chasing jump over him.

Joe sits back down to ironic, slow-clapping applause.

Gordie flutters his eyes and makes his voice falsetto. "My hero."

"Quit it, Gordie."

The minivan circles away from the terminal and speeds along the access road that Joe finds vaguely familiar. The traffic is heavy. Soon, they're going down Great Eastern Highway, with a dozen cars trailing in their wake. A few try to pass them, the kids hanging out the windows, whooping and laughing.

The driver blows the horn. "These bloody kids are mad. Are you guys a rock band or something?"

Anita looks straight ahead. "We're SINC."

"Never heard of ya. You gotta an album out?"

"We're not a band. We're simplicity Incorporated."

"Still never heard of ya."

A car zooms past, the kids waving from the windows.

"It looks like someone has."

They take the Graham Farmer Freeway, skirting the downtown. Joe sees the spires of glass and steel he found so uninspiring, what, seven, eight years ago. It looks like nothing has changed. He's sure that progress has brought subtle variations, a few renovations and coats of paint, but the city still seems locked in time. The sky is blue, the sun warm, the air tinged a smoggy, camel yellow. The eight lanes of the freeway are packed with cars: vans, utilities, trucks, SUVs, old cars belching blue smoke. They're bumper to bumper, so close he can't read the license plates. The cars that followed them from the airport seemed to have given up the chase or got lost amongst all the traffic.

Francois, sitting next to Joe, gives him an elbow. "This place is worse than LA. Nothing but roads."

"You wait till you see the beach. The coastline here is incredible."

Francois lowers his voice. "You think Gordie's giving us up?"

"Maybe. It could be any of us."

"Not me. That shit at the airport scares me. But you got them under control. You could've tossed them a rope and told them to pull the bus and they would have."

"They're just bored."

"But they listen to you."

"For now they do."

They pass pockets of greenery, a large lake dotted with ducks and black swans, a few parks and playing fields, but down Scarborough Beach Road it's mostly gas stations, fast food joints, shopping malls and car dealerships. All seven of them let out an appreciative sigh when they crest a hill and the dark blue of the Indian Ocean comes into view.

Cheryline stands up. "Oh, it's beautiful."

Joe looks out the window. There's the backpackers where he stayed, crammed into a sandy, smelly room with five surfers from Denmark who had been living there for six months, which he thought rather defeated the purpose of the place being a backpackers. Why didn't they find somewhere to live? There's the stop where he took bus 400 into the city only to find there was nothing much to do and the day would have been better spent reading on the beach. There's the bike shop where he paid a ridiculous amount to rent a crappy Scamaha for two weeks. There's the other backpackers he stayed in when he got back from down south.

The minivan pulls into an apartment complex and they pile out. Anita heads inside.

Joe stretches and looks at Cheryline. "You all right?"

She's got one hand on her stomach. "I hate buses. That moron was all over the road."

Xav grabs his suitcase. "He was trying to shake our followers."

"He succeeded. And I'm well shaken."

"At least no one knows we're here."

"Not yet."

Joe goes to the side of the minivan to help the driver with the luggage. Francois helps as well. The others stand and wait for their bags and then head inside. Joe gets the feeling that everyone's a little sick of each other. That's understandable. He decides to take a trip during the week off. Alone. Pay another exorbitant amount for a rental bike and head down south again. Drink some wine, eat some cheese, hike, hide.

Francois wipes the sweat from his head. "It's like full summer."

"All those cars, Francois. And I think the hole in the ozone layer is right over Perth, so you better wear a hat if you want to protect that sensitive skin of yours."

Anita comes out and holds up a key card. "You guys are in the Seahorse apartment with Xav and Gordie. Xav's got the other key. Where's Gordie?"

They look through the glass and see Gordie still sitting in his seat at the back of the minivan, his phone pressed to his ear. He pockets the phone and stands up.

Gordie speaks from the doorway. "Yo, where our digs at?"

"Third floor. Xav's got a key as well. You'll have to figure a system to share. Joe, your interview's in twenty minutes."

"Make sure you tell them my family's off limits. And for the last time, I'm not Australian. All this Aussie Joe crap is just wrong."

Anita heads inside. "I told them that in Melbourne, and Adelaide. Not my fault they want to stick their flag on you."

Gordie stands next to Joe, his backpack slung over one shoulder. "Now that I don't get, bro. Why do they care so much that Max was an Aussie?'

The three of them haul their bags inside and join Anita in the elevator. It's playing an upbeat, instrumental version of Radiohead's *Karma Police*.

"Credit. That's what they want. To claim simplicity as their own. But I'm not answering any more questions about Max."

Anita puts her Bluetooth set in place. "Just push the event. We sold twice as much advertising as in Adelaide."

"Just as long as we've got our priorities straight."

"I wouldn't complain if I were you, Joe. You've made more in a week in Australia than you probably made the whole last year."

Gordie taps his phone. "When are we gonna see some of that green? I wanna raise, and I still say we should all be living the life a bit more. Let's take this upmarket."

"We're still building our fan base. There's a lot of work to do, but the advertising is where we're making money. We'll be reviewing finances back in Montreal. Until then, we should stay focused on what we're doing. And these apartments aren't cheap, Gordie."

"Excuse me, sweetness, but we're all underpaid. Not just me. I don't see why Joe's getting everything."

Francois laughs. "You're right, Gordie. It's not like he started the whole thing and he's the one everyone wants to see."

"We're all in it."

"Face it, junior. He's the rock star. We're the entourage and roadies."

"I'm not a rock star."

"And I'm not a roadie, aight. Fucking straight."

The elevator doors open.

Anita leads the way. "Once we get to Montreal and review, we'll all be much wealthier than when we left. Everyone will get their share, especially the six of us who started it."

Gordie swaggers down the hall, doing his cool limp. "We should still be living it up. Where are the parties? The SINC groupies?"

"Give it a rest, Stan. We're all exhausted."

Anita stops at the door to the Blowfish apartment. "Joe, get yourself ready. I'll send Jana in to touch you up."

"Super duper."

Anita smiles. "Your biggest fan."

Francois slides the card into the door. Inside, there's a cramped living room and kitchenette, with two sofas pushed into an L facing the TV. The very low coffee table is scattered with magazines and has probably scarred many a shin in its time. Through the glass door, Joe can see Xav standing on the balcony, his back to the ocean, his head bowed over his phone. Xav sees them and comes inside.

"This is great. But fuck me if it's not hot. Isn't it supposed to be winter?"

Francois looks at the two doors. "Which room did you take?"

Xav points.

"Okay, so that's the snorers' room."

"I don't snore."

"Like a dying elephant."

"You lie."

"Gordie, you're in there too. Joe, we're in this room."

Gordie falls into a sofa and flips open his notebook. "Why does Anita always put us four in the same apartment?"

Joe puts his satchel on the kitchen counter. "Probably because we're all friends and she thinks we won't kill each other."

"We should be crashing with the girls. Why are we always separated? What are we, teenagers at camp? It's that spinster bitch's fault."

Joe follows Francois into their small bedroom. It has two single beds, half a metre apart. There's barely enough clearance between the ends of the beds and the wall to get around.

Francois smiles. "Intimate."

"Like a prison cell."

The knock on the door makes Francois turn. "That'll be Jana."

Joe rubs his eyes. "We gotta get rid of her. It's too freaking awkward."

"Isn't it fascinating that someone who's pushing thirty can still have a schoolgirl crush?"

"They need to get their hearts broken early on. That would sort them out."

"You shouldn't have slept with her."

"She practically raped me. Came into my room when I was half asleep."

Francois laughs. "And fully drunk. So call the police."

Joe hears Xav open the door. "Jana. Are you here to give us a rub and tug?"

"You're disgusting, Xav."

Francois laughs. "She's got balls."

"If only. That would make things less awkward between us."

"Probably more so."

Joe lets out a sigh. "We need a break from all this shit. Get away."

"We got it. After the event tomorrow. Eight free days. What'll you do with it?"

"We haven't stopped since Montreal. It's like we're in some kind of reality TV race."

"So we hang out here for a week?"

"I'm going down south. There's a place around the corner that rents bikes. I'll get one and head for Margaret River. It's nice down there. Wineries, beaches, forests."

"Sounds good."

"Joe?"

They turn to see Jana in the doorway.

"You're on."

Joe sighs again and heads into the bathroom. Jana follows him step for step and closes the door. He sits on the toilet, facing a long vanity mirror. In this familiar position, he gets the strongest urge to pee.

"This'll just take a minute."

"That's all we've got."

She goes to work, pushing her breasts against his left shoulder as she stands at his side. "That was some scene at the airport."

"They knew we were coming. Pretty soon, they'll know we're here."

"I was scared, Joe."

"They're bored. And there weren't that many. They were just loud."

"They were so aggressive. I thought they were gonna flip the bus over."

"They've been trapped inside for half a decade. Spent their childhoods staring at screens. They're like dogs let off the leash."

"Hold still."

She applies some make-up just below his eyes, getting very close to him and leaning forward so the crevice of her cleavage is on display. He tries to turn away, to be certain she won't catch him staring.

"Why do you think they're bored?"

"Maybe they've got nothing interesting in their lives, nothing that sets them apart from everyone else. They come out to the airport for something to do, to be part of it. Probably just to be able to tell people they were there."

"It was crazy. But you took care of it. You were amazing."

She does his hair, concentrating hard, eager to get it right. In the mirror opposite, he sees her small frame, once again so well-presented. Her hair is brown and cut short, streaked with blonde highlights like the keyboardist of an eighties new wave band; backing up a better looking singer and always trying to get attention. She's very plain, apart from her rack, which seems to vary in perkiness according to her mood, or choice of support undergarment. Like always, she's well styled, well organised, her colours, make-up and accessories well chosen. She puts together a good package, and it struck him positively at first, but it now looks to him like it took quite a lot of effort and cultivation to get it right; perhaps a decade of trial and error and experimentation with different looks. He wonders what she looked like in the business suits she wore as Anita's interning assistant at Natrofield.

He thinks of the pill game and chuckles.

"What?"

"Uh, it's nothing. A lot changed this year."

"Yeah, simplicity's really taken off."

"Has it?"

"Sure."

"I thought the fans were just getting louder. More aggressive. Like the kids at the airport."

She runs her stubby fingers through his short hair. "It was really great the way you handled it."

"Thanks."

"It's so impressive how they all listen to you."

She dabs cream on his cheeks, rubs it in with her thumbs, softly, massaging. She leans close again, giving another flash of crevice, squinting and feigning to inspect her work, to get the mix right. He smells airline food on her breath.

"I think Gordie likes you."

"What? He can't even remember my name."

"He's shy."

"No way."

"And insecure."

"The way he talks, I thought he hated women."

"That's because he's shy and insecure. He compensates by being all macho and sexist. He thinks girls like a man who's the boss."

"He watches too much TV."

"It's not that. It's the music."

"I know, hip-hop. Girls as accessories. As bling to be bought, sold and traded. And thrown in the trash when no longer needed."

Joe smiles, suddenly liking her a little more. "Yeah, but around you, he's a bundle of nerves. I know my brother and that behaviour means he likes you."

She puts some product in his hair and gives the fringe a few flicks. "He's not my type. He's a scared little boy."

"What is your type?"

She leans back, crosses her arm under her breasts, smiles plainly, almost bitterly. "That's obvious, isn't it?"

There's a knock on the door.

Joe stands up. "That's them."

"Show time."

"Thanks for trying to make me beautiful, Jana. An almost impossible task."

In the living room, there's another TV crew: a reporter in a very short skirt, two cameramen, and this time some kind of manager brandishing a clipboard and with a hands-free set clipped to her shirt. The room feels very full. He hears the door close as Jana slips out.

"Hi, I'm Joe. Where do you want to set up? On the balcony?"

The manager shakes his hand. "Too windy. Let's take the sofas."

"Okay. If you haven't all met, that's Xav, head of products and merchandise, Gordie, event management, and Francois, our image maximiser."

"You'll all have to leave. We can't have any background noise."

The three of them head for the door.

Joe holds it open. "Sorry, guys. There's a great ice cream stand down by the beach. And I wish I was coming with you."

"Sure you do, bro. You hate all this attention, don't you?"

Joe shakes his head as he closes the door.

"Doug, set up over there. Martin, you're on Sam. Make sure you get close ups, of the hands too. He's got no wedding ring so be sure to get that in the shot."

The cameramen get to work.

Joe walks up to the manager. "I didn't get your name."

"It's Carla."

"Nice to meet you."

"Thanks for your time. Did you just arrive?"

"Yeah. Long flight."

"Hi, Bob, we're interviewing him now...We'll make the late news... Yes, we got footage at the airport...Sorry. It's a big country. It takes a few hours longer flying west because of the wind."

"That's what I told everyone."

"You've been here before?"

"Yep. Long time ago. Not much has changed though."

"Perth's nothing like it was ten years ago. It's the best city in Australia. Now, we're not going to mike you. The room's quiet enough. It sounds more natural that way, and looks better too. You guys ready? Sam?"

Joe sits down on the sofa. Carla tells him to change seats and he moves to the other corner. He crosses his legs and drapes an arm along the back of the sofa. Sam sits forward, elbows on crossed, bare knees. Joe watches her put on her camera face. She takes a couple of deep breaths, adjusts her skirt, then offers him a smile that's all shiny teeth.

Carla lurks behind the cameramen, writing on her clipboard and whispering into her hands-free set. "Get straight into it, Sam. We'll do the filler later. Okay. We're rolling."

"Congratulations on a successful tour of Australia."

"Thank you. The support's been incredible."

"Your home state gave you a great welcome."

"What do you mean?"

"At the airport. A big crowd came out to welcome you home."

"A few die hard fans, yeah. That was great. But we're just visiting. This isn't my home."

"Your father, Max Solitus, was from Western Australia."

"Yes."

"So, your roots are here. Welcome home."

He tries to smile. "Well, my dad came from here, but I was born and raised in New Hampshire. America. I've only been to Perth once, and that was for a holiday."

Sam leans forward, eyebrows sympathetically diagonal. "Do you feel that Max is with you now?"

"Excuse me?"

"In spirit. You've been very open about saying that Max is the inspiration behind simplicity, the philosophy and the book. How was it for you when he died? How did it feel?"

Joe looks at Carla. "I'm sorry, but I'm not answering any questions about Max."

"They said you would."

"Who's they? Anita?"

"They said they wanted to show your emotional side. Bad comments online, hate email, or something. Can we continue, please? We're on a schedule. Sam, go on."

"Your father died in tragic circumstances. You were just seventeen. How was it for you?"

"How do you know all this?"

Carla whacks a pen against her clipboard. "Joe, the camera's rolling. Answer the question."

"It wasn't meant to happen. It was someone else's fault."

"Is that why you've always campaigned against cars? Because of the accident?"

"I don't campaign against cars. People can drive if they want."

"A car hit your father. What was going through your mind when you saw him lying on the road?"

"Who told you this?"

"We have our sources."

He stands up and walks out of the apartment. Doug follows him.

In the hallway, Joe bangs on the door of the Blowfish apartment. Jana opens it. He pushes her aside.

"Close the door and don't let them in. Anita? Anita?"

"What's going on?"

"What the fuck, Anita?"

She holds up her hands, confused. "Joe, calm down."

"They're only asking about Max. They know everything. What did you tell them?"

"Nothing. I don't know anything about Max to tell. I told them there should be no questions about the family. Keep it on SINC and the event."

"They're way off, over the line. Somebody told them something. Cheryline? Jana?"

The girls shake their heads.

Cheryline shrugs. "I don't know anything about your family, Joe. I got nothing to tell them."

"Me neither."

Joe nods. He rubs his forehead. Jana puts a hand on his shoulder, but he walks away from her.

There's a knock on the door. "Joe? Joe?"

"Don't let them in."

Anita goes to the door. "I'll put a stop to this."

As the door opens, Carla pushes the two cameramen inside, and then blocks the door, only letting Sam past. The cameras get in Joe's face. Sam holds up a microphone.

"How did the accident change your life? Did you try to get revenge on the driver? Why won't you talk about it? How did it affect your relationship with your brother?"

Joe puts a hand over the camera lens. "Gordie."

"Why did you go to Europe instead of the funeral? Are you in contact with your uncle?"

"Uncle? What uncle?"

"Trevor Solitus."

"Who?"

Anita steps in front of the cameras. "Carla, this is not what we talked about."

"We did some research. This is the interview the world wants."

Anita and Carla start shouting at each other.

Joe gets between them. "Okay. OKAY! That's enough. Look, let's just take a minute. Yeah, this interview's a good idea. But let's do it properly. I've got some photos in my bag."

Anita looks at him. "Do you?"

"Carla, I'll tell you everything. I just need a few minutes in my room to find the photos and put them in order. Anita, offer them something to drink. Maybe make them, uh, some tea. Yeah. Some tea. Put the kettle on. I need five minutes, and then we'll do the interview. Yeah. Right. I'll come back when I'm organised. I'll tell you everything."

Carla taps her clipboard. "Hurry up. We're on a schedule."

He goes out of the room. Anita follows him.

"You know what you're doing?"

"Keep them occupied. I'll knock on the door when I'm ready."

"Okay."

He strokes her shoulder. "You know, Anita, I'm really sorry it didn't work out. With us. Boston, Barcelona, Oregon, you restored a lot of things in me I thought I'd lost."

She looks at him strangely. "Great. Now get it together."

"You're one of the good ones. Remember that. Thanks for everything. You did all of this."

"We're just getting started, Joe. It's good you're doing the interview. The world would find out soon enough. And it'll be better coming from you."

"That's right. Nothing's private anymore. Five minutes?"

She nods.

He goes into the room and out onto the balcony. The drop is too far, and there's a crowd of about a hundred people below.

They chant: "Aussie, Aussie, Aussie, Joe, Joe, Joe."

His bags are still packed. He shoulders his backpack and loops his satchel over his neck. He slowly opens the door, peers out into the empty hall and runs for the stairs.

Down south with the Deleted Family

The hammock creaks as he shifts his position, putting his right hand under his head.

Tell me about it. You never talk about it.

I don't? The highlight of the day was when work stopped and everyone went to the pub. It's probably still like that.

It's boring here, too.

No, no. No, Jonah. Even this small town has a cinema, a theatre, some restaurants and cafes. There are churches too, but we won't talk about them. There's always something going on here and the locals expect it. And they get involved.

Is that why you left? Because there's nothing to do?

Yes. No. It always bothered me. But there was no one I could talk to about it. My friends didn't understand. They all thought I was little off. My folks didn't get me at all. They wanted me to be happy with what they had, like that was enough. They thought I was fruity.

Crazy?

Gay. And that's not really something you can be in small town, WA. Maybe that's changed. I hope it has.

They both take long sips of their beers.

What are you gonna do now, Jonah? School's just about dusted. We haven't spoken about it.

Don't know. Travel a bit, like you did.

He smiles, seeming to recall all those forays across the globe, the hitch-hiking trips, the motorbike rides, all those stories he would only tell if asked.

I was your age when I started out. It was good for me, to get out of that house and that town, away from all those fixed ideas about how things were. My old man, he wasn't a bad bloke, but he was a couple of decades behind. He decided how things were back in the fifties and stuck with all those ideals and beliefs. Religious too. He used to pray for rain. Him saying grace before dinner was like getting the most desired weather forecast. And all that praying and church-going never brought the rain when he needed it, and it didn't keep some drunk idiot from ploughing into them coming home from the trots.

Sorry, Max.

That kind of stuff happens every day. And because it happens, to believers who pray and do all the right things, it proves there's no God. How could there be? Awful things happen to good folks and good things happen to bad folks. If there's some almighty fella up in the clouds dispensing justice, He's doing a terrible job at it.

Yeah.

Don't listen to me, Jonah. Make up your own mind. You might go out into the world and have experiences that make you think there is a God, or that there's something. You're allowed to believe whatever you want, and you're allowed to change those opinions. People change over time and so do their opinions. A certain experience might make them think there is a God, or make them change Gods, or make them stop believing altogether, or confirm the fact there's nothing to believe in. You've always been free to go to church with your ma.

I know.

But you never go.

I'm not interested.

Len's been trying to convince me for years. He's barking so far up the wrong tree, but I think that just motivates him more. The biggest conversion will give him the biggest reward, so he thinks. He's not a bad guy, but his motivations are wrong. He thinks he's doing it for me, but he's really doing it for himself. Still, you've got to admire the force of his convictions. The only question is, where does it come from? Religion is completely illogical, something invented to fill the void. And Len's a doctor, a man of science. You'd think with all the death and disease he's seen, all the unfairness, that he'd approach life in a more rational way.

Maybe it gives him a reason, to go on, despite everything.

You got those smarts from my side of the family. That's what it's all about, Jonah. Having a reason. Justification. When we came down from the trees, it wasn't enough for us to eat, drink, hunt and be merry. There had to be more to it. We discovered fire, then we discovered worship. And it was probably around then that everything started to go wrong. My God's better than your God means war, destruction, invasion, crusades, genocide. Saul telling David to go out and bring him a hundred Philistine foreskins as a dowry for his daughter. And a thousand other examples. The Christians putting the Muslims to the sword. Empires, missionaries, invaders, inquisitions, converting the heathens. Who told them to do all that? Who's to say they're right? All these wars of belief versus belief. People dying for theories. All these people saying God is on their side. God gave me the strength to score a touchdown. God helped me win an Oscar. Bullshit. They need to simplify. Get rid of the Gods and focus on what really matters, on things that are real. On what they know and can touch with their hands, and the things they can control.

He reaches out a hand and pushes against the porch railing. The hammock swings and creaks.

Ah, but we love battle. Even if there were no Gods, we'd find something else to kill for. Oil and gold and land. Chess, Jonah, is a great metaphor for life. The guy who invented chess had his finger on the pulse of humanity. The king is the most important piece, but the queen is the most versatile and useful. And the queen is also the one that can be replaced if it gets taken. But there's only ever one king. The pawns are cannon fodder. The knights and bishops do all the dirty work, all the dinking and weaving, working the angles. Getting taken means getting killed. Chess, it's war.

I don't like chess.

That's because Gordie always beats you.

I let him win. You know what a sore loser he is.

That's very big-brotherly of you, but bad for his development. He's going to lose at some point in life and he'll be badly prepared for that day. By letting him win, he's gonna grow up expecting everyone to let him win. He'll think his life will be full of second chances and forgiveness, that no matter how badly he plays and behaves, he'll win in the end because someone will let him.

Okay. He wins because he's better. Chess is boring. There are better things to do, like go to the pool.

Or take a run.

Yeah.

Gordie can run. He's letting that talent go to waste. He's quick. Very economical stride, like me. He was born to be a miler. Or a five K champ.

He wants to get off the topic of Gordie. Can I ask you something, Max?

Anything.

Why did you start running? Did you run at school?

No, I played cricket and footy like everyone else. My old man wasn't good at sports, but he was into it, came to all my cricket matches and footy games. Put pressure on me, analysed my performance, but not too heavily. He wanted me to do well. I think he wanted someone to brag about, someone who compensated for his lack of sporting prowess. But I wasn't that good, and the sporting club culture didn't really suit me. In Australia, the team is a bit like an army unit. Very insular. I didn't think the team or those weekend games were worth dying for, or worth getting paralytic drunk post-game, win or lose. I guess, in the Aussie sense, I'm not much of a team player. The drinking was out of control, and we were teenagers. When you're in the team and you don't drink, you're in trouble. And there are a lot of other obligations too. You see it even in professional sports. Gang rapes by rugby league teams, organised fighting at footy training, extreme homophobia, drunken idiocy on end of season trips, guys getting arrested. An Australian sports team, pro or amateur, has the potential to do anything.

Do you miss it?

The sport? No. I started running when I was on the road. Ha. I ran away from home and just kept on running. It was another way to see the sights. I ran past all the wonders of the world, Jonah. Well, a few of them.

I mean Australia.

He turns and looks at the line of trees on Hassock Hill. An hour ago, they'd pounded the tracks through the forest, stopping after every two mile loop to do ten push-ups and twenty sit-ups.

It's similar. Here, I mean. The trees, the lay of the land. I think that's why I settled here so easily. No, never homesick. It's much greener here. And the people are nicer, more open and accepting. The only difference is the climate, and I don't miss that. The house used to sweat in summer. The school rooms too. What I like here are the changing seasons. You can see time moving forward just from coming out here each day and looking at the trees. These small subtle changes that are happening all the time, if you look for them and notice them. You don't get that in Australia. Time doesn't go in a circle like it does here. The time just runs, and you never really know where you are.

I wanna go there.

You should. It's part of you, and it's worth seeing, especially the south west. The cities are nothing special. Buildings, offices, suburbs, a few million people just trying to get by and do enough so others don't ask questions. They could be cities anywhere. But the landscape, the Nullarbor, the Kimberley, the coasts, up north. It's incredible. I miss that.

Let's go together.

He shakes his head. Would love to, Jonah, but I've got to finish the new elementary school in Meredith. Anyway, that's the kind of trip you should do on your own. If I came, you'd just see it all through my eyes. There'd be no discoveries for yourself. I tell you what. I'll spot you the flight, but only if you're back in time for college in September. That'll give you about three months there.

Deal.

They shake hands.

You earned it.

Another beer?

Why the hell not. All a man can do is eat, drink and be happy in his work. That's from the bible, Jonah. In among the hoarding of foreskins, the slaughtering of heathens and your namesake getting swallowed by a whale, there's a few good bits. Some of those fairytales are worth reading. The Old Testament, not the new. The New Testament's rubbish. It's advertising. Jesus was a spokesman. Change testament for testimonial. The gospel of the world's first brand manager. And his disciples got the naming rights for all the churches built in his honour. They made a killing.

He picks up the label maker that's lying on the porch. Joe watches him bang out a label.

Here.

Eat, drink and be happy in your work.

Simple as that, Jonah. Now, get me another beer so I can drink and be happy.

~~~

He wakes. The bed creaks and twangs as he sits up and stretches. A puppeteer pulls all the strings attached to his lower back at once, all in different directions. Or are Enora and Supe digging needles into a little Joe doll in an open-plan office in Montreal?

He stands and groans. "A swim would sort that out."

The best he can do is a hot shower. Well, a lukewarm shower. The
~~~

cubicle is orange with rust, around the drains and where the taps connect to the wall. The bricks behind the taps are exposed, flaking and chipped away; all those meaty farmers' fists yanking at the taps, wanting more hot water. The tiles glow with mildew the colour of rotten avocado. The thin motel soap dissolves in his hands after a couple of rubs. The water cuts from lukewarm to cold and back again. He misses the consistent banality of the Mayola, of life in Montreal, Popov and his apartment, where he ate, drank and was happy in his work. Relatively happy.

Dressed, he goes outside, his hair still wet. The morning is bright and cool, the sun close to the horizon and a very pale yellow.

"Excuse me. Is there a cafe around here?"

She points. "There's a bakery near the post office."

"Thanks."

He heads in that direction, down the town's one main street. He passes a second-hand clothing shop, then a small supermarket, a hardware store, a real estate office, a hairdressing salon. He touches his hair, wondering if he should dye it.

The bakery has a warm crusty smell, like the bottom of the family toaster after a loaf of Wonderbread has gone through it. He orders a sausage roll and a jam donut.

"Do you have any tea?"

"From the machine."

It looks dismal. He grabs a half-litre carton of orange juice from the fridge, pays, goes outside and sits down on a bench next to the Anzac memorial. He chews on the sausage roll and smiles, remembering all the sausage rolls he ate in Sydney and in various bakeries around the country.

"Should go to the Dunsborough Bakery while I'm here."

He takes another bite, the pastry flaking, the steam escaping, the grease staining the paper bag where he touches it, leaving fingerprints.

A few seagulls land at his feet.

He wonders if the event will go on without him. Who will make the speech? Who will organise the crowd? Who will be the centre of attention? Who the fuck cares?

He wonders if they're out looking for him. Maybe they contacted the police, already know he got a rental bike and checked into a motel in Busselton. Maybe Cheryline has already twisted it into some kind of marketing ploy. Where the hell is Joe? Or *Where's Joe?* picture books, like Waldo. Or something like that; something that increases brand awareness and offers cross-channel marketing and multi-profit revenue streams.

He grunts with distaste.

He wonders if there's a pool around here. He's certainly not going in the ocean. The last time he did that here, he got stung by jellyfish, and two fishermen hauled him out and peed on him before he could stop them.

He laughs with his mouthful.

He wonders why Max never mentioned Trevor. Come to think of it, he never said anything about his family, except that his parents died in a car accident. Why did he lie? Why did Trevor never call or visit? What else did Max lie about?

He wonders how far it is to Nannup. Will Trevor be there? The phone book in the motel was ten years old.

He wonders what goes into a sausage roll. It tastes like meat, looks like meat. Probably best not to know.

He finishes it, takes a swig of orange juice and hoes into the sugar-covered donut.

He wonders if the locals get bored with blue sky and sunshine every day. Does it dull their senses and make them walk around in a daze?

He wonders why everyone here has a dog, with big teeth and shabby coats, and why none of them are on leashes. He misses Popov.

"I wanna go home, Pops."

Donut finished, he licks the sugar from his fingers, wipes his hands on the paper bag and chugs down the last of the juice. He walks down the other side of the street, back to the motel. Another hairdressing salon, another real estate office, a boarded-up bakery, the local police station, an ancient-looking telephone box with one glass side broken and a pile of glass at the bottom. He swings the door open, lifts the receiver, pumps in a few coins and dials. It rings.

"Hello?"

"Uh, hi. Is that Trevor Solitus?"

"Who wants to know?"

"Are you Trevor?"

"Look, I'm not answering any more bloody questions about me brother."

He hears the chime as the receiver is slammed back in place, like it's an old rotary dial phone. He goes into the newsagent and buys a map. He locates Nannup and plots a course.

The ATM inhales his Visa card and exhales five hundred dollars. An assortment of those weird plastic notes. Money for dummies, colour-coded: two green hundreds, four yellow fifties, three red twenties and four blue tens.

"Beats the hell out of greenbacks. They all look the same."

He pockets the money and the card. They'll track that, he thinks, if they want to. And they probably already know about Nannup.

At the motel, he takes a dump, flushes three times to get rid of it, waiting each time for the reservoir to fill and then yanking the chain like he's trying to start a lawnmower. It makes the sound of a dam bursting, but has little impact. In the next room, he can hear someone else having the same problem. Their flushes follow one after the other, an echo of poor plumbing.

He brushes his teeth, packs and pays the bill with his Visa. Backpack and satchel shouldered, he gets on the Kapowasaki. It lets out a couple of burps and then squeaks to life. The seat set-up is all wrong, the angle terrible for carrying a backpack. He has to hunch forward like he's on the race track, legs behind. The satchel swings in front of him. But it was all they had.

He gets out on the highway and heads south.

It's a ridiculously beautiful day.

***

The house is down a narrow street that slices between the Vasse and Brockman Highways. He brings the Kapowasaki to a shuddering, farting halt out front. He gets off, straightens and unsticks the backpack from his sweaty back.

The house is now a youth hostel. A half dozen cars are parked by the fence, so close that doors can only half open. Station wagons and vans coated with red dust and filled with stuff. Surfboards dimpled with wax are lashed to roof racks. Bikes are tied loosely to back doors, with door and bikes about to fall off. Camp stoves, burned pots, enamel plates and charred cutlery scratch at the insides of back windows. The license plates are all eastern states, the cars most certainly headed back in that direction, if the occupants can face another cross country drive, if the car will make it. They'll head north for the long way around, or take the Nullarbor to Adelaide. Maybe some will venture down the Gunbarrel Highway for a climb of Uluru.

The door of the van next to him slides open. A dishevelled kid, still carrying the scrawniness of a teenager, his inverted-bowl stomach showing the results of a frugal, cash-saving road diet, stumbles out, bathroom bag in hand.

"Morgen. It's full."

He slips on a loose t-shirt, opens the gate and takes the path towards the house. Another guy climbs out of the van, equally scrawny, equally young. He sits in the doorway and pulls one knee under his chin. His toes poke out of the holes in his socks. He smells, as does the van.

"Your bike?"

"Yep."

"Nice."

"Thanks."

"What your pack weigh?"

"Maybe ten kilos."

"Must be bad to carry that."

"It is."

"Why don't you have, you know, side bags?"

"Saddle bags."

"That's what I said."

"Had no time. I left in a hurry."

"Where you from?"

"Montreal. You?"

"Rotterdam. Have you rode from Perth?"

"Yesterday. Spent the night in Busselton. What about you?"

"We came from Manjimup. Fruit picking."

"How long?"

"We've been there three months. We got here last night, but it was full."

"Crap."

"We wanted to make Margaret River, but it was dark. Our lights don't function."

Joe laughs. "Sorry."

"It's dangerous at night. Can't see something. No streetlights."

"Yeah, but you're probably safer. No animals are gonna get caught in your lights."

"Do you think that's funny?"

"How long you been here?"

"I told you. We got here last night."

"I meant in Australia."

"Almost a year. We buyed the van in Zydney. Drove north. Brisbane, Caaarns, Darvin, down the west coast."

"That's a long way."

"It was boring. So boring. Just roads. Nothing to see."

"Why'd you do it then?"

"Our friends back home can believe not what we done."

He reaches into the van and pulls out a small notebook. He flips it open.

"Are you heading back to Sydney?"

"Over the Mullarbor."

"Nullarbor."

The kid snarls, but doesn't look up. "That's what I said."

"Sorry. Look, do you know if the owner's around?"

"No chance. It's full."

"I just wanna talk to him."

"Try inside."

The kid connects a small camera to the computer and manipulates the track pad, his concentration intense. Joe leaves him to it.

He opens the gate. "All those kilometres just to brag to people back home."

The house has a narrow veranda around it. He'd like to think it looks familiar, but it doesn't. The wood is paler and thinner, the roof lower, the whole house much smaller. The beams on the floor are splintered and cracked, gnawed at in places by ants and rats, or maybe by starving backpackers who slept on the veranda because the hostel was full. The fly-screen squeaks as he opens it. Inside, the house has a lived-in, unloved smell, like the bottom of a never-washed sleeping bag, or a mouldy tent folded away and forgotten in a damp basement. A few people are scattered around the living room and kitchen, which is one big open area. They're hunched forlornly over bowls of cereal, or are staring at their phones with a minimum of enthusiasm. No one talks. They all look tired, worn out and fed up with the whole travelling enterprise. He wonders if, given the chance, each one of them would go home right now.

He goes into the kitchen and puts the kettle on. There's a disorderly collection of tea bags that a few hundred hands have rifled through and flipped. All the strings and labels are tangled. A couple of tea bags looked used, dried out and thrown back in. He finds a green tea, with vanilla. It's a little yellow at the edges, but he drops it in a chipped mug. The kettle slowly comes to a boil, filling the kitchen and living room with noise. A few people look at him with the fuzzy fury of hangovers. He smiles and shrugs, and turns the kettle off before it reaches its crescendo and wakes the whole town.

He holds it up. "Anyone else like some tea?"

"Got any coffee?"

He looks at the bare contents of the free food shelf. "There's just tea, and some of it looks older than me."

No one laughs, or responds. One girl brushes past him and dumps her cereal bowl in the sink; really drops it so the spoon rims out of the bowl and clangs against the metal sink. She trudges into a dorm room, her hiking boots thumping the wooden floor, the open laces picking up small bits of dried bread and what look like brown flakes of onion skin.

He lifts the tea bag out of the mug and puts it in the bin labelled "Kompost". He sits down at the table and blows on the mug. Two beefy young guys are working their way through a loaf of white bread, toasting it and spreading red jam on it, with no butter or margarine. They both fold the toasted slice over itself and eat it in two bites, toasting two more slices as they chew.

"How's it going?"

One guy nods. The other mumbles: "Good."

"The owner around?"

"Place's full."

"I know. I don't need a bed. I wanna talk to the owner."

"Why?"

"He's an old friend."

"Must be a long time ago because he's now a she."

Both guys laugh, opening their mouths to reveal half chewed messes of white bread and pink jam.

"Huh. I guess he's not here anymore."

"You an Aussie?"

"Yep."

"Where from?"

"Sydney. My dad's from Nannup. What about you guys?"

"Capetown."

"Nice."

"Have you been there?"

"My dad has. Said it was a great place. It's on my list. You heading home or just starting?"

"We live in Perth. Just down here for a holiday, but there's nothing to do. Any tips?"

"You got wheels?"

They chew and nod. The other guy loads the toaster with two more slices.

"If you like hiking, head over to Pemberton and Walpole. If you want the beach, go to Yallingup. You could dive an old battleship in Dunsborough. If you're feeling adventurous, head for Esperance."

They spread jam on toast, fold, bite and chorus unappreciatively: "Thanks."

"You're welcome."

A middle-aged woman enters carrying a big file. "Morning, all."

"That's the owner."

"Shaved her legs and then he was a she."

"What?"

Joe stands up. "Nothing. Have a good holiday."

He goes into the living room and sits down next to her.

"Sorry, we're fully booked. Even the tents and caravans out back are chockers."

"I don't need a room."

"Good, cause I don't have one."

He lowers his voice. "I'm looking for Trevor."

She doesn't look up from the file. "Not here."

"Where is he?"

"Not here. Elsewhere."

"I need to talk to him."

She looks at him sharply. "You a reporter?"

"No."

"This place was crawling with reporters yesterday. All looking for Trevor. I told em all to get stuffed. That's why he went out to the farm."

"I'm not a reporter. Look, can we talk outside?"

"I got work to do."

"Where's the farm?"

She offers him a plain, steady look. "What farm?"

He leans close and whispers. "I'm Joe. Joe Solitus."

She stops writing in her file and stares at him. Her eyes narrow. "I saw him on telly last night. Very briefly. Head of some religious cult or other. Angry looking fella. Kept putting his hand in the camera. Anyway, a guy came here yesterday saying he was you. I told him and everyone else to get stuffed. Bloody reporters."

"What did he look like?"

"Like I said, angry looking fella. Looked like no one had ever loved him."

"I mean the guy that came here."

"Oh, brown hair. Short. Weird accent. Couldn't understand a word he said. He kept saying he was looking for the farm hoose. Wouldn't leave until I threatened to call the cops."

"Xav."

"Said his name was Joe."

Joe pulls out his passport. "Here."

She flips it open and squints at the photo. "I haven't got me glasses on. What's Trev's middle name?"

"No idea."

She tosses the passport in his lap. "Then you're not him. The guy yesterday couldn't answer that question either."

"Twenty-four hours ago I didn't even know there was a Trevor Solitus. That I had an uncle."

"And an aunt."

"Are you his wife?"

She nods.

"Where is he? I gotta meet him. Talk to him."

"About what?"

"I don't know. Everything. I wanna know why Max never said anything."

She looks around the room. So does Joe. Everyone is looking at them. Doors from adjacent rooms and bathrooms have opened and heads pop out, some dripping. The girl in the chair opposite takes a photo of Joe with her phone. She starts tapping feverishly at the screen.

"Max was a selfish bastard. Just went and left when people needed him. Weak. Always was. Ruined everything round here."

"Steady on. That's my dad you're talking about."

"There's a lot about Max you don't know."

"Tell me."

"Why should I?"

"Because we're family."

"That was never good enough for Max."

"I'm sure he had his reasons for whatever he did."

"Don't defend him."

"I just wanna talk to Trevor."

"I'm not even sure you are Joe Solitus."

"Don't I look like Max?"

"Not really. That was years ago. You look a bit like Ben, but all you young fellas look alike to me."

The girl who took the photo leaps in the air. "Ohmigod! It's you. It's really you. I love SINC."

She lifts her sweater to show her white 'Simplicity is the answer' shirt.

"No, no. I'm not him."

"Yeah, you are. I checked your photo on idntphi. It's you. Ohmigod! We're driving to Perth for the event today."

Suddenly the room is alive with voices.

The woman stands up to protect him, swishing her folder back and forth. They edge towards the fly-screen. "Everyone just settle down. It's not him. I'd know me own nephew."

They raise phones in his direction, filming and taking photographs. A few people are talking on their phones. Joe sees the two South Africans at the table standing and staring at him, confused and still chewing. Two slices pop up in the toaster. Joe backs out the door. The woman follows him.

"We'll take my car."

But Joe is already through the gate, his backpack on and satchel swinging as he gets on the Kapowasaki.

She stands at the gate, blocking it. "Brockman Highway. Half way to Bridgetown. There's a windmill on the right side of the road, broken in half."

"Call him. Tell him I'm coming."

A couple of kids fight each other to get through the door and down the path, some holding car keys in the air, ready for the chase. The woman stands in front of the gate. One guy tries to jump the fence, but doesn't quite make it. He lands face first in the dirt. Joe spins the bike around. From the corner of his eye, he sees the Dutch kid look up from his notebook, still sitting in the doorway of the van.

***

He turns down the gravel road, weaving between the potholes. Every bump sends a wave of pain through his lower back. The road seems to lead nowhere, bending left and right, following dried out fields that haven't seen a crop in decades. He wonders if the woman, his possible aunt, has deliberately sent him way off track. And at the end of this narrow road is some yokel's house where he will be made into a house pet, or beheaded and mounted on the wall as a trophy.

The sun is high and hot, the paddocks dry and cracked. It looks like it hasn't rained all winter.

That's why they prayed for it, he thinks.

This land, that was once touched by man, ploughed and planted and ploughed again, over and over, is now just scraggly scrubs, all about waist high. A few dirty looking sheep are scattered under a paddock's lone tree. He passes a dam running low on milky green water.

The track goes straight and then bends right, over a cattle grill that feels like it shatters all his lower vertebrae. Up ahead is a house.

The house.

The big veranda supported by thick beams, the perfect pyramid roof, the square front with the door flanked by two double windows.

"Huh. You said it was in town."

The track widens closer to the house, and flattens, has fewer holes. A couple of dogs come from around the back, baring their teeth and snapping at the wheels of the bike. He wonders again what it is with dogs in this country.

He kicks at them. "Fuck off."

He stops the bike in front of the house and the dogs settle down a little. At least, they stop looking like they're going to eat him and are now just growling. They circle him warily, lifting hairy lips to show their canines, long and sharp.

He takes off his helmet and gets off the bike. "Popov has so much more class than you."

"Who's Popov?"

He looks up and sees a portly man with thick grey hair standing on the porch. His hands are tucked into the bib of his overalls, just near his armpits, which have damp patches that make Joe think the man was working. The front of the overalls is covered with grease, and it looks like he has a few streaks of it in his hair as well.

"Are you Trevor?"

"Depends. Are you really Joe?"

He shrugs off the pack and puts it between himself and the dogs. "You wanna see my passport?"

"Tell me something about Max no one else would know."

"Uh, like what?"

"He fell off a motorbike when he was thirteen. What did he break?"

"He never told me about that."

Trevor sniffs, rocks on his feet a little. "Not a good start. You do look like him, though."

The dogs bark. One tries to jump up at Joe, with dirty front paws that grab at his belt. Joe raises his arms.

"Geddown, Rosco."

"He never told me about you. He said you lived in town, in a house just like this. He built a copy of it in Harbrook. Where we lived."

"This isn't our house. It belongs to Bev's family. Whole farm does."

"Is Bev the woman at the hostel?"

Trevor nods. "That's our house. I kept the phone number because me mum's memory is shot. She only remembers that number, and she dials it whenever she picks up the phone, no matter who she wants to call."

Joe laughs at this.

"That's not funny, mate."

"Sorry. Is your mother still alive?"

"What did Max say?"

"They both died in a car crash."

"Only dad did. Mum survived."

"Huh."

Trevor unhooks his hands from his overalls. "You better come inside and have a cup of tea. Don't worry. They're too old to bite."

The dogs growl as Joe walks up the stairs and follows Trevor into the house. Once inside, with the fly-screen closed, both dogs collapse on the veranda panting, their bulky sides going up and down like ventilators.

The layout of the house is the same as the Harbrook homestead: living room, dining room and kitchen all in one open area, separated by furniture, counters, tables and strategically placed shelves and chests of drawers. There's the hallway leading to the various bedrooms and bathrooms at the back, four and two surely. No attic, no basement, no stairs. A simple, easy to navigate house with communal areas and private spaces. It reminds him how cramped the hostel was, with the small living room and all the bedroom doors opening into it.

Trevor gestures at the big kitchen table. "Have a seat."

"Thanks."

Trevor lights one of the burners of the massive cast iron stove, which still has a slot in the front where wood can be fed in, and puts an old-fashioned kettle on it, blackened at the bottom. He leans beside the stove and slides his big hands back into the bib of his overalls, thumbs hanging out.

Joe looks at him and decides he's Max's brother. Same thick hair, same physique, only a bit taller and not as lean. Everything about twenty years older than he remembers, but with more meat and a lot less happiness. Those lines on Trevor's face, he thinks, are not from smiling.

"I know what happened. It's a while ago now, but I'm sorry."

Joe nods. "That sounds like it's hard to say."

"It is. Milk?"

"No, thanks."

Joe watches Trevor dive his baseball-glove hand into the huge jar of tea bags, extracting two. There seems to be enough tea in there to last a decade.

"How do you know what happened?"

"Your mum called."

"Ma? She knows about you?"

"She didn't, until Max died. I think she found some pictures."

"She never told me."

"Maybe she thought that was best."

The kettle whistles. Trevor wraps a tea towel around the handle and lifts it off. He pours water into two mugs.

"What do you know about me? And Gordie?"

"Max used to write. When the letters stopped, I thought he'd given up. You see, I never wrote back. But he wrote for twenty-five years, so something must've happened. I asked me grandson to search this internet thingy and that's how I found out about the accident. Then I got the call from Tessa. Our family doesn't seem to do too well in cars."

"Max wasn't in one. He was hit by one."

"I know. Sugar?"

"It's fine as it is."

Trevor brings the mugs over and places one in front of Joe. He sits down and sips his milky white tea, then spoons sugar inside from a bowl on the table.

"So, Joe, I'm Trevor Solitus."

"I'm really sorry. I know nothing about you."

Trevor nods, the lines on his face working into furrows as he moves his jaw from side to side, like he's chewing the tea. "I guess he lied about everything. Or, didn't mention it. Can't blame him."

"Why?"

"Dad threw him out."

"He said he left."

Trevor chuckles, the mug close to his lips. "Believe me. Dad threw him out. Literally. Picked him up and tossed him off the veranda."

"What did he do?"

"He was a mean old bugger, got meaner as he got older. Bitter, like the whole world had done him wrong. But Max deserved it. We thought he'd come back after a few days, apologise and set things straight. Take responsibility. Dad used to sit on the veranda every night, waiting."

"Take responsibility? For what?"

"Bev told me not to say."

Joe sips his tea. It's strong and bitter. He wonders how old the tea bags are. "That's really helpful."

"Sometimes it's not good to go digging around in the past. You might not like what you find."

"I found you. That's good."

Trevor smiles thinly. "Yeah. I guess it is."

"At least tell me what Max did."

"He made a mistake."

"What?"

"If Max didn't say anything, he probably had his reasons."

"That's a great attitude. So we all live and die without even getting to know each other."

Trevor snorts. "Just like Max. Always spoke his mind. Left nothing behind. I guess he lived his whole life that way, and was too bloody stubborn to come back home and fix his mistakes."

"What happened?"

"Look, I suggest you get on that bike of yours and go back to Perth. The reporter said you've started something, some new religion."

"It's nothing. Not that big, and not a religion."

"I didn't have a clue what she was on about. Simple Simon, or something."

"It's just a fad. A trend. Anyway, I'm out of it."

"I thought you started this thing."

"It's out of control."

Trevor chuckles, bitterly this time. Outside, the dogs start barking.

Trevor stands up. "Expecting someone?"

"It's probably Bev."

"She didn't say she was coming."

Joe follows Trevor out onto the veranda. A white hatchback, dirty at the sides and around the tires, is parked next to the Kapowasaki. Xav gets out, talking on his phone. He looks dishevelled, as if he slept in the car.

"Found him. We'll be back in a couple of hours...Yep, We'll make it."

The dogs jump up onto Xav.

"Get down, you stupid mutts. Heel. Heel."

"What are you doing here, Xav?"

"Let's go, Joe. If we gun it, we'll make the event. We can go straight there. Make a big entrance."

"I'm not going anywhere."

"We'll put your bags in the car."

Trevor steps forward and stands next to Joe. "If he doesn't want to go, he doesn't have to. Do you understand?"

"Woah. I don't want any trouble. He knows he has to come. He's expected. Let's hustle, man."

Joe sits down on the top step. One of the dogs comes over to him and whines. He pats the dog on the head. "They're all going for themselves. Not to see me."

"Bullshit. Simplicity is all about you. The minute you leave, it'll start to fall apart. It already has."

"Forget it, Xav. I'm out."

"You wanna tell Anita that?"

Trevor looks down at Joe. "Who's Anita? Your wife?"

"She's the boss of our company."

"Your boss is a woman?"

Xav laughs. "What century are you living in?"

"One word, mate, and these dogs'll eat you alive."

"They so much as breathe on me and I'll sue you for everything you got, which doesn't look like much."

"You're on my property."

"Joe. We're already mega late. And there's a meeting tonight with some people who want to set up SINC Australia. You have to be there."

"I'm not going, Xav. I'm sorry. For me, it's over. It's out of hand."

"It's just starting."

"Nuh. I suggest you get in your little Lego car and go back to Perth. You shouldn't have come here."

"Gordie said you'd be here. He was dead right."

"Gordie's also been selling us out. Telling the press our travel plans, where we're staying and giving them family information."

"He wouldn't do that."

"He did."

Xav shakes his head. "No way. Gordie's pure, you know that."

"He's far from it. Get up in the middle of the night and see if he's playing online poker. Me and Len have already bailed him out. I bet he's been selling information and using that money to fund his gambling."

"Who's Len?"

Joe looks up at Trevor, standing again with his hands in his overalls. "He married my ma. Tessa."

Trevor's face somehow works itself into a smile. It looks like work. The muscles on his cheeks seem to cramp. "You don't like him. And little brothers, nothing but trouble, right?"

"Gordie's a mess. I've spent most of my life trying to fix his. Rescuing him, picking up the pieces, cleaning up all the mess he makes. My own fault too."

Xav's phone rings. He answers it. "Hey...No, we haven't started yet...Fine. You talk to him then. Here. It's Anita."

Joe takes the phone, reaching across one barking dog whose jaw is a few centimetres from Xav's crotch. "Hello, Ms Rudolph."

"How's it going, Joe?"

"Good. Really good. Best I've felt in ages."

"Are you on the way back?"

"No. I need a few days."

"You said five minutes."

"Time has slowed down here, in the outback."

"You find your uncle?"

"Yep. Call it a family emergency. You don't need me anyway."

"Gordie's already nominated himself to take your place."

"Huh."

"Look, Joe, do what you need to. You won't make it back in time for today's event anyway. You catch up with us when you're ready. We've got the break for it."

"Thanks."

"And, uh, Joe?"

"Yeah?"

"In case the family stuff doesn't work out, and you wanna forget it all and get back to who you were, I slipped something into your satchel to help you."

"Release?"

"I had a feeling your past would catch up to you at some point."

"How did you know that?"

"Gordie told me some of it. Warning me, so he said. We should've fixed that earlier, but it's too late now."

"Fucking Gordie. But what makes you think I wanna forget any of this?"

"Don't know. Intuition. I put them in your bag in Adelaide. You looked really distressed during the press conference there. I thought maybe you might wanna forget the family, or whatever it was that was troubling you. Your reactions were damaging our brand."

"It's a good thing you didn't give them to me then."

"Why?"

"I would've taken one."

"And not now?"

"Don't know yet. So Release is real. Wasn't just rumour marketing."

"It was both."

"Look, I'll be in touch in a couple of days. I gotta sort some things out."

"Take care, Joe."

"Thanks, Anita. And thanks for the magic beans."

He hands the phone back to Xav.

"What did she say?"

"She said it's too late, for today's event. You might as well start, Xav. I'll try to get back to Perth for the flight."

"Joe. Listen to me, Joe. We're leaving right now. Or I'll call the police to say you've been kidnapped."

Trevor goes down the steps. The dogs flank him. "You're gonna leave, or I'm gonna call the police. And you're gonna leave Joe alone until he's ready to go back to Perth. You don't own him. He's free to do what he wants. Now, get in your little car and rack off."

Xav pauses, seems caught. "I thought we were a team, Joe. That we were all in it together. You always said that."

"Yeah, simplicity belongs to everybody. That's why it doesn't need me."

"You're wrong."

"Bye, Xav."

Xav gets in the car. He reverses and drives down the narrow road. There's a chunk-a-chunk as he crosses the cattle grill. Then he goes around the corner and all the dust slowly falls to the ground.

Trevor sits next to Joe. He pats both dogs at once, one hand covering each head. "You're a wanted man."

"Only by people who want something from me. I better go."

"To Perth?"

"I can't stay here. He's probably on the phone telling everyone where I am. And if Gordie knows, then this place could be a media circus in a couple of hours."

"Then it might be better to go somewhere else."

"Where?"

"Augusta. You can stay with Denise. Bev's sister. Yeah, that's a good idea. I think she'd like to meet you."

"Can you give me her address?"

"She runs one of the caravan parks there. You'll find her. Ask around. Everyone knows Denise."

"All right. Thanks."

They stare at the sun shining on the paddocks. One lone sheep is crossing slowly towards the water trough. The sheep stumbles once, falls, and gets back to its feet.

"Our house was just like this. I used to sit on the steps with Max, talk about everything. He had a hammock on the left side. Sometimes, he'd lie in it all night and play the guitar. All these sad old songs."

"When did he learn to play the guitar?"

"He always knew."

"I guess there's a lot about Max I don't know."

"Me too. But, think about it, with all that happened, we finally got to meet. It's really nice to meet you. Do I call you Uncle Trevor?"

"Just Trev. You call Max by his first name?"

"Yeah."

Trev nods. "That fits. We used to talk about it. We shared a room, when were kids. We both agreed that we would grow up to be the complete opposite of our dad. We promised to stop the other from doing any dad-like things. Shame he wasn't around to stop me from becoming just like the old bastard. Was he a good dad?"

Joe sniffs. One dog puts its jaw on his right shoe and whines. "Yeah. And I gotta be honest. I never really got over it. I keep thinking I'm gonna see him. He's just...away."

"I used to pretend he was in the car with me, whenever I was driving on me own. I could have all those conversations I could never have. You talk to him too?"

"In my head. To my cat. In my sleep, dreaming, you know."

Trev stands up. "If you're still there on Friday, we'll come visit."

"That sounds good."

Trev extracts a meaty paw from his overalls and extends it. Joe stands and takes it.

"Nice to meet you, Joe. I'm sorry I was cold at the start. There's no reason for me to hold a grudge against you for what Max did. All that had nothing to do with you."

"Thanks, Trev, but you still haven't said what happened."

"Maybe Denise'll tell you. I can't. It's all too hard. But it's probably hard for you too."

"It is."

"Think about how it is for me. Looking at you, it's like looking at Max. The only difference is you're here, in this moment. Max was always somewhere else in his head. You could see it in his eyes. The girls seemed to love him because of it. A real dreamer. A romantic."

Trev says more about Max, but Joe isn't listening. He flips opens the satchel and finds a small envelope in the front pocket. Written on the front is "In the event of a mental emergency. Ani." Inside, there's a package of small green pills. The packaging is unmarked. Through the clear plastic, he can see small black Rs on the pills.

He shoulders the backpack, trying not to grimace. He loops the satchel over his neck and climbs on the bike. "I'll see you in a couple of days."

"Hope so."

"If anyone asks for me, tell them I'm on the way to Perth."

"Right."

He puts on the helmet and fires up the Kapowasaki. The dogs bark, a friendly farewell this time. He raises a hand to Trev who just nods and slides his hands into his overalls.

***

The head wind is brutal. It blows the Kapowasaki all over the road. He stops a few times to stretch his back and put on another sweater.

It's mid-afternoon when he gets to Augusta. The sun is bright, but the wind is biting. The angles of the tree trunks, the branches growing northeast, convince him the wind blows all the time here, strong and in one direction.

There are two caravan parks next to each other at the front of town. The reception at the first is closed. The man hunched over the open bonnet of a banged up utility tells him in a British accent that Denise runs the park next door.

Before going into the small office, he checks himself in the Kapowasaki's mirror. There's dirt, sand and dead flies lodged in the stubble of his three day growth. The too-small helmet has pushed his hair flat and forward, like a military cut a few weeks into basic training. There's a tap next to the office. He uses it to wash his hands and face. He cups some to drink.

"I wouldn't do that if I were you. That's bore water."

He turns. "Bev?"

"Denise. We're twins. Trev didn't say that? Hah. He likes surprises. Like a big old kid."

"I'm Joe."

"I know who you are."

He wipes his hands on his jeans.

"Welcome to the wind capital of the world. Wanna cuppa?"

"Love one."

"You can use that to wash the flies outta your mouth."

He follows her into the office and drops his backpack and satchel next to the counter. A bulky monitor is perched just behind the counter, a blackened keyboard in front of it. The equally dirty mouse is on a blue pad shaped like Australia. Maps on the walls, some taped, others nailed. A disorderly collection of flyers for local eateries and things to do: fish and chips, horse riding, all-you-can-eat Chinese, mini golf, bus tours to Margaret River and the Yallingup caves.

He finds Denise in the room adjacent to the reception, separated by a line of beads hanging in the doorway. She's a perfect replica of Bev, a clone, from her round, frying pan face right down to her short wiry legs. Same face, same proportions, same movements, even the same dye and perm job on her unruly bob of hair, with the same white roots blending into the blonde curls.

She offers him a fold-out chair at the small table and busies herself in the kitchenette. There's a sink, a microwave, a kettle and a combination grill oven and toaster, but no signs that this room is a place where meals are cooked. No proper food smells, no cutting boards, no cupboards full of cutlery and dishes, no lingering burps of satisfaction. It smells of things made in haste, cup-o-soups and leftovers zapped in the microwave.

"What would you like?"

"Have you got any green tea?"

She flips through the various boxes, extracts one. "Hmm, it appears I do. Someone must've left this is in a caravan. You wouldn't believe what people leave behind. Once, there was this idiotic American couple who left their kid. And it took them a whole day to notice. They had to drive all the way back from Albany."

"Poor kid."

She shrugs. "He seemed okay with it. Maybe he thought he was better off."

"Maybe it was better for everyone."

"Hah. Milk? Sugar?"

"Honey?"

"You're a good half a century late for the hippy movement. And you won't get any free love outta me."

"It's good for you. For the circulation."

"Is it? Maybe I should try it."

"You have to drink a litre a day."

She pours her black tea into the sink. "A litre? I'll be peeing every hour. Hah. I'll have to drink it on the toilet."

"And that pee will be the colour of pure gold."

"I could bottle it and sell it."

"For sure. What you put into your body is what you get out. People don't think about that enough. They throw anything in and don't realise what it does to them."

"Max teach you that?"

"Yes."

"Max."

She digs the tea bags out with a spoon and drops them in the compost bucket under the sink. Among the collection of jars on the counter she extracts one. She puts her cup and the honey on the table and sits down.

"This is the real stuff. You want to put this in your body."

"Thanks."

She offers him her spoon. He twirls the chunky brown honey around it, stirs it into his tea and hands it back. She does the same, being a little more liberal with the honey.

He sips. "Oh, the nectar of the gods."

"A different sort of liquid gold. Ben has some hives."

Joe nods.

"My son."

"Huh."

She sips and looks into the cup. "Tastes strange. A bit like medicine. Can't imagine what it would be like without the honey. So, Max told you about good eating and drinking. What else did he teach you?"

"Lots of things."

"Was he a good dad?"

He nods, sips his tea, tries to swallow down all the crap caught in his throat.

"You can cry in here. There's no men around. Believe me, lots of tears have been shed in here."

"Sorry."

"Hurt. It can last a long time, can't it? It's like you tell yourself it'll get easier over time, but it stays with you. It's always there, just as intense."

"I miss him. A lot. Still."

"Shame."

"Yeah."

"Don't worry. Ben turned out fine."

Joe stares at her. "Why do you say that?"

"Max is his dad. His biological dad."

"What?"

"There you have it."

"Why didn't Trev say anything?"

"He loves his secrets."

"Ben is my brother?"

"Half brother."

"Look, Denise, you don't have to tell me anything, but I'd really like to know what happened. This is all news to me."

"Long time ago."

"And it still hurts, doesn't it?"

A bell at the reception counter rings.

"Excuse me, love."

She gives his shoulder a pat before going through the beads. He can hear her dealing with a customer, recognising the mundane in her voice, the repetition, the words said a thousand times. Hook-ups, showers, barbecues, prices, beaches, playgrounds, no loud music, no drugs, separate the recyclables, please, there's a golf course in town but there's a better one up near Prevelly Park in Margaret River.

He sips his tea. He has an older brother. A half brother, Ben, who makes honey from his own beehives. He picks up the jar.

"Buzzcut Honey, Gracetown."

She parts the beads and sits back down. "It's on the way to Yallingup. Up the coast. Not far. He's keen to meet you. He was gonna go to Perth today for your big shindig, but then Bev called, and then Trev, and he saved himself the drive. He's coming for dinner tonight."

He nods. "Is there a hotel in town, or a hostel?"

"You're staying with us."

"Huh. Thanks."

She leans back in her chair and folds her arms. "How old are you?"

"Twenty-eight.'

She waggles a matronly finger. "Don't ask. Yes, I was older than Max. Let's leave it at that."

"Were you a couple?"

"What do you think?"

"Well, you and Max, you had a kid together."

"He was well gone before Ben was born."

"Then, Max got you pregnant and was thrown out of the house. They were pretty religious, weren't they?"

"Madge still is. She goes to church every day, even though she's deaf as a post. She tries to sing along to the hymns she can't even hear. And she can't remember the words. It's hilarious."

"Max told me she died."

"If only. I think they're still getting hell ready for her. Wicked woman. She'll probably live forever. Jim threw Max out, but Lady

Madge was the one behind it all. She'll rot in hell, even with all the church-going."

"I'd like to meet her."

"You don't want to. Believe me. She'd probably try to stone you. Oh, it's all such a long time ago. The things I thought were important then."

"You've lost me. Can you start from the beginning?"

"You don't know any of this?"

Joe shakes his head. "Nuh."

"Trev say nothing?"

"Nuh."

"Coward. No wonder he can't sleep at night. Bev says he always gets up and walks around the house. He goes out and stands in the barn. That's where, ah, where me and Max used to meet. He used to ride his bike from town."

"Maybe he regrets not doing anything."

"He misses Max. We all did. Especially Jim."

"What about Madge?"

"She prayed. For all of us. Probably for you too."

"Were you in love with him?"

She looks into her cup. "No. But he was...he was...irresistible. Even as a skinny, spotty teenager. You couldn't say no to him."

"So, what happened?"

"It's complicated. I was engaged. To Wally Locke. Big farming family over near Manjimup. Bev was engaged to Trev. We were going to have a double wedding. The biggest wedding the south west ever saw."

"So, this was before you were married."

"I never married Wally."

"Because of Max."

"Because of Ben. The Lockes, they were also very religious. Still are. They wanted a virgin bride. When I started to show, things turned a little nasty."

"How did anyone know it was Max's kid?"

"It didn't matter who the father was, if it wasn't Wally. The wedding was off. My parents were angry with me, but only because we weren't going to be connected to the Lockes, which was what my wedding was all about. But they didn't throw me out. They expected the father to come forward and take responsibility."

"And Max didn't?"

Denise shakes her head. Her curls bounce. "Bev knew. We're twins. We told each other everything. But she told Trev and Trev told Madge. And then Max was gone."

"He didn't try to get in contact with you?"

"Trev was sure Max would come back. He kept telling me he would, right up until Ben was born. Then he gave up. Had his own kids to worry about. The farm as well."

"What about you?"

"Me? I got lucky. I met Bryce. He's a Pom, didn't care that I was, to use Madge's word, soiled."

"Where is he?"

"Next door."

"At the other caravan park?"

She nods.

"I think I spoke to him already. He was fixing a beat up old car."

"That's him. A fine fella. I was real lucky to meet him. Everything worked out all right. We had three beaut kids. Two are in Perth, one in Mandurah, which is pretty much part of Perth these days."

"And Ben's in Gracetown."

"He was in Sydney for a while, studying."

"When?"

"About six or seven years ago. He was a late starter. Didn't really know what he wanted to do with his life. He's a bit of a dreamer."

"Which university?"

"UNSW."

He laughs.

"What's so funny?"

"I went to UNSW. At the same time. We probably passed each other on the way to lectures. Maybe we had a tutorial together."

"If you were supposed to meet, you would have."

"Yeah. Yeah, that's right. Maybe the time wasn't right."

"That wasn't long after Max died."

He nods. Then suddenly, he starts to cry and covers his face with his hands. He feels her arms around him, clutching his shoulders. He cries into her chest. Really cries. His body shakes. He can't stop. She holds him tight and pats his head.

***

He sits at the table peeling potatoes. Outside, the wind slices through the trees, ruffling all the tents and rattling caravan doors.

"I haven't done this since I was a kid."

"Clearly. You're terrible at it. I won't ask you to help me gut the fish."

He looks up and sees Denise with her hands deep inside the fish, yanking out long slimy bits and flicking them from her fingers into a bucket.

"Pass."

"Your mum do all the cooking?"

"Max did. Ma's a nurse. She worked nights mostly."

"And Max?"

"He was an architect."

"I think Trev told me that. Ages ago."

"He did an apprenticeship as a carpenter and travelled and worked. He studied later."

"Self made."

"He built our house by himself. And it's an exact copy of your house, out on the farm."

She holds up handful of purple and red intestines. "Really?"

"You could call one house Bev and the other Denise because they're twins."

She flings them into the bucket with a splotch.

"He could make anything. He was like MacGyver."

"He teach you any carpentry?"

"Everything he knew. I worked on construction sites when I was a kid. All summer. Never went to camp."

"Ben might be interested to hear that. He's building a water mill. Trying to go completely self-sufficient. He's just missing one thing."

"What?"

"Rain."

"Maybe he should build a windmill instead. There's enough of that."

"That's what Bryce said. Ben's more ambitious than that, and I think he favours the beautiful over the functional."

The front door opens and closes.

"Speak of the devil."

"Anyone home?"

"In the kitchen."

Joe wipes his hands on a tea towel and stands up. Ben wheels a bike into the room. His shoes clap against the tile floor. He clips off his helmet.

"G'day. I'm Ben."

"Joe."

Ben reaches out a gloved hand and Joe takes it, feeling the padding of the bike glove.

"Nice to meet you."

They look at each other, searching for similarities, clues, connections, differences.

Ben grins. "No doubt about it. Definitely brothers."

"Like looking in a mirror."

"I'll take that as a compliment. What am I, ten years older than you?"

"God, Ben, did you ride here?"

"Head wind was a bitch. Felt like I was pedalling standing still. Good thing is, I'll have a tail wind all the way home."

She points a knife at him. "You're not riding back in the dark."

"You're not the boss of me. I'm old enough to make my own choices."

"I'll pay you to stay."

Ben leans close to Joe. "I'm just messing with her."

"That's mean."

Ben nods. "It is. Can I take shower, mumsy?"

"Did you bring some other clothes? You're not sitting at the table in that spandex get-up. You look like a clown."

"A fit clown. Fine. I'll wrap myself in a towel."

She herds him towards the bathroom. "You. You're nothing but trouble. Help yourself to your dad's clothes."

"I'm not wearing his ancient jocks. You've got a g-string that'll fit me, don't ya? Something in a leopard skin?"

Denise comes back into the kitchen. She shakes her head. "I'm sorry. Did any of that look familiar?"

Joe laughs.

"I'll take that as a yes. Now that I saw you next to each other, you do look a lot alike."

"Yeah."

"Don't get the wrong idea. He's serious about a lot of things. Not everything's a joke to him."

He peels the last potato and drops it in the pot. He brings the pot into the kitchen. "I'm done."

"A slaughter. Fill it with water and put it on the stove. Can you handle that?"

He does as he's told. "What else can I do?"

"Sit down. Have a beer. It's in the fridge. Ben'll have one too."

He watches her put long stalks of rosemary inside the fish, along with some chopped garlic. She wraps the whole thing in foil, puts it in the oven and sets the timer.

"Right. The fish is in the pan. I'll have a beer too, Joe."

He takes three cans from the fridge. He sees a collection of purple and green stubbie holders in a basket next to the toaster and puts each can into one. He sits down at the table with Denise. She cracks open her can and he does the same.

She holds it up. "To long lost family."

"I'll drink to that."

"And to letting go of the past."

Ben comes in, his hair wet. He's wearing baggy pants that drag along the floor and almost hide his bare feet, and a tight fitting polo.

"That's my shirt."

"All of dad's are too big. I tried some of your pants, mum, but they were all a bit too generous in the hips."

"Careful."

Ben opens his beer, twisting the ring ninety degrees to the side. He drinks. "Ah, I earned that."

"How far is it from Gracetown?"

"About sixty-five K. The head wind makes it feel like double. Then cuts it in half on the way back."

"Ben's training."

"For what?"

"Ironman WA. In Busselton."

"Ironman? That's impressive."

"It will be if I finish."

Denise shakes her head. "You're too skinny. You won't even get through the swim."

"I'm lean, mum. And mean."

His attempt at an aggressive face is comical. Joe and Denise laugh. They all drink.

Ben looks at Joe. "Well, this is weird, isn't it?"

"A bit."

"You see the news?"

"No."

"Your little event was on it."

"It was? What happened? No, I don't think I wanna know."

Ben gets up and retrieves his phone from the back of his bike jersey. He taps at the screen and points it at Joe. "Check it out."

The newsreader talks earnestly at the camera. "A large, disorderly group converged on Kings Park in the centre of Perth today as part of a flash event of simplicity Incorporated, known as SINC. Sam Nolan reports."

Cut to helicopter footage of Kings Park.

"The SINC circus has come to town and Perth has never seen anything like it. After the location was announced, there was a rush as people tried to get to Kings Park, with some abandoning their cars on Riverside Drive and Mounts Bay Road. The resulting traffic jams made it impossible for some people to get in or out of the city, bringing parts of the metro area to a standstill."

Shots of abandoned cars and gridlocked streets. Short interviews with drivers talking through open windows.

"Bloody selfish."

"Disgraceful. Shocking."

"They should throw them all in jail."

"We've been stuck here for three [BEEP] hours."

"Events like this should be banned from the city. This is not what my tax dollars pay for."

Aerial footage of police jumping out of cars and running towards Kings Park. Other shots of police trying to disperse the crowd.

"Local police were called in to control the crowd as things soon got out of hand. The unruly simplicity supporters tried to put out the eternal flame at the Kings Park Memorial and damaged the gardens. Order was soon restored, but not without a number of arrests and injuries."

Shots of people being arrested and put in police cars. Other shots of people sitting at the back of ambulances, holding bandages to bleeding heads. Someone strapped to a gurney being lifted into an ambulance.

"SINC founder and cult hero Joe Solitus refused all interview attempts."

The footage of Joe putting his hand in the camera in the apartment yesterday. Cut to an important looking policeman.

"An investigation is underway. We'll also be talking to SINC to assess what level of responsibility they have in terms of the injuries and damages, especially the attempt to put out the eternal flame. They simply can't come here and do something like this without there being consequences."

A final aerial shot of Kings Park, the grass barely visible because of all the paper and garbage.

"Those consequences include an incredible amount of rubbish that the city will now have to clean up. Sam Nolan, the *News at Six*."

Ben puts his phone on the table. "Glad I stayed home."

Denise looks at Joe. "Are all the events like that?"

"What? No. Not at all. The park looks like it was too small for that many people. And if the people who show up vandalise the park, drop garbage and fight with police, that's not our fault."

Ben shakes his head. "Only in Perth. What'll you do about it, Joe?"

"Nothing. I'm done with it."

"You quit?"

Joe nods.

"What's your plan? They might come looking for ya."

"Don't have one. Go back to Montreal, I guess."

"You think you can?"

"I haven't thought about it. This whole thing, it's pretty much ruined my life."

"Nuh, nuh, nuh, nuh. You've got it all wrong. Think about it. If you hadn't started SINC, you wouldn't have ended up here. You would never have known any of us ever existed."

Denise nods. "And you wouldn't have found out the truth about Max."

Joe sips his beer. It tastes watery and metallic. "None of this is random, is it? You know, Ben. I went to UNSW, around the same time as you."

"Fuck off."

"Language, Benjamin."

"God, mum, I'm thirty-six."

Joe smiles and leans back in his chair. "It was all supposed to happen like this. We could've met in Sydney, but we didn't. One small change anywhere along the way, and we wouldn't be sitting here."

Denise rubs her temples. “You’re making my head hurt.”

“I know. And get this. If Max hadn’t been thrown out, hadn’t run away, he never would’ve gone to the States and met Tessa. There’d be no me. No simplicity. No idiots going wild at flash events.”

Ben grins. “The world’s a funny old place. One minute nothing’s connected, then it seems everything is. When do we eat? I’m starving.”

The timer on the oven goes off.

Ben slaps his hands on the table. “The interconnectedness of all things continues. Where’s dad?”

Denise stands up and goes into the kitchen. “At the pub.”

***

“Can I ask you something?”

“Go for it.”

“Why didn’t you look for Max?”

“Simple. He was dead.”

“Denise told you after?”

Ben shrugs. “Understandable really. I’d probably do the same. All things considered. She was trying to protect me, and herself, and dad too.”

“I wonder why he never said anything. Why he just lied.”

“Maybe to protect you.”

“He always talked about the importance of honesty, being open and clear.”

“Sounds like your basic hypocrite, Joe.”

“Yeah.”

“You miss him.”

“I do, but not as much as I did this morning.”

Ben chuckles. “What about Gordie? How’s he feel about it?”

“He was always all right. He was too young.”

“I wanna meet him too.”

“He’s different. More like ma. A mother’s boy.”

“Aren’t we all?”

“Yeah. When’s the big race?”

“December.”

“You train a lot?”

“When I can. Mostly running and biking. It’s too cold for swimming.”

“Wear a suit.”

"I do, but I'm not into it. The swimming, that is. It's so boring, and hard."

"You're probably not doing it right. It's always like that. People hate swimming because their technique's all wrong. They make it so much harder for themselves."

"That sounds like me. You an expert?"

"I was a competitive swimmer growing up. When I lived in Sydney, I did about twenty K a week at the Icebergs."

"Yeah? I sat on the beach and got fat. Can you help me out?"

"Is there a pool in Gracetown?"

"I think you're overestimating my fair village. We could go to the rec centre in Margaret River. Or jump in the Indian."

"I stuck my feet in today. It's freezing."

"The water comes up from the Antarctic. It's warmer up the coast. I've got a suit that might fit you. An old surfing suit. It's all stretched and full of holes from shark bites."

"We could try. And don't scare me with shark stories."

"You wanna come to Gracetown?"

"Denise said you're building a water mill. Maybe I can help you out. I know my way around hammers and saws."

"From Max?"

Joe nods.

"He was an architect."

"A carpenter first. That's how he worked his way around the world. He called it his Waltz. He told me they still do such a thing in Germany. All these carpenters walking from town to town, working and picking up new skills. He did the same. He even had a pair of the flared black cords they wear, with these weird zip pockets."

"I think I saw a doco about that. Big hats? All in black?"

"That's it. It's amazing to think traditions like that still exist, in western countries."

"So, before becoming the spokesman for a generation, were you waltzing around the globe as well?"

"In a way."

"Doing what?"

Joe smiles. "Selling solutions."

"Is that American corporate lingo bullshit?"

"That's what my boss called it. I worked for Denoris. They make medicine nobody needs."

"I get it. The solution to your problem. A pill. And? You liked it?"

"When I started, I had all these noble ideas about healing the world, bringing medicine to developing countries and all that. That's what they showed us in the introductory video. But the reality was way different."

"Any company with an introductory video is bound to have the Prince of Darkness as CEO."

"It was definitely some kind of evil. Denoris would develop a pill, get it approved and then market it in a way that makes people think they have to have it. Convince them, put fear in them. Once it's popular, they jack up the price. That means people who might really need it can't get it because they don't have the right insurance, if it's not over-the-counter. The result is that medical care, which everyone should have an equal right to, gets polarised by wealth."

"Everything does."

"Sure, but what really pissed me off, and still does, is how the companies sell themselves. That they're helping poor people and developing countries, making medicine available for everyone. Like they're do-good charities. Wrong. They're companies, and all they're focused on are bottom lines and profit margins. You can't believe how much medicine there is out there that we don't need. There are all these medical conditions, a lot of them psychological and psychosomatic, that have been cooked up in order to sell pills."

"So why do people take them?"

"It's a quick, easy solution. Don't change your diet, just take a proton pump inhibitor. Don't reduce your amount of stress, take Sailiun. Can't get it up, take Liftomex. And on and on. The pill is your solution. You don't have to change anything, and if it doesn't work, it's not your fault. Then there's Release."

"What's that?"

"A miracle pill. Brand new. You can forget anything you want. A delete button for your mental hard drive."

"I think you're in trouble when you start fucking with people's heads."

"That's been going on for decades."

"Come on, Joe. Would you take something like that?"

"I was thinking about that this afternoon walking on the beach. A couple of days ago, I would've said yes. But being down here, meeting you and Denise and Trev, being confronted with all this stuff, it's reminded me that life is about experience. And discovery. Good and bad. If people just walked around with only good memories, having deleted all the bad stuff, they'd be zombies. Even more than they already are."

"Like the kids at your events. Technical zombies. Square eyes like computer screens, unable to focus on something for longer than five seconds."

"I know, but simplicity was supposed to turn all that around."

"Come on. It's huge online. I followed it from the start."

"I guess that makes me a hypocrite too."

"Like father like son. Can I ask you about Max?"

"Sure."

"What was he like?"

"As a father?"

"As a person. That's pretty much the same. One carries into the other."

Joe takes a deep breath. "Well, let me think. Generous, giving, opinionated. He loved TV and music. Quirky, off-kilter stuff. Hated stuff that was made for the masses. He was sort of a big brother to me. I always called him Max."

"You ever fight?"

"We argued. Max didn't like it when people didn't see his point of view. He didn't try to change people. He just wanted them to accept that he could have a different opinion. He was complicated, even if he always tried to simplify things."

"That's where simplicity comes from. I saw the videos of you in Montreal."

"Some of it. But now I think about it, in simplifying things, he might've missed the nuances and subtleties, all those little bits of complexity that make things interesting. You can't have life with just zero and one. And even with zero and one, the complex combinations are endless."

"Life's not black and white."

"For him, simplifying meant finding the easiest, fastest solution. For me, it's about focusing on what's important."

"And what's that?"

"It was reducing my dependence on technology, especially all the time I wasted online. And all this unnecessary, emotionless communication that takes place with phones and the internet. All this pointless back and forth. That's what SINC's about. Going low-tech."

"You failed. It's a great idea, impossible though. There's probably wi-fi in the far reaches of the Amazon now. If there is any of the rainforest left."

"You have it in Gracetown?"

"Sure. I need it for work."

"What do you do?"

"I install solar panels."

"Now that's something worthwhile."

"I hope so. I studied environmental science. When I graduated, everyone wanted to go off and save some obscure animal or plant. A few went to NZ to wage war with Japanese whalers. All that's fine, but it's not going to make a lot of difference in the long run. Now, sustainable energy, that makes a difference."

"Is it popular here?"

"For hot water systems, yeah, but no one really thought of it for powering a house or a factory or a whole town. It's changing. The technology's better and there are government subsidies available. Price incentives and such. But it's more about reputation than helping the environment. All the new resorts going up around here want to boast that they're eco-friendly, to get all the wannabe greenies from Perth to drive down in their gas-guzzling tanks for a carbon neutral holiday. With a resort, you can cover the roof with solar panels and no one notices. There's a couple that I've worked on that are off-grid, completely self-sufficient. And that makes a lot of sense down here because the power lines are above ground. A strong wind or a decent sized bushfire and everyone's blacked out."

"Solar is the answer."

Ben laughs.

The front door opens and closes. Bryce comes into the kitchen. He loops his jacket over a chair and gingerly sits down, still wearing the clothes Joe saw him in earlier.

He reaches a hand across the table. "Bryce."

"Joe."

They shake.

"I know who you are."

"What's up, dad? You look well sauced."

"Where's your mum?"

"In bed."

"I saw the news in the pub. You've got yourself a bit of a mess up there. And a war memorial is not something you want to mess with in this part of the world."

"Not my mess."

"Your name's all over it."

"It'll be all right, dad. Joe's coming up to Gracetown with me tomorrow. No one'll find him there."

"Nobody's looking for me."

Bryce nods slowly, clears his throat. "You might wanna have another look at the news. There's a crowd in front of your hotel. Half supporting, half protesting. They reckon it might turn ugly."

"It won't. But it won't be my fault if it does."

"What are you gonna do, Joe?"

He sits back, looks at his watch and yawns. "I think I'll go to bed. When do you wanna start tomorrow?"

"After lunch. When the wind picks up. I earned that tail wind."

Joe stands. "Thanks for letting me stay, Bryce. It's been great meeting you all."

"G'night, Joe."

"Night."

He goes to the doorway of the guest room and closes the door, leaving it just slightly ajar.

"How ya doin, Benny?"

Ben's voice is barely a whisper. "Feels weird, dad. Really weird. Like I woke up this morning in a parallel universe."

"I ate at the pub, to make easier for you. I know your mum still takes it all pretty hard."

"You didn't have to do that. By the way, can you help me out on the weekend?"

"The water mill?"

"Yeah."

"What about Joe?"

"I don't think he'll stick around. He'll go back to SINC. They'll leave Perth and it'll all blow over."

"Don't be so hard on him. He's dealing with all this too. Can't be easy."

"Just a gut feeling. He's a runner. When it gets too hard, he hightails it."

"Look, Benny, he's Joe, not Max. If Max ran away from things, that doesn't mean Joe will."

"He already has."

"Looks to me that he did the right thing. And he wanted to find his family."

"He starts this whole underground movement and runs the minute it goes bad on him."

"You know there's more to it than that. There's got to be."

"It's funny, dad. I always wanted to meet him, and Gordie, but I wanted them to find me. I figured that was the way it should be. I was the one abandoned. Why should I do all the work?"

"Me and Nisa were always there."

"I know. But I wanted him to come to me. To apologise. To look me in the eyes and feel guilty."

"Give him a chance, Benny. He's not responsible for what Max did."

In hiding with the Benevolent Buzzcut

He waits at the turn off. The wind billows the sand into the air, creating little eddies that twist into the forest and send the sand across the tarmac in slithers, like a magician scattering magic dust. The trees are tall and skinny, with the leaves and branches ruffling as the wind slices through. A few cars go past, speeding; economy-sized rentals in white or blue or red, some bearing the company's name on the front doors. Couples mostly, the men driving, off to hit some wineries in Margaret River, maybe do a tour of the caves, take photos down at the lighthouse at the southern tip, and then circling back to Dunsborough or Busselton or wherever they're staying.

It's vague, the memory blending into so many other highways and roads he's seen, but he rode this stretch. Caves Road, from Margaret River to Yallingup. Summer, ages ago. Probably went straight past this turn off and didn't even look. All through that trip, Gordie kept him updated about Christmas in Harbrook, with a constant stream of texts: what they were eating, the presents he got, the school parties, the drinking and drug-taking, pretty much every time he burped and farted. Read altogether, it sounded like a really lame Christmas rap, as Gordie always tried to make his texts rhyme. "Cut the beast down, an bling the tree, spread the gifts around, and they's all fa me. Check it."

He looks down the road, wondering what Gordie, Xav, Anita and the others will do to simplicity. This is their holiday week, but they won't even be able to get out of the apartment. And they're probably on damage control after what happened yesterday.

"Maybe they'll try to go to the airport."

He sees Ben coming towards the turn off, sitting up straight on the bike, his fingertips on the handle bars, to get as much of the wind as possible. Closer, he clicks his right shoe out of the pedal and comes to a stop.

"You're fast."

Ben pops his water bottle with his teeth and drinks. "Love that wind. I hope they change the Ironman course so it goes in one direction. North."

"Then you'd end up in Perth."

"Almost. How was the ride? That pack looks heavy. When you passed me, you looked like you were about to fall off."

"Geometry's all wrong. I miss my bike in Montreal."

"What have you got there?"

"An Indian Enfield. She belonged to Max."

"He was a biker too, just like you."

"Back home, I get around mostly on my racing bike. But it's not nearly as nice as yours. Is that a carbon frame?"

Ben nods. "I figured if I was gonna spend so much time on a bike, I should get myself a really comfortable one. It was worth every cent."

"I want one."

"I'm sure some of the SINC proceeds can go towards it."

"Is there a bike shop around here?"

"Big city fella. We're in the country. There's one in Busselton. But unless you're gonna live here, it makes no sense to buy one. Get it in Montreal. Are there good places to ride?"

"The city's dangerous. Once you get out, there's some nice tours."

"But you gotta ride thirty K just to get there."

"Sometimes, yeah. Are we nearly there?"

"Couple more clicks. You can go in front and break the wind for me. But no actual breaking of wind."

He loads up and gets on the Kapowasaki. They set off down Cowaramup Road, into the wind.

Ben shouts: "Faster."

They go around a bend. There's a nice looking bay with a white sand beach. Ben lets out a whoop as they fly downhill towards it.

"Woooo-hoooo."

Up another short rise, then the flat roofs appear between the dirty green trees and shrubs. Everything looks dried out and weather-beaten, even the people standing on verandas sipping tea, or others washing down boats on trailers on their front lawns, which are mostly sand.

As they enter town, Joe slows down and let's Ben get in front to lead the way.

"We are now entering the downtown area. If you look to your left, you'll see nothing. If you look to your right, you'll see a dog. No, he's not there today."

It's a ramshackle place, looks and feels like it was built in a hurry and then no one bothered to make it nicer or fix all those initial hasty mistakes. Rusting white utilities are parked on dry grass in front of shrunken, inverted-looking houses. The wind is blowing hard, sending loose paper and old milk cartons down the street. A couple of houses, off the main street, are more expansive and striking, with two storeys, balconies facing the ocean, slanted tile roofs and fresh paint, and some with big gates in front and manicured gardens constructed from terracotta and grass bought by the roll that never looks natural.

Ben rides next to him. "Most are holiday houses. For people inland, not from Perth. A big farming clan buys one and all the extended family uses it. Gets pretty hairy around here at Christmas and New Year, and Australia Day, and Anzac Day. Incredible amounts of alcohol get consumed and the more they drink, the more convinced they are that they can drive. And that fist fights can solve every family issue. Down here."

They leave the main street and head towards the water. Ben waves to a few people, crusty-looking folks raking up twigs, trimming branches, cleaning gutters or sitting on the veranda drinking beer. They call out each others' names with the familiarity of people who do it every day, maybe two or three times. One man, mowing his lawn with an old push mower, comments that Ben's looking good on the bike and then laughs.

"Have another beer, Phil. Ya fat bastard."

A good-looking woman of about forty gets out of her car and steps in front of Ben. He clicks out of the pedals and stops.

"Hey, Ben, can ya have a look at my system? Water's stone cold."

"Course, Rae. I'll be round in a jiff."

Ben gets off his bike and pushes it towards the small, yellow house next door. On the roof, Joe sees the metallic grey of solar panels. They glisten in the sun.

"Welcome to my humble home."

Joe brings the Kapowasaki to a halt and gets off. He drops the pack to the ground and groans.

There's a white van parked in front, with a ladder attached to the roof and Smart Solar written on the side in bright orange lettering. The O in solar is a smiling sun, with one eye closed in a wink. Near the small veranda, he sees wood sticking out from under a blue tarp held down at the corners by bricks. A workbench has been set up on the veranda, with an electric saw and other woodworking tools. He doesn't see any beehives.

"It's nice."

Ben wheels his bike up to the front door. "Getting there."

"How did you end up here? In Gracetown."

"Long story."

"It always is."

Ben pulls his keys from the back pocket of his bike jersey. "Actually, it's not. Uni girlfriend and I had big plans to move to WA and try to live eco-friendly. You know, self sufficient, without needing all these other systems and providers. Independent. She didn't last a week. Wanted to move back to Sydney, and when I decided to stay, she left. End of story."

"Sorry."

"Don't be. She wasn't cut out for it. I knew that coming in, but I didn't want to admit it. A lot of people aren't cut out for it. They miss all the comforts too much, and aren't willing to work or wait. And Connie, well, she was a city girl at heart, despite what she liked to think of herself, and what she told others."

"What's she doing now?"

"Heard she was working for Qantas. Okay, I didn't hear that. I searched her online. She's in PR. Big companies need people who can put an eco twist into everything they do. Green up their image. A lot of people I studied with ended up at big corps doing stuff like that. Come on in."

Ben carries the bike inside and slides it into the gap between the sofa and the living room wall. Joe drops his backpack, putting it neatly out of the way, because that's what the room is asking him to do. Be neat. Everything is very clean and orderly, bordering on neurosis. He gets the feeling that every object, piece of furniture and scrap of paper has its place. He could recommend some pills for Ben that would dull that need.

"Make yourself at home. I'm gonna wash up and change. Help yourself to anything in the fridge."

Ben goes into what Joe assumes is the bedroom.

"You want a cup of tea, Ben?"

"Yeah. I would. There's some fruitcake in the big tin on the counter. Rae made it. Have some."

In the absence of a visible electric kettle, Joe fills the steel kettle and puts this on the stove. He gets the gas burner going without setting anything on fire and starts searching through the cupboards. The tea is neatly stacked next to a row of herbs and spice, alphabetised, starting with something called arugula, then basil. He finds some green tea.

The water comes quickly to a boil, letting off a loud whistle like a steam train. It sends the dog next door into a barking fit.

He hears Rae: "Shut up, ya stupid mongrel."

He makes a pot with three tea bags. He's lifting these up and down as Ben comes into the kitchen, dressed in boardshorts and an extravagant Hawaiian. His blonde hair is wet and falling forward, even as he tries to push it back.

"Find the fruitcake?"

"Not yet. That's simplicity rule number twenty-six. When you're making tea, just make tea."

"Uh-huh. Sounds like an excuse for laziness."

"True."

Ben opens the tin and cuts a couple of slices. "Rae's not exactly flush. She repays my little solar favours with delectables like this. You want some honey?"

"Absolutely."

Ben grabs a half empty jar from the fridge.

"You keep it in the fridge?"

"Stays fresher. And it keeps the ants from getting to it. Can you imagine being an ant and finding a jar of honey? It'd be like finding a lake of pure gold."

Joe laughs.

"Or the ant doesn't want his mates to see and tries to hide it with his hands. What's in the big jar, Ralph? It's just dog piss, Sam, nothing you'd want."

They sit down at the kitchen table. Joe pours the tea. Ben takes a bite of fruitcake and spoons honey into his cup. He licks the index finger of his left hand and gets the scattering of fruitcake crumbs on the table on the end of it. He puts the finger in his mouth.

"Yeah, so, here we are. Nice cuppa. Mum told me you like green stuff."

"You drink it?"

"Sometimes. I'm caffeine free, as much as possible. I drink tea when I fast."

"You do that?"

"When I can't be bothered shopping. Or when the delivery trucks don't get down this far. I'm kidding. I do it once a year. Clean out all the crap. Reset the system."

"You wanna start on the water mill today?"

"Why not? I need to take care of Rae's prob and then we can get to it."

"What about your solar panel work?"

"I'm on call. If someone has a problem, I'll change into my superman outfit and fly to the rescue. I should go out and check the hives later. You wanna come?"

"I don't like bees."

"But you like what they make. They'll know that. We can take your bike, use the short cut."

"I don't know, Ben."

"Trust me. Bees know."

"All right."

Ben stands up. He goes outside, then comes back in unfolding a piece of paper. He spreads it on the table, bites into some cake and fingers up the crumbs.

"Here's what I wanna do. You see? It's not that big, but when it rains, the water runs off the gutters. Here. Down this funnel and into the wheel. On the other side of the roof, the water runs into my rain tank. The water spins the wheel and that moves this turbine and generates electricity. All hooked up to the main box. The water goes to a reservoir and gets used for the veggie garden behind the house. It's terraced, perfectly irrigated. I'll show you later."

"What's the point of this?"

"I know, I know. Ma and pa said the same thing. It doesn't rain enough, but I already generate more power than I need. My panels feed the main grid and I get paid for it. A pittance, but that's not the point. This will be a bit more. I thought about a wind turbine, but I was scared a gale might blow the thing clear off and the blades would slice the house in half. And look at it. Isn't it beautiful?"

Joe nods. "What first?"

"I've already built and attached the funnel. It rained a couple of days ago. I had a shower under it. Brilliant. Half the town watched. We need to make the wheel, the support, dig a big hole and put the whole thing together. Easy. Dad's coming up on the weekend and he's good with a shovel. As long as there's no meltdown of any solar systems, we should have it up and running by Sunday. Simple as that."

Joe bites into a piece of fruit cake. He stares at it. "This is delicious."

"Made with Buzzcut Honey. Rae has a dehydrator. All of the fruit in there, she dried herself. Tasty, yeah?"

"It's the best piece of cake I've ever had."

"That's how nature should taste. The sun grows the fruit, and the sun powers the dehydrator. The bees make the honey."

Joe helps himself to another slice. Ben gulps down the last of his tea and stands up.

"Back in a bit. There's a computer in the study if you want to check your email."

Ben cups another piece of cake in his hands and goes through the front fly-screen. Joe hears the van door slide open and the rattle of a tool box. He bites into the cake and goes into the study. He stares at the computer.

***

The veranda faces the road, not the ocean. But he can hear it, the waves crashing rhythmically, like the background music at a yoga class.

They sit there, nursing beers, admiring their work, what took them some of the afternoon yesterday and all day today. It creaks a little, moving on its axis when the wind gets around the house and catches the slightly angled slats, which still have little black labels on them so Joe and Ben could remember which piece was which. The ever useful Colonel Mustard.

"I tell ya, Joe. I think I'm in love."

"With a wheel? You need to get out more."

"I feel like we invented it. Reinvented it. Life's amazing, isn't it? You can take a pile of wood and create a thing of absolute beauty, and practicality. The first fella who ever built something like this must've thought he was God. Or touched by God."

Joe scratches the bee stings on his arms. "Simpler times."

"When I had the idea for it, I did some research. Water mills go way back. They were like the first machines. Making flour, crushing rocks, moving heavy stuff. I even saw a picture of how a water mill could power a giant saw. Really clever."

"The world's first engine."

Ben sips his beer. "You know, mate, sometimes I think that all the great stuff's already been invented, all the great things done. And all we're doing is rehashing everything, churning out all this crap we don't need and making stuff that's nowhere near as good as the original. Where are the ideas, the innovations, the world-changing inventions? We can't come up with anything original. We just copy and paste."

"There's no big war."

"What?"

"That's what...what Max used to say. The bomb, nuclear power, computers, mobile telecommunications, that all came out of the Second World War. He said all our technical advances, all through history, came from wars."

"That makes some twisted sense. What about Iraq?"

"That's a fight in a sandbox. They might as well throw stones at each other. And no one's paid any attention to it for years."

"Mission unaccomplished. But it's a horrible thought. War driving the human race forward."

"It's not like that anymore."

"What then?"

"It's about money and power. The world used to be about gods and beliefs and ideology and territory. Now, it's about wealth and information. Knowing everything and using that as a power over others. Wars are being fought by companies, not countries. Information is what they're fighting for."

"The internet."

"And everything else. Phones, TVs, texts, emails, gossip, rumour, opinion. Having information and using it to your advantage. All the technical advances of the last few decades have focused on that. The smartest people in the world are putting all their brainpower into stupid websites, worthless gadgets and time wasting games. They could be trying to find a cure for AIDS or cancer or figuring out a way to end hunger and poverty, but instead they come up with fancy social networking sites, filter-beating spam, all-access porn and shit like Second Life and the-t-wall."

"What's that?"

"It's a website where you can write anything about anyone. Like a toilet wall at school. No filters, no editors, and all anonymous."

"I don't wanna read any of that."

"Yeah, I can't imagine what's been written about me. I bet I've been crucified. But the-t-wall's just scratching the surface. There's all sorts of sites out there that are variations of that. Unvarnished, blogaboutanyone, don'tdatehimgirl, the list goes on. I could sit down at your computer and flood the internet with so much bad stuff about you that you'd never get a job, no girl would date you and no one would be your friend. I could ruin you in five minutes."

"Please don't."

"If I did, it would be there forever. Your kids would read it. Their kids would read it. The internet is mega powerful and I think a lot of people don't even realise just how powerful it is. All these sites are designed to get information and make money, and access private information about consumers. What they like, what they follow, what they think, where they go, who they're friends with, where they live, how many hours a night do they sleep, are they having financial trouble, is their relationship collapsing, whatever. I don't want to think what ceeville knows about all of us."

"I'm not on it."

"That's smart."

"Did you ever search for something online and then on the next page you go to, all the banners and ads are for that same thing?"

"That's been going on for years."

"Yeah? I thought there was some guy on another computer somewhere making that happen. Connected directly to mine. I shut it down straight away."

"Some really smart guy invented the software that makes that connection happen. The same smart guy who could've been building sustainable infrastructure in Africa."

"You know a lot about this, Joe."

"When I first went low-tech, I started reading more about the internet and what it's doing to our lives. It's changing us, rewiring our brains. You wouldn't believe some of the websites out there. And I don't mean calls for Jihad or child porn or right wing extremists. I mean stuff that everyone looks at. Plasher seems so innocent, but they have a direct line to what everyone in the world is thinking. Crowd sourcing. Can you imagine how that information could be used to influence us?"

"Enlighten me. I don't spend much time online."

"For starters, companies can use it to find out what consumers think of their products, and manipulate people not to buy rival brands. Elections, reviews, scandals, product launches, rumour marketing, whatever. For a lot of people, the first thing they do in the morning is turn their computer on. They're willing to engage in online debate before they even brush their teeth. You can rant and rave about anything. Everyone's got a voice and they all think they're experts, and they all want to be heard. And when you read all that stuff, all the comments and responses, it sounds like everyone on the planet is really, really pissed off. All these people who just want to vent their spleen."

"Were you part of that?"

"I used to be a troll on Plasher. I created ponds I knew would make people angry just to see how much invective people would let loose. How low they would go and how personal they make it."

"Such as?"

"My hate list. I hate cars. I hate breaststrokers. I hate winter. I hate cigarettes. I hate littering. I hate mobile phones. I hate hip-hop videos. I hate reality TV. I hate airports."

Ben laughs. "That's a lot of hate."

"Yeah. Hate gets you nowhere."

"What was the response?"

"More hate. Every online conversation seems to start out friendly enough, but soon degenerates into a shout-a-thon. The only difference is that there are no consequences. They can say anything, be as brutal and petty and mean as they want."

"You included."

"I just got them started. To see what would happen. I used to find it entertaining."

"What about your book? Is that full of hate?"

"I didn't write it."

"Still, that's you venting your spleen."

"It's mostly positive stuff. We wanted it to be a guidebook for living a simple, low-tech life. The simplicity bible. It was meant to help people, to get them off Plasher and ceeville and the internet and out into the world. I thought that people wouldn't argue face to face like they do online. They wouldn't have the balls. I was right about that. The events were always great."

"Except in Perth."

"Maybe that's the sign of change. The way we behave online starting to influence how we behave in real life. Everybody thinking they have the right to comment about everyone else. Nothing is private. Pretty soon, complete strangers will come up to you and give you their opinion on what you're doing and how you're doing it. Like your neighbour yesterday."

"Phil? He was just pulling my leg. He can't even use a computer."

"Lucky Phil."

"I think you're blowing the influence of the internet way out of proportion, Joe. If some people use it more than others, that's their choice. Some people watch too much TV. Some eat too much junk food. Some drink too much beer and smoke too many cigarettes. They work too much, don't spend enough time with their kids, take drugs to finish an ironman."

"I hope you're not doing that."

Ben shakes his head. "But I know guys who are. Come on, Joe. Amateur athletes with full-time jobs who are just marginally slower than pros? What do you think? They never get tested."

"Makes me wonder about Max?"

"Why?"

"He was a marathoner. Always finished near the top of his age group."

"You think he was on the juice?"

Joe sips his beer. "Could be. I'm starting to realise there's a lot about Max I didn't know. I thought I knew him, really well, but I actually knew very little."

"Maybe you knew a version of Max. And everyone here knew another."

"Max 2.0."

"Maybe there's more than that. You said he travelled a lot. Maybe he reinvented himself everywhere he went, left kids all over the place."

Joe manages a laugh, but the thought makes him shift in his chair.

Ben breaks the short silence. "Was he religious?"

"No way. He hated religions, any kind of big organised group."

"He'd probably hate SINC then."

"Yeah. He would."

"So, to summarise. We've got a cult movement based on the ideals of someone who hated movements and started by someone who hates technology, but it's only a huge movement because of the internet."

"And the movement says you should focus on what's important for you."

"Simplify choice."

"Right, but everyone just comes to the event to be part of it, not because they believe in what it stands for."

Ben smiles. "A movement that's popular just for being popular. From underground to mainstream."

"What do you think, Ben? Should I be proud of myself or disgusted?"

"Maybe you should go online and see where SINC's at."

"I don't wanna know. I'm done with it."

"I'm not so sure SINC's done with you."

"Anyway, I want to see this wheel in action."

Ben looks towards the sky, at the pink slithers the dusk is throwing into the clouds to the east. "We just need to dig a big hole, hook it all up and start dancing for rain. Warm tomorrow. Wanna take a swim?"

"Is it safe?"

"Sharks? I thought you'd be too fast for them. They'll feast on me and you can get away. Ah, but you shouldn't joke about that here. Surfer got killed not long ago. We'll stick close to the beach. I'd be more worried about stingers."

"I got stung in Busselton."

"Where?"

"All over my face."

"I can't see it."

"That was years ago. When I was first down here. On holiday."

"You've been here before?"

"Not in Gracetown. But I did a tour of the south west. All the way over to Esperance."

"On a bike?"

Joe nods.

"Maybe we passed each other."

"There was a white van that nearly killed me. Hmm. That orange lettering looks familiar."

"It could've been one of a thousand tradies. They hate anything on two wheels."

"Yep. If there is a God, he's a motorist."

"Can I ask you something about Max?"

"Sure. You've earned my trust."

"That didn't take long."

"You were the one operating the electric saw."

"Hah. Look, mate. You said Max wasn't religious. What kind of funeral did he have?"

"Don't know. I wasn't there."

"Where were you?"

"Somewhere over the Atlantic. Gordie told me later Len had organised a full Pentecostal burial. Max would've hated that."

"Who's Len?"

"A friend of Max. He married my ma a few months ago."

"That's weird."

"It's all right. It's good she got on with her life. Not like me."

"Why did you scarper?"

"What do you mean?"

"Why did you run from the funeral?"

Joe looks out into the darkening evening. The sun has set behind them and the trees in front of the house shimmer and ripple like green curtains. He feels the pleasant, familiar soreness of hard work, the aches in his shoulders and lower back, the raw skin of his hands. And there's the satisfaction of having built something, something he could look at, admire and say, I made that. The last time he'd pounded nails, chipped groves and worked a saw was in Sydney.

He smiles, realising he's sitting on the veranda, drinking beer, full from the roast chicken Rae made and feeling happy with his work. "This was a great day, Ben. I'd like this day to keep going. This feeling."

"You don't have to say it if you don't want to."

"No. It's just...I couldn't handle it. I had to get away, from everyone. They were all so, sympathetic. I didn't want their sympathy, and I sure as hell didn't want their prayers and charity. I wanted justice. Revenge. I wanted an explanation."

"For what?"

"It was completely unfair."

"Life sometimes is. What did you do, once you crossed the Atlantic?"

"Travelled around. Germany, Belgium, France. I was scared shitless most of the time, and pissed off. I flew down to Portugal. Met a girl. Travelled through Spain with her. I felt all right then, started to forget about everything. Until she broke my heart. Italy, Croatia, down the coast to Greece. It's all a blur now. I couldn't tell you where I went and what I saw. I do remember Croatia being really nice. Wanna go back there. Turkey, the Middle East, then just kept going east. I didn't know how to stop."

"Forgive me for being practical, but how did you pay for all that?"

"Max had life insurance. That came through later and covered uni. I used his secret stash for the trip. He had this hiding place under the floorboards in his bedroom. Kept a tin full of money in there, just in case."

"How did you know about it?"

"He showed me. He built our house, exactly the same as the farm house near Nannup."

"Interesting."

"Yeah, under the bed, he put this pin that looked like a nail. It popped up and the board came loose. When he died, I took all the money and hitched down to Boston. That's how it started. I worked sometimes too, carpentry and construction, on the road and in Sydney. Always for cash."

"So you left. You didn't get thrown out."

"Maybe it was the wrong thing to do."

"Too late now. How much was in there?"

"About thirty grand."

Ben coughs. "You didn't feel guilty? What about Gordie?"

"He would've blown it. He got into online poker. And I know he's playing now. He was selling information to the press for funds."

"Where does he play?"

"I caught him on a site called Raising Pokerzona. College kids mostly, and high schoolers. Low bets, so you never lose too much. He always has a player name that's some version of Gordie, and sometimes Stan, which was my nickname for him. And he's always a girl."

"Did he lose a lot?"

"Ma called me about five years ago and said Gordie was in some kind of trouble. This was just after I'd moved to Montreal. I rode down and confronted him. Found out he was on that site. So, I logged on and beat him. Badly. That was a mistake."

"He tried to win it all back?"

"From others, because I pulled out. He got into a massive debt, and Len and me bailed him out. Ma forced Gordie to get help, but I caught him playing again in Portland a few months ago."

"Maybe you should beat him again. Teach him another lesson."

"That didn't work last time."

"Wait. Max built a copy of the house?"

"He said it was what the house he grew up in looked like."

"Mum and Aunty Bev grew up there."

Joe laughs bitterly.

"What?"

"It never fails. A buddy of mine, he's got this theory that all men get their hearts broken before they're twenty-three. I guess that happened to Max too."

"My mum broke his heart?"

"And he built the house in Harbrook as a kind of shrine to her. Ma sold it, but the house is still there. Unless the new owner demolished it."

Ben stares into his can of beer. "Why don't you buy it back?"

"That's a good idea. I think I will."

"If it hasn't become a shrine to simplicity."

Joe looks at Ben, who's still staring into his beer, at the opener bent ninety degrees to the right. He flicks it with his index finger.

"And there it is."

"There what is?"

"You're thinking about the girl. Who was she and how old were you?"

"I was twenty-one. Rachel Anderson. She was the best friend of Leonie, my sister. Oh, fuck. You know, the incredible thing is that even now I can't say something mean to Leonie without her getting back at me with Rachel. She knows how much that hurts."

"The rule is, that once your heart's broken, that's it. You're done. You never love with the same intensity again, never give as much of yourself."

"I think I've heard that before."

"Yeah, it's from a movie, I think."

"It's a really depressing thought. But there's some truth to it. Don't go so far in, don't get so hurt. Learning from experience. Maybe that's what went wrong with Connie. What about you in Spain?"

"Terrible story. She was from Perth."

"Not such a good starting point."

"Ben, I tell ya, I was so into her. It was like the world had turned magical. You know, those moments when everything around you slows down and freezes. Remember that scene in *The Fisher King*, where he's following the girl through the crowded train station and everyone suddenly pairs up and starts dancing? Like that."

"What happened?"

"It's awful, even now. It should be funny, but it still hurts."

He tells the Barcelona story.

At the end, Ben raises his beer. "Well, for her, it's a very romantic story. Let's drink to that."

"After we split in Barcelona I went on a shagging spree. I fucked anything with legs. Mothers, old women, the ugliest girl in the bar. Fucked them and walked away."

"Any of that catch up with you?"

"I was lucky my dick didn't fall off. Or got cut off. A couple of times I had to do a runner. You know, the husband storms in and I jump out the window with my clothes in my hands."

Ben laughs.

"Or do you mean karma?"

"If you wanna call it that."

"It did. I was really lonely in Sydney. Didn't make any friends."

"Shame we didn't meet. I would've been your mate."

"I should've studied what you did."

"What did you study?"

"Biology. Ma wanted me to go into medicine. That was always the plan. Doctor Joe. But I couldn't stand all the blood and gore. And I don't like being around sick people."

A large utility comes down the street. It pulls into the drive and stops behind the van.

"That's Uncle Trev's car."

Joe stands. "Something's up."

Ben stands as well. They watch Trev get out of the car. The passenger door opens.

"Who's the goose in the cap?"

Joe sees Gordie hop down from the utility. "Stan."

Gordie walks towards the veranda. "Gotya, bro. Hiding out in this buttfuck town."

"Ben, this is Gordie."

Gordie shakes Ben's hand, then looks from Joe to Ben and back again. "Fucking straight. You guys look like twins."

Trevor comes forward. "Let's all go inside."

Gordie gives the wheel a push. "What's with the hamster wheel? Gonna put a kangaroo in there?"

"You're a moron, Stan. You fucked everything up."

Gordie holds his hands in the air. "Wrong, bro. This is all your fault and no one else's. You're not passing the blame onto me, aight. I saved you yesterday."

"What? You were leading the charge to put out the eternal flame."

"Nuh-uh."

Ben opens the door. "Let's take this inside."

Joe and Gordie sit opposite each other at the small round dining table. There aren't enough chairs. Trevor stands with his hands hooked under the braces of his overalls while Ben grabs his large inflatable ball from the study. He sits on this, bouncing a little, then leaning forward with his elbows on his knees.

Gordie spins his cap around and flexes the visor. SINC is written on the front in bright white letters. "Cool digs."

"What're you doing here, Gordie?"

"Looking for you, bro. And I found you."

Joe turns to Trevor. "You kept that secret really well, Trev."

"He's your brother. My nephew. That means something in my book. You're all brothers. And I'm your uncle. We're family."

Gordie reaches into his pocket and pulls out his phone.

"Put that away, Stan."

"I'm under strict orders to call Anita when I find you. She's got rocking news for you. Galaxy altering news."

"What?"

Gordie hands him the phone. "Ask her yourself."

Joe turns the phone off and puts it in his pocket.

"What the fuck, bro?"

"No one can know I'm here. Did you tell anyone?"

"Not yet. Okay, don't call Anita. I'll tell ya. We met some guys two days ago. The day you disappeared into the desert. They're gonna start SINC Australia. AuSINC they're gonna call it. We got offers from people in Europe too. And that means a change of plans. We're heading to Europe after New Zealand."

"Gordie, slow down."

"Everything's booked. Business class. I said we should rent a jet, but Anita's blocking expenses."

"How much are you down?"

"What?"

"Raising Pokerzona."

Gordie shakes his head. "You live so much in the past, bro. I ain't been there in years. I'm making the dosh now for real. You just gotta come back and make sure we all get our fair share. Anita's lined up all these licensing deals. It's mind blowing. So many fucking zeros, bro. We're gonna be millionaires. SINC has gone ballistic in the last two days. You going AWOL triggered it. And Perth was on all the big news channels, global coverage."

Ben bounces on the ball. "I thought Perth would ruin you."

"The total opposite, Ken."

"It's Ben."

"Yeah, sure. The Perth event was out of this world. It was fucking brilliant. It was like being in the centre of, right in the middle of mother-fucking history, being made right there. The net's flooded with it, people giving long accounts of what is was like to be there, posting vids and pics. Our site got so overloaded we had to shut it down. The book's a mega seller. Right now, there's some native sitting in a grass hut somewhere in the jungle watching a video of you in Montreal. All the occupiers have picked up on it too. Simplicity is also about equality, sharing the wealth and involving everyone. We're the ninety-nine percent and we're making some noise. It's...it's...exponential."

Joe sits back and rubs his eyes. His fingers are dry and cracked from handling wood all day. He scratches at the bee stings on his arm.

Ben smiles. "Congratulations."

"If you wanna get in on this, there's no place for you. Sorry, Ben. But if you got some champagne, break it out. Are y'all ready for this? Bing, bro. Bling-a-bling Bing! They made an offer for one of our slogans. 'Simplify choice.' They want to buy the rights to it. Anita and Xav are already negotiating with them."

Ben stands up and goes to fridge. "How much?"

"We're talking millions. More money than you'll see in a hundred lifetimes. For two words. For two mother-fucking words."

"My words."

"Our words, bro. And they's gonna make us rich. Like, Forbes top ten rich. Check it. 'I wanna be a billionaire so fucking bad.'"

"No longer the ninety-nine percent."

"Fuck that. Who wants to be poor?"

Ben returns to the table. "No champagne. But I've got beer."

"I'll take one."

"Me too."

Ben hands Joe and Gordie a beer. Trev holds out his hand.

"Are you planning to drive back tonight?"

Trev bristles. "Yeah."

"Then no beer for you."

"I guess I'll, I'll get going then."

"All right. Drive safe."

But Trev seems reluctant to leave. "You fellas gonna be okay?"

Ben bounces on the ball and clicks open his can, twisting the ring. "Yep."

"Well, it was, uh, nice to meet you, Gordie. Don't be a stranger."

"Thanks for the escort."

Ben gets up and takes Trev to the door. "Say hi to Aunty Bev."

"Will do. Let me know what happens. You know, Benny, the farm, it could really use some touching up."

Ben lowers his voice, but Joe still hears. "I don't think they're gonna dump a suitcase full of money on you just yet."

"Fair go. That's not what I meant. It's been a hard year."

"Drive safe."

Ben closes the door and parks himself on the ball again.

Joe sips. "Are they struggling?"

"They're fine. Bev and mum got the farm. It's worth a ton of money, even during a drought. No one's gonna farm it after them so they'll have to sell anyway. That's the best thing they can do."

"Man, I can't believe how much you two look alike. How old are you?"

"Pushing forty."

"You don't look it."

"That's because he's got hair, Stan."

"Fuck you, bro. In a coupla weeks, I'll buy myself a wig made of gold."

"Not if I fire you first. Then none of those zeros would be for you."

"Anita's the boss, aight. She's making all the decisions. And we're all in this. You too. Wanna head back tonight? Terry said you're on a bike."

"Trevor. He's Max's brother. Doesn't that mean anything to you?"

"Right now, not really. Sorry, bro, but SINC's what's happening. That's now. That's important. We go back to Perth, make some deals and we's rich, bitch."

"I'm not going anywhere."

"Bing won't wait."

Ben sips. "You're welcome to stay here, Gordie. Are you good with a shovel?"

"Someone die?"

"We're digging a hole, for the water mill."

"So that's what the hamster wheel's for."

"Forget it, Ben. He hasn't worked a day in his life. Those hands have never touched any tool other than his own."

"Whatever. When Bing comes through, I'll never have to work again."

"You'll just gamble it all away."

Gordie stands up quickly, knocking the chair over. "Don't push me, bro. Or I'll fuck you up."

"Sit down, Stan. You're not in a gangster computer game. This is real life."

Ben picks up the chair and lays a calming hand on Gordie's shoulder, but Gordie shrugs it off.

"Don't worry, Ben. He's all show. Sorry, Gordie."

Gordie pulls his pants down and slouches back into the chair. He sips his beer and sneers.

"Look, Gordie, all those deals will get made, with or without me, but you can't tell people I'm here. I don't want Ben's place turning into a zoo."

"That'd be great publicity. We're working on a competition. A back-up plan in case you didn't come back."

"What competition?"

"Find Joe. Winner gets ten tickets and an all expenses paid trip to H-Brook for the music fest in September. You know what? I won't tell anyone you're here. Then you can hit the road and the whole world can try to find you. Everyone'll be trying to find Joe."

"Gordie, you can't do that to me."

"You did this to yourself. It's either that or we head back together. We got a week. Let's chill here for a few days. Yeah. Dig a hole. Get back to nature. Build this hamster mill. Simplify, bro."

Joe exchanges a glance with Ben, who smiles and shrugs.

Gordie sips his beer. He picks up the pencil that's on the water mill's blueprints. He chews the end, then starts doodling. He draws a stick figure with a set of massive breasts and dollar signs for eyes.

"Yeah, we'll hang here. This town seems pretty fly. Where do all the chicks hang? Are there any clubs? They be all over us when they find out we's from SINC. Three bros on the tear."

Ben smiles. "There's a golf club in Margaret River. Or you could try the bowls club, but it gets pretty rowdy there after lunch."

Joe laughs.

***

"How's the fit?"

"I can barely breathe."

"You're not even zipped in. Pull back those arms, suck in that chest."

Joe does so. He groans as the zip reaches the back of his neck. He lifts his arms and tries a few strokes.

"I don't think I'll last very long."

"It'll loosen up in the water."

They walk down the short path to the beach. Ben is wearing his sleek wet suit, which has what looks like crocodile skin on the forearms. He's got a fleece vest over the top, a purple and green wool hat with Dockers written on it, and ugg boots on his feet.

"You look ridiculous."

"Bullshit. You could put me on the catwalk in Milan and say I'm wearing the next collection. Winter beachwear. With the right walk and the right pout, they'd all buy it. Anyway, you look like the love child of Aquaman and the Green Hornet."

"But with the right walk, I could conquer Milan too."

Ben snaps his fingers. "You got it. It's all about delivery and attitude. They'll believe it if you believe it. But who am I to be giving you advice like that?"

Joe lets that last dig hang in the morning air. The sun is out, but the sand is cold. Waves are breaking on the beach, crashing with rhythmic regularity. Further out, the water is dark blue and calm. No grey dorsal fins pop out and slice through the water. The wind is wafting, to Joe's surprise, from the east. It's warm against his neck. He starts to sweat in the suit.

Ben trudges awkwardly in the sand, like he's walking in ski boots. "So, give me your tips."

"I need to see you swim first. See what you're doing wrong, and right."

Ben nods. He swaps his wool hat for a swim cap and presses his goggles into his eyes. He kicks off his uggs and unzips his fleece. He puts it all in a nice neat pile, rolling the fleece into a tube and sliding it into one boot, putting the hat in the other. He puts the towel, which looks like it was ironed into a perfect square, on top.

Joe holds up his ear plugs. "You'll have to shout at me."

"That'll scare the sharks off. Hah. Sorry. No more jokes. Why do you wear them?"

"I get water in my ears. Hate it."

"I never get that."

"You breathe on one side?"

"Yeah. Is that bad?"

"We'll have to fix that. Bilateral breathing means your body turns in the water."

"So?"

Joe makes a side-to-side movement with his hand. "There's less resistance. You go through the water instead of directly against it. And it means you can get a longer reach, like this. Ow. I should've showed you before I put this on."

"It feels so weird to breathe on the right side."

"You'll get used to it. Francois said the same thing and he does it now."

"Who's he?"

"A buddy in Montreal. He's in Perth, part of simplicity. He's the one with the under twenty-three theory."

"I hate him. That kept me up for hours last night. I relived every horrible moment with Rachel. I took her to the school ball and in the car she said, 'You know, Ben, we're just friends, right?' Oh, man."

"That's bad, but not as bad as seeing a guy on one knee proposing to the girl you're in love with."

"Those two girls will spend an eternity paddling the rivers of hell."

"It wasn't the proposal. It was the look she gave me. Like she'd been waiting all this time for someone better to come along so she could drop me in the garbage like a soiled pair of underwear."

"That's harsh."

They walk towards the water. A wave crashes and sends wash up the beach. It hits Joe's toes.

"Oh, fuck."

"Come on, you girl. It's good for you. Does Gordie swim too, or is he just an Olympic snorer?"

"He was never into sports. He was a good runner, but he lacked the required motivation and commitment. Never went to training.

Thought it was all a waste of time."

"He takes some getting used to. He doesn't seem to like me much."

"Gordie's got only one focus. Gordie. He doesn't have the attention span to factor in anything and anyone else. Unless they have something to offer him."

"If I didn't know already, I'd never pick you two as brothers."

"We looked similar when we were younger. But when he hit puberty, he went in another direction. I came back from uni and he looked completely different. I think he wanted to, cultivated the look."

"How old is he?"

"Twenty-two."

"He's losing his hair. His snoring woke me up last night and I went into the living room to throw a towel over his head, to dull the sound. His cap had fallen off and it was hello monkey's bum."

"Yeah, a few more years and he'll have nothing."

"Not you."

"Or you."

They're up to their waists now, having got past the shore breakers. The water sneaks into Joe's suit through the holes in the legs. He takes a deep breath and dives in. The water is freezing against his face. Contrary to what Ben had said, the suit seems to constrict, tightening around his chest and shoulders. He can barely move, but he is warm. They both pop their heads out at the same time.

"Phoar. Good morning world. You all right?"

Joe nods frantically. "Yep. Let's go before I lose motivation."

"No pissing. That's my favourite surfing suit."

"Show me your form."

Ben launches into a splashy freestyle. Joe coasts next to him, watching above and below the water. Ben makes all the classic mistakes: crossing his arms in front of each other, kicking too hard, struggling from head to toe. Joe reaches out and grabs his leg.

"Argh. Shark. Shark."

They stand in the water.

"And? How bad is it?"

"Better than I thought. Okay. One, straight arms. Like this. Reach from the shoulder straight out, bend the elbow a little, try to grab the water with an open hand and plough all the way to your hips. Reach, grab, pull, push. Easy."

He demonstrates and Ben copies him.

"That's it. Always from the shoulder. It's easier to do that movement breathing on both sides. So, that's the second thing. Even if it feels totally wrong, do it. You'll get used to it and you'll find getting the straight arm rhythm easier. Third, don't kick so hard. It's not a sprint. Kick too hard and you'll wear yourself out. Think of your kick as keeping your body on the surface, making it easier for you to swim. Your arms are doing all the real work."

Ben nods. "Long reach, bilateral breathing, girly kick. What else?"

"This is the hard part. Relax. When your technique is better, it makes it easier, but it's also about attitude. You can't struggle. You can't feel like you're sinking or getting nowhere or fighting for air. It has to be smooth and relaxed. You have to think that it's easy."

"How do I do that? It's too bloody hard."

"Try counting your strokes. Distract yourself and find a rhythm. One, two, three, breathe, one, two, three, breathe. Your body will fall into that rhythm and stick to it."

"Let's do it. We'll swim to that buoy and back."

"Remember. Straight arm. Smooth. If you get stuck, look at me."

Ben starts. To Joe's surprise, he immediately applies what Joe said, and even tries to breathe on both sides. It looks awkward, but he sticks to it. Compared to before, he now looks like he's swimming in slow motion, but going faster. Joe swims alongside him. Ben looks over a few times and Joe slows his stroke so they swim in the same rhythm. Joe counts his strokes, then counts his breaths, up to ten and back down to one. They swim in water that's barely a metre deep. He sees small white fish near the sand and they scatter when he gets close. He thinks he sees the silvery outline of jellyfish, but puts his head down and keeps counting.

They reach the buoy and swim back to the south end of the bay. When they get there, Joe stands up and takes out his ear plugs.

"Looks great."

Ben checks his watch. "I was faster."

"Yep. And you don't need an oxygen mask."

"Thanks, coach."

"I gotta get out. This suits killing me."

"I'm gonna do another lap. 'Smoke me a kipper. I'll be back for breakfast.'"

"*Red Dwarf*."

"You watched that?"

"Max loved it."

Ben dives back in and starts swimming to the buoy. Joe unzips the suit as he walks out of the water, pulling and yanking to get his arms out of the sleeves. He sees Gordie sitting on the beach, wrapped in a blanket, his green SINC cap low on his head, visor shading his face.

"S'up eco-Spiderman."

"How did you sleep?"

"Ben's computer's broke."

"We unplugged everything."

"What the fuck for?"

"You know why."

Joe bends the suit down to his waist. His upper body is striped and indented with stitched lines.

"Edward Scissorhands. All stitched up and nowhere to go."

"It's Ben's suit. A few sizes too small."

"I thought you only swim in Sydney. That ice place."

Joe towels himself down and slips on a shirt. "I gotta confession to make, Gordie. I never stopped swimming. Even when I was travelling in Europe. I found a pool wherever I went or I swam in the ocean."

"You lied all this time."

"You don't look very shocked about it."

Gordie shrugs.

Joe manages to sit in the sand. "Ow. Man, this thing's tight."

"What else you lie about?"

"I got the scholarship."

"So?"

"But that had nothing to do with you. That was more to punish ma. I hated it that she got together with Len. Straight after. Tried to make it look like it was nothing. Waited ten fucking years to get married."

"Hey, bro, leave Len alone. After you fucked off to Europe and abandoned me, he really stepped up and helped out. He was a rock."

Joe sniffs. He wants to shove that SINC cap down Gordie's throat. "Good old Len."

"At least he's interested in me. With Max, it was always about you. Why can't you be like Jonah? Watch and learn from your brother. Become a star athlete like fucking Jonah. Jonah knows what he's doing. He's got it together. Fuck that shit."

"That's not how it was."

"You can remember it however you want. That's why I gave you up to the press. I wanted you to tell the truth. If only to get over it all, move on. It was for your own benefit."

"So I should be thankful?"

"What are you pissed for? You lied about swimming. I lied about the press. Everyone lies. And I was trying to help you."

"I think this is a little different."

"There's degrees to lying? Please. A lie is a lie."

Joe looks at the water, watching Ben swim back towards the beach. His form is good, but he's really trying to force himself to breathe on both sides. He needs practice.

"I'm going back today. I don't like Ben."

"Because he looks like Max?"

"He doesn't care about us. These country hicks just want our cash. That's why they're being friendly."

"You're way wrong."

"Fucking straight. You coming back or does the world get to play Find Joe?"

"Neither."

"Xav said you promised to come back."

"I'm out, Gordie. I can't do that anymore."

"What? We're gonna make millions."

"Don't blow it all online."

"Fuck you, Joe. We don't need you anyway."

"Are you gonna take my place?"

"I already did. In Perth and at the meetings."

"Good luck to you."

Gordie stands up. "I want the phone back."

"No."

"Fine. Keep it. I'll use a public phone."

"You know how?"

"Douchebag."

"Wait, Stan. I got another confession to make. I was the one who took you for thirty grand on Raising Pokerzona. I did it in front of ma to prove to her what shit you were in. I gave her that money to bail you out."

"What?"

"And I used to let you win at chess. Sorry for that."

Gordie drops the blanket and walks away. "Go fuck yourself, bro. It was only ever about you. Fucking straight."

"Gordie, wait."

But he's already off the beach and heading for the house.

Joe sighs. He looks at the water. Ben is walking towards him, pulling off his goggles and cap, looking pleased with himself. He shakes the water from his right ear.

"What happened?"

"Nothing. We just, uh, opened a book of revelations. Family stuff. More skeletons out of the closet."

"Maybe it's a good thing. Where's he gone?"

"He just needs a minute to cool off. He's all show. I'm the one who should be pissed."

Ben picks up his towel and unfolds it. "On a happier note, you've changed my swimming life. I felt great in the water. I actually enjoyed it. That counting trick made me forget about everything. I swam past the buoy. Didn't even see it."

"That's great."

"Don't worry, Joe. Gordie's probably making us breakfast as we speak."

"Not unless you've got just-add-water pancake mix."

"Screw that. I'll make us real pancakes. Rae'll give us some eggs, freshly laid this morning. We'll need our strength to dig that hole."

Ben extends a hand and helps Joe up. They start walking up the beach. Ben puts his wool hat and fleece on but carries his uggs, one hand inside each boot. Joe carries the blanket.

"Are you and Rae, you know, together?"

"Kind of. We're not in love, at least, not in movie love. Running to airports to stop each other from leaving or that kind of thing."

"Hollywood love."

"Not like that. But we like each other, and like being together."

"Why don't you live together?"

"Not that easy. She's a widow, likes her space. She and Tony lived in that house. All of his stuff's still there. When we see each other, she comes to my place."

"What does she do for work?"

"She's a sales representative for Buzzcut Honey. And she's working on being self-sufficient."

"Huh. You're in it together."

"The honey was her idea. She knew all about it. I provided the muscle."

They walk up the short path to the vegetable garden. An engine starts. Joe looks at Ben and then runs around to the front of the house. He watches Gordie bunny-hop forward on the Kapowasaki.

***

Ben picks up the satchel. "'The universe is trying to help. Don't panic. Exercise your soul.'"

"I shouldn't have put the keys in there."

"He take the phone too?"

Joe stuffs clothes into his backpack, his hands shaking a little. "Yep."

"I guess he'll tell everyone your whereabouts."

"Or start this Find Joe competition. That'd be worse."

"You just gonna scarper?"

"I have to."

"Look, Joe, I know SINC's getting popular and what Gordie said last night about Bing and everything, but you're stretching it if you think thousands of people are gonna come to Gracetown just because you're here."

"They won't, because I won't be here. This thing's out of control. There was only a few hundred people at the first event in Montreal, but now...thousands at the event in Perth."

"That still doesn't mean they'll all come here. We're barely on the map."

"I don't wanna go, Ben."

"Then stay. It's a free country."

Ben peers inside the satchel. He pulls out Colonel Mustard and plays with it. "You just gonna walk into town?"

"Yeah. Flag down a truck or jump in a bus."

"I could drive you to Perth."

"I'm not going that way."

Ben starts making a label. Joe hears the familiar whirr and click.

"And no cars."

"Well, that's complete and utter bullshit, Joe. It all is. Uncle Trev's dad was killed in a car crash and he still drives."

"That's different."

"How?"

"It's just different. You don't understand."

"Try me. We've understood each other pretty well so far."

Joe closes the pack and pulls the straps tight. He goes into the living room and looks around to see if he's forgotten anything. Back in the kitchen, he finds Ben holding Colonel Mustard, the long black tongue of a label sticking out.

"Max wasn't driving. He was hit."

"Happens a lot."

"Not on empty country roads."

"So what? You've still got to get on with your life."

"I've done really badly at that. I've made more steps forward in the last three days than I did in ten years."

"Stop hanging onto all that old stuff. How do I cut this thing?"

"We used it yesterday."

"I forgot."

"Pull it up."

Ben does so, freeing the label. "Ah. I like this. What did you call it?"

"Colonel Mustard."

"Yeah, I'm a fan of you, Colonel."

"Keep it."

"Really? Thanks. Here, in exchange, another label for your bag."

Joe takes it. "'Follow the sun.' That's good."

He sticks it to the satchel. They both look at it.

"You've got yourself a good philosophy there, Joe. But how can someone possibly function in society without getting in a car?"

"It's hard, especially to keep people from asking questions. I always used to play the eco card. Tell everyone their pollution mobiles are fucking up the planet."

"That's good coming from someone who rides a motorbike everywhere."

Joe laughs. "Yeah, isn't it? Pathetic."

Ben snaps his fingers. "Raelene. Maybe she can help."

Still wearing his wet suit, the sleeves dangling at his sides, Ben heads outside. He jumps the low front yard fence and goes up to her door. Joe watches from the veranda.

She opens the door in her dressing gown.

"Sorry to bother you so early, Rae."

"No biggie."

"You still got that bike in the garage?"

"Yeah."

"Does it work?"

"Used to. Most of the time."

"Can Joe buy it off you?"

"It's worth a lot."

"He'll give you thirty grand."

Rae laughs. "Not that much. He got all that in his pockets?"

"He'll transfer the money to me and I'll give it to you."

"You're mad, Ben."

"Yep, but he needs a bike. Now. Hey, Joe."

Joe walks to the fence.

"Can you do that?"

"On the computer, yeah."

Ben jumps the fence, slapping Joe's shoulder as he passes. "I'll fire it up. You sort out the bike."

Rae walks down the short path of the front yard. She's wearing rabbit slippers. "You can have it for nothing. It's just falling to bits in there, like everything else."

Joe follows her to the garage. "No. Thirty grand, like Ben said."

She opens the garage door. "Trying to make a fast getaway?"

With the door open, a cloud of dust comes out. Rae steps back and swats at the air.

"I think we might need a gun to go in here. Spiders and snakes and God knows what else. You go first."

He edges inside. There's an old workbench next to the door, some dusty tools, jars of nails and screws, some papers turned brown. On the ground are dried oil circles from a car that was reversed into the garage. There are also the piled up wooden remains of what might have comprised a baby's crib. A set of golf clubs, a lawn mower, other garden tools, and hoses hanging from the wall that he hopes aren't massive snakes curled up asleep. On the far side, in the dark corner the light from the one window doesn't penetrate, there's something big and bulky under a tarp heavy with sand and dust. He pulls it back and coughs. Rae steps forward to help him and they get the tarp off. A few spiders scurry away, making Joe jump.

"You yanks are such pussies."

They both cough some more.

He touches the handle bars, the curved expanse of the tank, the dried, cracked leather of the seat. "A Bonneville."

"Tony loved this bike."

"What year is it?"

"Dunno. He had it when we met. It was a hunk of junk back then. Used to break down all the time, but Tony got it working good."

"She's beautiful."

"The keys are in it."

He looks at the ignition, sees one key on a ring with a model version of the same bike.

"You think it'll start?"

Rae pulls her dressing gown around her. "Try it."

"Better wheel it outside."

Rae pulls up the main garage door, letting in more light and sending more spiders into retreat. Joe guides the bike out. She's not as heavy as Eddie. Near the door, he sees a pair of saddle bags.

"Can I have those as well?"

She smiles. "I'll clean em up for you. Scare all those nasty spiders away."

"Thanks."

She hands him a brush and he starts sweeping away the dust. The seat has a long crack in it, revealing the dried foam underneath. Part of him hates Rae for abandoning this thing of beauty in her garage, but he assumes she had her reasons. He climbs on the bike and moves it a little from side to side, hearing the petrol swill in the tank.

Ben comes back over the fence. "Suits you, sir."

Rae looks as well. "Start it up."

He turns the key, holding his breath, and gives it a kick, hoping the bike doesn't explode. It putters and farts at first, not catching. He pumps the accelerator and tries again. It makes an incredible bang, roars, then cuts.

Ben laughs.

Joe pumps the accelerator a few more times. "This beast has got some character."

He kicks it again, another sonic bang, another roar. He puts the bike in gear and edges down the drive. On the street, the engine sputters a couple of times, making the bike lurch and tilt, especially when he tries to get some speed up. After a couple of laps of the street, it already starts to improve. He pulls back into the drive, kicks the stand, cuts the motor and jumps off.

"She just needs to be ridden."

Rae puts the bags next to the bike. She's also found an old-fashioned skull cap helmet, some dirty goggles and a pair of well-worn leather gloves.

"Take it. It's about time I got rid of all this stuff."

Ben stands next to her. "You want some help?"

She nods, then turns and faces the garage. "Let's clean out the whole bloody thing."

"I'm in."

She looks at Ben. "I think we both better put on something a little more appropriate. You wanna cuppa?"

"Yeah."

"I'll make a thermos of coffee. Sort him out and then we'll get started."

Joe picks up the saddle bags and goes into the house. He starts transferring everything from the backpack into the bags. There's more than enough space.

Ben snaps his legs out of the wet suit. "Don't forget the computer. I wrote my bank details on a piece of paper on the desk."

"Roger."

He finishes packing, goes into the study and plonks himself on the ball. He quickly does the transfer, from one of the SINC accounts, and puts a hundred grand into his own online account. He shuts down the browser, stands up, then sits down again. He goes to ceeville. SINC has just over a million ceevillians.

"God."

He writes: "SINC founder going on spiritual journey. Simply, to follow the sun and get back to what's important in life."

He shuts down the computer and swivels on the ball. Ben is standing behind him.

"Is that what you're gonna do?"

"Yep."

"You think they'll try to find you?"

"Maybe. Don't know. Depends how they market it."

Ben reaches into the top drawer of the desk. He takes out his passport and opens it. He looks at Joe, at the passport, at Joe.

"Get some more blonde put in your hair in Busselton. You should be able to pass for me. This photo was taken about ten years ago."

Joe looks at the picture. "You think that'll work?"

Ben nods. "There's a bike shop in Busselton. You might wanna get your hog checked out before getting out in the Aussie wilderness. It's desert in every direction from here. Except west. You can take care of all the paperwork in Busselton too. Put it in my name. Here."

Joe takes the driver's license and the passport. "Thanks, Ben. When did you learn to ride a motorbike?"

Ben sighs. "When I was trying to win the heart of one Rachel Anderson."

"Say no more."

"Dye your hair. And grow a beard. No one'll know. I'll get myself a new license. It's just about expired anyway."

"Thanks, Ben. Really."

"Which way will you go?"

"North. I never went there."

"Good idea. It's nice up there. And there's no one. One computer for every hundred people, and that's being generous. Great place to get lost."

They move into the living room.

"Get to Darwin, take a ferry to Indo and then you can disappear."

"Not for good, but for a while."

"Maybe by the time you get to Darwin, this'll all have blown over and you can come back."

"I hope so. But I doubt it."

It's a little awkward, but they hug.

"Stay in touch."

"I will."

"You've got my address. It's on your driver's license."

"I'll write you a postcard. Dear Ben, from Ben."

Outside, Joe fixes the saddle bags to the side of the bike. He puts on the helmet, goggles and gloves. It all feels very right.

Ben stands with his hands in his pockets. "You look like someone from a silent film."

"Thanks. Going back in time. What about the water mill?"

"Also taking me back in time. Dad's coming up tomorrow to help out."

"You were right. I didn't stick around."

"Yeah, but you're leaving for different reasons."

"I'd stay if I could."

"You'll just have to come back. Someday. In the meantime, send me some postcards. I don't do email."

"Give my best to your folks. And to Trev."

A loud crash comes from the garage. Rae laughs, coughs and laughs some more.

"I think I better help her."

Joe gets the bike going. Again it bangs, sputters and chugs. He has to rev hard to keep the engine from cutting.

"I hope I make it to Busselton."

"You will."

Joe revs the engine and clicks it into gear.

Ben grimaces. "Music it's not."

Joe edges the bike down the drive. "But it's alive."

"Take care, Brother Joe."

"You too."

Rae waves from inside the garage, Ben from the drive. The bike's a bit reluctant, but Joe gets her into second gear, waves, then third, and soon he's cresting the hill out of Gracetown, leaving the broad bay behind, the wind at his back, the sun in his eyes.

Reaching acceptance with Flower Power

"Hello?"
"Hey, Francois."
"Joe?"
"How's it going?"
"Joe! How the hell are you?"
"Good."
"Where the hell are you?"
"Where are you?"
"Your home town. For SINC Live. And we've already had a few Joe Solitus sightings this morning, so this better be you."
"It's me."
"Prove it."
"The code word is Emmanuelle."
"Bastard. You in the area?"
"No."
"Are you coming? You should."
"Why?"
"There's someone here who's being trying to contact you."
"Gordie? I really need to make peace with him."
"You do, but I mean Iris."
"Yeah? She should be at uni."
"Well, she's here."
"Huh."
"You wanna talk to her?"
"Pass. No, wait. Put her on. But tell her to go into another room."
"Sure. Hey, Joe. I miss you, buddy."
"Yeah, you too."
"But to be honest, I miss our life in Montreal more. We had it better than we thought."
"The simple life of anonymity. A bee in the hive. One of millions, unnoticed, undetected, unnecessary."
"You still swimming?"
"Whenever I can. You?"

"No time, and I lost my motivation."

"Sorry."

"Your fault, Joe. The Icebergs was the last time."

"You ended on a high note. Don't worry. We'll get in the pool again. Life will get back to normal, eventually."

"Are you living in a cave?"

"No, but I haven't been paying much attention to the news."

"What have you been doing?"

"Following the sun."

Francois laughs. "Here's Iris."

"Joe?"

"Hi, Iris."

"Is this really Joe Solitus? We get lots of people calling and emailing saying they're you."

"It's me. Why aren't you in Victoria?"

"There's a ceeville suicide pact with the plan to all kill themselves if you're not found by the final day of the festival."

"What? You're joking."

"It sounds a bit like you."

"Rusticity. The long run. Brutal Beach."

She lowers her voice to a whisper. "Where are you?"

"Well, I was in Victoria looking for you."

"I came to Harbrook looking for you. The net is full of rumours that you're gonna make a surprise appearance."

"More rumour marketing."

"The town's already full. Tents everywhere, people sleeping on the ground, in the forest. And more are coming. The roads are jammed."

"Listen, are you on your own?"

"Am I single?"

"Is anyone around?"

"I'll go out the back of the house."

"What house?"

He hears Iris walk the floorboards, the sounds of many voices talking, some shouting, the opening and closing of a door.

"Your house. Gordie bought it. We set up camp here."

"Yeah? What's your role?"

"IT stuff. Social media monitoring. Cleaning up our internet image. Keeping tabs on cults. Online and mobile updates."

"Are you hooked into the system?"

"Got a direct line to it."

"Then I need your help."

"With what?"

"I want to make a special announcement. I was gonna get Francois to do it, but it sounds like you've got a better chance. But you can't tell anyone."

"So the rumours are true."

"I just want to send a message to everyone, on the day the festival starts."

"That's tomorrow."

"Promise me you won't tell anyone."

"I promise."

"I'd ask you to pinky swear, but that's hard to do on the phone."

"You remember that?"

"Sure."

"Then you also remember you owe me a story."

"I know. You'll get it. Listen, Iris. I'm gonna send you a package. There'll be a USB stick inside with one file on it. All you have to do is attach that file and send it to all the phones and computers signed up with SINC."

"Sounds dangerous."

"It's nothing. Just a message. You can send it with the announcement of the first acts."

"Attach the file and send. Easy, eh?"

"Yep."

"Where have you been, Joe? Nobody's heard from you for weeks."

"On the road. How is everyone?"

"Busy. Really busy. They're a great bunch of folks. Cheryline and Anita are very cool, but Jana hates me. I think I scare her."

He laughs. "I miss them. But don't tell them I called. We'll all catch up eventually."

"You better come here or a large number of SINC fans might start dropping like flies."

"That won't happen. It's not worth dying for. You should know that."

"Speaking of dying. Your cat died."

"Popov?"

"I'm sorry."

"What happened?"

"Some idiots kidnapped him and tried to hold him for ransom. You didn't read about that? You could've done something. When you didn't show, they killed him."

"These people are fucking mad."

"You shouldn't have left him there."

"I shouldn't have left at all. And I only thought we'd be gone for a few weeks."

"You were way wrong."

"Ah, Jesus. Popov."

"He's just a cat."

"No. He was Popov."

"You can't bring him back."

"What about you? What about university?"

"Anita's offered me a full-time job. Social media analyst. But I don't know if I'm gonna take it. I can't stand working with Xav. He thinks he's the boss. Crap, Joe. All these people here, they really owe you a lot, but they all act like you're gone and never coming back. And they act like it's all about them."

"What about Gordie? Can I talk to him?"

"He's not here."

"Where is he?"

"Montreal. He went to pick up your bike."

"Eddie."

"Who's he?"

"Eddie's a she. My motorbike."

"Gordie's riding her back. He was on the news this afternoon. Half of Canada's following him. The police had to clear the highway. A SINC convoy."

"Fuck."

"What about this package? When's it coming?"

"Uh, wait. Change of plans. Forget the USB. I'll send you a phone. Plug this phone into the system and use it to forward that message to everyone else."

"Okay. Send me the phone. Maybe you'll be here to give it to me?"

"Maybe. Nice talking, Iris."

"Yeah. Be nice to do it in person. Another run. Another beach."

"Hope so."

"Bye, Joe."

He hangs up and turns to Fab. "Will that work?"

Fab adjusts his thin glasses. His left shoulder jiggles up and down a few times. "Why are you whispering?"

The Sticky Solutions ideas lair is empty.

"Sorry. I'm nervous."

"Relax. It's just a virus. Yeah, so if the same text gets forwarded, it should work. We infect the phone and then it goes to all the others. Better than a USB. Totally unreliable. Cool. Phone virus. Never been done before."

"If it works. What'll happen if it does?"

"It should fry the phone. Make it eat itself. It might fuck up a lot of phones, like a domino effect, if people forward the message on without thinking. All the phones connected to SINC will get blasted. But if people get wise and turn off their phones or don't open the message, it'll stop."

"Let's hope people open the message. Shut down a few million phones."

"Sweet fuck. Better keep it all a secret."

"I've got the solution for that. Here."

"What's this?"

"A magic pill."

Fab puts it in the palm of his right hand and looks at it. "Cyanide?"

"Better than that. Take it when you want to forget all this. You need to swallow it and concentrate on this moment. On this specific memory. Keep concentrating on it until it disappears."

Fab laughs. "Are you for real?"

"It works, especially if you want it to. That's the point."

"But why would I wanna forget this glorious achievement?"

"So you don't go to prison."

"And what do I get in return?"

"Good karma. For bringing all this shit to an end. You get to free the world from this fucking movement. It's out of control. They killed my cat, Fab."

"Who's they?"

"Crazy sincophants."

"Yeah, right. Can you put my secrecy into dollars and cents?"

"Aren't you already rich?"

"How about that bike you came here on, when you were first here in the spring?"

"The Enfield?"

"Yeah, the Bullet. I want it. I could have a hundred of them, but I want yours."

Joe scratches his beard and nods.

"And I'm also the winner of Find Joe."

"I found you. Anyway, you can't tell anyone I was here. One word gets out, then no Bullet."

"Deal."

Fab hooks up a phone to his notebook. He taps at the keyboard.

"How do you know so much about this stuff?"

"I was a teenage virus maker. I've been saving this doozy for a special occasion. It's fun trying to bring down other networks. I once infected every computer at my high school, and the virus spread to all the students as well. All their computers."

"Bully revenge?"

"You got it. I called it Kill Bull. The second one was even more potent. Kill Bull Volume Two. That shut down half of Pittsburgh. Caused a three day blackout. The only problem with this kind of genius, you don't get credit for it."

"Well, this time you can forget about it altogether."

"If I take your magic pill."

"That's part of the deal."

"Why do you wanna take SINC down anyway? You made it."

"I just wanna be free from it. And to free everyone else from it."

"You are."

"But the whole world's still looking for me."

"How did you beat that? Change your name?"

"Grew a beard."

Fab laughs.

"I took this pill and forgot who I was."

"You seem to know now."

"It has to be stopped."

"I don't see why you should care. Sweet fuck. You make a ton of money from it and you don't even do anything."

"I don't want to make money. I just want my life back. I want the world back the way it was. I don't want everyone wearing baseball caps and chewing straws."

"Whatever. Everything underground is cool until it goes mainstream, right? What do you want to call this virus?"

"Release."

"Like the pill that's coming out?"

"Yep."

Fab picks up the little green pill. "That's what this is. How did you get it?"

"A friend gave it to me."

Fab taps the keyboard and unhooks the phone. "Release 2.0. Done. Hah. Maybe Natrofield will get the blame for it. 'Release. Focus on what's important for you.' That line was in your book, wasn't it? *Simplicity Rules.*"

"I think nearly every word of that has been sold to sell something."

"Anita. Clever bitch. You hit that, yeah? I read about that online. Someone posted a sex tape of you two, but it was a fake. Man, it must suck to be you. Every girl you ever kissed and every guy you knew came out of nowhere looking for a piece of your fame."

"I'm not online. Haven't been for weeks."

Fab looks at him incredulously. "Sweet fuck, you don't know any of that?"

"I'm low-tech. No computers, no cell phones, no emails, no texts. I only know about the slogans because of the billboards I've seen."

"You need to have a look. You've been crucified online, by a lot of your supporters no less. Hung out to dry. Everyone I know on ceeville buried you in their cemeteries."

Joe shrugs. "Back from the dead."

"What you been doing?"

"Travelling."

"Where?"

"Rode across Australia. Cargo ship to San Fran. Up the coast to Canada, diagonal to Florida, then straight up here."

"Following the sun."

"Are you signed up?"

"Isn't everyone? I'm going to the concert tomorrow."

"Don't open the message. And take the pill afterwards to forget your involvement."

"I'll open the message and then I'll take the pill. I wanna see for myself if it works."

"Why would you open it?"

"I can't be the only guy in the whole crowd who doesn't suffer. Here. It's all set. That's the number."

Joe handles the phone like it's a bomb. He wraps it in paper and puts it in his satchel. "Thanks, Fab. I knew you'd be able to help."

"You recognised genius when you first saw it. Simple as that. How can you get the Bullet here?"

"I'll bring her down. It's in Harbrook."

"So it's true. You are making an appearance at the fest."

"No. That's all rumour."

"Hey, you said you rode here, but the Bullet's in Harbrook. What are you on?"

"A Triumph Bonneville."

"Is it outside?"

"Yeah."

Fab follows Joe out the door and up the short steps. Toni is glowing under a streetlight on Beacon Street.

"Oh, she's gorgeous. I'll take her too."

"Now you're getting greedy."

"Two bikes or I'll tell the world, Joe."

"And I'll tell the world you made it."

"And I'll take your little pill and won't know anything about it. Beat any polygraph."

"You want both my bikes?"

Fab crosses his little arms. "I don't think you're in a position to negotiate."

"Bad karma for you."

"Screw that."

"Karma is important."

Fab shakes his head. "There's no such thing."

"All right. I need this one for a few days. After that, I'll bring her and the Enfield to you."

"Wait. If I take the pill and forget the memory, won't I wonder why I'm getting the bikes?"

"I'll say it's payment for services rendered."

"Who cares? I just want your bikes. I don't care how I get them."

They shake hands.

"Going to Harbrook?"

"Montreal. To pick up my stuff."

"People are camped in front of your building. It's a circus. Has been for weeks."

"I had all my stuff moved just before that crap began."

"Cool. So, two beautiful bikes for a mega potent virus."

"Thanks, Fab. You've done the world a favour. And if you wanna save yourself, take the pill."

***

He wakes. Outside, a garbage truck is lifting and emptying the dumpsters. He hears the rattle, shake and crunch of all those recyclables thrown into the trash: Styrofoam coffee cups with plastic lids, jumbo soda bottles, scrunched-up beer cans, a thousand candy wrappers ruffling and fluttering, plastic bags that will last a hundred years; an orchestra of all the crap America consumes. Now landfill.

He gets up, stretches and scratches.

Mayola. Concord, New Hampshire.

He presses his hands into his lower back, where his spine fought against and finally succumbed to the curve of the hotel bed. All those people who had misshaped the mattress way beyond any discernable flatness, all those out-of-shape travelling salesmen.

He takes a piss, standing, smelling all the old urine, aiming at the slither of rust in the bowl; or at the leftover streak from the dump of the previous occupant. It's hard to tell. Either way, it's disgusting. This is easily the worst Mayola he's ever been in.

He washes his face and brushes his teeth. He strokes his beard and considers shaving it off. He looks older with it, the beard flecked with a few strands of grey, like Max on vacation when he left all his shaving gear at home.

"What did you call it? Tackle. Shaving tackle."

He puts on his bike clothes, the leather pants, jackets and boots that have seen so many miles. He checks himself in the mirror, and smiles. He shoulders his satchel and picks up the two saddle bags. It's all he has in the whole world and that feels fine. Soon, the bike will be gone too and he can start again. Total reset.

Outside, the morning is warm and bright. Under the small roofed bay for motorcycles, Toni has some drops of dew on her cracked seat. He sweeps them away with a gloved hand and then rubs the seat with his forearm. Saddle bags attached, he dons helmet and goggles and climbs on. Toni lets out her familiar bang and roar, alerting the world to her presence. She settles down to a low purr that reminds him of a very content Popov.

"I'm sorry, Pops. Gotta move on."

He wheels the bike backwards with his feet, turns forward in a slow, wide arc and gets onto Loudon Road. Out on I-93, the traffic is heavy, all going north. Every car is crammed with heads, a lot of them in green caps, with music blaring from lowered windows. It creates a cacophony of sounds where no one song can be clearly heard.

He scoots down the side, just next to the line of the stopping lane. Kids shout at him as he passes. One person opens a passenger door and he just gets around it, as they laugh. Rowdy kids hang out the windows with bottles and phones in their hands, like they're on spring break. They wear SINC shirts and whoop and holler and almost fall out.

Was it really just three months ago that Xav sold those shirts in the park in Montreal? That tech-free Sunday that never was, with just a few hundred people in attendance. It seems like a decade ago, a generation ago. Even the movement seems dated, those shirts now retro.

The traffic comes to a standstill. The chorus of horns is deafening. Everyone shouts as well, leaning out windows to give their opinions. Other people comment about other people's comments and soon everyone is shouting at each other. Two guys get out of the same car to start fighting.

People stare at him, the bearded biker, riding off the set of some seventies road movie.

He shoots down the stopping lane, weaving between those people who have got out of their cars, a lot of them to pee, and then takes the exit to Laconia.

The other side of the road is jammed, with more cars trying to get on I-93. Some do wild u-turns and head back the way they came. More horns, more shouting. The going is slow through Laconia. All the cars are trying to take roads heading north, the drivers on phones as they work the wheel and the gear stick.

He goes straight through, coming out the empty east side, knowing he can take the back roads around the lakes, the dirt tracks if necessary; the kind of roads that don't show up on navigation systems.

He stops for a swim at Squam Lake, but just paddles around, scared to swim too far and leave all his stuff unguarded on the beach; that ticking time bomb. The beautiful motorbike which took him across the globe, and which will soon no longer be his.

He dries off, gets dressed and sits down to eat an apple. He looks at the water and thinks.

It's all right that people make mistakes.

It's all right that people lie.

It's all right that Popov's gone.

It's all right that Max's gone.

"I can't change any of that. And simplicity isn't the answer."

Helmetless, he rides Toni around the side of the lake, down a hard dirt track that's already strewn with yellow and red leaves. There are the marks of bike tires, paw prints, even the deep half circles of horseshoes, and all the assorted shit that dogs and horses leave behind.

He used to follow Max on these tracks, pedalling his bike and trying to keep up, and then when he was older, running and trying to keep up. He'd give so much that he would be wrecked at swim training the next morning and Mr Smythe would berate him, yell at him in front of everyone, always emphasising that Joe was letting the team down.

Out of the forest, away from the lake, the sun is high. He gets out onto the road, sees the familiar roll of the land, but only between all the heads. People are walking quickly towards Harbrook, stopping to point and stare at the house and pose for photos out front, but more intent on getting into town to where the concert is being held. He wonders where exactly.

He turns the bike and rides back into the forest, passing a few girls crouching behind trees and looking slightly ashamed. One girl talks on her phone as she pees; another taps her fingers at the screen, writing a text. He sees a guy peeing who's filming a couple who look to be fucking against a tree.

He parks Toni between some trees and then covers her with his tent fly, putting some branches on top as well. He changes out of his riding garb and puts on jeans, a t-shirt and sunglasses. He carefully loops the satchel over his shoulder. Back on the road, he joins the throng heading towards his house. He assumes they abandoned their cars out near the highway – maybe on the interstate – and have walked the rest of the way. They buzz with energy, talk a lot and loudly, but they also look like they're struggling, not having ever walked more than a few miles in their lives, and many wearing the wrong shoes.

Or they're high, he thinks. Or drunk. Or both. Or everything: high, drunk, out of shape and badly-shoed.

Kids mostly, teenagers, some college kids. There are a lot of tweens, gathered in large groups, sometimes with a parent among them, two heads taller and in a SINC shirt and cap, trying hard to look relaxed and cool, like they're an older sibling; a few of those parents are chewing straws and look even more ridiculous for it. There's a palatable excitement in the air, the feeling of an experience about to happen, something memorable, something worth talking and bragging about.

A barricade has been set up in front of the house, where the driveway meets the road, and this is attended by a couple of security guards in dark suits, sunglasses and headsets. He stops at the barricade and looks through it. There's a helicopter behind the house, its blades turning slowly.

Suddenly, everyone reaches for their phones. The collective buzzing reminds him of that evening visit to Ben's hives, getting stung a few times and eating honey straight off his finger. Ben grinning as the bees crawled over his face like friends. Ben laughing, joking, enjoying everything.

The crowd starts to surge towards town, a charging army in white shirts and green caps. Joe gets out of the way by holding onto the barricade.

A security guard grabs his shirt. "Get off!"

He gets thrown into the crowd and has to shuffle along with it before grabbing the barricade again further down, where there are no guards. After a while, the crowd starts to thin a little – now in the hundreds instead of thousands – and he works his way back to the main gate. He goes up to the guard. Behind the house, the helicopter takes off.

Joe has to shout: "I've got a package for Iris Dowler. It's very important she gets it."

He reaches into his satchel and takes out a small box. The guard seems unconvinced. Joe puts a hundred dollar bill on top. The guard sneers, but takes it and squeezes through the gate. Joe watches him take the steps up to the veranda and then knock on the door. He sees Francois standing in the doorway. He's struck by how the house is an exact copy of the farm house near Nannup. Max built it entirely from memory.

"Maybe he had photos."

He waits. There aren't as many people running as before. They go straight past him, the guy who started it all, without even looking at him.

He takes out the pre-paid phone he bought in Boston and

punches in the number Fab gave him, for the infected phone.

He writes: "simplicity guru Joe Solitus to make surprise appearance at SINC Live."

He presses send, then dials another number.

"Hello."

"It's Joe."

"Where are you?"

"I need Eddie. Get me the keys and meet me at the gate."

"You're here?"

"Yep. And I don't have time for this. Now, Francois."

"Okay."

He hangs up and pockets the phone. He sees Francois jump down the steps, run towards the gate and look around.

"Joe?"

"Over here."

They hug.

"Look at you. The missing link. What the hell happened? You been in the jungle?"

"In hiding."

"No wonder no one could find you. But you're here. Man, it's great to see you."

"Where's Eddie?"

"In the garage."

"You got the keys?"

Francois shakes his head. "Gordie's got them. He went with Anita and the others in the helicopter."

"Crap."

"What's going on?"

Joe fumbles in his pocket. "I've still got a key. Here."

"I don't know how to ride. I think Xav does, but he went in the helicopter."

"Xav can ride?"

"He grew up on a farm."

"Yeah, that's right. And that means Iris did too. Maybe she can ride. Give her the key and tell her to get Eddie."

"What about you?"

"I'll wait here."

"You're not staying? I'll call Anita and tell her you're here. That'll make a lot of people happy, and it'll save us the hassle with that fucking suicide pact. Our lawyers are really sweating on that. Wait. That's my phone."

Joe looks at his phone too. Nothing happens. "I'm not signed up."

Francois checks the message. "Well, it looks like the surprise is over. Did you send that message? Hey, what the fuck?"

Joe sees Iris run down the steps towards the gate.

Francois taps at the screen of his phone. "It's dead."

A lot people stop in the crowd to look at their phones. Their joy and excitement turns to confusion.

Iris runs towards him like she's going to tackle him. Once embraced, he feels her taught body, her stiff ribs rubbing against his chest, her arms almost cracking his shoulder blades.

He pulls back and gives her the key. "Can you ride a motorbike?"

"Sure."

"Then get Eddie from the garage and let's go."

"Where?"

"Away from here."

"Now?"

"Why not now?"

Francois looks at Joe. "What's happening?"

"It's over. The whole thing's over. Go back to Montreal. I'll be there in a couple of days and I'll tell you everything."

Iris runs towards the garage. Joe heads back to the road.

Francois shouts: "Joe, what the fuck?"

"See you in the pool on Sunday. Same time as always."

He walks along the side of the barricade, past all the kids who have stopped and are staring at their phones, showing them to each other, banging their fingers against them. A few throw them to the ground.

"Hey, loser, you're going the wrong way. Joe Solitus is here."

"No, he's not."

"You're still going the wrong way."

He sees Iris ride out of the garage and then waves to get her to follow him. He runs into the forest, with Iris close behind.

***

They lie on the bed, bodies entangled. The noises from Cambridge Street come through the closed window: glass breaking, people shouting, police sirens, maybe cars being overturned and set on fire.

Bostonians rioting like they just won the World Series.

"Sounds pretty hairy out there."

"You wanna watch the news?"

"No. It's all show."

"Come on, Joe. I wanna know what happened."

"It's one night of madness. Things will be back to normal tomorrow."

"What about the suicide pact?"

"Won't happen. They just want attention. That was more about them than about me or simplicity. Anyway, the whole world probably hates SINC now. Hopefully. It's over."

"And Gordie?"

"I want him to go back to Portland, to college. I'll talk to him."

"Gordie can't go anywhere without being mobbed."

"That was yesterday. Tomorrow will be different."

"You're way wrong. Listen to that. The world's gonna be a mega different place tomorrow."

"Maybe. Maybe not. All those phones can be replaced."

"Let's check the news."

"You should do that too."

"What?"

"Go back to college."

She sighs. "Yeah. One more year. Easy, eh?"

"I'd come. Victoria's pretty nice."

"Slow down, cowboy. This is just our second time together. Don't go planning our future just yet. If you come to Vic, then you gotta get your own place. Make your own life. Then we'll see what happens."

"Deal."

"Pinky swear."

He laughs and shakes her pinky.

"Or you come to Montreal after you graduate."

"Maybe."

"But you have to get your own place and make your own life."

"Deal."

"And I'd like to take you to Australia, one day."

"Double deal. Well, if we're not gonna watch the news, tell me the story you promised."

"It's good I didn't tell you the first time. A lot's happened since then, adds colour to it and makes it easier to tell."

She props herself up on one elbow, flexing the bicep. "Ah, you're over it."

"So are you."

"The day you left. I got it all out of me. You gave me perspective."

"That's good. It's not healthy to carry all that shit around. You were poisoning yourself for no reason."

She settles her head in the crevice between his shoulder and neck. "You should know. Begin."

"Where?"

"At the start."

He takes a deep breath. "Comfortable?"

"For the moment. I still wanna see the news after."

"Once upon a time there was a boy named Jonah."

"I don't want a fairytale. And no third person crap. I hate it when people talk about themselves in the third person."

"My name is Jonah. I was a swimmer who lived in Harbrook."

"I thought you were Joseph."

"No, Jonah."

"Nice name."

"Feel free to call me that. I'm sick of being a regular Joe."

"You're not that."

"Anyway, I grew up in Harbrook, New Hampshire. My ma was a nurse and my dad was an architect. We lived in this big house that Max built."

"Who's Max again?"

"My dad."

She yawns. "Continue."

"Max was from Australia. He lied a lot about his past, which I found out later. And it was good for me to find that out, because growing up, I idolised Max. He was more of a big brother than a dad. He was good looking, funny, fit, successful, well-travelled and everyone liked him. Everyone knew they could depend on Max Solitus. He rode a motorbike, an Indian Enfield Bullet he called Eddie. He said he bought her right off the line in India, rode her back to Europe and put her on a ship for the States. But I'm not sure that's true."

"Sweet Eddie. That was fun today. Down all those back roads, those weird covered bridges. I can't believe you gave her away."

"It was a present."

"Very generous."

"Not really. Both bikes belonged to other people. It was good to get rid of them. I freed myself from the past."

"How are we gonna get back to Harbrook?"

"We're not going back."

"I don't have any clothes."

"We'll buy you some. Start again from scratch. Or Francois will take your stuff to Montreal. It's not important. But back to the story. Max, my dad, told a lot of lies. He said he left home, but he was actually thrown out for getting a girl pregnant. He never went back and the girl, Denise, had a son named Ben. I was lucky to meet Ben and Denise in Australia."

"You checked into this B&B as Ben. Is that how you got away?"

"Me and Ben look very similar. I was able to travel everywhere on Ben's passport and use Ben's driver's license. I even managed to get new license plates for Toni in San Fran as Ben."

"That must've been a wild trip."

"It was hard for me, to accept everything, especially that Max had lied. But as I rode across Australia, I started to realise that knowing all of it actually helped. I didn't feel the hurt with the same intensity anymore. I could let it all go. And I could rationalise it, in some twisted way. Karma catching up with Max. It all made the tragedy not as tragic. It wasn't just some random accident."

"You really believe that? You're living in an illusory correlation fantasy."

"Yeah, I still think karma is important. And I like that things are connected. Some things. Finding out the bad stuff about Max, all the people he had disappointed and let down, made it easier for me to accept something bad happening to him."

"Whatever. Sip."

He grabs the wine bottle, gives her some and then has a swig himself.

"That's how I rationalised it and it made it all easier to deal with. So, when I got on the freighter in Sydney, I knew I was leaving Max behind. It would be easier to talk about. I could stop carrying around all the hurt and hate. I could also forgive my ma for having an affair and go and see her to patch things up and apologise."

"This is a great story. A soap opera."

"Don't fall asleep."

"I won't. I wanna see the news when you're done. You've got

about seven minutes to wind this up. How did Max die?"

"Well, uh, that used to be the big thing. The hardest thing. I used to dream about it, remember it any time I saw an accident or had contact with death. I became a bit obsessed with death and dying, and about the fairness of it. The unfairness. I was convinced some people didn't deserve to die and I wondered how that could happen. I started to fear death, never got into cars, and hated people who didn't look out for others, the people who are so caught up in what they're doing, they cause accidents that kill people. That's why I wasn't big on cell phones and music players and the internet and all those other attention-numbing gadgets. The technology created apathy and selfishness. Everyone tuning out and not willing to accommodate each other. The world suddenly full of line-jumpers, people who walk with their heads down, people filming and photographing and commenting on everything and posting it online. People who expect to get everything now and aren't prepared to wait. People swimming in the middle of the lane and not even letting you pass at the wall. I really hated the world and all the people in it."

"Poor boy. You really need to lighten up. The world's a great place."

"I went so far as to start a movement to try to change all of that. But now I know I was wrong, not the world. All the people were just living their lives, living as the world is today, using the technology as every generation has. The problem was that I went out every day looking for shit and that's what I found."

She yawns again, plays with the remote control in her hands and checks the bedside clock. "And now you look for beauty."

"I have you to thank for that. You changed my attitude."

She bites his neck.

"Ow. You got sharp teeth."

"From hockey. They're all chipped."

"Then no biting."

"How does this story end?"

"It has ended. I'm ready to start a new story."

"Doing what?"

"I had the idea of becoming a swimming coach. Running special courses that combine meditation and swimming. So people could get fit and relax in one course."

"Exercise your soul."

"That could be the slogan. It's one Anita never knew about, otherwise she would have sold it too."

"It belongs to Rusticity."

"That's right."

"Ah, everything's stolen. Nothing's original anymore."

"Meditation swimming would work for kids as well as adults. There's a lot about swimming that you can apply to life. A lot of good lessons you can learn in the water."

"And I'm sure there's a good buck in it."

"I'm not interested in money."

"Says the guy who has enough of it. Now. But you still haven't told me about Max."

"I never told anyone that story. I should have faced it a long time ago, should've told people, should've stayed for the funeral and helped out my family instead of abandoning them."

"What happened?"

"We were running on the road, from our house to the forest. There was a two-mile track where we used to do loops and stop after every lap to do push-ups and sit-ups. A car hit Max, sideswiped him and threw him off the road. The car kept going and then stopped about a hundred metres down the road. The driver got out, still talking on his phone, then got back in his car and drove off. Max was lying in a heap in the ditch. He died."

"You saw it?"

"Yes. I saw the pain, the struggle, then the relief. And now I understand why, and I also understand that not everyone dies with such a look on their face. It was what I wanted to see. But for Max, there was no more lying to do, no appearances to keep up. He'd lived an interesting life and he knew he was lucky to have done that. But he'd also made a lot of mistakes and he was sorry for that. The expression on his face, that look of relief, that was because Max had deceived a lot of people, including me. Especially me."

"Sounds like Max was no different to a lot of people. Everyone lies."

"Yeah, I get that now. I'm trying to change. The first step was to go low-tech. The second was to look for beauty instead of shit, to stop being so angry. The next step is to accept things as they are and let it all go. Like swimming. Straight arms, breathe on both sides, relax and don't fight. It's simple."

"Don't lose touch with reality. People will always want things from you, and you can't live without technology."

"True. I'm trying. I tried to change the whole world and that turned out to be a huge mistake. All the time, I should've been trying to change my own little world. That's what's important. Me. Jonah. Self-help. This is difficult because the world's constantly telling me what's important and what I should want and what I should be. The world's also offering me solutions to problems the world's telling me I have."

She raises her head. "Calm down. Don't go crazy on me."

"Sorry. I just wanted to say that out of all of this, I'm trying to live differently. Ignore all the noise and put myself in the middle."

"Simplify, focus on what's important. Where do I fit in to all of that?"

"You're important to me."

"Hey, what time is it?"

He takes a swig from the bottle. "Almost midnight."

"Time's up. You don't wanna watch the news?"

"No."

"Whatever you sent me killed my phone and it sounds like there's a riot outside."

"It'll be over in the morning. And your phone's replaceable."

"Yeah."

"Everything is. SINC will be blamed for it. Anyway, something else will come along."

"I've been monitoring that the last week or so."

"What?"

She picks up the remote. "Complexity. They're getting supporters on ceeville. They've got an event planned as well."

He yawns loudly and kisses her forehead. "See. There's already something else the kids can get into. God forbid that should look inside themselves. The summer of simplicity will be followed by the winter of complexity."

She turns the TV on. He hears her voice, between the gaps in the newsreader's. It's a hazy echo that rises and fades depending on the attention he gives it.

He closes his eyes and tries to tune out. The pillow is soft, the bed hard, the girl naked, the wine warm in his stomach. It's after midnight. A new day. Hopefully, a new world.

Something hits the window and he turns to look. Iris is still fixated on the television, commenting about the reports coming in from around the country. Phone networks down, something about a rampant computer virus, blame being put in SINC. This makes him smile. He knows the world will be different tomorrow. It has to be.

He will be Jonah Solitus, and that's a good start.

He won't get his Montreal life back, and he doesn't want it.

On the bedside table, there's one little green pill left in the packet. He looks at it and tries not to listen to the television.

Travel Page (cont.)

Lightning Source UK Ltd.
Milton Keynes UK
UKOW04f1225021213

222223UK00003B/27/P